All That Lies Within

D0708725

By
Lynn Ames

ALL THAT LIES WITHIN
© 2013 BY LYNN AMES

ISBN: 978-1-936429-06-6

OTHER AVAILABLE FORMATS

E-BOOK EDITION
ISBN: 978-1-936429-07-3

PUBLISHED BY
PHOENIX RISING PRESS
PHOENIX, ARIZONA
www.phoenixrisingpress.com

CREDITS
EXECUTIVE EDITOR: LINDA LORENZO
AUTHOR PHOTO: JUDY FRANCESCONI
COVER DESIGN: PAM LAMBROS, WWW.HANDSONGRAPHICDESIGN.COM

Dedication

To anyone who has ever felt marginalized or misunderstood, know that there are those who really see you and love you for exactly who you are. Let your light shine and show others the way.

Acknowledgments

The impetus for this novel is *Knowledge and Illusion*, a poem I penned in June 2012. It was published in the poetry anthology, *Roses Read*, edited by Beth Mitchum. An excerpt of the poem appears in Chapter Ten and is annotated with an asterisk. For the purposes of the story, I gave author credit to one of my main characters.

As with any of my novels, there are many details that must be factually correct or at least plausible. To my good friend, Audrey Evans, a film veteran who worked on such theatrical releases as *Thelma & Louise*, *Waterworld*, and *Zoolander*, and who provided accurate and essential insights into the workings of a movie set and movie making; to Doctor Jenni Levy, a childhood friend and expert in end-of-life care, who lent realism to some very critical scenes; to Katherine Fugate, screenwriter of such movies as *Valentine's Day* and *New Year's Eve*, who provided an essential bit of information at a crucial moment; to the counter guy at the Carnegie Deli in New York City, the contracts expert at the Writers Guild of America, the librarian at the Academy of Motion Picture Arts and Sciences, to Laura Nastro, who painted a vivid picture for me of attending a taping of *Late Show with David Letterman*, to the communications assistant at Middlebury College, and my college friend Lisa Kissinger-Kaplan who helped augment my memory of graduation—you all helped me infuse this novel with realism and plausibility and I am forever grateful for the assistance. Any potential inaccuracies in this book belong solely to me.

I am blessed to have what I think is the finest team in the history of novel-writing. To my beta readers who read through my manuscripts chapter by chapter during the creation phase and give me critical feedback—you have my eternal gratitude.

To my primary editor, Linda Lorenzo, in whom I have absolute, unshakeable trust—thank you for your infinite wisdom and patience. Having you guide my work is such a gift. I always know if you say it's going to be okay, somehow, it will be.

To the readers who continue to clamor for the next book—you make it all worthwhile.

Happy reading!

CHAPTER ONE

Wait until you hear this one—"

Dara Thomas held up a hand in protest. "I don't want to know. Thanks anyway."

"But this critic says, 'Her arresting blue eyes and flawless features guarantee any movie's success. Dara Thomas is box office gold!'"

Dara rose out of the director's chair with her name embroidered on the back.

"Where are you going?"

"Back to my trailer to work on my lines."

"But you haven't heard what they said about you in this week's *Enquirer*."

Dara sighed audibly and walked away. She pushed open the door leading from the sound stage and squinted into the midday sun, only to see her co-star, Luther Rollins, heading directly toward her. "Well, now my day is complete."

"Dara, sweetheart, when are you ever going to admit that you're madly in love with me? Or at least in lust? Your looks, my physique... Just think of the beautiful babies we'd make! Well, we wouldn't make babies, of course, cuz I'd wear a condom, but..."

"I don't know how I could resist such a...touching...offer. But I'll try." Dara continued on her way without breaking stride.

Once inside her spacious trailer on the Warner Brothers lot, she leaned back against the door and closed her eyes. She inhaled deeply through her nose and exhaled through her mouth until she found that peaceful place within—the place where she wasn't Dara Thomas, movie star, the place where she was just herself.

Since her next scene wasn't scheduled to shoot for a couple of hours, Dara plopped down on the sofa and picked up her laptop. She booted up, entered her password, and opened a file in Microsoft Word. After re-reading a few paragraphs, Dara began to type, at once lost in what she was doing.

She kept on typing until a knock on the trailer door startled her.

"Ms. Thomas? Two minutes."

"Oh. Really? Okay. Be right there." Dara checked the time on her laptop. Was it really possible that two hours had passed? She saved the document with the five new pages she'd written. Pleased with her progress, she backed up the file to a flash drive, shut down the laptop, and packed everything away in her briefcase. She would be shooting for the remainder of the day, so there wouldn't be any more time to spend on the project.

She rolled her shoulders to relieve the tension of sitting hunched over the computer and shrug off the remnants of the world in which she'd been immersed. She closed her eyes and took in a deep breath, mentally transforming herself back into Oscar-nominated actress Dara Thomas. Then she adjusted her posture to mirror that of the character she was playing in the movie. "Show time."

∽〰∾

"Come in, it's open."

A moment later, Carolyn Detweiler dropped her keys and briefcase on the kitchen island and stood with her hands on her hips, waiting for her best friend to look up from the laptop.

"What?" Dara finally said.

"What? That's what you've got to say?"

Seeing Dara's furrowed brow, Carolyn sighed in exasperation at her evident confusion. "How did you know I wasn't some crazy stalker person?"

Dara uncurled her long legs from underneath her, turned to put her bare feet on the floor, and placed the laptop on the coffee table. "Well, sweetheart, you're the only one I'm expecting, and I had a perfect view of you from the comfort of my couch."

Dara spun the laptop around so Carolyn could see it. On the screen was a series of boxes with views of the driveway and every entrance to Dara's new haven, a getaway beach house.

"If you push this little button here"—Dara manipulated the mouse over a command on the toolbar—"it unlocks the front door. So you see? I didn't unlock the door until I knew it was you. Feel better now?"

Carolyn came around the coffee table and kissed Dara on the cheek, then sat down on the couch next to her. "Much." She cast her eyes around the space, taking in the wall of glass that overlooked the ocean with the sliding glass doors in the center, the exposed beams, and the airy openness of the layout, and whistled. "I like the new digs."

"Yeah?"

"Mm-hmm. Very nice, indeed. Good thing you're the sexiest woman alive and the movie business is paying well these days." Carolyn realized her mistake too late, fumbling on the last two words when she saw the pained expression on Dara's face.

"It certainly is a good thing. I mean, how else could I ever earn such a lucrative living if it wasn't for 'the face that launched one thousand men's fantasies'?" Dara stood and walked to the glass doors.

Carolyn walked up behind her and wrapped her arms around Dara. "I'm sorry, sweetie. You know I didn't mean it that way. You're the most intelligent and accomplished person I know. You want to be a rocket scientist instead? I'm sure we could polish up the old résumé and make that happen." She could feel Dara's sigh against the cheek she had pressed between Dara's shoulder blades. "Forgive me?"

Dara turned in Carolyn's loose embrace and kissed her on the top of the head. "Always."

Carolyn gave one more squeeze for good measure and dropped her arms to her side. "Besides, I think you're going to love me again when I tell you the news."

"You could've told me over the phone or via Skype, you know."

"I know, but where's the fun in that?" Carolyn retrieved her briefcase from the kitchen island and walked back to the couch, motioning Dara to join her. She pulled out a sheaf of papers and fanned them out on the coffee table.

Dara leaned over and began to read. After several minutes, she looked up at Carolyn, her eyes wide. "Are they serious?"

"As a heart attack."

Dara reverently ran her fingers over the pages. "For real?"

"Absolutely. They loved the last book so much they want to lock Constance Darrow into another three-book deal."

"And they gave us what we wanted on the e-book royalties?"

Carolyn nodded, pleased to see the child-like glee in Dara's expression. "The film rights too."

"Why?"

"Why?" The question caught Carolyn off-guard.

"Every other writer is fighting tooth and nail to get a publisher to give them a fair piece of the electronic market, and we don't even have to break a sweat?" Dara scanned the contract again. "So yeah, why are they giving us this without so much as an argument?"

Carolyn laughed. "Do the words 'Pulitzer Prize for Fiction' mean anything to you?"

"Well, yes, they mean something to me. The question is, do they mean that much to the money men who carped about poor book sales?"

"Having Constance Darrow in their stable of writers gives the publisher credibility. It gives them gravitas. They don't care if she makes money for them."

Dara shook her head. "No. They always care about the bottom line."

"True. But in this case, they assume Constance Darrow's presence draws in other authors they want to land."

"So, they figure giving Constance movie rights and e-books won't amount to much; therefore, they aren't risking much financially and they keep her happy?"

"Pretty much." Carolyn slid the papers out of Dara's hands. "It's a really good deal."

"What about the personal appearance clause? Are they still insistent that they need to meet the author face-to-face and that she needs to do interviews? Or have they given up on that?"

"I reminded them that the mystery surrounding Constance builds her image as an enigmatic recluse, and it enhances the buzz. The fact that no one has ever photographed or seen her, that she refuses to do interviews or social media of any kind, that she works through a representative and not even her publisher has met or spoken directly to her, that she didn't even accept the prized Pulitzer in person... All that makes her even more inscrutable and appealing."

Dara pursed her lips. "They bought that?"

"Read the contract. It's written right in there. No public appearances required, no social media—nothing."

"Okay. Sign it."

"Yeah?"

Dara smiled that million-dollar smile. "Yeah. Why not? Besides, Constance is halfway through the next manuscript."

"I can't wait to read it."

∾∾

Professor of American Literature Rebecca Minton distractedly tucked a strand of hair behind her ear and turned the page of the hardcover sitting open on her cluttered desk. Gradually, she became aware of someone standing in the doorway. She smiled and looked up, assuming it was one of her students stopping by, even though posted office hours wouldn't begin for another thirty minutes. When she realized that it wasn't a student at all but her ex-girlfriend, her smile became a pained frown.

"What do you want, Cynthia? And why couldn't you have asked for it over the phone like a normal person?"

"Because, dearest, you don't take my calls anymore. Remember?" Cynthia sashayed the rest of the way into the office and looked Rebecca up and down as she wiggled into one of the visitor chairs.

"You needn't have bothered to sit down. You're not going to be here that long."

"Tsk, tsk. To think, you so used to look forward to my impromptu office visits. Some of the hottest sex we ever had took place right here, on this desk." Cynthia trailed her fingers across the glossy wood surface.

Despite her best efforts, Rebecca felt a blush creeping up her neck. She cleared her throat and shifted in her seat. "What do you want? Or did you just come here to reminisce? Because if you came here to relive old times, any happy memories I might have had of us went out the window when I found you in bed with our landscaper. What a cliché."

Cynthia threw her head back and laughed. She ran her fingers through her luxurious hair, a move Rebecca knew well.

"There was a time when that would've worked. That time is long past."

Without warning, Cynthia leaned forward and snatched the still-open book off the desk. This time the laugh was more of a cackle. "Well, dearest, perhaps if you had paid more attention to me and less attention to your obsession with Constance Darrow, I wouldn't have needed to look elsewhere for...entertainment."

Rebecca reached out and grabbed the book back. Through clenched teeth she managed, "I'll ask again. What do you want?"

Cynthia sat back and crossed her long legs, revealing quite a bit of skin. "I want the rest of my things."

"You already got everything that belonged to you. Now get out."

"Not true, dearest. How about those lovely three-carat diamond earrings you bought me last Christmas?"

"You're the one who left them behind. I believe you said, and I quote, 'Keep them. I'm sure I can get plenty more where those came from.'"

Cynthia waved her hand dismissively. "I was just hurt, that's all."

Rebecca narrowed her eyes, the pieces finally clicking into place. "You're broke."

Cynthia opened her mouth to speak, but what came out was a squeak.

"You want the earrings so you can sell them for cash. What's the matter, did the flavor-of-the-month kick you out?"

"You don't know what you're talking about."

"Is that so? Try this on for size. Get out of my office now, before I have security throw you out." When Cynthia didn't move immediately, Rebecca picked up the phone.

"All right, all right. I'm going. Besides, I have a date."

As Cynthia sauntered out the door, Rebecca muttered, "Heaven help the next victim."

∽◈∾

Dara sank into her favorite chair. Fleetingly, she wished she was spending the night at the beach house instead of here, but this was so much closer to the studio and her call for the morning was so early, the commute was impractical. She laid her head back and closed her eyes, letting the soothing jazz music from the sound system ease the stress from her tight muscles.

The day's filming ran over by four hours, the director was cranky because the fading daylight forced him to alter shots he had planned, and the subsequent adjustments required Dara and her co-stars to improvise dialogue, a fact that made the screenwriters apoplectic.

Tomorrow's schedule already was tight. Now Dara was waiting for the e-mail to arrive with the new script changes she would have to memorize before arriving on set at five a.m. She opened her eyes, yawned, and stretched her arms over her head, simultaneously rotating her upper torso to relieve the pressure in her upper back and neck. As she did so, she noticed the thick manila envelope her housekeeper had left for her on the coffee table. She smiled at the sight of Carolyn's neat, precise handwriting.

Once a week, Carolyn forwarded some of Constance Darrow's carefully screened fan mail to Dara. Every once in a while, when time allowed, Dara/Constance would type out a reply and send it to Carolyn so that it would go out postmarked from New York.

Dara hefted the envelope in her hands and slit open the seal to peer inside. Carolyn's usual handwritten note was on top of the pile.

My dearest Constance <g>,

I'm sorry that this week's pile is so thick. I culled out the dreck as best I could, knowing how busy your schedule is at the moment and wanting to spare you extra work.

There is one letter in here I think you'll find of special interest. It's from a professor of American literature. She's apparently quite a fan. At any rate, her points seem highly intelligent and

13

cogent. Her name is Rebecca Minton and her letter is first in the pile.

Have fun, darling. Talk soon. C.

Dara noted the embossed seal of Middlebury College above the words, "Department of English and American Literatures" and raised an eyebrow. Middlebury was an excellent liberal arts college, famous for the Bread Loaf Writers' Conference, the oldest writers' conference in America, and for the Bread Loaf School of English. The same School of English that had turned down an application from a very young and eager, up-and-coming writer named Dara Thomas. That was years ago, before she adopted the nom de plume Constance Darrow, and long before she went to Hollywood.

"I'll try not to hold a grudge."

Just as Dara opened the envelope, her computer chimed announcing the arrival of the new pages. She sighed. Rebecca Minton would have to wait. Dara Thomas, movie star, had lines to learn.

Rebecca's hands trembled as she turned the letter over and over. She hadn't dared hope that she'd hear back from Constance Darrow...and within several weeks too. She ran her fingers over the return address, which was ridiculous, she knew, since it wasn't even hand-written and it was only a post office box in New York.

"Oh, for goodness sake. Just open it and stop being a school girl."

Rebecca reached for the letter opener and made a neat slit along the top of the envelope. The paper was standard-issue letterhead, with the name Constance Darrow and the same address from the outside of the envelope centered at the top.

As she scanned the contents, she realized with a jolt that there was more than one page. Constance Darrow, Pulitzer Prize-winning author, had taken the time to write Rebecca a multi-page letter.

Ms. Minton,

Thank you for taking the time to write. I'm so pleased that you've chosen to key in on the complexity of the metaphor of weather for the condition of the human soul. I agree with you that this is critical to understanding the motivations of the protagonists throughout the novel.

However, I take issue with your assessment of Harold. I am intrigued that you characterized his relationship with God as one of disappointment. You are correct that he is a middle-aged man struggling to find and follow his path. The loss of his wife has left him questioning things he, heretofore, took for granted.

But, compelling as your thoughts on the subject are, I disagree with your conclusion. To my mind, Harold has not stopped believing in God. He's simply trying to reconcile what he knows of God and Heaven with his own personal experience, which seem to him to be at odds. I'm interested to hear your response to this interpretation...

Rebecca raised an eyebrow. Was Constance Darrow inviting her to continue their dialogue? She reread the passage. It certainly appeared that way. Rebecca squealed and held the letter to her chest. She wondered how long was appropriate to wait before replying. As she'd never replied to an author before, she was unaware of the protocol. Was there one?

"Rebecca, you're not some fan girl. You're a grown woman, a tenured professor of American literature. Act like it." Still, she couldn't help but wonder about the woman whose prose she so admired. She told herself it was because she was teaching some of Constance's works this semester, though she knew the interest went far deeper than that.

Rebecca had googled Constance, researched her copyrights with the Library of Congress, written to her publisher, her agent, and anyone else she could find who seemed remotely connected to the mysterious Ms. Darrow, explaining that she needed the information for the course she was teaching. And she'd come up completely empty. No one would tell her anything about Constance, and not a single picture of her existed anywhere that Rebecca could find. Apart from a bibliography of her work, a brief biography, and a vague description of a difficult and lonely childhood, Constance Darrow was as amorphous as a cloud.

Regretfully, Rebecca folded the letter and returned it to its envelope. Her senior seminar students would be filing into class at any moment. Rebecca locked the letter in her desk drawer, gathered up her lecture notes, and tried to get the enigma that was Constance Darrow out of her mind.

≅≅

"And, that's a wrap, people! Nice job," the director called.

The cast and crew broke into applause. Dara, who just had finished an emotionally grueling scene, blew out an explosive breath and rubbed the sore spot in the back of her neck. She blinked away the tears that had been required for the scene and looked around at the people she'd spent so many hours and days with over the course of the twelve-week shoot. They weren't a bad lot, really. But there wasn't one of them who knew the first thing about who Dara Thomas was, which made this set just like every other one she'd been on.

"Hey, pretty thing. Are you coming to the wrap party?" Luther Rollins sidled up to Dara and slipped his arm around her waist. "Leading man and his on-screen love. It'd make for great headlines."

Dara twisted out of Luther's grasp. Despite the smile still plastered on her face, she allowed the ice to show in her eyes. "I don't think so, Luther."

Then she walked away. *Not if you were the last man left on Earth.* Indeed, she would have to make an appearance at the wrap party; after all, she was the female lead and it would be bad form not to attend, but she would arrive solo, as she always did.

CHAPTER TWO

Ms. Thomas, you're the hottest box office draw and, some would argue, the most striking actress in Hollywood." The television interviewer leaned in closer, and Dara steeled herself for the inevitable. "Every man in America, and plenty of women, for that matter, would love to have you on their arm. Yet you consistently arrive at premieres and parties alone. Just yesterday, you showed up solo to the premiere of your new movie, *Rock Me Gently*. You've never been photographed with anyone 'special.' Why is that?"

Dara mustered her best aw-shucks look, even as the familiar pain stabbed at her heart. Despite her best efforts and no matter how many times she was asked the same question, Dara couldn't seem to prevent the sting of Sheilah's betrayal from piercing her well-developed emotional armor. Sheilah—the first woman she'd ever been with, the woman to whom she'd pledged her love and her life at the age of twenty-one. How naïve she'd been back then! She vividly recalled the moment all of her illusions were shattered.

"What in the world made you think it was acceptable to talk politics?" Sheilah whispered fiercely in Dara's ear.

"You told me you wanted me to have a good time. I thought—"

"You thought? What in the world gave you the impression I was interested in you for your mind?"

Dara cleared her throat and focused on the interviewer. "I'm sorry, what was the question?"

"I asked why you're never photographed with anyone special? You're a beautiful woman…"

"Listen," Sheilah hissed, *"when's the last time you looked in a mirror? You're gorgeous, even first thing in the morning. Nobody,*

17

including me, cares what's in your head. They just want to look at you. To covet you. I love that other people want what I have. Why else do you think I've kept you around the past few months? You're great for my image."

"But you told me you loved me."

"Would you have stayed if I hadn't?"

With a practiced air of ease, and no hint of the angst she was feeling, Dara answered the interviewer. "I'm picky." She sold it with a wink and a saucy smile.

The rhythmic slapping of the waves against the shore did little to soothe Dara, so she ran harder and faster. She understood that there were some things that could not be outrun, and a heart still broken after ten years was one of those things. But she'd be damned if she wasn't going to try.

Sheilah was Dara's first female lover and it was only natural for the first to hold a special place in her heart. But the newness of the experience and her budding sexuality weren't the only reasons the aborted relationship with Sheilah left such lasting scars. Sheilah encouraged Dara to share her deepest desires and dreams and held out the promise of a lifetime spent fulfilling them together. Her interest and support seemed so genuine and Dara's trust in her promises was so absolute that she poured all of her heart into the relationship.

In the beginning, it had been magical. Sheilah was the only person apart from Carolyn who accepted Dara for who she was and encouraged her to be herself, or so Dara thought. They spent hours lying in each other's arms talking about Dara's childhood. Sheilah was nurturing and compassionate, and Dara was so relieved to let her guard down for the first time in a romantic relationship. Then Sheilah so callously revealed everything to be a sham, and Dara was cast adrift and once again betrayed by someone who purported to love her.

I could've done without reliving all that.

Dara gave herself the now-familiar pep talk designed to get her out of this brooding head space: her time with Sheilah had helped her to understand herself better. She had gained sexual experience that served her well. She had learned to guard her heart, and she had learned to be more discerning about people and their motivations.

By the time Dara returned to the beach house, she was physically spent. Unfortunately, her emotions continued to churn. She turned the key in the lock and let herself in. Normally, Dara welcomed the silence of the house. Now it was a reminder of how very alone she was. Apart from Carolyn, who'd been her best friend since nursery school, Dara had no close friends. Oh, there were plenty of people who wanted to be close. Fame and beauty tended to attract all kinds of potential hangers-on. But, like Sheilah, those people were more interested in what Dara was and what she looked like, than in who she was.

Finally unable to hold back or pretend anymore that it didn't matter, she collapsed on the floor in front of the sofa and let the torrent of tears flow until they lulled her into a restless sleep.

Dara didn't know how much time had passed when she heard the incessant buzzing and the sound of someone banging on the front door. She looked around at the dark shadows that had crept across the tile floor. How long had she been asleep? She wiped her bleary, swollen eyes and grabbed a tissue.

"Dara? Sweetheart? Are you in there?"

She recognized Carolyn's voice and the alarm in her tone and hustled to undo the locks and open the door.

"Oh, thank God." Carolyn swept her into a tight hug.

"W—" Dara cleared her throat, trying to erase the hoarseness from her crying jag. "What are you doing here?"

Carolyn pulled back and examined Dara's puffy face. "Oh, my God, sweetie." Carolyn reached out her hands and smoothed her thumbs under Dara's eyes. Without another word, she drew Dara closer again and rubbed her back.

Dara wanted to object, wanted to say that she didn't need to be comforted, to be consoled. But it felt so good to be held. She closed her eyes and soaked in the sensation. As always, her best friend knew exactly what she needed and when.

After several moments, Dara pulled back. She saw the caring and deep concern written on Carolyn's face and turned away. "I need to get cleaned up." She started toward the bedroom. Carolyn stopped her with a hand on the arm.

"Don't, Dara. Don't stuff your emotions. Don't run from me."

Dara stopped and reluctantly turned around. "I don't want to feel like an emotional midget who needs her best friend every time someone says something that hurts her."

"You're not and you don't. But I saw the interview and I knew I needed to be here."

"Last I knew, you were packing to tour the national parks with Stan. And now I feel guilty for dragging you away from your plans. Poor Stan. It's a wonder he stays married to you, you know that? You spend more time with me than you do with him."

"Stan knew who he was marrying and he knew you and I were a package deal. We have been since we were five years old. He loves you as much as I do."

"That's because he doesn't know anything about me."

"He doesn't know about Constance Darrow, that's true. But he knows who you are to me, and that's good enough for him. And stop changing the subject. I didn't come here to talk about my husband or our marriage. I came here because I know you. And I know what that interview did to you."

Dara sighed and led the way to the sofa. It was clear Carolyn wasn't going to let this go.

✧❀✧

Rebecca paused the interview she had recorded on her DVR to pull her dinner out of the microwave. Once resettled on the sofa, she picked up the remote to resume the program but stopped short of hitting the Play button. There, frozen on her big-screen TV, was Hollywood sensation Dara Thomas.

Despite her best efforts, Rebecca felt her pulse quicken. Who wouldn't be turned on by that kind of beauty? Even paused in mid-word, the actress had the most perfect features Rebecca ever had seen. It was the kind of face that was tailor-made for the movies.

But there was something else, maybe the obvious intelligence in the actress's eyes, that Rebecca found absolutely irresistible. Rebecca hit the Play button.

"Ms. Thomas, you've taken some interesting roles over the past few years." The interviewer consulted his notes. "A scheming woman scorned, a romantic ingénue, a cancer-stricken young mother, a fiery rock singer... Is there any kind of role you feel is beyond you?"

Rebecca's heart melted a little more when Dara Thomas flashed her megawatt smile.

"As an actress, it's my job to make the audience suspend disbelief. I love the challenge of stretching beyond my comfort zone. My goal is always for movie-goers to forget that they're watching Dara Thomas and become absorbed in whatever character I'm playing. I so admire Meryl Streep. She's my role model. Have you ever noticed how she becomes the character she plays? She's not playing a role. She *is* the role. That's the way it should be. So I like to push myself, to play a variety of character types so that I don't get too comfortable in any one archetype."

"Oh, SAT word," Rebecca mumbled. "I knew you were more than a just pretty face." Rebecca pulled her laptop into her lap as she continued to listen to the interview. She googled Dara Thomas, unsurprised to see that there were hundreds of hits.

After reading Dara's filmography on IMDb, Rebecca clicked to the actress's official website. She scrolled through dozens of pictures of Dara at movie premieres in glorious dresses that hugged her perfect body. Rebecca got lost in the movie trailers and the numerous incarnations of Dara for a time, and then moved on to her biography. "Huh. Yale, eh? Definitely no slouch in the brains department." In fact, Dara Thomas was a magna cum laude graduate of the Yale School of Drama. There wasn't much information about her life prior to college apart from the fact that she grew up in a suburb of New York City, left home for college, and never looked back.

Rebecca read on.

Dara was an understudy at the Williamstown Theatre Festival in 2002, the summer after her graduation from Yale. Rebecca paused and whistled. The Williamstown Theatre Festival featured some of the biggest names in the business. Many famous movie and television actors and actresses took roles there in order to hone their stage skills. That Dara was able to secure an understudy position right out of school said a lot about her talent.

It was during the run of the production of Under the Blue Sky, *starring Tate Donovan, Marsha Mason, and a young Vera Farmiga, that Dara was discovered. She filled in for Vera one night when there was a major Hollywood producer in the audience and the rest, as they say, is history.*

Rebecca returned her attention to the television just as the interviewer asked Dara about her personal life. For a fraction of a second, Rebecca thought she recognized in Dara's eyes the same pain she saw when she looked in the mirror every morning. And just as quickly, it was gone, leaving Rebecca wondering if she'd really seen anything there at all.

When the interview ended, Rebecca clicked off the television, rinsed her dish in the sink, loaded it in the dishwasher, and returned to the couch to curl up with Constance Darrow's latest book.

❧❧

Dara dredged herself up from a sound sleep and fumbled for the bedside phone as it rang for the third time. "Yes," she mumbled as she pressed the receiver to her ear. She spied the digital clock with her one open eye. It was 3:34 a.m.

"Is this Dara Thomas?"

The voice was male and unfamiliar. Dara pushed herself up in the bed. "Are you aware that it's 3:30 in the morning?"

"I'm sorry for the inconvenience, Ms. Thomas. You are Ms. Thomas?"

"Yes. Who's this?"

"This is Doctor Emanuel at Memorial Sloan-Kettering."

Dara sat up. "As in the cancer hospital in New York?"

"Yes."

Dara felt panic well up in her. Surely if Carolyn had been sick she would've said something.

"Ms. Thomas? Are you there?"

"Yes." Dara gripped the receiver a little tighter. "What is it?"

"I'm afraid it's your mother."

Dara closed her eyes in relief. It wasn't Carolyn, after all. That reaction was followed immediately by another—her arms broke out in gooseflesh. "My m-mother?" Dara tried to assimilate the information. Was her mother ill? It had been so many years since they'd been in contact.

"I'm sorry to give you the news this way, Ms. Thomas, but your mother has slipped into an irreversible coma. I don't believe she'll be able to hold on much longer. She gave explicit instructions not to bother you unless..."

Dara closed her eyes as a tear leaked out. "Unless she was dead or about to be." Her tone was flat. Even in her final moments, her mother would disavow her.

"As I said," the doctor's voice sounded a little less sure, "I have no reason to believe your mother will regain consciousness, but often even comatose patients are aware of our presence."

"I understand, doctor. Thank you. What room is she in?"

Dara found a pen and a piece of paper on the night table and wrote down the information. "I'll be there as soon as I can. Thank you for letting me know."

She put the phone down and swallowed down a sense of impending panic. Her mother was dying and she just agreed to go home for the first time since she'd left for college fourteen years ago. Dara wished there was a script for handling this situation.

"The themes in Ms. Darrow's novel—absolute faith in miracles beyond all rational evidence to the contrary, and the power of belief in unseen forces to light our path in this lifetime—speak to the main character's deep spirituality. These unwavering ideals propel Celeste with grace through experiences that would bring most people to their knees." Rebecca looked up from her notes and surveyed the lecture hall full of soon-to-be-graduating seniors. "We can all learn a lesson from Celeste. May your paths forward be filled with miracles. Good luck, everyone. It's been a pleasure teaching you this semester."

As Rebecca gathered up her notes, she was surprised to hear the sound of applause. She was even more shocked to see all of her students on their feet, giving her a standing ovation. She smiled and took a mock bow. Moments like this reminded her why she chose to teach.

Dara leaned her head back against the headrest in First Class. The plane would land at New York's JFK Airport in less than an hour. Her hands trembled slightly underneath the blanket and she clasped them together.

You're not that little girl anymore, Dara. She can't hurt you now. Go see her, take care of whatever needs to be done, and get back to your life.

"Can I get you anything else, Ms. Thomas? We'll be landing in just a little while."

"No, thank you." Dara smiled at the flight attendant. The poor woman had spent half the flight playing traffic cop, keeping gawking fans from disturbing Dara. "I really appreciate your interceding on my behalf. Sorry to be so much trouble."

"You were the easy part," the woman said. "On the other hand, all those passengers turning on their phones to take pictures and tweet them…" She looked at Dara sympathetically. "I don't know how you do it."

Dara shrugged. "Goes with the territory, unfortunately."

"Well, I can tell you. After watching what you had to deal with today, I'm crossing 'famous actress' off my list of dream jobs." The plane's intercom system chimed. "Oops. Gotta go."

When Dara deplaned and cleared security, several photographers stepped in front of her. *So much for privacy and flying under the radar.* She ignored the clicking of the shutters and strode past them to where she could see Carolyn and Stan waiting for her.

"Hey, sweetie," Carolyn said, as she hugged Dara. "You okay?"

"Mm-hmm." Dara turned to Stan and accepted his hug. "Long time no see, Stan. You're looking good."

Stan pulled away and put an arm around Carolyn. "My wife takes good care of me."

As always, Dara was struck by the unmistakable love her friends shared. It was so clear that they were meant to be together. Dara swallowed the lump in her throat and blinked back the involuntary tear that threatened to escape. Carolyn and Stan had something she likely would never know. She was so happy for them, but there were times like these when the sight of two people so in love left her longing for more in her life.

"I'll grab your bags. You two go to the car. That ought to cut down on the mayhem." Stan inclined his head to where a crowd started to gather.

"I've got just one bag. A twenty-seven-inch Louis Vuitton, black."

Stan laughed easily. "That ought to narrow it down."

Carolyn looped her arm through Dara's elbow as they walked away. "So now you can tell me the truth, because I know you were lying through your teeth back there." She tugged Dara a little, momentarily unbalancing her. "How are you, really?"

Dara sighed and leaned into Carolyn. "Honestly? I'm terrified, I'm nervous, I'm angry, I'm sad." She shrugged. "Pick one."

Carolyn nodded sympathetically. "I wish you didn't have to deal with this. I wish I could spare you."

"It isn't yours to do."

"Dara Thomas! Dara, over here!"

Dara ignored the plea of the paparazzo. She had no idea who already had leaked out word of her arrival in New York, but it didn't surprise her. No doubt someone had managed to send one of those tweets from the plane. She was glad she'd taken the time to shower, blow-dry her hair, and put on her makeup.

"Let's get you out of here." Carolyn tightened her grip protectively and steered Dara out the glass doors and across the way to the parking structure. "Where do you want to go first? You're going to stay with us, right?"

Dara shook her head. "I think I ought to stay in midtown, close to the hospital."

"Nonsense—"

"Car, please. I know you mean well, but I won't be much company and I don't want to feel badly about that." Before Carolyn could object again, Dara pleaded, "Please, let me do this my way."

Carolyn stared hard at her. "Okay, but I don't have to like it. When Stan gets here, I'll have him make the reservation under his name. He can go check in for you and the paparazzi will be none-the-wiser."

"For about five minutes." Dara kissed her on the cheek. "You're a good friend, you know that?"

"I do." Carolyn smiled at her. "It goes both ways." Carolyn unlocked the car. "Do you want to go to the hotel first, then?"

Dara considered. "Tempting. But I think I should head right to the hospital."

"I'll have Stan drop us off there and go to the hotel, then come back and get us."

Dara hugged Carolyn before getting in the passenger seat. "That's not necessary. You go with Stan."

"But I want to come in with you. You don't have to do this alone."

"I love you for that and for so many other reasons, but this is something I have to do by myself."

"Again, let me say I don't have to like it."

"Noted."

CHAPTER THREE

Rebecca put her feet up on the deck railing and sipped her second cup of coffee. School had been out for a week and she was relishing the respite and the peace and quiet. She watched as a buck approached the clearing, its head up, alert for any dangers. Apparently sensing none, it began grazing in the open field. As always, Rebecca marveled at the quiet majesty.

Carefully, she put the coffee cup down on the nearby table. She didn't want to make any sudden movements that would frighten her guest, nor did she want to spill the coffee on the envelope with the now-familiar return address. Unable to resist the temptation any longer, and frankly astounded that she had lasted as long as she had, Rebecca picked up the envelope and slit it open.

Dear Ms. Minton,

I'm glad your class enjoyed On the Wings of Angels. *I, too, hope they go out into the world and discover miracles of their own.*

I find it interesting that some scholars (thank Heavens you're not one of them) somehow view as incongruent the fact that Celeste is a non-religious individual who believes wholeheartedly in the existence of forces such as angels and ascended masters.

Setting aside issues such as religious affiliation or upbringing, let me start by saying that I have the utmost respect for people of all faiths and belief systems. I'm so glad that you accept that beings of light, i.e. angels and ascended masters, exist; as you've discovered, not everyone does. As you mentioned having heated discussions with peers on the subject as it pertains to this book, I offer you the following, in case citing a quote on the subject from

27

the author is helpful to you. I'd be most curious to know what you think of my argument.

Rebecca paused, lowered the letter, and heaved a happy sigh. After three letters back and forth, Constance Darrow wanted to keep the dialogue going. She raised the letter and continued reading.

First, I think it would be incredibly arrogant to think that we're the most evolved beings in the Universe, don't you? There is plenty of evidence to suggest otherwise. So, even for a non-religious person, it makes sense that there's something else out there affecting our fate. From this standpoint, it is easy to imagine that someone with Celeste's positive outlook and inquisitiveness would investigate the possibilities.

Next, let's consider and accept that ascended masters such as Jesus, Mother Mary, Saint Francis of Assisi, and Saint Bernadette (who had visions of the Blessed Mother that led her to dig in the dirt at Lourdes), were real people who existed on this earth at some point. The fact that these figures have been adopted by religions and worshipped as religious icons does not, and should not, diminish their power as great beings, period.

Celeste recognizes these historic figures as extraordinary beings that have ascended. She views them as non-denominational figures that belong to everyone. When your colleagues think about it, even from a religious perspective, do they think it likely that Jesus would ever say to someone, "I'm sorry, you're not a Christian, so I'm not going to help you?"

I don't know you that well, but I'm imagining you laughing at that idea. And so it is that Celeste can be simultaneously non-religious and a great believer in angels, ascended masters, and miracles. I hope this gives you all necessary ammunition to fight the good fight with your colleagues.

Until next time, happy summer vacation (assuming you get one).

Constance Darrow

"Wow." In just a few short paragraphs the author had given Rebecca all the explanation she would need to support her perception of the main character as a spiritual conundrum and that fact being a central theme to the novel. More importantly, for the first time, the author had allowed some of her personality to shine through. "Careful, Ms. Darrow, one might begin to guess that you have a sense of humor and a lighter side."

As she had many times since reading Constance's first book, Rebecca let her mind wander to the mystery that was Constance Darrow. "Who are you? What do you look like? Are you bookish and frumpy or a looker? Are you old or young? Blond or brunette? Gay or straight? Tall or short?"

It was a game Rebecca played with herself, since she had no real way to satisfy her curiosity. Innately, she knew that asking Constance anything of a more personal nature would bring an end to their correspondence. No. She would stick to talking about issues relevant to the author's work, much as she longed to know more about the woman.

Rebecca carefully folded the letter, returned it to its envelope, and pondered what she would ask Constance next.

Dara shifted, trying to make herself more comfortable on the hard seat. Machines and monitors beeped and whirred all around her mother's head and tubes fed from her hands and arms. She looked so frail, so small, not at all like the proud, larger-than-life figure from Dara's childhood. Her hair, once so long and lustrous, now was completely gray and splayed limply across the pillow. Her face, once exquisite, was a grotesque mask, her skin lax, and her mouth slightly agape.

Despite her intention to stay detached, an errant tear rolled down Dara's cheek. "Oh, Mother. You would so hate to see how you look right now."

Slowly, tentatively, Dara reached out and brushed a bruised hand with her fingertips, then just as quickly withdrew.

"It's okay to touch her." Dara jumped and put her hand to her heart. The nurse, oblivious to having frightened Dara, prattled on. "I like to believe she can feel that. In fact, I've had patients emerge from comas who've told me they were aware of their loved ones holding their hands."

"How long has she..." Dara waved in a gesture that encompassed all of the medical equipment.

"Been in a coma?" The nurse fussed with the sheets. "She stopped responding yesterday morning. Up until then, she was in full command of her faculties."

"I'm sorry if she gave you any trouble."

The nurse paused in her ministrations. "Your mom? She was great. Always asking about my kids and telling me to spend more time with them."

"*My* mother?" Dara pointed at the still figure in the bed. "That woman?"

Now the nurse turned fully to face Dara. "Of course. Why are you so surprised?"

Dara swallowed several responses. *Because she never bothered spending time with me. Because if they gave awards for the most distant and coldest person, she would win hands-down. Because to her, a child was meant to be seen and not heard—an ornament, a decoration, and a testament to her good genes.*

If the nurse thought Dara's silence odd, she didn't show it. She resumed fluffing the pillows. "She talked about you all the time, you know."

Dara could just imagine what her mother might've said. "I'm afraid to ask."

Again, the nurse stopped what she was doing and looked at Dara quizzically. "Are you kidding me? Your mom was so proud of you. She bragged about you and said you were so much smarter than she ever was and that you could be anything you want to be." The nurse laughed. "I think if you'd told her you were going to run for president, she'd have said you'd win."

Dara blinked hard as her eyes again started to water. Who was this woman in the bed and what had she done with Dara's mother?

"She asked me to help her with a project," the nurse was saying when Dara tuned back in. "Wait here and I'll find it."

"Find what?" Dara furrowed her brow.

"I'll be right back." The nurse hurried from the room.

Dara studied her mother's face and wondered how much she really knew of this woman. It had been so long since they'd spoken. Was it possible that she had changed so drastically?

"Here it is. Took me a minute to find it. These dang flash drives are so small." The nurse held the USB drive out for Dara to take. She must've seen the puzzled look because she added, "Your mother made a recording for you. She asked me to give it to you if you showed up."

Dara looked from the drive in her hand to the nurse and back again. "I'm sorry?"

"I came in the other day to check on your mom and she asked me if I could help her with something. So I said, sure. She wanted to leave you an audio recording, but she had no idea how to do it. She told me technology was a mystery to her. So, on my next shift I brought in my son's laptop and set it up for her, plugged in the microphone, opened GarageBand, and hit Record."

Dara tried to imagine her mother sitting up in this bed, a laptop on her lap, talking into a microphone. She shook her head, unable to picture it.

"She rang the call bell when she was done, and I saved the file for her. Then she gave it to me for safekeeping and asked me to make sure it got to you. So here it is."

Dara closed her hand around the drive. "Thank you." She touched the nurse on the arm. "Thank you for taking such good care of my mother and for helping her with this."

"You're welcome. It's been my pleasure. Like I said, your mom was a special lady." The nurse patted Dara's hand and moved away. "I've got to look in on a few other patients. If there's anything you need, just ring the call button."

What would her mother have wanted to say so badly that she enlisted the help of a near stranger to do it? Nothing the nurse said sounded anything like the mother Dara knew. She stared at the drive in her palm. She was grateful that her computer likely was safely tucked away in the hotel room Carolyn and Stan secured for her. Otherwise, she might've been tempted to listen to the recording right now.

"Ms. Thomas?"

Dara turned to see a handsome, middle-aged man in a lab coat striding through the door. "Yes."

"I'm Doctor Emanuel. We spoke on the phone."

"Of course." Dara stood and extended her hand. "Thank you for contacting me."

The doctor glanced down at the iPad in his hand that contained her mother's medical files and nodded grimly. "As I explained to you on the phone, your mother's prognosis is not good."

"I understand."

"Your mother has a Do Not Resuscitate order on file." The doctor's look was compassionate.

"Okay." Dara let that information sink in. "What happens now?"

"That's entirely up to you. You are your mother's health-care proxy, so the decision is yours to make. What the DNR means is that your mother has asked that we not take any extraordinary measures to save her life."

Dara regarded all of the tubes and machines.

"These machines are not considered extraordinary measures," the doctor said gently. "They are simply maintaining her present condition."

"I see." Dara swallowed. "And if they were removed?"

"Most likely your mother would pass away within twenty-four to forty-eight hours."

"And if all things remain as they are right now?"

"You mean, if the machines stay in place?"

"Yes."

"She likely would continue as she is for an indefinite period of time."

"But it's your professional opinion that there's no chance of her recovering?"

"I've been involved in many cases similar to your mother's. I've never seen a patient in this circumstance recover once they've progressed to this stage."

"Oh." Dara slumped down onto the chair. After a few seconds, she asked, "Did you have a discussion with her about this? Did she say what she wanted?" Somehow, Dara felt unqualified to make choices for this woman who had been a stranger to her for so many years.

"I'm sorry, apart from the DNR and the health-care proxy, she left no specific instructions."

Dara weighed her options. What would her mother want? She glanced up at the doctor. "Do I have to decide right now?"

"No."

"If it's okay with you, I'd like to take a little time. This," Dara's gesture encompassed the room, "is a lot to take in."

"Of course." The doctor turned to leave. "I'm sorry to meet you under such difficult circumstances."

"Thank you, doctor."

When he'd left, Dara rubbed her tired eyes. "Mother? What do you expect me to do here?" Briefly, she wondered if having her make this decision was her mother's way of punishing her. Finally, she rose from the chair. She was too exhausted to think clearly. It was time to go to the hotel and rest. She gathered her things and rose. Impulsively, she leaned over and brushed her lips over her mother's forehead. Then just as quickly, she turned and ran out of the room.

≪≫

"What's the latest from your pen pal?"

"Who?" Rebecca feigned puzzlement. The steady sound of her running shoes pounding against the pavement gave her a familiar sense of comfort as she ran stride for stride with her colleague and closest friend, Natalie Runyan.

"Come on." Natalie shoved Rebecca playfully in the shoulder, nearly knocking her off stride. "How many pen pals do you have?"

Rebecca arched her eyebrows suggestively. "Maybe I have a secret life you know nothing about. A pen pal in every port."

Natalie chortled. "Nice alliteration, but I'm not buying it. Nor am I going to be dissuaded by your evasive tactics. Come on, Bec. Give."

Not for the first time, Rebecca regretted having told Natalie about the correspondence with Constance. It was a weak moment. She'd had one glass of wine too many and still was basking in the glow of the newness of the dialogue. Well, there was no way around it now. "If you must know, I just sent her another letter. At her invitation." Rebecca wasn't sure why she felt it necessary to add the last. *Probably because you don't want her to think you're stalking the poor woman.*

"She asked you to write again?" Natalie whistled, as they made the turn at the covered bridge. "Why don't you just ask the woman out, already?"

The blush crept up Rebecca's neck. "As if…"

"Hey, you never know. She might welcome the possibility."

Rebecca bristled. "First of all, we don't even know that she's a lesbian. Second, she's practically the most private person on the planet. I'm sure she'd run for the hills at the first hint of any personal line of questioning. And what makes you think I'm looking for a relationship with her? Maybe I just enjoy the conversation and accept it at face value."

Still, Rebecca's heart thudded a staccato beat at the idea of something more than a discussion about books with Constance.

❖❖

Dara sank into the in-room Jacuzzi and closed her eyes. Her laptop rested safely out of reach of the water on a wide ledge obviously designed for multitaskers like her. For several moments, she simply breathed in the scent of the lavender candle Carolyn thoughtfully left in the room for her. Her muscles and bones ached from so many hours spent sitting, first on the plane, and then in the hard hospital chair. Her head and heart ached from the emotional turmoil of the long day.

Exhaustion crept up on her and she forced her eyes open, fighting to stay awake. It wouldn't do for her to drown in a hotel Jacuzzi. She could just imagine the headlines. Her gaze settled on the USB drive sitting innocuously next to the computer.

Her mother always had been a technophobe. It took her five years after cable television came to their neighborhood to get it. Dara tried to imagine her mother using a computer to compose an audio message. It was unfathomable. What on Earth could she have wanted to say so badly? *There's only one way to find out.*

Dara dried her hands and picked up the drive. Her normally sure fingers fumbled as she tried to plug it into the laptop and she paused. *Breathe. You're not that little girl anymore. Nothing she says can hurt you now.*

It was a lie, of course. Dara understood that, but it was necessary. Otherwise, she wouldn't be able to listen to what her mother had to say.

She double-tapped the trackpad on her MacBook Pro to bring it to life, and double-clicked on the drive when it appeared on the desktop. There it was, a single file named, appropriately, "For Dara." Dara's heart fluttered and her nostrils widened as she sucked in air. It wasn't her mother's handwriting, but it might as well have been.

The arrow hovered ominously over the file. Just as Dara was about to double-click, her cell phone rang. "Oh, for goodness sake." The sudden buzz in the quiet startled her, and she practically levitated out of the tub. Carolyn. She accepted the call and hit Speaker.

"Hello?"

"Catching you at a bad time?"

"It's never a bad time for you, Car, although I will say, your timing is interesting."

"What are you doing? You sound like you're spelunking in a cave."

"I'm in the Jacuzzi. Thanks for the candle, by the way."

"You're welcome. I can call back later, if you want."

Dara considered. "No. It's okay. Are you sitting down?"

"Do I need to be?"

"Probably."

"Why? What's going on?"

"My mother recorded an audio message for me. I was just gearing myself up to listen to it."

"Oh." Carolyn drew out the word. "Do you need company? Want to wait for me?"

Dara closed her eyes. It was tempting. Nobody in the world understood the dynamic between Dara and her mother the way Carolyn did. How many times had Dara cried in Carolyn's reassuring embrace after another painful encounter?

"No. No, I can do this."

"Yes, you can. But you don't have to do it all by yourself. I'm here for you."

Dara smiled. "Always. I've given myself the pep talk. I'm good."

"You sure?"

Dara swallowed hard and mustered up her brightest tone. "Yes."

"Okay," Carolyn said, clearly not convinced. "But if you want to talk afterward, I'm keeping the phone on."

"It's late. You should turn it off and get some sleep. Poor Stan."

Carolyn's laugh was rich through the speaker. "Poor Stan has been sleeping in the recliner for the past hour. I'm pretty sure he's not missing me right now."

"Still, I don't need you to babysit me."

"Good God no, but I could use the pocket change. How much does the job pay?"

Dara smiled. "Whatever I'm paying you, it could never be enough."

"You know I'd manage your affairs for free, right?"

"You're a horrible businesswoman, you know that?"

"That's not what you say when I get you those great contracts."

"Point taken. But I'm not paying you to babysit me."

"Sweetie, this has nothing to do with our professional relationship. This is me, Carolyn, your best friend." Carolyn's voice was soft, comforting.

"I know. And I love you."

"Thank God. But I mean it, Dar. I'm right here if you need me."

"I hear you. I'll be fine."

"Okay. But if you're not…"

"I'll call you in the morning, okay?"

"Good night."

"Sweet dreams, Car."

"Dara?"

Dara halted her finger just before hitting the End button. "Mm-hmm?"

"Remember who you are, not who she wanted you to be."

Dara's lip quivered. "Right." She wondered if her voice sounded as small to Carolyn as it did to her. "Good night." This time she did disconnect the call.

Dara turned the jets in the Jacuzzi back on and double clicked on the file before she could over-think it anymore.

CHAPTER FOUR

D ear Dara. I don't know why, but I feel like this should start as a letter, since, in essence, that's what this is, I suppose. A spoken letter to my only daughter. To say the things I should've said a long time ago."

Dara closed her eyes. Her mother's voice sounded so weak and scratchy, not at all like the powerful, commanding tone she was used to hearing.

"Oh, Mother. What happened to you?" Age, Dara supposed or maybe it was just the illness. She did the math in her head. Her mother was forty-five when she'd given birth to her only child. That would make her seventy-six years old now. Still, the difference between the booming, self-assured, imperious woman Dara knew and this tentative, soft-spoken slip-of-a-woman was stark and difficult to reconcile.

Her mother's wracking cough brought Dara back from her musings.

"I'm sorry. I seem to lose my breath often these days. I have a feeling I don't have long to live. I don't mean to be overly dramatic, although I imagine if I were, that would be the woman you'd recognize best." Weak, self-deprecating laughter brought on another bought of coughing. "On with it, then, before I can't get this done."

The jets on the Jacuzzi shut off, and Dara reset the timer one more time.

"I regret many things in my life, but the one thing I will never regret—the one thing I know I got right—is you." Her mother sucked in a wheezing breath. "I bet that surprises you. But there it is."

Dara's eyebrows shot up. "Not surprised, Mother. Shocked might cover it," Dara mumbled.

"Please understand. Your father and I never wanted children."

"That, I can believe."

"When we got the news that I was pregnant, I panicked. I was so ill-equipped to parent a child. And your father... Well, your father wanted no part of it. Oh, how we argued. He wanted me to get an abortion. Can you imagine? Or I could put you up for adoption. Those were the only options he was willing to consider."

Dara squeezed her eyes shut on the tears. To hear exactly how unwanted she had been in such naked terms made her cry for that little girl.

"As my due date came closer, something shifted in me. I fought for you with a ferocity I barely recognized in myself. Your father gave me an ultimatum, and I stood up to him. He backed down and I was proud of myself.

"Then you were born. You were the most perfect little child. Your father fell in love with you as much as I did." Another, more powerful coughing spell rattled her mother's chest. "I'm sorry. I don't know how to stop and start this darned thing, or I would spare your ears."

Dara could hear the rustling of the hospital-bed sheets and envisioned her mother trying to get comfortable.

"Anyway, I'll get on with it while the getting's good. Neither one of us had a clue how to raise a child, no less a bright, inquisitive, sensitive child like you. It's not like you came with an instruction manual.

"As you began to talk, you would say the damnedest things. Not the kinds of words other little toddlers said, but really advanced, complete sentences. It was as if someone was putting the words in your mouth. You saw and noticed things nobody else did. We never knew what you would say in public. It frightened your father, I'll tell you."

There was a pause, and Dara heard her mother struggling to take in air.

"As for me, I had no idea what to make of it. I just wanted you to be like other children. Your difference put so much pressure on my marriage."

"*My* marriage," Dara scoffed. Now that was more like the self-centered mother she knew.

"Anyway, once you hit six or seven, you started talking about imaginary people who weren't in the room. When we corrected you and told you that you were making things up, you would get indignant."

Dara closed her eyes, remembering. "Making things up" was more genteel than what her parents would say. They accused her many times of being a little liar and a troublemaker. For a small child to hear such things from the people in her life that were supposed to love her was devastating. It shook her to her core. But she knew what she knew. She wasn't lying. She wasn't. Dara shivered even in the warmth of the Jacuzzi, feeling more like that little girl than a thirty-one-year-old woman.

The first time it happened, Dara was on the playground at recess, playing kickball with her friends. The ball sailed over her head and down an embankment. She chased after it. When she finally caught up to it, there was a boy standing next to it.

"What's your name?"

"I'm Timmy. This your ball?"

Little Dara shifted from one foot to the other. "Yeah. Wanna come play with us?" She pointed in the direction of the game.

"Sure."

Dara picked up the ball and they ran up the rise together. "Everybody, this is Timmy. He's going to be on my team."

Every single child, with the exception of her best friend, Carolyn, laughed at her.

"What's so funny?" Dara threw the ball back to the pitcher and put her little hand on her hip.

The children continued to laugh. "I'm sorry they're so rude," Dara said to Timmy. He shrugged.

"Dara?" The teacher motioned for her to come over.

"Wait here," Dara said to Timmy. "I'll be right back." She darted to where her first-grade teacher was waiting. "Yes, Mrs. Sparks?"

"Who are you talking to?"

"You mean Timmy?"

"Who's Timmy?"

"That little boy over there." Dara jerked her thumb in Timmy's direction. "He was down the hill all by himself, so I asked if he wanted to play with us."

The teacher followed the direction of Dara's thumb, then looked kindly back at her. "There's no one there."

Dara stood up a little straighter. "Of course there is. That's Timmy."

Mrs. Sparks put a hand gently on Dara's shoulder. "Dara, there's no little boy over there."

Dara felt her face grow red and she raised her voice and gestured again in Timmy's direction. "He's right there. His name is Timmy."

Mrs. Sparks shook her head. "Lower your voice, young lady. You need to take a time out. Go sit on the bench and take your imaginary friend with you."

"I'm not making him up and you're being rude. He's right there." Again, Dara gestured toward Timmy. "He's the one wearing the striped shirt."

"That's enough! One more word, young lady, and I'll send you to the principal's office."

Dara was shaking with fear at the thought of being sent to Mr. Ponterio's office. He had a brush cut and liked to pinch everybody's cheek. She marched to the bench and dropped down onto it hard, glaring at the kids happily playing. Timmy came and sat down next to her.

"I'm sorry I got you in trouble."

"S'okay. I'm sorry they're all so rude."

"Listen, I've got to go. Maybe I'll see you around sometime."

"Yeah. See you around." When he was gone, Dara folded her arms over her chest and brooded.

At the end of recess, Carolyn came and sat down next to her. For a moment, neither of them said a word. Eventually, Carolyn said, "We better get inside."

Dara nodded morosely. When they were almost to the building, she said, "You could see him, right?"

"Your friend, Timmy?" Carolyn asked.

"Yeah."

"No. But that doesn't mean anything," she hurried on. "You're probably the only one who can see him because you're special."

Satisfied with that answer, Dara bumped shoulders with her best friend and skipped the rest of the way to the door.

Dara clicked pause and rose out of the Jacuzzi. If she stayed in there any longer, she'd turn into a prune. She toweled off and tried to shake the memory. She would leave the rest of the recording for the morning. Right now, what she really needed was a good night's sleep.

༻ං

The invitation shook in Rebecca's hand. What had possessed her to accept? Whatever had she been thinking? *You were thinking that high school was a long time ago, you haven't seen or talked to any of these people in twenty years, and you're not that girl anymore. Suck it up and go inside. It won't help your case if they see you sitting out here in the car talking to yourself.*

She unbuckled her seatbelt and opened the door of the rental car. "I'm a grown woman—an accomplished professor of American literature at a prestigious institution of higher learning. I'm a... Oh, stuff it." Her heart sank as she saw someone get out of the car behind her and lurch in her direction.

"No, it can't be..." The man with the paunch and the balding pate squinted. "Hefty Becky? Is that you?" He wolf-whistled.

It was all Rebecca could do not to turn around, get in the car, and hightail it out of there. Instead, she threw back her shoulders and mustered her best inauthentic smile. She would not allow this Neanderthal to spoil her night this early. After all, there would be plenty of time for that over the course of the next few hours.

"Bobby." She acknowledged him with a small nod. "Are you here for the reunion, or are you still retaking Mr. Reistetter's geometry class?"

"Still a smart-ass. But damn, you look hot."

Rebecca did her best not to squirm under the inappropriate scrutiny of the school's number one jock and biggest bully. He was the epitome of every cliché about high school she could imagine. And he and his friends had made her life completely miserable.

"You must be like a hundred pounds lighter. And you ditched the dorky glasses." He undressed her with his eyes. "Damn. I could tap that."

Rebecca felt the bile rise up in her throat and a frisson of fear run down her spine. She forced herself to walk toward the entrance to the hotel. "Thank God. Now we know where all the blood is flowing, since it isn't being used elsewhere." She watched with amusement as Bobby tried to puzzle out her meaning. He still hadn't gotten it by the time they reached the hotel lobby.

According to the electronic sign in the lobby, the reception was in Ballroom A on the second floor. Rebecca spotted a ladies' room and peeled off in that direction. She braced both palms on the marble sink countertop and leaned forward. Her breathing was shallow and her cheeks were pale. "Of all the people I could run into first, it had to be the biggest asshole in the history of high school assholes. God, if this is your idea of a joke, I'm not laughing."

Rebecca jumped at the sound of a flushing toilet and blushed a deep shade of crimson when she looked in the mirror and saw a classmate exit a stall and wash her hands.

"You must be talking about Bobby Frasier."

"Sorry. I didn't know anyone else was in here."

The woman checked her lipstick. She met Rebecca's eyes in the mirror. "Would it have changed your opinion of Bobby if you had?"

Rebecca laughed. "No, but I might have kept the thought bubble in my head." She held out her hand. "I'm Rebecca. Minton."

"Sharon Glastonbury. Our lockers were almost next to each other."

"I remember. You were the prom queen." *And you look like you still could win a beauty contest or two.*

"And you were the class valedictorian. Smartest kid I ever knew. Oh, how I envied your brain."

Rebecca blushed again and lowered her eyes. "Oh, how I envied your looks. You're still beautiful, by the way."

Sharon touched Rebecca gently on the elbow to get her attention. "Keep your head up. You're a gorgeous woman.

Remember, looks fade, intelligence is far more useful. Combine the two together in a package like you and..."

Rebecca smiled. Was this woman flirting with her, or just trying to make her feel better?

"C'mon," Sharon said, looping her arm through Rebecca's. "Let's go face the masses together."

Rebecca allowed Sharon to lead her into the ballroom. The room was packed with well-dressed women and men in suits. Rebecca recognized several faces. Although names escaped her, she well could remember how she'd been treated by some of these classmates.

Sharon increased the pressure on the inside of her elbow, and Rebecca looked at her questioningly. "I can feel the tension vibrating off you. How about if we head directly for the bar and get ourselves something to drink? You know, to take the edge off."

"That would be fantastic." She covered Sharon's hand with her free hand and gave it a quick squeeze, hoping the gesture adequately conveyed her gratitude.

They ordered drinks and settled at a nearby table. Sharon stared at her appraisingly, and Rebecca willed herself not to look away. "I'm wondering what you do for a living, and I'm thinking I'll take a couple of guesses before I let you correct me."

"Okay."

"Hmm. I know you don't do manual labor—your hands are too soft and the manicure's too perfect for that." Sharon cocked her head to one side. "Pretty enough to be a model or an actress, but I think that would be a waste of your intellect."

Rebecca raised an eyebrow. "What makes you think actresses aren't smart? I would think having to inhabit so many characters and memorize all that dialogue would require quite a bit of intelligence."

Sharon waved a hand dismissively. "Yes, but not the kind of brain power you possess. I'd be terribly disappointed if you wasted all those smarts entertaining other people."

Rebecca had a fleeting image of Dara Thomas, Yale graduate, and thought about what Sharon said. If she weren't an actress, what would Dara Thomas be doing?

"Well, I suppose some people would say it's part of my job to be entertaining."

Sharon's eyes lit up. "Ah, so you're willing to provide hints. Excellent." She tapped a finger against the side of her head. "Are you self-employed, or do you work for someone else?"

"The latter."

"Good." Sharon nodded her approval.

"Why?"

"Someone as lovely as you shouldn't be sitting home by herself. It would be a waste."

Definitely flirting. "Although large chunks of my job are spent in blessed solitude."

Sharon squinted her eyes, re-evaluating. "I see. I know you wouldn't be anything as mundane as a bank loan officer or a salesperson that spends a lot of time in the car."

"God, no."

"Do you train other people?"

Rebecca pursed her lips. "In a manner of speaking."

"Well, damn, girl. This isn't as simple as I thought it would be."

"You're the one who wanted to guess."

"True." Sharon waved a white cocktail napkin. "I surrender."

"That was easy." Rebecca laughed.

"So?"

"I'm a professor."

Sharon slapped her hand on the table. "Teacher. Why didn't I think of that?"

"Is that a noble enough profession for you?"

"Absolutely. Is it an Ivy League school?"

"Middlebury College."

"In Vermont?"

"That's the one."

"Great school. My niece went there. Second smartest kid I ever knew, after you." Sharon's fingers brushed Rebecca's forearm. "What do you teach?"

"American literature."

Sharon nodded. "I can see that."

"So, is that a waste of my talents?"

"No. No, I think that's perfect. Challenging and shaping the next generation to take over the world? I like it."

"I'm so glad you approve. So, your turn."

"Guess away."

"Not me," Rebecca said. "I'll take the straightforward approach. What do you do for a living?"

"Really? Just like that? No foreplay?"

Rebecca feigned mock surprise. "Is that what you were doing?"

"As if you didn't know. You're too savvy not to have figured that out already." Sharon batted her eyelashes suggestively. "Any interest?"

Rebecca shifted in her seat. Sharon was a remarkably attractive woman, and it had been so long...

"I'm sorry if I misconstrued." Sharon started to rise, and Rebecca stopped her by grabbing her hand.

"Don't go." Sharon sat back down. "You didn't." More quietly, Rebecca said, "If I was in the market, I'd jump at the chance—"

"I should've known someone as hot as you would be taken."

Rebecca shook her head. "It isn't that. I'm single. It's just—"

"You've been burned."

"Badly," Rebecca agreed.

"Been there, done that, myself." Sharon looked at Rebecca earnestly. "I'm not asking you to marry me. I've had a crush on you since freshman year in high school. I figure now is a good time to tick one of my fantasies off my list."

"You. Had a crush on me?" Rebecca blushed.

"Is that so hard to believe?"

Rebecca thought back to the chubby, ill-at-ease, self-conscious, socially inept girl she'd been back then. The idea that a girl that every boy in school lusted after harbored a secret interest in her... Well, it simply was inconceivable.

"Frankly, yes."

Sharon put her hand on Rebecca's leg under the table and Rebecca's stomach flipped. "I'm telling you the truth. I meant what I said. Your brain was so sexy. I just wanted to sit and listen to you talk."

Ah, so it wasn't sexual, after all.

"I know what you're thinking," Sharon said, removing her hand. "It wasn't like that. I was attracted to you for your brain, but

45

make no mistake about it, I would've jumped your bones in a heartbeat if I'd known what the hell I was doing." Sharon's laugh was self-deprecating. "I had all these feelings for girls and I had no clue what that meant."

This was something Rebecca could understand. "Me either. I just knew I wasn't interested in boys. But then, they weren't interested in me, either, so that sort of made it a moot point."

"Well, look around the room, honey. Every man in the room is drooling over you now."

Rebecca glanced around dubiously. There were heads turned in their direction. "I suspect they're looking at you, not me. It was true then, and it's true now."

"Thank you, but you're selling yourself short." Sharon's eyes were alive with appreciation. "So what do you say? You want to blow this pop stand? Go someplace more private? I've got a room upstairs."

Rebecca glanced around, then down at her watch, surprised. They'd been sitting there, nursing their drinks for the better part of an hour. "Don't you think we ought to at least pretend to be engaged?"

"I thought that's what we were about to do—become more engaged." Sharon's voice was smooth as honey.

"I was talking about the event, as you well know. Don't you think we ought to at least mingle for a little bit before we take off?"

"You afraid people will talk?"

Rebecca shook her head. "Why would it bother me if people I never cared about speculate that I left the party with the most attractive woman in the place? I would think that would be the ultimate revenge."

"Is that what you're looking for? Revenge?" Sharon's voice was quieter now.

"No. These cretins don't mean anything to me. I don't give a fig what conclusions they draw."

"Then come with me now, Rebecca." Sharon took Rebecca's hand under the table. "I promise not to put any pressure on you. I swear this is a bucket list thing. Consider it an act of mercy."

"Pfft. As if." Rebecca thought about how much she didn't want to know anything about these people or get caught up on their lives. She could go back to her own hotel and read. Or she could spend a lovely evening with Sharon. Really, there was no decision to make.

"Let's go."

CHAPTER FIVE

L ittle Dara held tightly to her mother's hand. The room was packed with people, all dressed in black, many of them holding handkerchiefs and blowing their noses. As she peeked around her mother's dress, Dara spied her Uncle Charlie, her Aunt Charlotte, her older cousin Georgia, and her mother's best friend, Tessa. Just past them was a big, shiny black box. Her mother had called it a casket.

Everyone who came in stopped by the box, and then came to kiss her mother on the cheek and cry. Dara thought it an odd ritual. All the while, her grandfather stood ramrod straight next to the box, alternately beaming or brooding at the people standing in front of the box. As Dara never had been particularly close to him, she was happy to keep her distance.

A man Dara didn't know bent over to whisper in her mother's ear, pointing in the direction of another room. Her mother sniffled a little and nodded.

"Ladies and gentlemen," the man said, straightening up, "if you would please take your seats in the chapel, we'll be getting started momentarily."

Dara's mother waited for the room to clear, and then gave Dara's hand a tug. They moved in the direction of the box. Her mother let go of her hand and leaned into the box. Dara wasn't tall enough to see inside, so she watched her grandfather warily as he leaned over and patted her mother on the back as she sobbed.

After a few minutes, her mother turned to her. "Do you want to say goodbye to Granddad?"

"Why? Is he going somewhere?"

"Dara, we talked about this." Her mother's voice was stern. "Granddad has gone to heaven to be with Grandmom."

Slowly, Dara shook her head, watching her grandfather out of the corner of her eye. "He hasn't left yet, Mother. He's right there." Dara pointed.

Her mother gasped and grabbed Dara by the shoulders, her fingers digging into Dara's flesh.

"You're hurting me." More frightening to Dara was the look on her mother's face. "How could you?" Her mother shook her shoulders. "Why do you want to hurt me?"

"I-I don't want to hurt you, Mother." Tears began to roll down Dara's cheeks. "Granddad is right there. He's been watching the whole time. He called Mr. Sandstein a-a something-monious son-of-bitch."

"Augh. You are a hateful child. I wish I'd never had you."

The slap stunned Dara and left her cheek stinging, but the words hurt more.

"What's going on here?" Dara's father strode into the room.

"She's insisting that Dad is over there, perfectly fine and watching. Why must she torment me?" Dara's mother hid her face in a handkerchief.

"I'll take care of this."

Dara's father lifted her into the air. Suddenly, her head was rushing downward and she closed her eyes. When she opened them, her upper body was hovering just above the inside of the box. She was nose-to-nose with someone who looked vaguely like her grandfather, only more pinched and sunken. She slammed her mouth shut on a scream.

"That," her father hissed, "is your grandfather. He's dead. Here." He used his free hand to yank Dara's hand and place it on her grandfather's cheek. It was freezing cold to the touch. Dara struggled to pull back, to get away.

When her father put her down, Dara bolted for the exit. She ran out the door and into the parking lot, her eyes wild and her little body shaking with fear. She found their car and pulled frantically on the door handle. The door was locked. She heard a noise and turned to see her father walking toward her, his face a mask of anger. Again, Dara yanked on the handle.

When her father was a few steps away, Dara simply slid down to the ground, crouching and cowering.

"What are you doing?" her father asked.

Dara's lip quivered. "I—"

"Never mind. You want to be out here so badly? Fine." Her father unlocked the front passenger door, then reached around and unlocked and opened the back door. "Get in." He made a sweeping motion with his hand. When she didn't move, he gave her a quick shove.

Dara stumbled into the back seat. Her father closed the door and locked the car.

"You can stay in there until the funeral is over. I'm sure your mother will be much relieved."

When he was gone, Dara curled up on the vinyl seat and cried. After a short while, she fell asleep. She awoke to see an angel watching over her. She was radiant. Her hair glistened in the sunlight. She wore a flowing bright white robe that matched the feathers on her wings.

"Don't be afraid, my child, for we angels are here, watching over you. Always."

"I'm not afraid of you." Dara jutted out her chin.

The angel smiled. "I'm glad."

As she looked into the angel's kind face, Dara's resolve crumbled and tears pooled in her eyes.

"It's okay to cry." The angel wrapped her wings around Dara, and she knew a comfort unlike any she'd ever known.

"Everybody thinks I'm crazy. The other kids make fun of me and my parents hate me."

"They don't hate you, dear. They simply cannot see the things that you see and so they do not understand. For instance, they didn't see your grandfather standing next to the casket, but you did. Most of your classmates didn't see Timmy on the playground, but you did."

Dara looked up into the angel's face. "You know about Timmy?"

"Of course. We see everything."

Dara scrunched up her eyes. "You said 'most' of the kids couldn't see Timmy."

"That's right."

"Does that mean that I wasn't the only one who saw him?"

The angel laughed delightedly and hugged Dara to her. "You're a very bright little person. Yes, there was one other little girl who saw, but she wasn't as brave as you in speaking out."

Dara frowned. "I don't want to be brave. I want to be like everyone else."

"I want to be like everyone else. I want to be like everyone else. I want to be like everyone else..." Dara's head flailed from side to side on the pillow. She gasped and shot up as she came awake in the hotel bed. Sweat dripped between her breasts. She buried her face in her hands as her heart continued to pound. *You're not that little girl anymore. That was a long time ago. That time is done. Let it go.*

Dara turned and put her feet on the floor. The bedside clock read 5:55 a.m.

After a trip to the bathroom and a splash of cold water on her face, she lay back down. Dara didn't want to sleep—no, that would be risking another dream. Besides, her mind still was racing. She hadn't recalled those childhood memories in a very long time, but it wasn't hard to figure out what had triggered them.

The laptop sat on the table in the corner. The last thing Dara wanted to do was subject herself to more of her mother's confessional tale. But today Dara would have to decide whether her mother lived or died. At the very least, she owed it to this woman she barely knew to hear her out.

"How about if I call room service and have them send up some champagne?" Sharon asked, as she dropped her purse on the dresser.

"Sure." Rebecca stood just inside the door, wondering what the hell she was doing here.

"You are planning to come farther into the room, aren't you?"

Sharon's delicate hand rested on her hip, inviting Rebecca's scrutiny. The fingers were long and tapered, and...

"I'll take that for a yes," Sharon said, acknowledging Rebecca's stare. She approached slowly, deliberately, maintaining eye contact.

Rebecca swallowed hard, rooted to the spot, mesmerized. Then Sharon was standing in front of her, running a finger across her lips, and all thought fled in a rush of blood to Rebecca's center. She knew exactly why she was there. It had been too long and she badly needed to restore her confidence. A very attractive woman wanted her—her, the chubby, awkward kid—apparently to satisfy a teenage fantasy. Well, she certainly could help with that.

She sucked Sharon's index finger into her mouth. As Sharon's eyes fluttered, Rebecca pulled her close, released her finger, and claimed her lips instead. They were soft, intoxicating, and Rebecca happily lost herself in the kiss.

As if in a dream, she walked Sharon backward toward the bed, never relinquishing her lips, and unzipped her dress as they moved. Rebecca was vaguely aware of Sharon's hands kneading her ass. It spurred her on. She grazed her fingertips along Sharon's spine, pausing to unhook her bra and release her breasts as Sharon gasped in pleasure.

Emboldened and on fire, Rebecca eased the dress and the bra off Sharon's shoulders in one motion and let both garments fall to the floor at their feet. She felt a rush of air on her skin and barely had the time to wonder how Sharon had managed to de-frock her without her being aware of it.

When Sharon covered Rebecca's nipple with her warm tongue, Rebecca pulled her closer, tumbling both of them onto the bed.

Sharon was relentless. She recaptured Rebecca's breast, further teasing her already-taut nipple. If Sharon kept this up much longer, Rebecca would lose the upper hand. And after being dominated and used by Cynthia for too long, Rebecca very much wanted to be the one in control.

She slid her thigh between Sharon's legs and rocked against her damp panties.

"If you keep that up," Sharon said, in between licks, "I'm going to lose my place."

In answer, Rebecca wrapped her arms around Sharon and rolled them over. Then she got to her feet and stood alongside the bed. "I'm sure you'll find it again, but right now I've got other ideas." She slid her fingers inside Sharon's panties, brushing her thumb lightly over Sharon's clit. "Help me get these off?"

Rebecca indicated the underwear and Sharon lifted up to facilitate their removal.

"You too."

Rebecca complied, pleased at the look of admiration in Sharon's eyes. "You like what you see?"

"What's not to like? You're a knockout. Surely you know that now."

Rebecca smiled wryly. "It's always nice to be reminded. Now, where was I?" She maintained her position by the side of the bed, enjoying her vantage point. She trailed her fingers from Sharon's jaw, down along the curve of her neck to the hollow of her throat, where she leaned over and planted a soft kiss. Sharon reached for her, but Rebecca evaded her touch.

Sharon groaned in protest.

"You'll get your turn. All in due time."

"I didn't figure you to be sadistic." Sharon's eyes followed Rebecca's every move.

"Your idea of sadism and mine must be very different." Rebecca resumed her exploration, allowing her fingers and tongue to roam freely over Sharon's body, creating a trail of goose bumps in their wake. She'd never made love to anyone while standing over them. The feeling of power was exhilarating.

"Please," Sharon pleaded, reaching again for Rebecca. "You're killing me."

"You want me to stop?" Rebecca grazed her teeth over the pulse point in Sharon's neck.

"God, no. I want you to take me. Now, please."

Sharon's breathless plea was all the encouragement Rebecca needed. She entered Sharon with two fingers, simultaneously circling her clit with her thumb. In seconds, Sharon was rising off the bed to meet her thrusts. Sharon's face was the picture of rapture. She came on a strangled cry, a light sheen of sweat covering her body.

When Sharon's breathing slowed, Rebecca gently extracted her fingers. Sharon sighed. "That was…different." She rolled on her side to face Rebecca. "Any chance I can get my hands on you now?" Her tone was light, but Rebecca had no trouble hearing the undercurrent of desire.

In truth, although Rebecca was incredibly turned on, she wasn't inclined to be touched. Not by a stranger. But Sharon wasn't really a stranger, was she? After all, they'd known each other once, many years ago, hadn't they? Still, sex with a virtual stranger was not something Rebecca did. Sex was an act of love, not of lust. And yet, here she was, having just brought this woman to climax in a hotel room after only an hour's worth of conversation. What was she doing?

Sharon cleared her throat, and Rebecca snapped back into the moment. "Should I take that as a stinging rebuke?"

"No." Rebecca motioned for Sharon to slide over, and she sat gingerly on the side of the bed. "It isn't you." Rebecca ran her thumb across Sharon's bottom lip. "Heaven knows you're sexy, and I'm completely soaked."

"But?" Sharon propped herself up on an elbow.

"But this isn't me." Rebecca struggled for the words; Sharon deserved her honesty. "When Cynthia cheated on me—"

"Ouch."

"Exactly." Rebecca fidgeted with the sheets. "Anyway, when she cheated on me, I think I lost my confidence. I no longer trusted my judgment and I felt so...I don't know...unattractive. It was like being that teenager all over again."

"I totally get that." Sharon's eyes were kind. Rebecca noted that she made no move to cover herself.

"I think maybe tonight, this," Rebecca indicated the two of them, "was my way of reminding myself that there are women out there—remarkably attractive women—who might want me."

Sharon nodded sympathetically, but did not try to touch her.

"I'm really sorry. I shouldn't have let this go so far." Rebecca started to get up. Sharon stopped her with a hand on her wrist.

"Hey. It's okay. I don't want you to feel badly about this, Rebecca." Sharon covered her hand with her free hand. "I'm a big girl. As I told you up front, I was just looking to mark the experience off on my bucket list. I'm not deluded enough to think this was ever going to be anything but a pleasant diversion. And it certainly was that." Again, she eyed Rebecca appreciatively. "You are very beautiful. And that Cynthia, whoever she is, is an ass."

"Still, I feel like a cad."

"Stop it. I'm well satisfied, my body feels great, and I've got a wonderful memory to tuck away in my mental journal of outstandingly fun experiences. I promise you, this is one reunion I'll remember quite fondly."

Rebecca rose from the bed, leaned over, and gently kissed Sharon's lips. "You're an amazing woman. Whoever ends up with you will be very, very lucky."

"I'm not planning to settle down anytime soon, but thank you for the compliment. Now you'd better get going before I forget my manners and decide to ravage you anyway."

Rebecca caressed Sharon's cheek with her fingertips, and then planted a kiss there. "I'd tell you to keep in touch..."

Sharon laughed. "I promise if I'm ever in Vermont, I'll look you up."

"Good. Seems I owe you that champagne we never got around to ordering."

"Good point. Goodbye, Rebecca. I hope you find everything you're looking for."

"You too, Sharon. You too."

Sharon rose and disappeared into the bathroom. Rebecca understood that this was her way of allowing Rebecca to dress and slip out without any more awkwardness. And she was grateful.

Rebecca managed to get out of the hotel and back to where she was staying without running into anyone from the reunion. She let herself into her room, tossed her purse and the room and car keys on the dresser, and stepped out of her clothes on her way into the bathroom. She still was aroused, and the fact that her hands smelled like sex didn't help.

She stepped into the shower and allowed the hot water to flow over her back as she soaped herself. Her breasts were sensitive, and the slightest touch sent pinpricks of pleasure shooting directly to her center. She slipped a finger into the wetness and groaned. That's when she saw Cynthia's face in her mind's eye. Rebecca withdrew her finger, rested her forehead against the coolness of the shower wall, and cried. It had been more than a year since the ugly ending with her ex, and in all that time, Rebecca had successfully brought herself to orgasm exactly once.

Rebecca wondered if that wasn't the real reason she had resisted Sharon's touch. How embarrassing would it have been to fail to reach orgasm with a woman as attractive as that?

"This is ridiculous." Cynthia certainly wasn't having any sexual dysfunction over the break up. Rebecca was certain of that. The woman had no conscience. "What did I ever see in you?" Rebecca wondered aloud.

She knew the answer. Cynthia was sleek, and confident, and very, very persuasive. She had the ability to make any woman think she was the center of the universe...until she got bored or got everything she thought she could get out of the relationship.

Rebecca finished her shower, toweled herself off on the bathmat, and stood looking in the mirror. Her breasts were high and firm. Her belly was flat. There was no hint of the overweight, awkward teenager she'd been, except in her head. In her head, she couldn't shake the memories of the taunting cruelty of her peers, the very same peers who most likely were still, at this moment, laughing it up at the reunion, every bit as immature and insufferable as they had been twenty years ago.

Again, Rebecca wondered what had possessed her to come to the reunion. Then her mind flashed on the image of Sharon, head thrown back, lost in a moment of pure pleasure, and she smiled. The connection with her made the trip all worthwhile. Despite the way the night turned out, Rebecca easily could envision Sharon showing up one day in her Middlebury office, offering to take her to dinner. And it wouldn't be the least bit uncomfortable.

Rebecca snorted. Maybe by then she'd be sufficiently recovered from the Cynthia trauma to truly enjoy herself.

CHAPTER SIX

The arrow rested ominously on the Play button icon as Dara's finger hovered above the track pad. She was fully dressed for day two at the hospital and had been for an hour. Several times, she'd clicked on Play and then, just as quickly, on Pause. Although she'd been up for a long time, she'd been unable to shake off the remnants of the dream. The idea of listening to more of what her mother thought she ought to know had her stomach in knots.

Dara thought about her time at the hospital yesterday. The person the nurse described was nothing like the mother she remembered. It was possible her mother's monologue would get better. Wasn't it? Shouldn't she give her the benefit of the doubt?

She rubbed her damp palms on her pressed slacks. Visiting hours would be starting soon and she needed to get back to the hospital. There was no point putting it off any longer. Dara pushed Play and resigned herself to hearing her mother out.

"Anyway, I don't want to dwell on all that." Her mother was wracked by another coughing spasm. "It was a long time ago and there's no use revisiting what I'm sure must be painful memories for both of us."

The covers rustled and Dara's mother groaned in pain.

"Yes, I suspect it might come as a surprise to you that I recognize how difficult that time must've been for you. I wasn't completely unsympathetic, Dara, despite what you might think. I was simply out of my league when it came to dealing with a child. Period. And you weren't just any child. You were bright, inquisitive, head strong, and that imagination... Well, who could keep up with it, or you? In the end, it just seemed easier to give you a wide berth than to constantly fight with you."

Dara paused the recording, closed her eyes, and willed herself not to cry. Again. All the familiar feelings of loneliness, isolation, and abandonment, all the days and nights when she'd longed for her mother to take her in her arms and tell her she was loved and valued—every painful moment bubbled up from deep within her, threatening to swallow Dara whole.

"Enough." She'd shed enough tears over her childhood. That time was done and gone. There was no sense mourning it at this late stage. Dara got up and poured herself a glass of water and took a big gulp before sitting back down. She could get through this. She had to. She pressed Play.

"I'm not proud of myself, Dara. I know I wasn't the mother you needed or the mother I should have been. Every day I looked at your unhappy face that was abundantly clear. You seemed so lost, so solitary in your own world. I hated being constantly reminded just what a failure I was at this nurturing thing. Often, I wondered if you wouldn't have been better off if I had listened to your father and put you up for adoption."

Dara gasped as a renewed blast of pain bloomed in her chest. What kind of mother tells her daughter that she should've gotten rid of her when she had the chance?

"Damn it." This time the coughing lasted for several minutes and left her mother gasping for breath. "There I go getting off track again. I'd blame it on all these darned medications making me dopey, but the fact is, I'm old and I get distracted easily." Her mother cleared her throat. "On with it, then. I didn't decide to make this tape to justify myself to you. There are things I want you to know. Things you should know."

Dara's heartbeat accelerated. She wasn't at all sure she could take any more of her mother's revelations.

"I'm very proud of you, Dara."

"What?"

"There. I said it. I know I can't take any credit for the woman you've become, but I want you to know that I burst a button every time I read about something you've done, whether it's using your fame to raise money for charity, or conducting yourself in an interview. You have such grace and poise. I know that's not just your acting, either. I know you well enough to know the genuine you when I see it. Of course, I've seen all of your movies. You really are quite good. In a way, you remind me of a young Kate Hepburn."

Dara nearly choked. Katherine Hepburn was her mother's favorite actress. How many times had she sat with her mother watching Hepburn and Spencer Tracy or Hepburn and Bogie? It was the closest she and her mother ever came to bonding. Those were the moments when she first decided she wanted to act. She'd watched as her mother sat riveted to the screen and wanted nothing more than to command that kind of attention and evoke those types of emotions. As much as she didn't want to admit it, there were moments in the middle of one of her movie premieres when Dara secretly wished her mother was in a theater somewhere watching with that same expression she remembered seeing as a little girl.

The sound of her mother's coughing and gurgling brought Dara back to the present.

"I'd better wrap this up while I still have the breath to talk. I want you to know that I regret things turned out the way they did between us. I'm sorry that you couldn't see your way clear to come home once in a while after you left for college. I'm not blaming you. I just wish it could've been different. I know that I'm as much to blame as your father for you thinking you needed to stay away. In case you're wondering, he passed away eight years ago. But maybe you knew that. I tried to find you to tell you. I even contacted that friend of yours, Carrie. But... Well, I guess you didn't want to be found."

Dara turned her head to look out the window. This day looked very much like the day she learned her father had passed away. Dara had been on her way out to an audition, when Carolyn unexpectedly showed up at her door. Carolyn wanted to tell her the news in person. They sat down on the front stoop of Dara's small townhouse in Burbank and talked. Carolyn didn't pressure her to go home for the funeral, a fact for which Dara was very grateful. She hadn't shed any tears for the man who never treated her as more than an inconvenience and a tax deduction.

In the end, she went to the audition, channeled her churning emotions into the scene, and got the part in her first major movie. After that, she'd never looked back. But now the past beckoned.

"If you're listening to my ramblings, it must mean I'm at the end of my rope. I'm sorry to burden you with me at this late stage, but as you know, there's no one else. So I'm going to try to make this as easy as possible for you. If I'm unable to speak for myself, to hold a conversation, to live with dignity... Well then, I hope you'll be kind and compassionate, even if you don't think I deserve those things, and end my suffering. The young woman I've witnessed you to be in those instances when I've been able to catch glimpses of you here and there, leads me to believe you're a bigger human being than I ever was. I'm sure I'm in good hands."

Dara didn't want to care. She didn't want to feel grief or despair or anything at all for this virtual stranger who'd given birth to her. But she did. She put her hand to her chest where her heart ached. "Oh, Mother."

"I don't know if you can, but I hope you'll find it in your heart in the end to forgive me all my shortcomings. Please know, Dara, that in my own way, I loved you very much. I always did. I'm sorry I wasn't very good at it and I'm sure it's cold consolation to you now, but it's the truth. I've lived the past eight years all by myself, but somehow I was never bothered about being alone until now. Now, I'm scared. I'm scared that I'll die all alone and no one will care."

Dara covered her mouth as a sob escaped. This woman she knew so little sounded so small, frail, and frightened. All Dara wanted to do was to bring her comfort.

"I-I just wanted to be sure that the last words you ever hear from me are these: I love you, Dara. I'm proud of you. I'm so proud to be your mother, even if I never deserved you. I hope you'll forgive me and I hope you'll go on to be the greatest actress of your generation. But more than that, I hope you'll find lasting happiness and love. You deserve all that and more. Goodbye, Dara. I love you."

Tears streamed down Dara's cheeks as she listened to her mother weakly call for the nurse to show her how to stop recording. She clicked out of the program and shut down the laptop.

62

"Goodbye, Mother."

The movie theater was packed, despite the fact that it was a matinee. Rebecca found herself a seat on the aisle and dug into the popcorn bag. Since her flight home wasn't scheduled to depart until that evening, she decided to take in *Rock Me Gently*. Dara Thomas's face and lithe body filled the screen. She was wearing a body-hugging leather ensemble, her hair flying wildly around her face as she paced a concert stage in stiletto-heeled boots. Rebecca silently sighed. This would be a most pleasant distraction before her flight.

She wondered if Dara actually was doing the singing or if she was being voice-dubbed. *If she's faking that, she's an even better actress than I gave her credit for.* Watching Dara play a self-indulgent, hyper-exposed, but vulnerable rock star, Rebecca flashed back to Sharon's dismissive inference that being an actress would be a waste of intelligence. Here was a Yale graduate on screen—the antithesis of an airhead, and watching her bring this character to life reinforced Rebecca's belief that it required plenty of mental acuity to play a role that she imagined must be so different from the actress's reality. Rebecca happily lost herself in the performance. Catching this movie might prove to be the best part of her trip.

"Are you on your way to the hospital?"

"Yes." Using her shoulder, Dara held the phone against her ear as she put in her earring. She hoped Carolyn couldn't hear how relieved she was to hear from her.

"Don't come downstairs."

"Why not?"

"Because there's a pack of paparazzi camped out in the lobby."

"Do I want to know how you know that? Please tell me you're not here."

"Okay, if that's what you want to hear."

Dara sighed. "You're here."

"Of course I'm here. I'm your best friend. Where else would I be?"

"I can think of dozens of places. I have to get to the hospital, Car. What do you suggest?"

"I'm working on alternative exits right now." Dara could tell by Carolyn's breathing that she was on the move. "Looks like you could take the elevator to the second floor. There are some ballrooms there. The hotel staff services them from the back via a service elevator from the basement kitchen. Looks relatively quiet, but it probably won't be for long. Most conferences start at 8:30 or 9 a.m."

"That gives us about a ten-minute window."

"Exactly. Are you all dressed and ready to go?"

Dara spared one more look in the mirror. Even with her makeup expertly applied, she could see the dark smudges under her eyes and the telltale signs of stress. She knew Carolyn would spot them too. "As ready as I'm going to get."

"Okay. I'll meet you on the second floor."

"Carrie?"

"What is it?" Dara heard the concern in Carolyn's voice and understood why. She rarely used her best friend's childhood nickname.

"I... Thank you."

"You're welcome, sweetie. Hurry down here so I can give you a hug."

The elevator opened on the second floor. Dara literally got one foot out and Carolyn grabbed her by the hand and was propelling her around the corner. "This way."

"What happened to my hug?"

"Only if you want it splashed all over the social media sites." Carolyn glanced back over her shoulder. "One of the conferences started early. It's a geek conference. Want to place a bet on how many cell phones and tablets are walking around here right now?"

"I'll take your word for it." Dara hustled to keep up with Carolyn's determined steps. It was obvious she'd scouted the precise route.

"This way, ladies." The massive man in a server's uniform held a door open.

Carolyn handed him something that Dara assumed was money. She mustered up her best megawatt smile and met the server's eyes. "Thank you."

"Don't thank me yet. We've still got to get you out of the hotel, Ms. Thomas."

Dara knew it shouldn't surprise her after all this time that people recognized her, but somehow it always did. "I have faith in you."

"Thank you, ma'am. I'll sure do my best." He led the way through a back corridor and around a corner, then through a set of double doors and to a service elevator.

When they stepped out of the elevator, they were in the basement. People were hustling everywhere. Dara smelled the scent of freshly made coffee and bacon and her stomach growled.

"I brought you some fruit and a bagel," Carolyn said. "Somehow I doubt breakfast was high on your list this morning."

Dara threw her arm around Carolyn's shoulder. "Please tell me my stomach wasn't loud enough for you to hear."

"Okay. Your stomach wasn't loud enough for me to hear."

"Placater."

"Maybe."

Dara released Carolyn. She was aware that heads were turning in her direction, but she ignored them. Early on in her career, she made a point of acknowledging those who acknowledged her. Then she'd experienced her first serious stalker. The consultant Carolyn hired to review Dara's security insisted she immediately stop engaging the public so openly. Reluctantly, Dara acquiesced. Rudeness was a foreign concept to her. The idea that people might think her cold or aloof pained her and she said as much. She remembered the consultant's response quite clearly.

"You have a choice. You can either be friendly and dead, or aloof and alive. Pick, because you can't have it both ways."

"When we get through this next door," the hotel staffer was saying, "you'll be in the parking garage."

"Thank you," Dara said. "I really appreciate your help."

"No worries, Ms. Thomas. I'm a big fan." He smiled sheepishly.

As promised, Dara and Carolyn emerged on the ground floor of the parking structure. Dara paused for a moment to let her eyes adjust to the darkness. A flash went off in her face, momentarily blinding her.

Carolyn lunged forward, and Dara grabbed her by the arm. Two more flashes, and the photographers faded into the shadows.

"Don't. It's not worth it."

"I hate that. I'm sorry, honey. I thought I had a foolproof plan."

"It was a good plan. There's always going to be one. Don't worry about it." Dara waited a beat. "But I do hope they got my good side. Also, I was hoping to avoid them following me to the hospital, so let's see if we can't shake them."

Carolyn led the way a short distance to her car and they managed to get inside and drive out of the garage without further incident.

Two blocks away from the hotel, Carolyn reached over and caressed Dara's hand. "Want to talk about it?"

"About what?" Dara knew it was a weak dodge but honestly, what was there to say?

"About how you're feeling. When we hung up last night, you were about to listen to your mother's message. You haven't said a word about it yet and you look like little Dara Thomas this morning, not the confident, strong woman I know you are."

Dara closed her eyes and rested her head against the headrest. "How is it I can fool everyone else in the world, but not you?"

"Probably because I've known you longer and better than anyone else in the world." Carolyn paused. "And maybe because I lived through your story and watched your pain every day. For the first time in fifteen years, I see that same look in your eyes this morning."

For a fleeting moment, Dara considered remaining mum. She had no desire to relive the dream she'd had last night or most of what her mother had to say in her message. But this was Carolyn, the one person from whom she'd never kept anything and who deserved an honest answer.

During the remainder of the drive to Sloan-Kettering, Dara recounted all of it. She left nothing out. She watched as Carolyn's expressions changed from sad to angry to outraged and back to sad.

When Dara finished, Carolyn turned to her. Tears glistened in her eyes. "I wish there were words to make you feel better, but I know there aren't. I wish I could change so many things about your childhood for you, but I know I can't. Most of all, I wish I could take away your pain, but I know I can't do that, either."

"I don't expect—"

"Let me finish." Carolyn held up a hand. "I'm glad your mother told you how proud she was of you and that she loved you. When she called me looking for you that day that your father died, I considered not telling you. You were doing so well, coming into your own and you had such a big audition that day. I just knew in my bones that you were going to get the part and that it would be the start of great things for you. I didn't want the news to be one more thing you had to overcome. There had already been too much. In the end, I think all of those swirling emotions helped you nail the part."

"You were right about that."

"What I never told you was something your mother shared with me on the phone."

Dara shifted in her seat to fully face Carolyn. "You kept something from me?"

Carolyn nodded mournfully. "I knew how you felt about your parents and I just— You didn't need to hear it."

"Hear what?" Dara wasn't sure she could take any more revelations right now.

"Your mother wanted me to tell you that your father had set aside some money for you for when you came to your senses and gave up, as he called it, 'this foolish acting notion.'"

The comment should've made Dara angry. Instead, what she felt was resignation.

"Obviously, based on what was on the recording, your mother doesn't feel that way anymore. I mean, she compared you to Katherine Hepburn and your father's remark eight years ago was before you landed your first big role."

"Car, it's okay. Don't worry about it. That was just who my parents were."

"I'm sorry, sweetie. I'd change it in a heartbeat if I could."

"I know. There is one thing that's been bothering me."

"Only one?"

"Okay, more than one, but one thing that puzzles me. How did the hospital get my phone number? Even my own mother didn't have it."

"Actually, she did. Sort of." Carolyn glanced at her. "Because she knew I would never give it to her, your mother had her lawyer call me a few months after your father died to get your number. He needed it for some legal documents your mother was having him revise. I gave it to him with the stipulation that your mother would never try to contact you directly. I'm sorry. That's my fault."

"No. It's okay. I can see why you did it. I just wondered how they found me directly."

Carolyn pulled the car into the hospital's parking garage.

"What are you doing?"

"Parking the car. What does it look like I'm doing?"

"No."

"Dar—"

"No. This is mine to do. I've got it."

Carolyn pulled into a space and cut the engine. "I'm not going to let you deal with this by yourself, I don't care what you say." She opened the car door and stepped outside, arms crossed, feet spread shoulder-length apart, ready for battle.

Dara joined her. "I appreciate your loyalty. You know I do. But I really think I need some time alone with mother. Until yesterday, I thought I'd made peace with her and left that time of my life in my rearview mirror."

"And now?"

Dara stared off into space and shook her head. "I don't know. Today the decision to let my mother die lies in my hands, and I believe that somehow, before I make that call, I have to find a way in my heart to forgive her, to see her as a flawed human being, not a…"

"Cold-hearted bitch?"

Dara slowly shook her head. "More like a supremely unhappy, miserable, emotionless woman."

"Same thing, nicer dressing."

"Anyway, I need clarity here."

"And you think my being there makes that harder?"

Dara smiled kindly. "I think this could take a little while and I don't want to feel like I'm holding you up."

"I already said—"

"I know what you said. Please, Car, help me out here."

Carolyn relaxed her stance, and Dara knew she would capitulate. "Really? You're not just letting me off the hook?"

"I am not."

Carolyn fingered the key fob. "You're sure?"

"Positive."

"You'll call me if you need anything and let me know when you're ready to go so I can pick you up?"

"Pinky swear." Dara held up the digit in question and wiggled it.

"Well, if it's a pinky swear…"

Dara leaned forward and gave her friend a warm hug. "Love you, girlfriend."

"Love you too, sweetie. I won't be far away."

"I know." Dara disengaged, waved, and headed for the doors to the hospital.

CHAPTER SEVEN

R
ebecca took her time browsing in the airport newsstand. Her flight wasn't for another two hours and she'd finished all of the novels she'd brought with her. She picked up the latest Steve Martini book and flipped it over to read the synopsis. Sufficiently intrigued, she held onto the book and moved on to scan the newspaper headlines. A delivery person dropped a bundle of newspapers on the floor in front of her and efficiently sliced the plastic tie holding the pile in place. She saw that it was the *National Enquirer*—something she would never stoop to read. Still, although she tried not to pay attention, it was hard to miss the big, bold, banner headline. "Dara Thomas's Private Pain."

"Not so private if you're broadcasting it all over the front page," Rebecca muttered. A picture of the movie star accompanied the headline. She looked incredible, even dressed casually as she was in designer jeans and a light sweater.

"May I?" She indicated the stack.

"Whatever," the worker said as he pocketed the box cutter.

Rebecca picked up the rag and opened it to the promised story on page two. Inside, there was a second snapshot of Dara, obviously taken at the same time as the first. Farther down on the page was another photo, this one of an elderly woman in a hospital bed. Tubes and machines surrounded her and her face was in shadow. The quality of the picture made it clear it had been taken surreptitiously, most likely with a cell phone camera.

"Oscar favorite Dara Thomas is dealing with off-screen tragedy. Her mother, from whom Thomas mysteriously has been estranged for many years, is apparently dying of cancer. Thomas

71

flew to New York yesterday to be by her side. No word on how long the actress plans to stay in town, but sources tell us that her mother could die any day now."

Rebecca closed the paper and returned it to the stack. She didn't know whether to believe the article or not, but either way, she felt sorry for Dara. She couldn't imagine what it must be like to be her—to have your most intimate emotions and moments plastered across the pages of a tabloid for the world to see and dissect. She was glad she'd never need to know.

∽᳭ᢒ

"Good morning, Ms. Thomas." The nurse looked up from adjusting the bed covers.

"Good morning." Dara noted that her mother's cheeks appeared even more sunken and ashen than they were yesterday. "How…how is she?" Dara realized this was probably a foolish question. It was abundantly clear how her mother was.

"No change, I'm afraid."

"I guess that was a silly question."

"There are no silly questions when it comes to losing a loved one." The nurse regarded her compassionately. "Doctor Emanuel spoke with you yesterday, right?"

"He did." It struck Dara that perhaps she should at least move all the way into the room instead of standing like a statue in the doorway. She approached the bed and looked down at her mother, but stopped short of touching her. The memory of the recording was still too fresh in Dara's mind and on her heart.

"Do you want me to get him?"

"The doctor?" Dara knew she was stalling. Who else could the nurse have been talking about?

"Yes."

"I—I don't think I'm quite ready just yet." Dara made eye contact. "Is she in any pain?"

"I don't think so. She's on a morphine drip and she's shown no indication of discomfort."

"Good." Dara hesitated. "Is there anything more she needs right now? I mean…"

"No. I'm done here. I imagine you want some time alone with her." The nurse headed for the door. "If you need anything, I'll be around."

"Thank you." When the nurse was gone, Dara dragged a chair to the side of the bed and sat down. Now that they were alone, she had no idea what to do.

For a while, she simply sat and watched her mother breathe. The frail chest rose and fell faintly, and the pulse point in her neck seemed to stutter periodically. After a time, the machine noises faded into a steady hum in the background.

"Mother." Dara reached out and touched her mother's hand. "I don't really know what to say. I'm not sure you can hear me. And even if you can, I'm not sure what you..." Dara paused as an unexpected wave of long-buried emotions threatened to swamp her. Her lips trembled.

"Why couldn't you have loved me, Mother? Was I so unlovable? Really? I tried. I tried to be a good girl. I tried to stay out of your way and to be an easy child. I tried to... Damn." Dara fumbled in her pocketbook for a packet of Kleenex. She blew her nose, deposited the tissue in the waste basket by the side of the bed, and prayed for composure she wasn't sure she could find. She took a deep, settling breath. It wouldn't do to stay stuck in the past. She should focus on the things her mother said about her career and stick to the present.

"Thank you, Mother, for letting me know that I haven't turned out to be the disappointment I'm sure you thought I'd be." Dara slid her hand underneath her mother's so that their palms were touching. "I'm glad you saw my movies. I'm glad you liked them. Kate Hepburn, eh? High praise, indeed. Thank you, for giving me something positive to hold onto.

"I don't know what my next project is just yet, but I know what I'm hoping for. If you liked my other work, I know you'd really love me in this role, if I can get it. It's an adaptation of the Pulitzer Prize-winning Constance Darrow novel, *On the Wings of Angels*. I think I could really connect with the material and do it justice."

Dara smirked. "I don't suppose you've read the book, Mother, have you? I hear it was pretty good, but that the author is a complete mystery." She studied her mother's face, but there was no change in her expression. Had she read the book? And if she had, would she have made the connection between Dara and Constance? Dara didn't think so. After all, they'd been estranged for so long that the last written work her mother had seen was most likely a high school term paper. She probably wouldn't have been able to recognize her style.

Would her mother have been proud of her career as an author? Dara felt an unexpected twinge of sadness as the realization dawned that her mother would never get to see anything more of her work or to know about her alter ego, Constance. How ironic. Until last night, she hadn't even known, or thought she cared, that her mother had seen her movies. Now... Now she deeply regretted that her mother would likely miss her best work as her career continued to take off. Why on Earth should that matter to her? After all this time?

The sound of someone clearing his throat startled Dara, and she jumped.

"I'm sorry. I apologize for interrupting." Doctor Emanuel walked around the bed and checked the IV connections without looking at Dara.

"No, it's okay. I...I was just keeping her company."

A second man entered the room and stood off to the side.

Doctor Emanuel cleared his throat again, and Dara realized that he seemed profoundly uncomfortable. Although she had only met him the day before, he didn't strike her as the nervous type.

"I want you to know..." He continued to fiddle with the IV line. "I want you to know how deeply angered I am personally."

"I'm sorry," Dara withdrew her hand from her mother's. "What are you talking about?"

Doctor Emanuel looked at the other man, and then at Dara for the first time since he'd come into the room. "You don't know?"

"Know what?"

"About the photos and the article."

Dara's heart sank. "What photos? What article?" For the first time, she noticed that the other man held a newspaper folded under his arm.

"This is Gerry Nuland. He is the Vice President of our hospital's Quality Assurance Committee."

The man stepped forward and handed the newspaper to Dara without comment.

The first thing Dara saw was the shot of her at the airport yesterday and the big, banner headline. Her heart flipped. She opened the paper to the next page and felt the bile rise in her throat as she spied the shot of her mother in the hospital bed. She dropped the paper on the floor. "Who?" Her voice shook. "Who took this?"

The doctor started to answer, but the other man interrupted him.

"We deeply, deeply regret this incident, but we are not at liberty to discuss confidential personnel matters. This hospital does not tolerate such breaches. Rest assured that this matter has been investigated and dealt with swiftly and decisively."

Dara felt sick. She knew she shouldn't do it, but she picked up the newspaper again and read the brief article. With each word, despair at the indignity to her mother threatened to bring Dara to her knees. She was used to the loss of privacy for herself, but the picture of her mother on her deathbed...that was a violation of basic human decency.

"As I said, we are very, very sorry about this," Doctor Emanuel said. "It never should have happened, and I assure you, it will never happen again."

"It's a little late for that, isn't it?" Dara mumbled, as much to herself as to the two men.

"The full committee will meet this afternoon to discuss this matter and evaluate how and where protocols might have been compromised. If there is a determination that changes should be made to our current systems, they will be instituted immediately."

"That's all well and good...Mr. Nuland, is it? But it's not going to give my mother back her dignity now, is it? Or me my privacy?" It was so rare for Dara to lose her temper that the heat rising in her chest frightened her. She closed her eyes and took a deep breath, praying for patience and control. So many things were happening at once and her emotions were on overload. "I'm sorry. I don't mean to be difficult. I'm normally pretty even-keeled. Everything is just a bit much for me right now."

"Of course it is," Doctor Emanuel said.

"I'm sure you and the hospital will take all necessary and appropriate actions."

"What happened is regrettable. I wish it hadn't happened. I assure you, I would change it if I could, Ms. Thomas."

"I know you would."

"Do you have any questions, Ms. Thomas?" Nuland asked. If not, I'll leave you and Doctor Emanuel to discuss your mother's condition."

"Honestly, right now all I want is to focus on my mother."

"Very well. If you decide later on that there are questions you'd like to ask specific to this…unfortunate…situation, here is my card."

Dara took it.

"Again, I'm sorry for the lapse and I'm sorry about your mother."

After he left, Dara and the doctor stood awkwardly facing each other.

"Well, then, let's talk about your mother."

As if on cue, Dara's mother groaned, and Dara took her hand without thought. "Is she…?

Doctor Emanuel shook his head. "Vocalization is a common occurrence." He removed the stethoscope from around his neck and conducted his examination.

When he'd finished, Dara asked, "Any change?"

"Not of the kind you're looking for, I'm afraid. Her breath sounds are more shallow and her lungs are filling with fluid."

Dara felt the tears well again in her eyes and she willed them not to spill onto her cheeks. "I suppose… I suppose it's only going to get worse from here, right?"

Doctor Emanuel nodded.

"And if I authorize you to remove all life support now…"

"I can't say for sure."

"If she was your mother, what would you do?"

"I can't make this decision for you. Only you can do that."

Dara tried to read something, anything in the doctor's expression. All she saw was compassion. "There's no chance for improvement?"

"No."

"Okay." Dara entwined her fingers with her mother's. "Let's do it, then. I authorize you to remove all life support."

Doctor Emanuel nodded. "Do you want to be here for that? It will take about half an hour or so."

As much as Dara wanted to say no, she felt that she owed it to her mother to bear witness. "I'll stay."

"Very well. I'll call the nurse and she'll take care of gathering the respiratory therapist and the rest of the team, and we'll get this done right now." As Doctor Emanuel was about to leave the room, he turned around. "I promise you that we'll continue to provide your mother with morphine for the pain and anything else she needs to keep her comfortable."

"Thank you, doctor."

"Do you want me to call the chaplain for you?"

"No, thank you."

"Very well then, I'll start the process right away."

When it was done, Dara sat alone with her mother. The door was closed to give them some privacy and the room seemed so much more peaceful without the noise of the machines. In the quiet, the sound of her mother's labored breathing seemed so much louder.

Dara took her mother's hand again and held it loosely. Perhaps it was her imagination, or maybe wishful thinking, but her mother seemed more at ease now—more peaceful and serene, despite the rattling breath sounds.

As the hours passed, Dara's eyelids began to grow heavy. The restless, memory-filled sleep last night, combined with all of the emotion of the past two days, was taking its toll. Still, she wasn't ready to leave her mother's side. No one, not even her mother, deserved to die alone. So Dara scooted the chair a little closer and laid her head on the side of the bed. If she could just rest her eyes for a few minutes, she could rally again. Within seconds, she was asleep.

The angel was large and luminous and light radiated everywhere around him. Dara watched as he effortlessly lifted her mother in his arms. "It's time, Dara. It's time for your mother to go home."

Dara felt a comforting hand on her shoulder. She smiled, enjoying the dream. Then someone squeezed her hand and her eyes popped open. She lifted her head in time to see her mother looking at her. She was certain that she must still be sleeping, but her mother squeezed again. This time, Dara squeezed back and covered her mother's hand with her other hand.

Her mother mumbled something, and Dara leaned in closer. "What, Mother?" She put her ear right next to her mother's lips.

"I'm...glad...you came."

"Me too." Dara's eyes watered.

"You...were...right."

"Right? Right about what?"

"There really...are...angels."

At that, Dara cried. She watched as her mother left her body. Indeed, the radiance of the large angel Dara saw in her dream enfolded her mother. She wanted to say something, but the words, "I love you" wouldn't come. Instead, she said, "Goodbye, Mother. Safe journey."

And then the hand holding hers went limp. Dara looked back to her mother's face. It was peaceful. She was gone.

৵৶

"How was your reunion?" Natalie asked Rebecca as they passed the Morgan Horse Farm on their way up the hill.

Should she share about the night with Sharon? What would Natalie think of that? Unconsciously, Rebecca picked up the pace. "It was...interesting."

"Oh. Cryptic. Interesting in the cluster fuck sense, or interesting as in you met someone and are madly, deeply in love, or at least in lust."

Again, Rebecca stepped up the pace. She took satisfaction in hearing Natalie struggle to breathe. Maybe it would keep her from asking any more questions. "Interesting, as in interesting. As in, not boring."

"I remember when you used to be fun, you know that? And are you trying to kill me, or what?"

"Or what. Although the thought does have some appeal," Rebecca joked. "Crazy killer kilometers kill popular professor. It has a nice ring to it."

"Well done, but you're obfuscating. You met someone, didn't you?"

"I met a lot of people."

Natalie growled in frustration. "Why are you being so difficult about this?"

"Difficult? Who's being difficult?"

"You are. You had all that angst trying to decide whether or not you wanted to go, and now you won't even talk about it?"

Rebecca frowned. Natalie was right, of course. She'd spent weeks agonizing about attending the reunion, and Natalie had been with her every step of the way—literally, since it had been on their runs that they hashed through the pros and cons. Surely she deserved a real answer.

"It got off to a rough start. The first person I ran into was the one I least wanted to see."

"The moronic bully you told me about?"

"Yes. Him. Took him all of three seconds to revert to childhood."

"Maybe he never left."

"Probably. Anyway, he was predictably inappropriate, gross, and disgusting."

"But you stood up to him, right?"

"I did."

Natalie squealed and clapped her hands. "Excellent. See? I told you you could do it. I'm proud of you." After a beat she added, "It was probably lost on him, though, huh?"

"Pretty much."

"Please tell me the night got better from there."

"Okay. The night got better from there." Rebecca smiled as Natalie grunted in exasperation. "I met a woman—"

"I knew it!"

"It's not what you think."

"Oh, how disappointing."

"I mean, it is what you think, but it's not."

Natalie laughed. "For someone as eloquent as you are, you seem to be having a hard time articulating, Professor."

"It's complicated." Was it? When Rebecca thought about Sharon and what happened, it really seemed rather simple. So she explained about the brief encounter and her reaction to it. What she didn't expect, was to be met with stone-cold silence. "You're not saying anything."

"I'm busy seething at Cynthia."

"Oh."

"That woman screwed you fifteen ways to Sunday. I'd love to put my little hands around her neck and—"

Rebecca shook her head. "She doesn't deserve the energy you're giving her by thinking about it."

"I may be giving her the energy, but you're giving her power by letting her stand in the way of you and any potential love interest that crosses your path. How long are you planning to let that wench control your life?"

Rebecca started to object then stopped herself. Natalie was right. Even in her absence, Cynthia cast a long shadow. It was time to stand in her own power. Hadn't that been the problem growing up—that she'd let everyone else determine how she felt about herself and how she lived her life? Well, that time was over.

"No more."

"I'm sorry? I couldn't hear you." Natalie playfully put her hand to her ear. "A little louder and with more authority, please?"

"No more," Rebecca shouted, her words echoing in the stillness of the summer air.

"That's more like it. So, do you have Sharon's digits?" Natalie waggled her eyebrows suggestively.

"I do not. It wasn't that kind of connection. I mean, don't get me wrong, she was gorgeous and nice, but..."

"But not the kind of girl you bring home to Mother?"

Rebecca pondered the question. "Nah. It's not really that. I mean, I wouldn't bring her home to *my* mother, but then again, I wouldn't subject any woman to my mother. Still, I suspect Sharon would hold her own in most settings."

"So, what's the deal with her."

"It's the intangibles, you know?"

"Nope. Clueless."

Rebecca searched around for what she was trying to say. "Whoever is next for me, I want her to be 'the one.' Does that make any sense?"

"You mean like some idealized, romanticized image from one of the novels you teach? A love to exceed all others."

"Something like that," Rebecca agreed. "Let me guess. You think that's nothing but a bunch of literary rubbish."

"Hey. I may not be the most romantic woman in the world, but I can agree that it's possible for others to find that one, perfect match."

They finished the run in silence. But Rebecca found that her thoughts were anything but still. For reasons she knew she'd never share with Natalie, the enigma that was Constance Darrow filled her mind to overflowing.

CHAPTER EIGHT

I have something that'll cheer you up," Carolyn said, as she helped Dara sift through her mother's papers. They were sitting at Carolyn's dining room table three days after Dara's mother passed away. Carolyn had no trouble convincing her best friend to check out of the hotel and come stay with her and Stan, especially after the press outside the hospital mobbed her. Apparently, after the *National Enquirer* story, every newspaper, tabloid, and entertainment magazine and several syndicated television shows staked out positions in front of the hospital and hotel.

"Hmm?"

"What are you reading that has you so engrossed?" Carolyn peeked over Dara's shoulder. "Your mother kept old love letters between her and your father?"

"So it would appear."

"How romantic."

"Remarkably, they are. I didn't think either of them had an ounce of passion in their souls. I was wrong."

"Something came in the mail for you today." Carolyn dearly wanted to make some clever connecting quip as a segue, but she feared it would call attention to something she was sure Dara wasn't seeing…yet.

"It did?"

"Uh-huh. Another letter from your favorite Am Lit professor." And there it was. Dara looked up and smiled. It was brief, but Carolyn caught it. Over the past few months, Constance Darrow and Rebecca Minton had exchanged no less than a half dozen letters. Since Carolyn was the conduit, she bore witness to both sides of the correspondence. In the past couple of letters, Carolyn noticed that Dara had begun to soften and allow glimpses of her wicked sense of humor to shine through. That was a first with any admirer, not to mention the fact that this now qualified as the longest-running correspondence Dara and/or Constance had maintained with any one fan.

The last time Dara let her guard down was with that witch, Sheilah. In the ten years since, Dara hadn't so much as looked at another woman.

When Sheilah first came on the scene, Dara was so filled with joy, and Carolyn was grateful. Dara had led such a lonely, solitary life. That she should find great happiness was everything Carolyn hoped for her friend. Then Sheilah broke Dara's heart and Carolyn's heart broke for her. She watched the wariness slip back in and the light go out of Dara's eyes.

Until now. That was what Dara hadn't yet recognized. Rebecca's letters breathed new life into her. Without realizing it, Dara had begun looking forward to them. Carolyn didn't know where, if anywhere, the correspondence would lead, but she loved seeing the light back in Dara's eyes. For now, that was enough.

She handed Dara the unopened letter. As anticipated, Dara's expression was quizzical.

"You didn't review it?"

Carolyn tried out her best nonchalant one-shoulder shrug. "I figured by now it was safe to leave you two adults unsupervised." She held her breath, hoping the implication wouldn't send Dara running from the room.

"You, trusting someone enough not to run interference? That's a switch."

"I vetted her. She is who she says she is. Her résumé is solid and she doesn't seem to have an agenda beyond being a really good Constance Darrow geek. I see no harm. Unless you want me to…"

"No. That's okay. I checked her out too."

"You did?"

"Of course. You don't think I'd keep answering her otherwise, do you?"

"I just figured you trusted my judgment." Carolyn gave a mock pout.

"Well, that too. Did you catch her last lecture? She had the kids wrapped around her little finger."

Carolyn hid a huge grin. She had seen the lecture. It was a great piece of theater. Before she could answer, Dara prattled on. "I can't believe they record the lectures and put them on YouTube like that. And from several camera angles too. Then again, it might just have been a student-led effort."

Carolyn badly wanted to ask whether Dara found Rebecca attractive, but she held her tongue. Carolyn certainly thought Rebecca was. *Not just attractive. She's gorgeous.* "I'm glad you're participating in your own security. I'm proud of you—knowing who you're talking to and all."

"Uh-huh. Don't patronize me."

"Me? I would never. Hardly ever." Carolyn winked. "I'm going to go start dinner. Join me in the kitchen when you're done in here."

"Mm-hmm."

As Carolyn walked out, she watched out of the corner of her eye as Dara turned the envelope over and over in her hands. Yes. This was going quite well.

✎✐

"No. Absolutely not." Dara jumped up from the visitor's chair and went to gaze out the window at the New York skyline.

"Dara, just think about this. It's Broadway, for chrissakes. It's a three-month run. Limited engagement, packed houses, you get to go back to the live stage and show your acting chops, and you have room in your schedule to do it. What's not to love?"

Dara turned and glared at Rick Church, the man who had been her agent since she signed her first movie contract ten years ago. She started ticking items off on her fingers. "It's New York. It's three months. It's New York."

Rick threw his hands up. "What do you have against The Big Apple?"

Dara opened her mouth to answer, then thought better of what she'd been planning to say. She shook her head. "I told you a long time ago I have no interest in being that close to my hometown." She crossed her arms over her chest.

"Be reasonable. You're already in New York, and it's Broadway. You have to finish closing up your mother's affairs anyway, right? Please." Rick pressed his palms together in a prayerful pose. "Please?"

"Why is this so important to you? Surely we've got plenty of other offers on the table that would be more lucrative than this."

"You've got the big Spielberg shoot coming up, and I'm trying to give you enough prep time for that. But this is a long-term strategic move for you."

"Seriously? That's what you're going with?"

"Hear me out." Rick gestured to the seat across from his desk. "And please sit back down. You're making me nervous as hell."

Reluctantly, Dara complied. "Let's have it."

"The backers for this show are the same guys who just took over 722 Films. You know, the ones who are fronting the mega-budget production of *On the Wings of Angels*."

Dara's heart skipped a beat even as she tried to limit her expression to one of mild interest. "The Constance Darrow novel adaptation I asked you to try to get me cast for?"

"That's the one."

"Very tricky." Dara whistled appreciatively. "You think by doing the Broadway show for them, that'll give me the inside track for the role of Celeste in the movie."

Rick nodded, a self-satisfied smile playing across his lips.

Dara squirmed in the chair. Just thinking about staying in New York, even for a brief few months, made her palms sweat and her head spin. But the opportunity to play her own title character on the big screen was something she'd been dreaming of since the publication of her debut novel. She tried to calculate her chances of getting the film role without the advantage doing the stint on Broadway would give her. "When do we have to commit?"

"Yesterday." Rick slid a sheaf of papers across the desk. "I've already reviewed the details of the contract and negotiated out most of the onerous requirements for practice schedules, et cetera. All you have to do is sign on the dotted line."

Is that all? Dara picked up the pen and began reviewing the document. Halfway through, she set down the pen and folded her arms over her chest. "Rick, you know I love you and I respect you. You've done fantastic things for my career. With you as my agent,

Colin as my PR guy, and Carolyn as my business manager, I've been in the best possible hands. I'm confident that I still am. But I won't take this play just in order to get a movie role. I won't. I'll either be right for the role of Celeste or I won't—on my own merits."

"I think you're making a big mistake, Dara. This is how the game is played—"

"I'm not interested in playing games. I'm interested in making powerful movies and playing great parts. Nothing more. Are we clear?" Dara noted the look of displeasure but chose to ignore it. "Are we?"

"We are."

"Good." Dara stood. "Anything else?"

"I spoke to Colin. He didn't want to bug you while you were dealing with your personal issues, and he knew we were going to sit down today. He tells me he has calls in to Dave Letterman and the network morning shows for interview slots. How long are you planning to stay in New York?"

"I'll be in town for the rest of the week. After that, I'm going back home where I belong. If Colin can get any of the shows lined up for the next few days, I'm in. After that, it'll have to be something LA-based."

"Okay. I'll let him know and one of us will be in touch."

"Sounds like a plan."

"Take care of yourself, Dara."

"You too, Rick. And say hi to that wonderful wife of yours."

"She'll be sorry she missed you."

"Me too," Dara answered, as she headed out the door.

Rebecca stood in line at the TKTS booth in the middle of Times Square waiting to get a half-price ticket to a Broadway show for tonight. This was her last getaway of the summer before the fall semester got underway and she was planning to make the most of it. A couple of Broadway shows via TKTS and a museum or three would make her very happy.

"Excuse me?"

Rebecca turned to see a cute twenty-something trying to get her attention. Normally, she would've ignored a stranger in New York, but this girl looked harmless enough. And she was wearing a T-shirt that identified her as a staffer for the David Letterman show. Rebecca had always wanted to be in the studio audience for something like that. "Yes?"

"What are you doing this afternoon?"

"You mean other than standing in this line?"

"How about if I gave you another option?"

Rebecca noted that she had pretty dimples when she smiled. "I guess that depends."

"Fair enough. You look like a smart woman."

"Thanks, I think."

"So, here's a question for you. Who said, 'Well-behaved women seldom make history?'"

"Seriously? That's your question?" Rebecca's eyebrows rose to meet her hairline. "Okay. Although the quote is widely attributed to Eleanor Roosevelt, it actually belongs to Harvard University Professor Laurel Thatcher Ulrich, who wrote—"

"Stop! You can stop anytime now," the woman said, laughing. "Color me impressed. I knew you looked smart."

"Thanks."

"How would you like to come sit in the audience for the Letterman show today?"

"What time?"

"Be there at 2:00."

"For real?"

"Yup."

"Who are the guests?"

"Oh, I think you're going to like this. How do you feel about the hottest actress in Hollywood?"

Rebecca's mouth fell open. Surely this woman didn't mean...

"You're telling me you don't know who Dara Thomas is, but you can fire off Laurel Thatcher Ulrich without thinking?"

Rebecca shook her head. "It's not that."

"So, you do know who she is?"

"I certainly do." Rebecca accepted the ticket being held out to her. "Thank you!"

"You're welcome. Happy to make your day."

Rebecca stepped out of line. Broadway would have to wait until tomorrow. She checked her watch. It was 11:45. She would have just enough time to get some lunch, change her clothes, and head off to the Ed Sullivan Theater on Broadway, eight blocks from the hotel.

ぐ&

Dara sat in the makeup chair and listened as the makeup artist talked about her boyfriend troubles.

"You know, I'm just an old-fashioned girl. I think the guy should pay for dinner once in a while. Don't you?"

"I do." Dara smiled in the mirror. "And I think you should stick to your guns. You are absolutely worth a dinner and a lot more."

The young girl stood up a little straighter. "Thank you. Next time he asks me to do something I'm just going to—"

"Ms. Thomas?"

"That's me." Dara watched the reflection as a trim, business-like woman with a dour expression approached.

"I'm Lucy Dunn, the show's producer."

"Nice to meet you." Dara noted that Lucy's fingers were white where they gripped an iPad. She imagined that being a producer on a show like David Letterman's must be incredibly stressful.

"You too. Um, I thought I'd go over a few things with you before you go out there and see if maybe there's anything in particular you'd like to chat about."

"Sure."

"Mr. Letterman may or may not have time to stop by and say hello before show time."

"I understand."

"Right. Well, Mr. Letterman wants you to be relaxed and have a good time. There'll be one commercial break during the segment. You're the primary guest tonight, so the interview will last approximately fifteen to twenty minutes. Of course, the idea is to entertain the audience."

"Of course."

"So, if there's anything you can think of that's quirky, or interesting, or funny that you'd be willing to talk about that maybe you haven't talked about in other interviews, that would be great."

Dara tried not to blink as the makeup artist applied her eyelashes. "I'm assuming the audience wouldn't find anything humorous about my mother's recent death." She enjoyed the horrified look on the producer's face perhaps a little more than she should have. "I'm kidding."

"Oh. Heh. Of-of course you are." The woman shifted from foot to foot and Dara almost felt sorry for her.

"How about if we talk about the day on set during the filming of *Rock Me Gently* when my leather pants split wide open in the middle of the big production number?"

"That will work."

"Do you want to know the details now?"

"No. Mr. Letterman likes to have some spontaneity in the interview." The producer checked her watch. "Okay, well. Fifteen minutes to show time. You'll head from here to the Green Room and I'll come get you from there."

"I'll look forward to it." Dara watched the producer's retreating form.

"She's wound a tad tight, that one, but she's good at what she does," the makeup artist said.

"I'm sure that's not an easy job. I don't envy her."

The makeup artist was about to answer, but whatever she was going to say died on her lips as David Letterman strode up to Dara's chair.

"Hi. I'm Dave." He put out his hand for Dara to shake.

"Dara."

"I know." His smile was boyish and engaging. "Listen, I'm glad you're here. I don't want to talk too much now. I prefer that our interactions are fresh for the audience. I just wanted to let you know I'm a big fan and I'm looking forward to this. You can stick around afterward for the other guest and the closing musical act if you want, or if you have someplace to be..."

"No, I'm good. I like Nickelback, so I'll stick, if that's okay with you."

"Love it. Well, I'm off to do the monologue. See you in a little while."

When he was gone, the makeup artist whistled.

"What?"

"You must really rate, that's what."

"What do you mean?"

"In the three years I've been working on this show, I've only ever seen him come back here to personally meet a guest twice. Once was Meryl Streep, and the other was President Obama."

Dara raised an eyebrow. "That's pretty heady company."

"My point exactly," the makeup artist agreed.

"In that case, I feel honored. But tell me, does he know your name?"

The makeup artist shook her head.

"Now if he did, that would've impressed me more." Dara winked.

"You're really sweet, you know that? Most big-time stars don't give me the time of day." She smudged Dara's eye shadow one last time. "We're done here, by the way."

"Thank you, Christie. You did a great job."

The makeup artist looked startled. "You know my name?"

"I told you—"

"But you never asked me, so how did you know?"

"I like to know who is making me look so good. So I asked the associate producer who brought me up here."

"Oh. That's super cool. Wow."

Dara smiled. "Glad I could make your day."

As if on cue, the associate producer appeared to escort Dara to the Green Room. She could hear the audience laughing at the monologue as they walked down the hall. She would be on in a few minutes.

✥

After an hour standing in line outside and another forty-five minutes standing in the lobby, the studio audience was ushered into the theater. By sheer luck, Rebecca got a great seat in the third row, just to the right of the center camera, and just to the left of the right-side camera. From this spot, she'd be looking directly at Dara Thomas.

She fiddled with her necklace, making sure it was perfectly centered. Why on Earth it mattered, she didn't know. It wasn't like Dara Thomas was going to see her out there or notice her. Still, for whatever reason, Rebecca was a little nervous.

She'd taken extra care when dressing and applying her makeup and had added a dab of perfume behind her ears and between her breasts. She'd never sat in the studio audience for a show like this, so she had no idea what to expect. She wished she'd thought to bring a sweater. The theater was freezing! Still, she knew she'd have chosen style over comfort for this event regardless, on the off chance that... *What, that Dara Thomas would meet your eyes across a crowded room? What's wrong with you?*

Fortunately, Rebecca was saved from her own thoughts by some comedian she'd never heard of, who came out first and told lousy jokes to warm up the audience. Then the band came out, and she immediately recognized band leader Paul Shaffer. Finally, the announcer intoned those famous words, "Ladies and gentlemen, David Letterman!" The crowd cheered and clapped.

The monologue was funny and Rebecca laughed along with everyone around her. When it was done, they went to a commercial break. Rebecca thought it odd that Letterman didn't interact with anyone. He simply sat down behind his desk and looked at his index cards. The band was playing and the sound was deafening, amplified no doubt by the smallish size of the venue.

The light on the camera to her left turned red, indicating that was the "live" camera, and Rebecca's stomach tightened in anticipation. She had no time to stop and analyze her reaction, though, because Dara Thomas was striding out from behind the curtain to her left and walking toward Letterman.

CHAPTER NINE

*H*oly Mother of God. Rebecca vaguely remembered to close her mouth. She was sure she'd never seen anyone, male or female, as glorious as this in all her life. Dara's dress was low cut, but classy. The fabric was smooth and silky and the material clung to her in all the right places. She was tall—nearly as tall as the host—and looked him in the eye as they brushed cheeks. Granted, she was wearing three or four-inch heels, but still, she was taller than Rebecca expected. When she sat and crossed one leg over the other, her dress hiked up just enough to reveal an expanse of toned thigh.

After Dara was seated, the crowd continued to clap and whistle for several minutes as she waved and motioned for them to settle down.

"I think they like you," Letterman said.

"So it would appear," Dara agreed. "Either that or they're cold and they're just trying to get their circulation going again."

Immediately, Rebecca was charmed by Dara's engaging manner. Her smile was easy and effortless and the bit of self-deprecating humor seemed genuine. Rebecca thought Dave was equally smitten.

"Good one," he acknowledged. "So, you don't mind if I just sit here and stare for a few minutes, do you?"

Dara gave the host a saucy look. "I don't. But I imagine it might get a little boring for your viewers."

"Don't worry. They're staring too." Letterman propped his chin in his hand and gazed at Dara for several seconds. The audience ate it up.

To Dara's credit, she didn't flinch.

"This feels a little awkward, doesn't it?" Letterman said.

"I don't know. I'm not the one staring."

Letterman laughed and sat up straight. "Touché. Still, I imagine you're fairly used to people staring at you."

"Why would I be?"

"Why would you be?" Dave asked, incredulous. "Why would you be?" He looked at the audience. "She looks like that and wants to know why folks would stare."

"Are you used to people staring at you?" Dara asked.

"Me? People don't stare at me. They avert their gaze."

"I highly doubt that."

"Oh, my, folks. She's stunning and sweet." He leaned over and took Dara's hand to kiss the back of it. "How is it that we've never had you on here before?"

"You haven't asked."

Dave ran his index finger inside his shirt collar. "Is that true? Well, remind me to fire myself later."

"Okay, but the network might object."

"Oh, I seriously doubt that," Letterman quipped. "Have you seen the ratings?"

Dara laughed, and Rebecca was enthralled. She was quick on her feet, had an excellent sense of humor, and the most radiant smile.

"Now that you've put me in my place, I'm so flummoxed I hardly know where to go from here," Letterman said.

"This is probably where you ask me a question," Dara offered helpfully.

"Can I just say, thank God you're here to help me out. I don't know how I've made it all these years, just bumbling along without you. If the actress thing doesn't work out, I'd absolutely give you a job as my sidekick."

"Good to know I have a Plan B to fall back on."

"Ah, yeah." Letterman paused for effect. "Alrighty, then. Where was I?"

"You were about to ask me something deep and probing."

"Well, when you put it that way…"

The audience cracked up as Letterman blushed. "Are you sure you don't want to rephrase that?"

"Are you sure you want me to?" Dara asked. Her voice was a throaty purr that reached all the way to Rebecca's gut and below. She crossed her legs and shifted in her chair. Suddenly the air seemed a little warmer.

Letterman wagged his finger at his guest. "You. You're trouble, you know that?"

"As a matter of fact, I did. But apparently you didn't get the memo."

"Apparently." Letterman cleared his throat, picked up his index cards, and pretended to study them. "I know. I know what I wanted to ask. Here it is, right here." He indicated one of the cards.

"Good that you wrote it down. I wouldn't want you to forget."

"Shh. Let me get this out before the rest of my brain leaks out my ears."

Dara folded her hands in her lap and affected a demure pose.

"You've played all kinds of roles. Obviously, you're not someone who wants to be typecast. So what's the one role or type of role you haven't played that you'd really like to sink your teeth into?"

Rebecca could've sworn she saw Dara's eyes light up.

"As it happens, I've been giving this a lot of thought lately. I really love complicated characters, women who have depth and passion. There's a rumor that casting is going to get underway soon for the screen adaptation of the Pulitzer Prize winner, *On the Wings of Angels*."

Dave nodded, although Rebecca barely noticed. She was too shocked to discover that Dara Thomas was familiar with Constance Darrow's work. What might've started as a crush for Rebecca was quickly ramping up to pure adoration.

"I've read the book," Letterman said.

Dara looked surprised. "You have?"

"Well, yes. I'm not a complete dolt, you know. I do know how to read."

"I didn't mean—"

"Yes, yes." Dave waved Dara off. "Anyway, you were saying?"

"The main character in the book is Celeste. She's this layered woman who is non-religious and yet has an abiding faith in miracles, angels, and ascended masters."

"And that appeals to you?" Dave asked.

Rebecca leaned forward in her seat, anxious to hear what Dara would say.

"I think it would be incredibly arrogant to think that we're the most evolved beings in the universe, don't you? There is plenty of evidence to suggest otherwise. So, even for a non-religious person, it makes sense that there's something else out there affecting our fate. I'd love the challenge of bringing the nuance of that to life onscreen."

If Dara said anything else, Rebecca didn't hear it. Her ears were buzzing and she felt lightheaded. It didn't make any sense. Or did it? How could Dara Thomas, Hollywood star, use exactly the same words that Constance had used in supporting Rebecca's understanding of Celeste. Unless... No, it couldn't be.

"Fair enough. I hope you get the part. Heck, I'd give you the part," Dave was saying. "When we come back, we're going to talk about Ms. Thomas's most embarrassing on-set moment. You won't want to miss this, folks. We'll be back in a minute."

The band started playing, indicating that they'd gone to a commercial break. Rebecca sat completely still, her eyes focused solely on the woman sitting in the guest chair as her mind continued to whirl.

"Rick called," Carolyn said as Dara changed out of the dress and into a pair of low-slung jeans, a designer T-shirt, and boots.

"I bet he did. Let me guess, he wasn't pleased that I overtly campaigned for the role of Celeste."

"That would be an understatement. I believe his exact quote was, 'What the fuck does she think she's doing? That's not done. Totally uncool. Now Colin and I have got to figure out how to walk that back. Fuck!'"

"My, wasn't he colorful?" Dara emerged from behind the partition carrying the dress in a garment bag.

"I'll take that." Carolyn relieved Dara of the garment bag. "He might've been right. Has that occurred to you?"

Dara paused with her hand on the doorknob and looked back at Carolyn. Her expression was no longer glib. "Do you think he was?"

Carolyn knew that Dara didn't want to be coddled. "Since you're asking me, and you know I'll always tell you the truth, I think it was risky." She rushed on before Dara could interrupt. "Not necessarily for the same reasons that Rick is freaking out. On that front, I think if Hollywood's top box office draw comes out and says she wants a role, then she gets the role."

"But?"

"I'm more worried about Dara Thomas being too closely allied with Constance Darrow. Have you considered that someone might make the connection?"

"Why would they?"

"Well, for one thing, you know you're going to inhabit that role in a way that nobody else can."

"That's the point. Don't you see? I'm the only one who can truly understand Celeste. I'm the only one who knows with certainty how she feels, what drives her—"

"And if you were to slip up on set and say something if the director wanted you to take the character in a different direction?"

Dara opened and closed her mouth, apparently rethinking what she was about to say. "We'd talk through it. Surely you trust me to stay professional."

"It isn't a matter of professionalism. It's a question of you getting carried away in the heat of the moment and saying something that tips your hand."

"It won't happen."

Carolyn was less certain. "You'd better hope not."

"Does that mean you think I'll get the part?"

Carolyn shook her head in wonder. "How can you ask me that? Can you imagine the backlash now if they cast anyone else after you said publicly that you wanted the role?"

Dara smirked. "They'd be pretty stupid, huh?"

"Total idiots," Carolyn agreed. "C'mon. Let's blow this pop stand and go get dinner."

They exited the dressing room and walked down the corridor toward the building's stage door. "You think there'll still be anyone out there waiting for autographs?" Dara asked.

"Is the Pope Catholic?"

"Good point."

"I suppose you're going to stop and sign."

"Don't I always?"

"Yes. Despite the objections of everyone who cares about you and your safety."

"There'll be security with me." Dara pointed to the burly guy in uniform standing underneath the Exit sign twenty feet ahead of them. "And the limo is out there, right?"

"Yes. I confirmed with the driver that he's idling at the curb."

"So there's nothing to worry about."

"That's what you always say," Carolyn said.

"And I'm always right."

"Except when you're not."

"Hey. I'm not going to be some arrogant snob. That's not who I am."

"I know. But I still worry. It's not safe."

They reached the security guard. Dara gave him her best, engaging smile and glimpsed his nametag. "You'll keep me safe, Charles, right?"

"Yes, ma'am."

"See? I'm safe."

"Just so you know, ma'am, there are a lot of folks out there waiting for you."

Dara nodded. "That's okay. I'm good with you staying nearby, but please don't interfere unless you can see that I'm truly in trouble. Understood?"

"Yes, ma'am."

"And you see this beautiful woman here?" Carolyn blushed and squirmed as Dara pointed at her. "Please keep the big bad wolves away from her too."

"Yes, ma'am."

Dara threw her shoulders back and ran her fingers through her hair one last time. "Okay. Let's do this."

The security officer opened the door and a surge of humanity strained at the barricades that had been put up to keep them corralled in one area.

Carolyn saw Dara hesitate at the top step. She knew it wasn't that her friend was afraid; it was more that, despite her success, Dara never understood what all the fuss was about.

As Dara descended the stairs and waved to the crowd, Carolyn moved to the side, trying her hardest to be inconspicuous. She watched as Dara made eye contact with each of her fans to let them know that they were seen. Then she signed whatever was thrust in front of her.

Almost everybody had a camera or a cell phone with which to take pictures. Never once did Dara's smile falter. And then Dara came to the last person in line and she became very still. Too still, Carolyn thought. Something wasn't right.

Carolyn maneuvered closer. When she did, she got a good look at the fan standing directly in front of Dara. *Oh, my God.* It was the professor. Carolyn recognized her from the lecture footage and her photo on the college's website.

Carolyn didn't know what to do. She could see that Dara's posture was stiff and tense. Surely Dara wasn't in any danger from Rebecca. Not any physical danger, anyway. Carolyn skirted around the barricade so that she could get close to Rebecca and hear what she was saying.

"I don't need you to sign anything, Ms. Thomas. I just want to say, in my opinion, I can't imagine anyone more qualified or appropriate to play the role of Celeste in *On the Wings of Angels*. It would be inspired casting, to be sure."

Carolyn swallowed hard. Although she hadn't said anything explicit yet, Rebecca left no doubt that she'd made the connection between Dara and Constance. This was a disaster.

To her credit, Carolyn noted, Dara didn't retreat and she never stopped smiling. Anyone who didn't know Dara the way she did might never figure out that anything was amiss. But Carolyn knew.

"I appreciate your support," Dara said. "If you'll excuse me, I've got to go."

"I didn't…"

Rebecca's shoulders slumped as Dara hustled away toward the limousine and Carolyn could see the confusion and despair in the professor's eyes.

Carolyn felt sorry for her. She seemed so deflated. But Carolyn's allegiance was to Dara, so she slipped away without a word and joined her friend, who by now was seated in the back of the limo.

Dara's hands were shaking. "You know who that was, right? That was Rebecca."

"I know."

"Did you hear the conversation?"

"I did."

"Of all the stupid, jackass, idiotic mistakes I could've made…"

Carolyn put an arm around her shoulder. "It'll be okay."

"You don't know that." Dara's hands trembled and she clasped them together.

"Driver, get us out of here, will you?" Carolyn gave him the address for the restaurant where they had reservations for dinner.

She waited until they were safely away and then turned on the seat to face Dara. "Listen. She could've given you away and she didn't. She was very circumspect. She made sure she was at the end of the line, and she kept her voice low so that no one around could hear."

"She knows."

"Yes. She does." Carolyn didn't see any sense in denying the obvious. "But—"

"But, nothing. No one was ever supposed to know."

After a few minutes of silence, Dara said, "It's my fault."

"How so?"

"I allowed the correspondence to go on. I got sloppy."

"You're human and you were enjoying the interaction. There's no crime in that."

"I should've answered her once and been done with it."

"You can't wall yourself off from all of humanity."

"I'd be better off if I did."

"That's bullshit and you know it."

Dara sat back and looked out the window, a sure sign to Carolyn that they were done talking for now. She thought about how crestfallen Rebecca seemed. *What a mess.*

∽∾

"What were you thinking? Did you think she'd just say, 'Congratulations. You got me. Brava?'"

Rebecca pivoted and paced in the opposite direction. The hotel room wasn't large, so it only took her six strides to reach the door before she had to turn around and head back toward the window.

"For a bright woman, that might've been the dumbest thing you've ever done."

She paused and looked out at the city lights without really seeing them. She'd planned to have a nice dinner out somewhere, but after her encounter with Dara, she'd lost her appetite. In truth, she felt sick to her stomach.

The last letter from Constance had shown glimpses of the woman inside the author, and Rebecca somehow held out hope that she and Constance were establishing new parameters for their relationship. Now...

Rebecca sat on the bed and buried her head in her hands. Now, she'd likely never hear from Constance again. She so looked forward to their exchanges. After the fiasco with Cynthia, her life had been utterly empty. The letters from Constance gave her something to look forward to.

Maybe she could find a way to make things right. Surely, Constance... *Dara,* Rebecca corrected herself. Surely, Dara understood that she would never violate her confidence. Hadn't she made that clear in the way she handled the revelation?

What makes you think so? It isn't like you said, "Don't worry. Your secret is safe with me." And did you see how quickly she took off? She couldn't get away from you fast enough.

Rebecca shook her head in dismay. She knew she'd crossed a line, an almost tangible one. If she had it to do over again, she knew she wouldn't have said a word. She would have said hello, told Dara how much she admired her without explaining why, and they could've gone their separate ways with Dara thinking her secret was safe and Rebecca maintaining her pen pal status with Constance.

Perhaps, in time, Dara would've come clean and revealed the secret on her own. *And maybe pigs really can fly.*

Rebecca flopped back on the bed and stared at the ceiling. The prospect of staying in New York now seemed so much less appealing. On the other hand, a good night's sleep and a Broadway show tomorrow might lift her mood. She checked her watch—11:56 p.m. As if on cue, she yawned. And then her eyes popped open wide. Letterman was on and his monologue was probably almost over.

Could she really bring herself to watch? *You'd pass up a chance to see Dara up close again? Who are you kidding?* She laughed, mirthlessly, scooted up to sit against the headboard, and grabbed the remote.

After a couple of commercials, Dave introduced Dara. With the advantage of the camera close-up, Rebecca could see that the dress matched Dara's eyes. Her breath caught as she saw an image of those eyes, looking directly at her. *A sight you'll never see again.*

Although she looked amazing on television, Rebecca thought Dara was far more attractive in person. And when Letterman began staring at her, Rebecca could have sworn she saw the bright smile slip a fraction. Rebecca wondered if she was reading too much into it. She didn't think so.

How wearing must it be to be Dara Thomas, movie star! Rebecca couldn't begin to imagine. Her mind wandered to the research she'd done on Constance. "Oh, my God. No wonder it was so hard to find out anything about her."

Finally, belatedly, the pieces fell into place. What would Rebecca do if everyone objectified her and nobody took the time to realize that she was a complete person, with an outstanding mind?

"I'd find an outlet where I could be taken seriously and I'd guard it with my life."

If Rebecca felt badly before, now she was beside herself. The last thing in the world she wanted to do was cause Constance any anguish. Somehow, some way, she had to make this right.

CHAPTER TEN

Dara sat in the dark, fully dressed, in Carolyn's guest room. She declined Carolyn's invitation to watch her Letterman appearance. All she could see was Rebecca and all she could think about was that her jealously guarded privacy was gone. If she was going to be honest, that was the correct order of things.

Dara frowned. About the former, she didn't want to care. But in the interest of more candidness, she had to admit that she really did. How did that happen?

Rebecca was even more attractive in person than her picture on the college website or in the video of her teaching. Her eyes were kind and luminescent. *Luminescent? What's that about?*

Dara sighed. Well, it was true. Not only that, but her energy was so open, so honest, and so sincere.

Carolyn was right—Rebecca didn't say anything overt about Constance. She didn't even mention the author at all. *Yet,* Dara reminded herself. She hadn't said anything, yet. Wasn't it only a matter of time before Rebecca leaked word to the press or sold the story along with copies of their correspondence, or...

"Hey," Carolyn said, peeking her head inside the room. "Can I come in?"

Dara motioned her acquiescence. There was no sense pushing Carolyn away. She'd just keep coming back until Dara agreed to talk about it.

Carolyn walked in, turned on the light, and sat on the side of the bed. "I recorded the show in case you change your mind about watching it. This chick, Dara Thomas, she wowed Letterman. Had him eating out of the palm of her hand. It was really something to see."

"Ha, ha."

"You really did do a great job. You were engaging, witty, and charming."

"Woo. The big three."

"Don't pooh-pooh it, Dara. This was an important moment for you and you nailed it." Carolyn paused. "Except when Dave started off by mooning over you. I thought you might punch his lights out."

"Was it that obvious?"

"Not to anybody but me. But then, I know how you feel about being treated like a piece of chocolate the day after Lent."

Dara snorted. "You have such a way with a phrase."

"Am I right, or am I right?"

"Of course you're right, and you know it."

"It's why you were so adamant that Constance not be connected to you. You wanted her to stand on her own merits."

Dara narrowed her eyes. "You did not just use the Letterman thing as a bridge into a discussion about Constance, did you?"

Carolyn winked. "I did."

"Seriously?"

"Seriously. You created Constance because you wanted a place to be your whole self. You wanted to be the person people admired for your intelligence and your depth instead of your cup size."

"My cup size is average," Dara pointed out.

"Don't equivocate."

"Oh. Big word."

"Did you have trouble understanding me? Would you rather I used a simpler term? Need a dictionary?"

Dara scoffed, and Carolyn pointed a finger at her. "See that look? That's what I'm talking about. You bristle when anyone assumes you're just a pretty face."

"Of course. It's insulting."

"Do you remember what you told me the night Sheilah revealed her true colors?"

Dara wrapped her arms around herself. She didn't want to do this. It was too painful. "I'm sure you'll remind me."

"I'm sure I don't have to, but if you want me to be the one to say it, I will."

Dara shook her head as a tear leaked out of the corner of her right eye. "I said I could never trust anyone but you again. No one but you ever loved me for who I was. Everyone else saw the shell and never the person inside. I said that I felt so alone, like a blind spot inside a lighthouse beacon."

"Exactly. And then you cried and sat down and wrote that poem. Do you remember it?"

Dara nodded. How could she forget? It was written from the depths of her despair. "'Knowledge and Illusion,' I called it."*

Dara closed her eyes and began to recite from memory.

Who will know me
When I am old and gray
Wizened by age
And wiser for the experiences?

Who knows me now
When the glare of the spotlight fades
And I am simply me?

Who understands that I am
At once so much more
and so much less?

Who sees me?
All of me
Not the fragments projected
On a screen
Or written on a page
Or frozen in images
That capture glimpses
Of things real or imagined...

"Blah, blah, blah." Dara waved a hand to cover another swell of emotion she didn't want to feel. When she looked up, it was Carolyn who was crying. "What?"

"That poem was achingly sad and poignant. And all these years later, you're still asking the same question, searching for the same thing."

Dara shrugged. "What's your point?"

"What if—"

Carolyn twisted her wedding ring, a sure tip off that she was nervous about her next words. Dara tensed in anticipation. She wasn't sure she wanted to know where this was going.

"What if Rebecca is the answer to the question?"

A rush of heat turned Dara's face beet red.

"Before you say anything," Carolyn rushed on, "consider what we know so far. Rebecca had no idea who Constance was and what she looked like when she wrote that first letter. It was obvious that she admired you for your writing." Carolyn held up her fingers and ticked off that item.

"Two. Rebecca never once in a half dozen letters asked you anything too personal or out-of-bounds. She didn't pry, she didn't flirt, she didn't push to meet you. She was at all times respectful and focused on your work."

Dara had to admit that everything Carolyn said was true.

"Three. You enjoyed the conversation. In fact, you enjoyed it so much that you let some of your real personality shine through. You showed glimpses of humor."

Again, Dara couldn't dispute what Carolyn said.

"Four. I know you realize this is, by far, the longest correspondence you've had with any reader. I want you to look me in the eye and tell me that if today had never happened, you wouldn't have continued the correspondence. I want you to sit there with a straight face and say that you were done with the conversation."

Dara slumped her shoulders in defeat. "I can't."

"So what's changed?"

"Everything!"

"How so?"

"How can you ask me that? You were there. She knows. She said as much. I'm no longer Constance Darrow to her now. I'm Dara Thomas, and she'll never be able to un-know that."

"Who says she needs to?"

Dara rolled her eyes. How could Carolyn be so obtuse?

"I do. Look, we know how this scenario goes. Now she treats me differently and, even if she says all the right things, I can't trust that she's not exactly like Sheilah and everybody else like her."

"Now who's rushing to judgment? You have no idea who Rebecca is or what kind of person she is or what her experiences have been."

Dara flashed back to the gentle kindness in Rebecca's open, honest face. She wished she could wipe that from her memory.

"At any rate, she'll probably take those letters to the nearest tabloid or entertainment show and sell me out."

"That's completely unfair. Again, I'll point out that, even though she had the chance, Rebecca didn't 'out' you as Constance. She didn't."

"Yet."

Carolyn growled. "What if she never does? What then?"

"Then she'll be different from all the rest. But I just can't take that chance. I won't risk it."

"What you mean to say is, you won't allow yourself to open your heart to the possibilities."

Dara stood up and strode to where Carolyn was sitting. She was vibrating with anger, and she couldn't explain why.

"What does my heart have to do with anything? She's just a fan who provided me with some momentary entertainment." Even as she said it, Dara knew it was a lie.

Carolyn stood up. "Wow. Really, Dara? You're full of shit. I saw the look on your face when I handed you that last letter. You couldn't wait to open it and see what Rebecca had to say. Don't deny it. There's no point. If you want to play it safe and live in your lonely, isolated world for the rest of your life, I can't stop you." Carolyn headed for the door. "But for the record, I think Rebecca is just the kind of person you were yearning for in that poem. I guess we'll never know now, will we?" She slammed the door closed behind her.

Rebecca sat at a table in Virgil's on West 44th Street eating barbeque ribs and mashed potatoes. Comfort food. The music from *Avenue Q* still reverberated in her head. Normally, a good musical would've had her spirits soaring, and it had helped somewhat, but Rebecca couldn't shake the sadness. She'd hardly slept at all last night after watching Letterman. The conversation with Dara played over and over in her mind. Rebecca tried to recall the expression on Dara's face when she mentioned Celeste. Had there been any wariness in her eyes? Any fear? Was there any chance at all that Dara walked away only because she was caught off-guard? *As if.*

"Can I get you anything else?" The waiter asked.

"No, thank you. I'll take the check whenever you're ready."

When she'd paid, Rebecca walked back to the hotel. Along the way, she continued to run through her options. By the time she used the keycard and entered her room, she'd made up her mind.

She flipped open the laptop and logged onto the Internet. In the Google search box she typed, "Dara Thomas representation." Nearly nine million hits popped up. Wikipedia showed up on top, but Rebecca ignored that. Instead, she clicked on a link for WhoRepresents.com. She grumbled at having to register in order to get any information, but her outlook brightened considerably when she realized the gold mine she'd found. Every major actor, actress, and director was listed alongside his or her respective talent agents, lawyers, business managers, and public relations representatives.

In short order, Rebecca was able to determine that Dara had three key team members—a talent agent named Richard Church, a public relations representative named Colin Lafferty, and a business manager named Carolyn Detweiler. A few more keystrokes and she had copied contact information for all of them and saved it on her hard drive.

Logic would dictate that the public relations rep was the most likely contact point, but Rebecca didn't like the idea of using a man as a go-between for such a delicate matter. So she googled the business manager.

Carolyn Detweiler, CEO of Detweiler Enterprises, represents an elite group of clients, including best-selling thriller king Randall Nabors, the reclusive Pulitzer-Prize winning author Constance Darrow, Oscar-winning director Peter Davidson, and mega box-office star Dara Thomas, who is described as her best childhood friend.

Rebecca sat back. "Bingo. You're exactly who I'm looking for." Now if she could just figure out what she wanted to say.

Carolyn read the e-mail for the third time. Still, she couldn't decide what to do. She knew she should make Dara aware of it. *You know what she'll say. She'll tell you to turn it down out of hand.* Carolyn rubbed her temples where the beginning of a monster headache was forming.

She already was going to be on thin ice when Dara realized who the featured artist was at the gallery exhibit opening they were slated to attend tonight.

Again, she scanned the contents of the e-mail. It wasn't as though Rebecca was asking to meet with Dara. She wanted to sit down with Carolyn. Carolyn was an adult, fully capable of taking a meeting with anyone she so chose. Technically speaking, this had nothing to do with Dara. *You keep telling yourself that, Car.*

Before she could reconsider what she was doing, Carolyn typed out a quick response, then closed out of her e-mail, grabbed her suit jacket off the hangar on the back of her office door, and headed down the hall toward the elevator.

Rebecca checked the address again for the Carnegie Deli, then glanced at her watch. Carolyn said she'd be there at 11:45 a.m. and would give Rebecca a half-hour window to make it. It wasn't much notice, but Rebecca didn't care. She picked up the pace and arrived a few minutes later.

The deli was packed to overflowing. Rebecca wondered how in the world she would find someone she'd never seen before in such a crowd.

"Lookin' for someone, hon?"

Rebecca eyed the young hostess. "I am."

"Lemme guess. Carolyn Detweiler, right?"

"Yes."

"She's waitin' for ya. Follow me." The hostess led Rebecca through the tightly packed seating area to a corner table in the back.

"Thank you," Rebecca said to the hostess's retreating form. When she turned around, she was face-to-face with a woman who might have been indistinguishable from any businesswoman in the restaurant, save for the expensive and well-tailored clothes.

"You must be Rebecca." Carolyn put out her hand for Rebecca to shake. Her grip was soft, but firm, and her smile was warm.

"And you must be Ms. Detweiler."

"Call me, Carolyn, please. Have a seat." Carolyn indicated the seat opposite her and Rebecca took it.

"Thank you for seeing me. I'm sure your schedule must be ridiculously busy."

"You made it sound important." Carolyn handed Rebecca a menu. "Best to get our orders in. This place is insane at this hour."

"Right." Rebecca opened the extensive menu and glanced up at Carolyn as she perused her own menu. "What do you recommend?"

"Everything is huge and to-die-for. If you like that sort of thing, the Reuben is phenomenal, as is the roast beef." After a second, Carolyn added, "You're not a vegetarian, are you?"

"Me? No. Nope. I'm a meat-lover from way back." Rebecca's leg bounced up and down underneath the table and she struggled to be still. Could she sound any more nervous? Now that she was sitting here, she wasn't sure contacting Carolyn had been the right thing to do. What was it she really wanted to say? What did she want to ask for? And how could she do it without sounding asinine?

"You know, I think I'll just have a cup of coffee." As nervous as she was, Rebecca couldn't imagine keeping a sandwich down now.

Carolyn arched an eyebrow. "Okay, coffee it is." She motioned for the waitress.

As Carolyn ordered two cups of coffee, Rebecca used the opportunity to study her more closely. Something about her seemed familiar... Then it clicked. Carolyn had been there during the exchange with Dara. She had shouldered her way into the crowd, nudging Rebecca's arm in the process. Had she heard the whole thing?

When the waitress left, Carolyn folded her hands under her chin. "So, what can I do for you, Rebecca?"

Rebecca picked up her napkin and put it in her lap as she struggled to collect herself. "As I indicated in my e-mail, I'm a professor of American literature. I've been studying and teaching Constance Darrow's work to my students." *Don't waste time rehashing things she knows. Get to the point.*

"Several months ago, I wrote to Ms. Darrow and we began a correspondence." Rebecca forced herself to make eye contact. "Perhaps you already know that?"

"I do."

"Of course you do. It's naïve of me to think that someone as famous as Constance Darrow would open her own mail. I'm sure it probably goes through several filters. I apologize for my ignorance."

"It's okay. And it's not ignorance. We in this business rarely advertise the way things work behind the scenes." Carolyn's tone was sympathetic—not the least bit condescending—and her smile was kind.

The waitress came with their coffee and a huge slice of cheesecake that Rebecca hadn't heard Carolyn order. There were two plates and two forks.

Rebecca's eyes widened and Carolyn laughed.

"This could feed half the population of a third-world country."

"Welcome to New York, where everything is larger-than-life. Shall I?" Carolyn indicated the cheesecake and a knife.

"Sure." Rebecca held the second plate still as Carolyn slid half of the cheesecake onto it.

"I'm a firm believer that life is short, we should eat dessert first."

"That works for me."

"Best cheesecake in town," Carolyn said. "Go ahead, try it. If you don't love it, I'll... Well, I don't know what I'll do, but it will be dramatic." She chuckled.

With a start, Rebecca realized she really liked Carolyn. She was accessible and easy to be around. "May I," Rebecca started, then stopped to gather her courage. "May I be completely honest and frank with you?"

"I would love that. It would make you such a refreshing change from most of the people I have to deal with every day."

"I bet." Rebecca put her fork down and took a deep breath. "Now that I know what you look like, I recognize you. I mean, I recognize your face. I saw you after the taping of *The Letterman Show*. I know you were standing close enough to hear what I said to Ms. Thomas." Rebecca swallowed hard. "You did hear, didn't you?"

Carolyn nodded, but said nothing.

"Right. Well, I didn't get a chance to say so, because it all happened so quickly, but I want Ms. Thomas to know that I would never, ever, violate her privacy. I would never say anything to jeopardize her in any way." Rebecca faltered, as tears welled in her eyes. She looked around to make sure no one nearby was paying attention to them, composed herself, and continued.

"She's brilliant. I have so much respect for her and *all* of her work. I'm not the kind of person who goes around shooting off my mouth. She has absolutely nothing to worry about from me. I'll never say a word. I promise."

Rebecca fumbled in her purse for a Kleenex and dabbed at the corners of her eyes. She was surprised when Carolyn reached across the table and put a hand over hers.

"I believe you."

"You do?"

"Yes."

"Oh." Rebecca was overcome by a rush of gratitude. "Why?"

That startled a laugh out of Carolyn. "You're unique, you know that?"

"I've been called worse."

"Call it intuition. Call it an educated guess. I believe you're telling the truth." Carolyn leaned forward. "So, in that spirit, I'm going to explain something to you."

Rebecca leaned forward, as well. "Okay."

"Dara's life hasn't been easy. She's been badly hurt before. It's difficult for her to trust that someone wants to know her. *Really* know her." Carolyn held Rebecca's gaze.

"I can't even begin to imagine," Rebecca said. She checked again to make sure their conversation was private. It was, but she still wanted to be as circumspect as possible. "I can see why she would keep the two 'things' so separate. The 'other' gives her something of her own—something not connected to the face the public sees, a place where her soul can shine honestly and on its own merits."

Carolyn sat back. A slight smile played on her lips. "Exactly. And, might I add, quite eloquently stated."

"I meant it."

"I believe you did."

"When I researched the author for my course, I was frustrated that I could find next to nothing about her. After all, most literature illuminates the experiences of the author or vice versa. With no context to work with, it made discussing the origin and genesis of the material rather...challenging."

"That makes sense."

"But knowing what I know now, I understand so much more. The author is such a gifted writer, a real student of human nature. A great observer. Her characters reflect a bone-deep knowledge of what motivates people." Rebecca was warming to her favorite subject. "And yet, her protagonists almost always yearn for something more. It's as if the life they lead is not real and what is real, what they truly yearn for, is always just out of reach. There's such depth, such passion in the prose." Rebecca stopped talking when she realized she'd slipped into professor mode. "I'm sorry. I tend to get carried away."

Carolyn chuckled. "I can see that. Nothing to apologize for. I'm certain the author would love to know her work inspired such strong enthusiasm."

Rebecca's stomach dropped and her heart stuttered. "No, she wouldn't. Not now." She felt the lump rise up in her chest and into her throat. "If I had it to do over again, I never would have said anything. I can't explain what I was thinking, except to say that I wasn't thinking. If I'd only kept it to myself. I should've realized..." Rebecca stopped and blew out an explosive breath.

"Anyway. I can't imagine I'll ever get another letter from Constance. I just wanted her to know that she doesn't need to be looking over her shoulder. There is no other shoe that's going to drop. I'll never bother her again."

Rebecca reached into her purse, pulled out enough cash to pay the bill, and stood. "Please..." She couldn't choke back a sob. "Please tell her how much I admire her heart and soul and her intellect. Please tell her how much I enjoyed our correspondence and how much it meant to me. And please tell her I wish her all the best. She's an extraordinary gift to the world, in all ways."

"Rebecca—"

Rebecca couldn't look Carolyn in the eye. "Thank you so much for seeing me. I didn't think you would. I'm so glad you did. Thank you for listening. And you were right, this is the best cheesecake I've ever had. Take care, Carolyn."

Rebecca didn't wait for a reply. She simply ran, dodging tables and patrons along the way, her heart aching with every step.

CHAPTER ELEVEN

Tell me again why we're going to a gallery opening for a Southwestern landscape photographer?" Dara asked.

"I'm sorry. What?" Carolyn maneuvered through the early evening traffic on the way to the Everest Priest Gallery on the East Side.

"Hello? Earth to Carolyn. Where the heck are you?"

"What do you mean?"

"I mean you haven't said two words since we got in the car and you're lights on, nobody's home. What gives?"

"Nothing." All afternoon, Carolyn hadn't stopped thinking about her meeting with Rebecca. She wasn't ready to tell Dara about it; she hadn't finished fully processing it herself. "What was your question?"

"Why are we going to a photography gallery opening?"

"Oh. Well, the work is breathtaking. I thought you might want something for the beach house."

"And?" Dara's stare was penetrating.

"And, what?"

"How long have I known you?"

"As long as I've known you."

"Cute. There's more to it. If it was just a matter of decorating my house, you'd have gone yourself, found something you knew I'd like, and bought it."

Carolyn knew she had to come clean about tonight. Dara would know soon enough, anyway. "We know the artist."

"We…know the artist?"

"Yes."

Dara turned to face Carolyn. "If it was someone I liked, you would've told me long before now. So, who is it?"

Carolyn took a deep breath and said a silent prayer. "You remember Renée Maupin?" Carolyn could feel Dara seething. "Look. All of that was a long time ago. We were just kids. Renée has changed. She's grown up."

Carolyn chanced a glance at Dara's face. Her expression was completely closed. "Say something."

"I'm contemplating who I should kill first, you or her."

Carolyn winced. "Hopefully, neither of us."

"How could you possibly think I'd want to see her, never mind support her work?"

"I'm telling you, she's a completely different human being than the sullen, mean kid we knew in school."

"She wasn't just sullen and mean, Car. She was a bully. She made my life a living hell."

Carolyn considered it a positive sign that Dara hadn't asked her to turn the car around and allowed the ensuing silence to linger. After several minutes, she peeked over and saw that Dara's face held so much sadness. She reached out and patted Dara's leg.

"I'm sorry. I know this has been an incredibly emotional week for you, and this just adds a whole new layer."

"That's an understatement. It's just...I'm not sure I can handle one more thing, you know?"

"I know. But in a sense, this week is all about healing the past. When Renée read about your mother's death and saw that you were in town, she contacted me and specifically asked if we would stop by the opening."

"Why?"

"Good question. She said she had something she wanted to say to you. I told her she could say it to me and I would be happy to pass it along. But she said it was time for her to revisit the sins of her youth and make amends. Since you're leaving tomorrow, this is the only chance."

"And to think, I almost got away."

"I spent a while talking to her, Dar. I couldn't believe this was the same person. You'll see." Carolyn pulled up in front of the valet parking area. "If we get in there and you don't agree, we can turn right back around, okay?"

Dara didn't answer. She simply shook her head in resignation and stepped out of the car.

≪⑥❧

The first thing Dara noticed was a massive image of a snow-covered canyon vista. The picture covered an entire wall and took Dara's breath away.

"This is my favorite, as well."

Dara turned to see a gorgeous Native American woman standing beside her and smiled.

"To be fair, I can't say that it's my favorite yet, since it's the only one I've seen."

"I am Yazhi Begay." The woman held out her hand and Dara took it.

"Dara Thomas."

"I know. Thank you for coming. Renée wasn't sure you would. I assured her you'd be here. She'll be quite pleased."

"You're a friend of Renée's?"

Yazhi's laugh was easy and soft. "I am her wife."

Dara struggled to keep the shock off her face. She wasn't sure she succeeded.

"Are you more surprised that Renée is gay, or that she is married to me?"

Yazhi's eyes shone bright with mirth and the good humor was contagious.

"Um…Can I have some time to think about it?"

"Take all the time you need. I will get Renée."

Dara moved on to the next image as her mind continued to swirl. It was a mystery how a woman whose energy felt as gentle as Yazhi Begay's could love someone like Renée Maupin.

The title on the next photograph was "Fated Encounters." The walls of a slot canyon were iridescent.

"I snapped that the day I met my wife. Hence the title."

"Renée."

"Dara." Renée was Dara's height, so they were eye-to-eye. "Thank you for coming. I really appreciate it and I know it was probably the last thing in the world you wanted to do."

"Your work is stunning."

"Thank you for saying so."

"It's the truth."

Dara thought Renée seemed subdued and almost humble. It was hard to ignore that she'd grown up to be a very attractive woman. Still, Dara knew a thing or two about judging the content of one's character based on physical beauty.

"Carolyn tells me you have something you wanted to say."

"To the point and forthright. Just as I remembered. But then again, you always had more courage than I did. A *lot* more courage than I did." Renée fussed with her cufflink. "All right, but I'd like to do this someplace a little more private. Please, follow me."

The office was well appointed and softly lit. The chairs looked comfortable, but Dara wasn't planning on staying long enough to find out. She stood just inside the door and folded her arms across her chest. "Okay. I'm listening."

Renée nervously licked her lips. "When I met my wife, I was a lot like you remember—I was a complete bitch. I was angry at the world, I was bitter, and the only thing or person I cared about was myself." She moved to the corner of the desk and leaned against it. "Yazhi changed everything. She taught me to embrace all of who I was and not to be afraid of it anymore."

"I'm glad for you." Dara didn't know what else to say.

"That's where you come in." Renée finally made eye contact. "Do you recall how, whenever you talked about seeing people who had passed over, I was the first one to give you shit?"

Dara flashed on an image of Timmy. "Yeah. Being made to feel like a complete pariah and a freak is not something a kid easily forgets."

"Right. First, I want to apologize for treating you that way and for encouraging others to do the same. I was a jackass."

Dara raised an eyebrow. She didn't know what she'd been expecting, but an astonishingly frank self-assessment and apology wasn't it.

"I know, right? Who thought I'd ever become self-aware enough to admit that." Renée shook her head. "But wait, there's more."

Dara unfolded her arms and consciously assumed a less hostile posture. "I'm listening."

"I want to explain why I was the way I was. It doesn't excuse anything," Renée hastened to add, "but it does shine a little light on the whys and wherefores."

"Okay."

"The truth is, I was more like you than I wanted to admit. Those things that you saw—the kid on the playground, the old teacher in the classroom—I saw them just as clearly as you did."

"What?" Dara felt a wave of dizziness sweep over her and she lowered herself into the nearest chair.

"I saw the exact same things you did. The difference between us was that you were brave enough to say it out loud. I was too afraid of the consequences."

Dara tried to assimilate the information. It was mind-boggling. Slowly, anger rose up from her gut and into her chest, where it bloomed.

"You were afraid of the consequences? Do you think I wasn't? Do you think it was easy being the butt of everyone's jokes? Having people—including, and maybe especially you—say horrible things about me?"

"I'm sure that it wasn't." Renée's voice was quiet and contrite. "As I said, you were a much better person than I was. You had the courage of your convictions."

"I went through my entire childhood thinking there was something wrong with me. I felt so isolated and alone. You…you used my pain to make yourself more popular. 'Let's make fun of the weirdo who sees things that aren't there.'" The adult Dara realized, even as the words poured forth, that the distress she was feeling belonged to the small child inside her, but she couldn't seem to stop herself.

"You're right. I wish I could go back and undo it all and do everything over again. But I can't. I can't take away the pain and anguish I caused you. The pain and anguish you're still feeling right now. I would if I could, I promise you."

Renée came and sat in the chair directly opposite Dara. She leaned forward and clasped her hands together, her forearms resting on her thighs. "I don't know what it was like growing up in your house. It isn't like you ever invited me over. Not that I blame you," she added immediately. "But in my house, it wasn't safe to be who I was. My mother thought I was Satan's spawn. She was convinced I was possessed and threatened to send me away."

Almost against her will, Dara felt her anger melting away. It was as if she and Renée were twin daughters of different mothers.

"My parents were the same way."

Renée nodded grimly. "Then I'm even sorrier. My answer to the situation was to shut down my abilities and pretend like they weren't there. Like a homophobe who is a self-loathing homosexual and doesn't want anyone to know. The easiest way to draw suspicion away is to be the loudest detractor."

"Not being honest about what I saw never occurred to me."

"As I said, you were far stronger than I was. I was so in awe of you. You were just the coolest person I knew. But I couldn't be you. And that made me hate myself even more."

For the first time in her life, Dara understood Renée. She still couldn't fathom being the bully Renée had been, but she could empathize with her, nonetheless. And that was enough.

"I get it. And I'm sorry for the way things were in your family. Heck, I'm sorry for the way things were in my own family."

"I'm sorry about your mother, by the way," Renée said.

"Thanks. I hadn't seen her in years. When I left for college, I never looked back."

"I can understand why."

Dara studied Renée's face. Now she looked relaxed and at peace. "Why did you want to tell me all this now? Why not just leave it all alone?"

"Yazhi is such an incredibly gifted healer and spiritualist. She recognized right away that I had stuffed down and rejected all of my abilities. She helped me to see what a gift they are and to get in touch with them again. I'm so glad I did. I'm so much more centered and aware."

"She sounds like a really special woman."

Renée's face lit up. "She is. Anyway, we went to see one of your movies. It was really good." Renée blushed, shifted uncomfortably in her seat, and cleared her throat. "Afterward, I told Yazhi the story of our childhood and what an idiot I was. She helped me to see how important it is to heal what's in our auric field."

"Like I said, it sounds like she's a keeper. I'm glad you've got her in your life and that you're happy." Dara felt a pang of loneliness. For reasons she didn't want to examine, Rebecca's face flashed before her eyes. Just as quickly, she dismissed it.

"I really wanted to make this right, Dara. And not because you're famous, either. It's just time, you know?"

Dara could see that Renée was sincere. "I appreciate your reaching out. That took a lot of guts."

"Yeah, well... Anyway, I have something for you." Renée stood up and Dara followed suit. "Wait here a sec."

Dara did as she was told. Her head was swimming, but one thing was certain—Carolyn was right. This was not the same girl she knew growing up.

"This is for you." Renée handed Dara a gorgeous, museum-mounted image of a lone tree framed by a glorious sunset with the remaining rays of the day's light reflecting off the red rocks in the background.

"It's incredible." The beauty of the shot transfixed Dara.

"The tree is you. Standing strong and true. May you always walk in the rays of a perfect sunset and remain as courageous and steadfast as you were when we were kids."

Dara opened her mouth to speak but nothing came out. So she tried again. "I—I don't know what to say. That's a lovely sentiment."

"I mean it."

And Dara could see that she did.

Renée continued, "I know it's unlikely, but if you ever wanted to keep in touch, I'd like that."

She was back to fiddling with her cufflink, and Dara realized this wasn't easy for her.

"I'd like that very much. I don't come to New York much, but next time I'm in town maybe we could all get together for dinner. Likewise if you ever come to LA, assuming I'm in town."

"That'd be great."

They started to walk out together. "I'm glad I came," Dara said.

"Me too."

Dara didn't know how much time had passed, but when they cleared the hallway and entered the main gallery, the place was packed.

"Oh, my. I didn't mean to take you away from your fans." Dara gave Renée a hug. She could feel her surprise. "Thank you for the gifts. I'll treasure all three of them always."

"Three?"

"The photograph, the apology, and your friendship."

"Oh." Renée stepped back. "You're welcome on all counts. Number two was way overdue."

"You'd better go mingle. I've got to get going anyway. I've got an early flight tomorrow."

"Safe journeys, Dara. I wish you every success."

"Likewise."

Renée disappeared into the crowd. Within seconds, Carolyn was by Dara's side, a self-satisfied smirk on her face.

"Don't gloat."

"Well? Was I right or was I right?"

"You were right. Now take me home before I turn into a pumpkin."

"I'd pay to see that."

"I bet you would."

⤙🙣⤚

Rebecca shuffled papers around on her desk. Class would start soon, and yet she couldn't seem to muster any enthusiasm for it. Traditionally, the first lecture of the semester was her personal favorite. She enjoyed seeing all those eager faces, alert and ready to learn.

Since her visit to New York, she'd made a few adjustments to her course on "Constance Darrow and the Modern American Heroine." As she'd explained to Carolyn, being able to study the author and factor in the author's background and experiences did much to illuminate the subtext of the work.

The fact that the author was Dara Thomas made all the difference in the world. Still, Rebecca was careful not to include anything in her presentation that would make the connection between Constance and Dara.

Rebecca felt the now-familiar ache in her heart at the thought of Dara. *Constance.* She needed to continue to think of her as Constance so that she didn't slip and reveal anything.

It seemed ridiculous that the absence of a woman with whom she'd shared a few letters and a bond over well-written literature should leave such a gaping hole in her life, but it did.

Rebecca eyed the clock on the wall. "Pull yourself together. It's show time." She gathered her papers together and headed for the lecture hall.

<ᢒᢙ

"They loved the table read you did with Sam. You got the part!" Rick Church's voice was an octave higher than normal, as was usual when he was excited.

"Good," Dara said. She was sitting on her back deck, watching the waves wash in against the shore.

"Because of the response to your interest in the project, everything's being fast-tracked. Filming is set to start in two weeks. I'm having the script messengered to you right now. Rehearsals start next week."

"Okay."

There was a pause on the other end of the line. "I don't understand you lately. You should be thrilled."

"I'm jumping up and down on the inside."

"Very funny. For more than a year, ever since Jessica Howland got fired from the role, you've been telling me how much you want to play Celeste in *On the Wings of Angels.* Now I tell you the part is yours, and you've barely got a pulse."

"As I recall, you wanted me to do a Broadway show to improve my chances. I'm sure glad I had confidence in my ability to get the part on my own." Dara heard the sarcasm in her own voice and frowned. "I'm sorry. That was shitty."

"It was. Which, I might point out, also is not like you. But I still love you. And if you'd listened to me instead of going on national television and openly coveting the role, they might still be diddling around instead of getting it done."

"You weren't too fond of my taking it public at the time."

Rick's laughter echoed through the cell phone connection. "That was before you got the part. Now? I'm thrilled. Good call." "I'll remember that next time I do something that freaks you out."

"No you won't, and that's okay. I'll talk to you later."

"Bye, Rick." Dara closed the Bluetooth and tossed it on the small table beside her chair. For several minutes she simply sat, mesmerized by the rhythmic slap of the water on the sand and the call of the gulls.

Rick was right, she should be thrilled and doing a happy dance. So why wasn't she? Playing the role that she wrote was a dream come true. She wouldn't have to worry about whether the actress could do justice to a character so near and dear to the author's heart. She was the actress. Everything rested in her hands.

"Almost everything." Dara corrected herself. The screenwriter, and most especially the director, would have a lot to say about how the book got brought to life. A scene shot this way or that, a choice of camera angles, a deleted line here or there—all of it contributed to the final product.

Still, Dara had the part. Rebecca would be overjoyed to know. Dara groaned. That was the problem. She'd never get to tell her in a letter or in person and watch her reaction, to see those vibrant eyes light up... *Stop it. You're torturing yourself. Let it go.*

In the week since she'd come back to LA, Dara had replayed those few seconds with Rebecca dozens of times. What if she had stayed long enough to hear what Rebecca would say next? What if she hadn't gotten so terrified and run? Why couldn't she bring herself to write to Rebecca now?

"Because you're afraid she's just like all the others and you don't want her to be." Dara shook her head in disgust. "And now you're so pathetic you're talking to yourself."

At the sound of the warning alarm that a car was in the drive, Dara got up and went back inside. No doubt, the script had arrived. She would be grateful for the distraction.

CHAPTER TWELVE

W elcome to *Entertainment Tonight*. Our top story comes out of Hollywood, where *Entertainment Tonight* has learned that Tinseltown's torrid affair with actress Dara Thomas won't be cooling off anytime soon."

Rebecca froze with a forkful of honey balsamic salad in mid-air. Her mouth went dry.

A video clip showed Dara looking spectacular in a flowing indigo gown. Her hair was swept up in a French knot. Cameras flashed from every angle as she smiled and posed. Rebecca marveled at how calm, cool, and collected Dara appeared despite the frenzy around her.

"I bet you hate that," Rebecca muttered. The thought sent a renewed spasm of pain through her. It was yet another reminder that she would never again be privy to Dara's thoughts or see those now-familiar flashes of humor.

"Thomas, seen here at last night's star-studded benefit for the AIDS Foundation in Beverly Hills, reportedly has signed on to play the role of Celeste in the troubled big-screen adaptation of the Pulitzer Prize-winning novel, *On the Wings of Angels*. The film languished in limbo for a long time following the very public firing of A-list actress Jessica Howland over her reportedly lackluster performance as the title character. With Thomas taking over the role, shooting on the film will begin in less than two weeks."

It took several seconds for the substance of the report to sink in. When it did, Rebecca's heart fluttered on a surge of pride. Dara would get to play Celeste, after all. "I'm happy for you."

How the director ever could have thought Jessica Howland was right for the part was beyond Rebecca. Dara should have been the clear choice all along. But maybe her schedule hadn't allowed for it.

Rebecca turned off the television and picked up her copy of *On the Wings of Angels*. Rereading it somehow made her feel closer to the author. As she focused on Celeste's spiritual journey, she imagined the dialogue being spoken by Dara. Yes. There really was no other choice for the part. She knew that when the movie made it to the big screen, she'd see it many times. It was as close as she was going to get to be a part of Dara's life again.

≪≫

Dara tossed the script down on the table. "This is never going to work."

"What's wrong?" Carolyn asked.

"What's wrong? Are you listening to these lines? This isn't Celeste. I don't know who the hell it is, but it isn't Celeste."

Carolyn lowered her copy of the script. "It's the screenwriter's version of Celeste," she said practically. "You know as well as I do that when Constance sold the rights, she lost any say over the film version."

"It wasn't practical for me to write it. It wasn't like Constance was going to be able to be on set to consult with the director, now was it?" Dara went to the refrigerator and yanked the door open. She looked inside for something to eat, decided she didn't want anything, and slammed it shut again. When she returned to the living room, Carolyn was sitting there, patiently waiting for her.

"Are you done having a temper tantrum?"

Dara laughed. "It did sound a little like that, didn't it?"

"It's been sounding a lot like that ever since you left New York." Carolyn's voice was gentle, but her message was unmistakable.

"We're not going to go there. You know that, right?"

"You and I both know you've been miserable ever since the encounter with—"

"You are so going there." Dara shook her head.

"Am I wrong?"

Dara didn't want to answer. They both knew it was true. "What do you want me to say?" She threw up her hands.

"I want you to acknowledge that in the two weeks since, nothing has happened. Zero. No tabloids have run anything, no entertainment shows have broken the story. No magazines are talking about it."

"Yet."

Carolyn jumped up. "There is no 'yet!' For God's sake. In that timeframe the whole world knows you were cast to play Celeste. Don't you think that if Rebecca wanted to cash in, she would've outed you as Constance in that context? Really? Could there have been a better time for her to do it? A more profitable time for her to do it?"

Dara took a step back. She couldn't remember ever having seen Carolyn this animated. "What's this really about?"

"What's it about?"

"That was the question, yes."

"You're being incredibly unfair. This woman hasn't done anything to harm you. On the contrary, she's respected you and your privacy. You, on the other hand, haven't shown her anything close to respect. You've judged her without even letting her have her say."

"She had her say outside the studio."

Carolyn gave her a withering glare.

"Change the subject," Dara said.

Carolyn shook her head in disgust. "I've got to go. I'll see you tomorrow."

When she'd left, Dara stood in the middle of the room wondering what the hell had just happened.

Carolyn drummed her fingers on the steering wheel. She'd come perilously close to blurting out that she'd spent time with Rebecca and that the woman didn't have a disingenuous bone in her body. Now, she was wondering what had stopped her from saying so out loud. She wanted to tell Dara about the meeting. She did. *Who are you kidding? No, you didn't.* As angry and cranky as Dara had been since Letterman, Carolyn couldn't envision an upside to disclosing the meeting. She didn't think Dara could hear her.

"And yet, here you are feeling guilty about keeping your mouth shut," she mumbled.

True to her word, Rebecca hadn't tried to contact Dara or explain herself. She'd simply disappeared. Carolyn wondered how she was doing, and whether she was as ornery as Dara was right now. "Probably."

Maybe she should reach out to Rebecca. *And say what? That you're sorry Dara's being a butthead? That maybe she'll come around? You can't guarantee that.*

Carolyn pulled into the parking lot of her West Coast offices. When she took on other LA-based clients in addition to Dara, she decided it was time to establish a beachhead on the left coast. It wasn't much, just a small boutique setup convenient to the major studios in Burbank so that she could be present for her clients in their hours of need. She also rented a condo nearby. As much as she and Dara loved each other like sisters, they each needed their own space.

She checked her messages, returned phone calls, and answered e-mails. Then, unable to resist, she checked to see if there were any new videos of Rebecca's classes online.

Sure enough, the newest entry listed in a YouTube search was Rebecca's opening lecture for the semester in her "Constance Darrow and the Modern American Heroine" class.

An hour later, Carolyn was still sitting there, her chin propped up on her palm. The lesson was smartly crafted and the insights showed a remarkable command of the material, but... But, something was off. It was Rebecca. The passion from her previous semester's classes was missing. The spark in her eyes had gone out.

"You're every bit as miserable as Dara." The problem was, Carolyn wasn't sure she could or should do anything about it.

෯෧

"No, no, no!" the director, George Nelson, yelled. "Stop!"

The actors and actresses halted in the middle of the third rehearsal scene. Dara turned her head from side to side trying to relieve the tension. She could've told him the scene would never work as written. But it wasn't for the actress to speak up in this situation; that was between the director and the screenwriter, in this case, Cal Whiting.

"Cal, this just isn't working. If this is what we shoot tomorrow, we'll be wasting money and time."

"It isn't in the words, George. I'm not sure what you want me to do here."

The director pulled the screenwriter off to the side, but Dara didn't need to hear them to know what was being said. No doubt the screenwriter was complaining that the actors were underperforming. The director wouldn't want his actors to be uptight before the shooting even began, so he would defend them and order the writer to figure something out.

"Okay, people. Let's move on to the next scene, shall we?"

Dara noticed the writer hustling away. *Revisions to follow, I'm sure.* She only hoped the changes would bring Celeste closer to the complicated, conflicted woman as she'd written her.

They moved on to the scene where Celeste meets Harold, a middle-aged man who has just lost his wife. He's questioning his existence, pondering what kind of God could take the love of his life in her prime, and trying to find his way in the wake of his loss.

"Dara, Sam," George said. "You're up. I'm planning to shoot this scene in tight, so I want to see plenty of emotion from you, Sam. Dara, how were you planning to play this?"

Constance's Celeste also was searching for something more after years of stumbling through life, never really finding any solace or meaning in her days. This script's version wasn't anywhere near as nuanced.

"I think Harold and Celeste have a lot more in common than meets the eye. Although Celeste is much younger than Harold and hasn't experienced nearly as much, she's also questioning what the universe has in store for her."

"Sounds lovely," the director said. "Except that's not really the way it's written. If you take her in that direction, it throws off almost every other scene between these two characters. Poor Cal would have to rewrite the whole script."

Dara badly wanted to point out that Cal never should have written the script that way in the first place, but that would be too far out of the norm for any actor to suggest.

"Tell me what you have in mind and I'll make sure I deliver it." She smiled the sweetest smile she could muster. Dara prided herself on being a team player. No one had ever accused her of being demanding or difficult on a set, and she intended to keep it that way.

The day progressed on in much the same fashion, as they blocked out and rehearsed the most critical scenes in the movie, going over motivations and mindsets, filling out the details that would bring the words on the pages to life. Finally, after eleven hours, the director told everyone to break for the day. Shooting would begin tomorrow.

As Dara headed to her car, she dialed Carolyn's number. "Hey."

"Hey, yourself. How'd it go?"

Dara groaned in response.

"That good, eh?"

"You have no idea. Do you have time for dinner, or did you already eat?"

"I had a feeling I'd be hearing from you, so I waited. I'm starving, though, so hurry."

"Where do you want to go?"

"I'm already there."

Dara raised her eyebrows. "Where's there? Your condo?"

"Nope. Actually, I'm at your place. I figured you'd be beat and with tomorrow being the first day of filming, I thought I'd make this simple and bring in something light."

Dara was quiet for a moment.

"But, if that isn't what you want..."

"No. I was just thinking about what a thoughtful gesture that was and how much I don't deserve it. I know I've been a total bitch all week."

"Almost three weeks, but who's counting."

Dara agreed. "I'll be there in about fifteen minutes."

In the end, she was there in ten. Carolyn already had everything on the table. "If Stan ever gets tired of you, you'd make a great wife."

"I already make a great wife, and I'm taken. Sorry, you're going to have to go out and find your own."

Dara felt the edges of loneliness creep in. She'd spent enough time there in the last few weeks. "Nah. I'm good."

Carolyn frowned, but said nothing more on the subject. Instead, she asked, "So, how was the last day of rehearsal?"

"In a word? Aggravating. George actually asked how I wanted to play that really crucial first scene between Celeste and Harold."

"Uh oh."

"What do you mean, uh oh?"

"I mean, I read the book, and I ran lines for this scene with you. They bear precious little similarity to each other."

"My point, exactly."

"I suppose you told George that?"

"Sort of."

Carolyn covered her eyes and peeked out between her fingers. "What?"

"I'm afraid to ask how that went."

"I suggested the proper way Celeste should be played."

"And?"

"And I got shot down."

Carolyn made a sympathetic noise. "It's going to be a long three months, isn't it?"

"It's looking that way."

"Remember, you wanted this."

"I did. But that was before I read the script."

"Please tell me you haven't changed your mind."

"Okay. I haven't changed my mind."

"Now say it like you mean it."

"I do mean it, Car." Dara leaned forward. "But I can't say it's going to be easy."

"Your life seldom is, so why should making this movie be any different?"

"This is different. This is my creation. My heart and soul are in those pages."

Carolyn got up to clear the plates. "You could always come out as Constance and suggest changes to the script."

Dara choked on the water she was drinking.

"Well, you could."

"That's not an option."

"Why not?"

Dara went to the sink and nudged Carolyn out of the way. "My house, I do the dishes. Besides, you got dinner."

Carolyn leaned against the counter. "You haven't answered the question."

"I didn't think you were serious."

"I wasn't. But if it's going to be such torture for you, it's worth revisiting."

Dara turned off the water and faced Carolyn. "You're my business manager. How can you ask that? Can you imagine how it would look to know that I campaigned to star in the adaptation of my own book without giving full disclosure? The press would have a field day, and George certainly wouldn't want me on his set after that. There'd be too much tension. Do we follow the director's lead, or do we go with the author/actress's interpretation?"

"Mm-hmm."

"But you knew all that already, didn't you?" Dara said.

"Of course."

"So that was for my benefit?"

"You needed to get to a place where you understand why you're only the lead actress on this set. Otherwise, you're going to be miserable. You have to let go of this one and trust the writer and director to get it right."

Dara eyed Carolyn appreciatively. "That was pretty deft, you know that?"

Carolyn winked. "I sure hope so."

"Is that why you're really here tonight?"

"I live to serve." Carolyn bowed.

"Right. Now get out of here before I kick you in the ass."

"That's the thanks I get?"

Dara leaned over and kissed Carolyn on the cheek. "Nope. That's the thanks you get."

"That and five bucks will get me a latte. I'm out of here." Carolyn gathered up her things and waved as she headed out the door.

To the empty room Dara said, "Slick. That was very, very slick."

Carolyn was right, of course. Dara needed to stop fighting with the material and just suck it up and do it. She wasn't in charge here; she was just a hired hand. It would be a struggle, but she'd try to remember that tomorrow. She turned out the lights and headed for bed. A 5:15 a.m. makeup call meant she needed to get a good night's rest.

༖

"Professor Minton? Why do you think someone like Celeste, who is young and vibrant, wants to spend all her time with a washed up, beaten-down guy like Harold? What's in it for her?"

Rebecca considered how to answer her student's question. It was the second class of the semester, and she was pleased to see that the kids were invested in the material. Today, they were discussing the nature of Celeste and Harold's relationship.

Rebecca threw the question back. "What do *you* think is in it for her?"

"Maybe she's into older men," one of the guys said.

"Or maybe she feels sorry for him," one of the girls offered.

"Or maybe," Rebecca said, "she has more in common with Harold than she does with a lot of other people her age. What do we know about Harold?"

"He's a wicked sad dude who misses his dead wife and doesn't know what to do with himself," the male student said.

"True. And what is he looking for?"

"Someone to hang out with."

"A friend."

"An escape."

"Meaning."

Rebecca pointed enthusiastically at the student who said the last. "That's right. He's looking for meaning. He's looking for something to hold onto, some force larger than himself to explain why things happened the way they did and why his wife died so young. He's having trouble understanding how a merciful God could take such a good woman."

"Professor, Celeste is just turning thirty. I don't see what she's got in common with Harold except that he was probably thirty at one point in his life too."

Rebecca laughed. "That's because you haven't turned thirty yet. Trust me, it's a life-changing event worthy of mourning. I draped my house in black for a week when I turned the big three-O."

All of the students laughed. "Aw, you don't look a day over fifty, Professor M."

"Who said that?" Rebecca pretended to look around. "Nobody? Nobody wants to own that? Bunch of chickens." Rebecca wadded up a piece of paper and playfully threw it in the direction of the student who made the crack.

"What Celeste and Harold share is a spiritual journey. They're on a spiritual journey, each seeking meaning. Celeste is looking for something to believe in that makes her existence worthwhile. Harold always found meaning in his relationship with his wife. Now he's trying to puzzle out the spiritual purpose of his wife's death and a way to hold on to his faith now that she's gone. They're both adrift." Rebecca waited a beat. "Kind of like all of you look right now. Get out of here, everybody. See you next week."

Rebecca closed the folder on the lectern. As she turned to leave, she watched a student break down a Go-Pro video camera on a tripod in the corner of the room. "What's that for?"

"YouTube."

"You're taping my lecture for posterity and uploading it to YouTube?"

"Yeah. Been taping them for a while. Haven't you noticed before now? It's part of a college Excellence in Education program we're putting together."

"Don't you need my permission for something like that?"

"Um. The department head and Old Chapel signed off on it."

"The administration gave you permission to use my image?"

"Yeah." The student rubbed the back of his neck nervously. "You're down with it, right?"

"Do I have a choice? I guess if it's okay with them, it's okay with me. Just make sure you get my good side."

"Which side is that?"

"I'll leave that up to you."

As she walked away, she muttered, "YouTube." She spent a second fantasizing that Dara would somehow see one of the lectures and want to talk to her about it. *Yeah, right. Keep dreaming.*

CHAPTER THIRTEEN

"Okay. Dara, Sam, one more time. Sam, this time I want to see the rawness of the emotions. You just buried your wife. You're all alone without a plan, just sitting on this park bench, trying to keep it together. Dara, you spot him and you're intrigued, wondering what his story is. At first, you sit down on the bench across from him. Then, you simply can't resist. So you get up and move next to him." The director motioned to the "B" camera. "I want you in tight on Sam, so close we're looking at the red in his bloodshot eyes. Places, everyone!"

Dara's body vibrated with tension. She slid her jaw from side to side to ease the pain from clenching her teeth. This was the twelfth take and none of them yet had been worth a damn. Out of the corner of her eye, she could see that her co-star was struggling with the contacts he had to wear to get his eyes to look sufficiently bloodshot. *Poor guy.* She liked Sam Rutledge. He was a great actor with a well-deserved reputation as a hard worker and a professional. He showed up on time, knew his lines, and never complained.

"You okay?" she asked.

"Yeah." Sam smiled at Dara. "These buggers suck, but I'll get through it. Thank God I don't have to spend the whole movie wearing them."

"Tell you what. How about we nail it in this take so you can get the heck out of those things."

"Sounds like a plan to me."

In the end, they shot another eight takes before the director yelled, "Cut! And print it."

Dara leaned back and said a silent thank you to the universe.

Audrey Eaton, the first assistant director on the film, yelled out, "That's a wrap for today, folks. We're going into turnaround."

Since Dara didn't have a watch on and they were inside on a sound stage, she was surprised at the pronouncement. Going into turnaround meant that they were getting close to being within eight hours of when the crew had to be back on set. Contractually, if they didn't get at least eight hours off, the studio would have to pay more than time-and-a-half to anyone the rule applied to. Despite the fact that this was a big-budget production, no one wanted to waste money on a turnaround violation.

"Damn. That was a long day," Sam said, as he and Dara walked off the set.

"No kidding."

"What do you think we'll be shooting tomorrow?"

Dara shrugged. "My guess is unless George magically falls in love with today's dailies, it'll be more of the same in the morning."

Sam groaned. "Another day of those blasted contacts. Please, God, let George and the studio love the dailies."

Dara laughed. "Good luck with that, but I'm happy to pray with you. A girl can sit on a bench for only so long before her ass gets flat."

Sam conspicuously checked out Dara's butt. "Nope. It's still round."

Because Dara knew Sam was happily married and not the least bit lecherous, she played along. "Well, thank God for that. For a second there, I was worried."

"Glad I could help ease your mind, though having to do the research was a hardship."

They reached Dara's trailer. "Uh-huh. Say goodnight, Sam."

"Good night, Sam." He winked. "See you too early in the morning, Dara."

"You got that right." She climbed the steps and entered the trailer—her home away from home during the three months it would take to shoot the film. As she started to change out of her costume and into her street clothes, the exhaustion set in, followed closely by the depression. They'd been filming for a week, and it wasn't going well. She wished she could see the dailies. She hoped they were better than the takes felt.

But that was never going to happen. Traditionally, actors never got to see what had been captured on film that day, because directors worried that seeing them would affect the actor's work. Dara grabbed her jacket and purse on the way out the door. A good soak in the Jacuzzi would do her a world of good. The call sheet for tomorrow's shoot should arrive by e-mail in another couple of hours, but she imagined that it would be much like today's—a 5:15 a.m. date with the makeup chair.

❧❧

"Rebecca Minton, please."

"Speaking." Rebecca shifted the phone so that she could continue organizing the papers on her desk and transferring them to her briefcase.

"My name is Randolph Curtain. I'm a movie producer."

Rebecca stopped what she was doing. "How can I help you?"

"I'm producing a new movie. It's based on a Constance Darrow novel, *On the Wings of Angels*."

The room spun, and Rebecca reached out for her chair, barely sliding into it before her legs gave out. Dara's movie.

"Are you there, Ms. Minton?"

"I'm here."

"Anyway, it's come to my attention that you are the top Darrow scholar, and we're in need of some help."

"What kind of help, exactly?"

"How do you feel about coming to Hollywood to meet with me and Director George Nelson?"

"I don't—"

"It's Friday. If you can get on a very early flight tomorrow morning, you'd be here in time for lunch. Of course, we'd make all the arrangements. We can have a car pick you up at your home and drive you to Logan. There's a 7:20 a.m. American Airlines flight that gets you into LAX at around 11:00 a.m. We'll have another driver pick you up and bring you to our offices. We'll put you up for the night at the Beverly Hills Hotel and get you back on a flight on Sunday so you'll be right on time for your Monday morning class. What do you say?"

Rebecca's head was spinning.

"Ms. Minton? Are you still with me?"

"Yes. I'm just trying to wrap my brain around this. What is it you think I can do for you?"

"We'd really rather discuss it in person, Ms. Minton. So, can I schedule a driver to come get you? We realize this is very short notice, but, heh, it's Hollywood, after all, and this is how we roll."

Did he really just say that? "I guess there's no harm in meeting with you." *It's not like I had anything planned for the weekend.*

"Excellent! I'll have my assistant call you in just a few minutes with all the arrangements. Look forward to meeting you in person. See you tomorrow."

The line went dead, and Rebecca sat for long seconds still holding the phone to her ear. What had she just agreed to?

∽∾

Even though she'd had only three hours sleep, Rebecca was too nervous to nap on the plane, and by the time she arrived in Los Angeles, she was running on pure adrenaline.

Before exiting security, she stopped in the bathroom to check her lipstick and hair. Eyeing herself critically in the full-length mirror, she wished she'd worn the purple blouse instead of the red. *Red is a power color. It tells them you won't be trifled with.* Rebecca snorted. She didn't even know why she was here, how could she assume that she needed to look tough?

When she arrived in baggage claim, she saw the official-looking driver holding up a sign with her name on it. Since she didn't have anything but an overnight bag, he relieved her of that and escorted her to the car—a nice, shiny black limousine. *Good to know the movie has a big budget.* Or maybe this was simply that legendary Hollywood excess she'd read so much about.

In the car, she allowed herself to daydream that she and Dara were riding together, heading out on the town, or to a gala.

"We're here, Miss."

"Oh." They drove through the security gate on the Warner Brothers lot and past a series of large warehouse-like buildings that Rebecca assumed were sound stages. A few turns later, they were outside a building that resembled a bungalow. The driver put the car in park and came around to open the door for her.

"Thank you."

"You're welcome, Miss. Enjoy your stay."

When the driver stepped away, a second man stood waiting for her.

"Ms. Minton, I'm Randolph Curtain. We spoke on the phone. Welcome to 722 Films."

He was a little man, far smaller than Rebecca had envisioned. She shook his hand. "Please, call me Rebecca."

"Right this way." He led her into the bungalow, which was surprisingly roomy on the inside. "We're in the conference room."

The room was jam-packed with technology. There was a large-screen television on one wall and speakers mounted in every corner. On a long oval table sat six iPads, two laptops, five conference speakers, and a telephone console.

Sitting at the table were three people, two men and one woman. They were in the middle of a spirited discussion when Randolph and Rebecca walked in.

"Everybody, this is Professor Rebecca Minton, the foremost scholar on the author Constance Darrow and her work."

Rebecca blushed. "I don't know—"

"We've seen some of your lectures, Professor. Very impressive." The woman nodded in Rebecca's direction.

Something that had been niggling at Rebecca's brain shoved its way to the forefront. "Can I ask how you all know about my lectures and my scholarship on Ms. Darrow's work? I mean, I'm not exactly a household name."

"It's fair to say we had an inside track," Randolph said from his position standing next to her.

"What does that mean?"

"The student who has been taping your lectures is my son."

The young man who was doing the college Excellence in Education project. *So that's why I'm here?* Rebecca frowned as the picture started to take shape. "Jeffrey is your son?"

"He is," Randolph said proudly. "When I spoke to him last week, he went on and on about your course. It was all he talked about. When I told him about the movie, he could hardly contain himself."

"I'm here because your son likes my course?" Rebecca felt the edges of anger creep in. If this guy thought she would give his son a better grade because he was some hotshot Hollywood producer, he was badly mistaken.

"No, Ms. Minton," the balding man at the other end of the room said. "You're here because we're in a heap of trouble and we need your expertise."

"And you are?"

The man laughed. "I'm George Nelson, the director of this mess." He stood up and came around the table to shake her hand. "I'm glad you're here."

"I'm not sure what you're looking for and what it is you think I can do."

"Here's the situation," the other man said. "By the way, I'm Eric Jordan, the other executive producer on this project."

Rebecca turned to the woman.

"Oh, I'm Audrey Eaton, the first assistant director."

"Nice to meet you all," Rebecca said.

"Come in all the way and sit down." Randolph motioned her to a nearby chair.

"As I started to say," Eric said, "we've been shooting for a little more than a week now. The dailies look horrible."

"The dailies?" Rebecca asked.

"Every night the director, the editor, and someone from the studio, meaning us producers, review the footage shot that day," Randolph said.

"And what we've seen up until this point is very concerning," Eric added. "We're spending a lot of money on this movie, and we need it to be box office gold."

"At the moment, it's more like box office blah," George said.

"Again, I'm not sure what it is you think I can do for you."

"We need help with the script. A lot of help with the script," George admitted. "Normally, in a situation like this, we'd approach the author of the original work and ask for their assistance."

Rebecca's heart tripped as the nature of the dilemma hit home. "You can't do that, because you can't reach Constance Darrow."

"Bingo," Eric said.

"Surely you must have some way to find her," Rebecca probed. She needed more information. She needed to know what they knew about Constance.

"Even if we could, it wouldn't do us any good."

Rebecca turned her attention to Audrey, who'd made the comment. "Why not?"

"Because we need someone on the set who can help us make adjustments on the fly."

"When they sold us the rights to the work, Ms. Darrow's representatives made it a stipulation of the contract that she would not be required to meet with anyone connected to the film," Eric said.

"It was weird." Randolph shook his head. "Most authors want to be consulted. They want to be part of the process. This is their baby and they want to make sure we stay true to the material. Her? She didn't want to have any part of it."

That's because she would've given herself away, and her privacy was too important to her to risk that. Oh, Dara. This must be killing you. "Okay. So I am, what? A stand-in?"

"To be honest, you're the next best thing and maybe our only hope to get this piece of junk back on track," George said.

"How do you know I'm right for this?"

"Let's find out, shall we?"

Audrey got up and shut the blinds and turned off the lights as George punched keys on one of the laptops.

"This is the footage from yesterday. It's a scene between Celeste and Harold. See for yourself and tell us what you think."

The first time Rebecca saw Dara on screen as Celeste, her pulse throbbed with excitement. She *was* Celeste. But as she watched take after take, Rebecca felt increasingly sick inside. This wasn't Constance's Celeste. When it was over, Audrey turned the lights back on.

The room was quiet until Rebecca broke the silence. She couldn't contain herself anymore. "Let me start by saying, I don't want to insult anyone."

"But?" Randolph asked.

"But that woman on the screen isn't Celeste. It isn't Dar—the actress's fault," she hastened to add. "It appears to be the way the scene is written. Is there any chance I can see the script?"

Audrey slid a copy of the script down the table to Rebecca. "Start on page seven."

Rebecca flipped to page seven and read what the screenwriter had written. *Oh, my God, Dara. I'm so sorry. You have to be going crazy inside.* "Can I be frank here?"

"Please, God, yes," Randolph said.

"I'm not sure who wrote the screenplay, but this isn't even close to what Ms. Darrow intended. If you want to make a movie about some woman who isn't Celeste, this might be the ticket, but if you bought the material with the idea of bringing Constance Darrow's work to life, then you've got yourself a big problem."

Rebecca pointed at a section of the script and held it up for everyone to see. "This? This interaction right here is all wrong. The thing that motivates Celeste in this interchange is her recognition of Harold as a kindred soul. The way this is written, we don't see any of that. This is absolutely critical because it sets up the nature of the bond between the two main characters. It's the underpinning of the entire story and it's just not here." She slapped the script back down on the table.

In the ensuing silence, Rebecca wondered if she'd gone too far. She glanced around at the faces, trying to read their reaction.

"Professor?" George was the first to speak. "What are you doing for the next ninety days?"

Rebecca raised an eyebrow. "Ninety days?"

"That's how long we're scheduled to shoot and I don't see how we can go forward without substantial revisions to the script."

"I—I'm not a screenwriter. I've never written anything that wasn't academic in nature." Rebecca felt the panic rise up in her throat.

"We're not asking you to write it," Eric said.

"What we need is for you to do what you're doing right now. Read it, and doctor it. Edit it so that it matches the author's original intent," Randolph said.

"You understand these characters and the nuances of this story. You've studied it extensively."

And I've had the advantage of conversing with the author. But Rebecca had no intention of mentioning that out loud. "I have, but, as I said, I have no experience with movies or writing screenplays, or even doctoring them."

"Professor, we really, really need you," George pleaded. "Without you and your insights, there's no point even shooting another minute of tape. It's a waste of the studio's money."

"We might as well fold up shop and cut our losses," Eric agreed.

Rebecca was torn. Even if she ignored the fact that the semester had barely gotten underway and she couldn't just walk away from her teaching responsibilities, there was the matter of a learning curve. She was certain there was one, and they already were in the middle of production. There would be no time for her to figure out what a script doctor did and to learn enough about the business to feel competent at what they were asking her to do.

Something else occurred to her. "You'd want me to be on the set every day?"

"Most days, at the very least. We'd need you there to re-imagine scenes if necessary, and to advise me as we shoot," George said.

If she agreed, Rebecca no doubt would be face-to-face with Dara. The thought simultaneously thrilled and terrified her. What would Dara think about that? How would she feel? There's no way Rebecca could even entertain saying yes until she knew the answers to those questions.

"Can I have a little time to think about it? This is all very sudden. I would have to take a leave of absence from my teaching position, which would require a conversation with my bosses. Then there's the matter of relocation."

"We'd rent you a condo for the time you're out here. And get you a car so that you could get around," Randolph said.

"And the consulting fee would be substantial," Eric threw in.

Money's not the issue here. I need to know that this is the right thing to do for Dara. That thought triggered another question. "Would the actors be made aware that someone was coming in to rework the script?"

"They'd be made aware, sure," George said. "But they'd have no say. You'd be working primarily with me, with Audrey, and our editor." His tone left no room for discussion. It appeared that on set, the director was king.

"As I said, I'd really need a little time to think this through and make sure this is the best thing for me."

"Your flight tomorrow is at 7:00 a.m. We can give you until then. Shooting resumes Monday morning," Randolph said.

"That's not a lot of time. Less than twenty-four hours."

"Time is money, Professor. Time is money."

"Okay. You'll have your answer before I board the plane."

"Good enough," Randolph said. "My assistant will give you all the contact information you need and I'll have terms messengered to your hotel for your consideration."

As the meeting broke up and Rebecca started to leave, George approached her.

"You know, I was against bringing you here. But I don't hold the purse strings, so I didn't have much choice."

Terrific. A hostile work environment and I haven't even said 'yes' yet.

"But after watching your lectures and listening to you today, I realize I was wrong. I believe in this film. I signed on to direct it because I was impressed with the depth of the emotions and the intricacies of the plot. This is a story that really, really needs to be told. That isn't going to happen without your help. I don't want to be overly dramatic here, but the fate of this movie rests on your shoulders right now."

"No pressure here." Rebecca kept her tone light, even as a knot the size of a softball formed in the pit of her stomach. She had so much to think about and roughly seventeen hours to figure it all out.

As she was being driven to her hotel, Rebecca mapped out a strategy. There were two phone calls she needed to make. One was to the head of department at Middlebury. But even before that, she needed to reach out to the one person who might be able to guide her in this situation. She needed to call Carolyn Detweiler.

146

CHAPTER FOURTEEN

The hotel lobby was crowded with tourists, no doubt hoping to catch a glimpse of a favorite star. Carolyn found Rebecca sitting in a high-backed chair, her Kindle in hand. She was completely absorbed in whatever she was reading.

"Hi." When Rebecca looked up, Carolyn noted the bags under her eyes that the makeup couldn't quite cover. Her expression was a cross between deer-in-the-headlights scared and kid-caught-with-a-hand-in-the-cookie-jar guilty.

Rebecca scrambled to her feet and tossed the Kindle into a briefcase. "Hi. You look great."

"I bet you say that to all the girls." Carolyn noted the resulting blush creeping up Rebecca's neck and silently congratulated herself on obtaining confirmation of Rebecca's sexuality. Rebecca never actually outed herself to Dara in their letters and Carolyn wanted to be sure, especially since Dara continued to mope around in a way that told Carolyn that she was missing Rebecca. *Even if she still refuses to admit it.*

"Thanks so much for coming on such short notice. I didn't know you had an office out here, but that's certainly fortuitous. I thought we'd just be talking on the phone."

"I always prefer face-to-face whenever possible." That was certainly true in this case. Carolyn wanted another opportunity to get to know Rebecca a little better. She gestured for Rebecca to walk with her.

Rebecca seemed so nervous that Carolyn practically could feel her vibrating next to her. The only thing she said on the phone was that she needed to talk about a time-sensitive matter of great

147

urgency. "It's too loud in here, don't you think? Have you eaten lunch?"

As if on cue, Rebecca's stomach rumbled loud enough that, even in the hubbub, Carolyn heard it. She laughed. "I'll take that for a no."

"I haven't had time."

"I know a great place around the corner."

After they'd ordered, Carolyn said, "Okay. I'm listening. What's so important?" It wasn't really the first question Carolyn wanted to ask. She wanted to know how Rebecca was doing and if she was missing Dara as much as Dara was missing her. She knew she couldn't ask it, but once she sat down across from her and had a chance to study Rebecca's face more closely and in better lighting, the stress and sadness were written in the lines around her mouth and in the depths of her eyes.

Rebecca began shredding a napkin. Her hands were trembling and Carolyn felt sorry for her. So sorry that she reached across the table and stilled her hands. "Whatever it is, Rebecca, it's going to be okay."

"I hope so." Rebecca looked up with tears in her eyes. "I don't know what to do. I feel like I'm damned if I do, damned if I don't."

Carolyn withdrew her hand. "Why don't you start at the beginning?"

By the time Rebecca finished her tale, they'd finished eating and were drinking coffee.

"Say something, please?" Rebecca pleaded.

"Wow."

"Tell me you've got something more than that?"

Carolyn's mind tumbled over the possibilities and implications. She tried to organize her thoughts.

"I didn't ask for this," Rebecca said.

Carolyn realized that Rebecca mistook her silence for disapproval. "I know that. There's a lot to sift through here." She took a deep breath. "Okay, for starters. I'm going to put on my business manager hat for you. I can't help you officially, not without talking to Dara first. And I don't think any of us is ready for that. But I do want to make sure this is even feasible for you and professionally in your best interest. I won't let anyone take advantage of you. Did you receive a contract offer yet?"

Rebecca reached down next to her chair and fished around in her briefcase. "Right here."

Carolyn removed the document from the envelope and read through it. The offer was both generous and fair.

"Well?"

"It's a good deal. There's nothing in here that would raise a red flag for me. If you were my client, from a business standpoint, I'd tell you to sign it."

"Good to know. Thank you. And the rest?"

Carolyn pursed her lips. This was so thorny and delicate. Dara would be completely rattled to know that she was going to have to face Rebecca again, never mind see her at work on a regular basis. Then again, Dara was dour without Rebecca's letters and putting the two of them together in one place might be just the thing to give them a romantic shove toward each other. Beyond that, there were the business aspects of the situation to consider...

"Earth to Carolyn?"

Carolyn realized with a jolt that she hadn't answered Rebecca's question. "I think it's complicated."

"Tell me about it."

Really, there's only one thing to do. "You said you fly out first thing in the morning and they want a decision by then?"

"That's right."

"What are you doing for dinner tonight?"

"Didn't we just finish eating lunch? Is that all you Hollywood types do, eat?"

Carolyn recognized Rebecca's teasing tone and matched it. "Nope. Occasionally, we drink too."

"Of course you do."

"Well?"

"It's not like I know anyone in this town. I don't have any plans other than to collapse into a soporific stupor."

"Nice alliteration."

"It's a habit. My friend, Natalie and I..." Rebecca started to explain. "Never mind, it's not important."

It was the first time Rebecca had mentioned another woman, and Carolyn thought it was *very* important. Before she could stop herself, she asked, "Is Natalie your..."

"Girlfriend?" Rebecca's tone was incredulous. "Oh, my God, no. We'd kill each other. She's just my best friend. A colleague and running buddy." Rebecca narrowed her eyes. "What makes you think I'm gay?"

Busted. "I—I didn't. Really. I—Isn't it..." Carolyn threw her hands up. "I'm sorry. That was an inappropriate question."

"For the record, I am gay. And no, I'm not in a relationship. The last one nearly destroyed me."

"I'm sorry." Carolyn meant it. "You're not giving up on commitment, are you?" *Please say no. Please say no.*

"No." Rebecca sat back. "How did we get on this topic?"

Carolyn sat back too. It was time to get this conversation back on less personal ground before Rebecca got around to asking why Carolyn wanted to know about her sexuality. Dara had never come out, and, apart from some mild speculation no doubt caused by her non-existent love life, very few people knew she was a lesbian.

"I want you and Dara to sit down together and talk about this," Carolyn blurted out. She watched as Rebecca's visage morphed from shock, to fear, to horror. "Before you say no, hear me out."

"No."

"What did I just say?"

"No. No. No."

"Rebecca, listen to me. I know Dara better than anyone in the world."

"You saw her reaction to me the first time."

"And what do you think her reaction would be if you showed up on the set as a script consultant without any forewarning?"

That notion seemed to make Rebecca stop and think. Her shoulders slumped. "She hates me."

Carolyn scoffed. *Quite the opposite. She just doesn't know it, yet.* "She doesn't hate you. She's afraid of what you represent."

"Her loss of privacy. Her ability to have something that is disconnected from the movie star persona. And that's what it is, isn't it? A persona. She's so much more than what's visible on the surface."

Carolyn's eyes gleamed. Yes, Rebecca definitely was as smitten as Dara. Now if she could just get both of them to see it.

Rebecca leaned forward again. "In Constance's letters to me, I could see a genuine, gentle, thoughtful, vulnerable woman. The prose in her books represent Dara yearning to be seen as the complete human being she really is, not someone else's sophomoric fantasy, but an intelligent, caring, deep, passionate, complicated woman." Rebecca clicked her jaw shut. "Sorry. I got carried away."

"Don't be." Carolyn's voice was husky. Sitting in front of her was the first person ever to truly understand her best friend. She wanted to laugh and cry at the same time. Instead she reached across the table again and took Rebecca's hand. "Come to dinner at my place tonight. Please. I promise to run interference and to make this okay."

"I don't have a way to get there."

"I'll have you picked up and dropped off."

"I have nothing to wear."

Carolyn could see that Rebecca's resistance was weakening. "I'll take you shopping right now."

Rebecca still looked uncomfortable and dubious.

"Please? This may be the one chance you have to set things right with Dara." She knew that was a low blow, but these were desperate times.

Rebecca chewed her lip. "Are you sure it's a good idea?"

"Positive." Carolyn released Rebecca's hand, threw some money down on the table, and stood. "Let's get you something smashing to wear."

❧

Dara glared at Carolyn's reflection in the mirror as she put on her makeup. "It's my night to rest and recoup. You know I hate to go anywhere on the weekends when I'm shooting. I'm wiped out."

"I know. I wouldn't insist if this weren't vitally important. And you can rest tomorrow. I promise I'll leave you in absolute peace and quiet. Not even a phone call or a text."

"Who are we meeting, again?"

"It's a potential colleague. Someone who could be a great ally."

"To you or to me?"

"Both of us."

Dara turned to face her best friend. "Why are you being so cagey about this? I can tell when you've got something else going on, and you, girlfriend, definitely have another agenda." Dara looked back in the mirror to apply her lipstick. Suddenly, a horrifying thought occurred to her. "You're not setting me up on a date, are you?"

Carolyn's eyes opened wide. "A date? No. I told you, this is about business."

"Well, there's something fishy going on here. You won't even tell me where we're going and you're acting weird."

"You mean weirder than usual?" Carolyn checked her watch.

By Dara's count, that was the fifth time she'd done so in the last ten minutes. Something was definitely going on.

"Okay. I'm ready. Let's go."

Carolyn practically ran out the door in front of Dara.

The whole set up gave Dara a sinking feeling. That sinking feeling turned to ice cold dread when Dara realized that they were in Carolyn's neighborhood. "You're taking me to dinner at your condo? And you had me dress up?"

"Business casual doesn't count as dressed up." Carolyn parked the car. "Now, when we get in there, I want you to be open-minded. Don't freak out on me."

Dara grabbed Carolyn by the arm before they reached the front door. "I'm going to ask you one more time before I turn around and take your car back to my house. Who are we meeting?"

"Rebecca," Carolyn mumbled.

Dara's pulse quickened and her eyes opened wide. "What? I could've sworn I heard you say, 'Rebecca.'"

"That's because I did."

Dara brought them to a complete stop inches away from the front door. "I'm not going in there."

"Dara, please."

"How could you?" Dara's voice vibrated with anger and indignation. "You have no right—"

"This really is about business. I swear. Rebecca is in town on business and it affects you. I felt it was in your best interest—my client Dara Thomas's best interest—to take this meeting."

Dara tried to swallow, but suddenly she was having difficulty. "How did she know who you were?"

"It's not like that's rocket science. She Googled your rep, found my info and called me."

"Rebecca called you and asked for this meeting?" She crossed her arms over her chest.

"No. She called me and asked for my advice. When I heard what proposal she was being offered, I asked her if she would meet with you. She doesn't want to be here anymore than you want her to be. She's in a tough spot, Dar. Together we can work this out. Please don't let your fear get in the way."

"Fear? What do I have to be afraid of? I'm not afraid." Dara's heart raced and she fought the urge to bolt. "I don't know what this is, but I don't want any part of it." Somewhere in the recesses of her mind, Dara registered that she was making a scene on Carolyn's doorstep, but she didn't care.

"I just need you to listen."

"I have no intention of talking to that woman, ever again. Am I clear?"

"You're perfectly clear," a quiet, quavering voice said from the open doorway of the condo. "I'll just be going now. You have a lovely place, Carolyn."

Both Dara and Carolyn stared open-mouthed as Rebecca ran past them down the driveway and out into the empty street.

Shit. Dara ran after her. "Wait. Rebecca, wait." She was surprised that she wasn't gaining any ground. It was obvious Rebecca was in shape. "Please." Dara picked up the pace, her longer strides eating up the pavement. Finally, she caught up to Rebecca on the next block.

Tears streamed down Rebecca's face, and Dara's heart broke a little.

"Please. Don't cry. Please don't cry. I'm sorry." Without thinking, Dara pulled Rebecca to her and held her, rocking her from side to side. "I'm sorry." Rebecca shook in her arms, and all Dara wanted was to make it better.

"I never should have let them fly me out here. Never. I knew better. I knew it was a mistake. I never intended to bother you, ever again. I wanted you to have your privacy. I wanted you to feel secure and to know that Constance's secret would always, always be safe." Rebecca took in a shuddering breath. "I'm the one who's sorry."

"Shh. It's okay." Dara tried to make sense of what Rebecca was saying, but it made no sense at all to her. As Rebecca's sobs subsided, Dara used two fingers to lift her chin. Under the streetlight, she could see, beyond the pools of tears, that Rebecca's eyes held much pain and grief.

Rebecca sniffed and tried to catch her breath. "I'm so, so sorry. You'll never see me again, I assure you."

She started to pull away, out of Dara's arms, and Dara was shocked to realize that she didn't want to let go. "Hang on a second." She loosened her grip just enough to give Rebecca a little space. "What do you mean, you should never have let them fly you out here? Who flew you out?"

Instead of answering, Rebecca sobbed again and shook her head. "It doesn't matter now. I'll be on a plane first thing in the morning and we can pretend this never happened. Really, it's like a dream anyway. More like a nightmare, really."

"Rebecca?"

"Hmm?"

"Please tell me, who flew you out here?"

"The studio."

Dara's eyes opened wide. "The studio, as in who, specifically?"

Rebecca cleared her throat. "Randolph Curtain." Her voice was hoarse from crying.

Goose bumps popped up on Dara's arms. "Randolph Curtain, the producer of my movie, flew you out here?"

Rebecca nodded.

"Why?"

Rebecca's laugh was hollow. "He couldn't get Constance Darrow. So he, his partner, and the director decided I was the next best thing."

Dara tried to put the pieces together, but they just wouldn't fit. "What am I missing?"

Rebecca's body finally relaxed, but Dara still didn't relinquish her hold.

"The really short version is that they determined that the script sucked. They wanted the material to be closer to the original intent of the author. Since the author is a recluse"—Rebecca chuckled mirthlessly—"they wanted to hire what they called 'the top Constance Darrow scholar' to help doctor the script."

The light finally dawned for Dara. "Oh, my God. They wanted to bring you in to re-interpret the scenes as Constance would've done it."

"Yes. Only I told them I needed time to consider the offer. Without telling them why, of course." Rebecca wiped an errant tear away. "I didn't know how you would feel about it. I wasn't going to take it if you objected. Now I know you object. So I'll give them their answer tonight and be on my way."

This time Rebecca did pull away, much to Dara's dismay. "As I said. This was a bad idea. I didn't know what they wanted from me until I met with them this afternoon. If I'd known, I probably never would've made the trip and I could've spared all of us this drama. I'm very sorry." Again, Rebecca turned to go.

"Wait!" Dara moved in front of her and put her hands on Rebecca's shoulders. "Where are you going?"

"Back to my hotel, I guess."

"How are you planning to get there? Walk? It's not safe."

"I have a cell phone. I'll call a cab."

"Please don't. I want you to stay." With a start, Dara realized she really meant it. "Let's go inside and have a nice dinner, and we can talk about all this, okay? We'll sort it out."

"It's not what you want, Dara. That's abundantly clear. What's the point? You don't need to be polite or nice to me. I'm an interloper, an intruder in your life. And I never wanted to be that." Rebecca hung her head.

Dara couldn't stand to see her so sad. She looped her arm through Rebecca's. "Please. Let's start over and try this again, okay? I was out of my mind and I was an ass. For the record, I'm not usually an ass. I just seem to be one around you."

"I tend to bring that out in people. It's a gift."

Dara laughed delightedly. She'd seen glints of humor in Rebecca's letters, but being a party to it in person was so much better.

Carolyn was inside sitting at the breakfast bar when they got back to the condo. She jumped to her feet, a look of pure surprise on her face.

Dara reluctantly disentangled her arm from Rebecca's and moved an appropriate distance away. "Car, please tell Rebecca I'm not always a class 'A' jerk."

"Nuh-uh. You're going to have to prove that one to her all on your own." Carolyn cocked her head. "Everything okay, you two?"

"I've used my considerable charm to convince Rebecca to stay for dinner and talk through what's going on." Dara glanced sideways at Rebecca. "I have convinced you, right?"

"I guess that depends."

"On?"

"What's for dinner?"

Dara and Carolyn both laughed. "A woman after my own heart. Car? What's for dinner?"

"Lasagna, salad, and garlic bread."

Dara and Rebecca looked at each other. Dara said, "What do you say?"

"I guess I could stomach that." She winked, and immediately Dara felt lighter.

"Excellent. What can we do to help?"

"Offer your own services," Rebecca said. "I'm sure I look like I've been hit by a freight train. If one of you would point me toward the ladies' room, I'll try to see if I can create a miracle to repair the damage."

Dara wanted to tell Rebecca that she looked just fine. Even with a tear-streaked face. In fact, she looked stunning. Instead, she said, "Second door on the left down that hallway."

When she was gone, Dara turned toward Carolyn, who was standing next to the oven. "You don't have to say it. I'm a total jackass. I know."

"What makes you think that's what I was going to say?"

"Oh, you weren't?"

"No. I definitely was. Hear her out, please. I know you don't want to, but—"

"Actually, I do." Dara said, surprising herself.

CHAPTER FIFTEEN

W hat made you want to become a professor?" Carolyn asked, as she pulled the garlic bread out of the oven. She felt horrible for Rebecca, and it was all her fault. She should've handled the whole situation a lot differently. If she'd told Dara what the plan was for the evening back at Dara's place, Rebecca never would've been subjected to the ugliness outside the condo.

Now they had to find a way to get past the awkwardness. Carolyn sent up a silent prayer that Rebecca wouldn't retreat into her shell—that she would show Dara some of her personality. As for Dara, Carolyn couldn't remember a time when she'd ever seen her friend act like such a complete jerk. She hoped that Dara wouldn't put up a wall to shut Rebecca out. Maybe Dara would see that with Rebecca, it was safe to be herself.

"Growing up, I had a hard time. I was the odd kid, the one who never quite fit in. I was heavyset and shy, my self-esteem was non-existent, and I got bullied. A lot. So I disappeared into books, where I could be whoever and whatever I wanted to be. I could inhabit someone else's world and forget the bullies and the popular kids who never gave me the time of day unless they wanted me to do their homework for them."

Carolyn chanced a glance at Dara, who was sitting at the breakfast bar, watching Rebecca intently. She hoped Dara was recognizing some of the parallels in her own life.

"By the time I reached college, I was better read than some of my professors. So, I would sit in the lectures and think about how much better I would teach the subject, whatever it was, than the professor who was giving the lecture. I was constantly analyzing

159

the literature and finding nuances I was certain the professors had missed in their reading." Rebecca smirked. "I was insufferable. I often wonder if the kids in my classes are doing the same thing." She shrugged. "Probably. Anyway, I started to gain a lot more confidence in myself. I got in shape and lost the weight. I made friends with other kids who were like me. And I found my purpose in life, which was to educate young minds and encourage them to think for themselves and to dream."

"Dinner is served, ladies. If you'll retreat to the main dining room," Carolyn said.

Dara picked up the basket of bread and Rebecca grabbed the salad bowl. Carolyn watched from behind as the two women walked side by side. Maybe this would be okay, after all.

When they were seated, Rebecca addressed Dara. "I imagine you had the exact opposite problem."

"What do you mean?" Dara visibly stiffened.

"Um," Rebecca blushed, "where people only saw me for my brain and completely dismissed my looks, I suspect most people didn't recognize your obvious intelligence and depth of character. They probably never got past the surface. Which would've been their great loss. You're one of the most insightful, sensitive, caring, passionate people I know. That's why you created Constance, isn't it? A place where you could allow yourself to be all that you are and be accepted for it?"

Carolyn held her breath, waiting to see how Dara would react. To her great relief, Dara's smile lit up the room. A real smile—not one for the cameras.

Dara pointed her fork at Rebecca. "You're too sharp for your own good, you know that? If you ever decide to give up your teaching job, you could make a lot of money as a counselor."

Rebecca's laugh was rich. "Oh, Heavens no. I'd end up being more of a head case than my clients." She fixed Dara with a serious look. "Before anything else happens here, there's something I want to say." She cleared her throat. "I want... No, I *need* you to know—" Her voice broke and she took a second to compose herself.

Rebecca directed a questioning glance in Carolyn's direction and Carolyn started to panic. If Rebecca revealed that they had met in New York... Ever so minutely, Carolyn shook her head.

In response, Rebecca returned her attention to Dara. "I would never, ever violate your privacy or share what I know about you and Constance. Never. That goes against everything I believe in." Her voice shook with emotion and her eyes welled with tears. "I can't even begin to imagine what it costs for you to be...well, you. Constance is your haven. I would never, ever... That's a lot of 'never, evers,' isn't it?" Rebecca joked to lessen the tension. "What the hell, what's one more? I would never, ever take that away from you. Whatever else you think of me, I hope you believe that."

Carolyn watched as, to her great surprise, Dara's eyes filled with tears, as well.

"I..." Dara choked up and shook her head. She rose and walked around the table to where Rebecca was sitting and lifted her up into a hug. "I believe you. Thank you for understanding and sharing that. I'm pretty sure I've never known anyone like you." She kissed Rebecca's cheek, and held her for another moment longer.

Carolyn wanted to cry, herself. Instead, she rested her chin on the backs of her hands and heaved a happy sigh. "Well, now that we've got that cleared up, it's a perfect time to segue into the issue at hand."

Dara released Rebecca and returned to her seat. Maybe Carolyn was imagining things, but she could've sworn she saw reluctance when her friend relinquished the body contact.

"The way I see it, we've got several factors that we should weigh." Carolyn pointed at Dara. "You're miserable with the way the shooting is going and you're beside yourself that you risk too much if you point out all of the problems with the script."

"Too true on all counts there. Cal Whiting isn't a bad guy. He's written some really nice original screenplays. But this is his first adaptation. And, frankly, it sucks."

"I only read a few pages of the script," Rebecca chimed in, "but already I can see that he has no understanding of the nuance of the story. He doesn't 'get' Celeste at all. What he's written is some female character with angst and a chip on her shoulder. That's not Celeste. I saw the dailies from yesterday. All I could think was how much it must be killing you inside to play her that way."

For a second, Carolyn thought Dara would come around the table and kiss Rebecca again. Joy bubbled up inside her.

"You have no idea," Dara said. "I thought I would lose my mind."

"Which brings me to the next point," Carolyn interjected. "If we allow the movie to go forward as is…"

"I'll regret selling the rights to it for the rest of my life."

"There is that. Worse, if it bombs at the box office and with the critics after you campaigned publicly to get the part, it could also be a career-wrecker."

"They already told me they'll pull the plug if it doesn't get any better," Rebecca pointed out. "The way they were discussing it today, if I don't come on board, they're going to scuttle the film."

Dara groaned. "What a cluster."

"I'm sorry, Dar. Moral of the story, next time I negotiate one of these things for Constance, I write in a clause that the author gets final say over the screenwriter and the script."

"Good luck with that," Dara said.

"Listen," Rebecca said. "None of us wants this project to fail. I want the movie to be everything Constance wants it to be." She chuckled. "Why am I talking about Constance like she's not you? Yikes. And you're a phenomenal actress, which sounds like kissing up, but I promise you it's not. Celeste is an amazing vehicle for your talents…if she's properly realized."

Carolyn smiled behind her hand. Rebecca truly was adorable, and she could see that Dara was thoroughly charmed.

"Anyway, here's the bottom line. Let me say upfront that I know nothing about script doctoring. Zilch. Zero." She looked at Carolyn. "That book you saw me madly reading on my Kindle in the hotel lobby was a 'how-to' book on the subject. That was right after the interview I watched of a panel of screenwriters talking about the script revision process during the actual shooting of a film."

Carolyn laughed. "Good research skills, Professor."

"Thanks. So, as I was saying, I know nothing about script-doctoring. Still, the powers that be seem to think I'm the answer here. Since it appears my coming on board is the only way they'll move forward, and since we all want the movie to be everything it should be, I could agree to take the assignment. Then, I can go over the script with you"—Rebecca pointed at Dara—"every night so that I'll know what you want the scene to be for the next day. They'll think I'm a genius, Constance will get to re-imagine the script the way it should've been written, Dara gets to play Celeste the way only she can, and no one except for the three of us will ever be any the wiser."

Carolyn raised an eyebrow. Really, it was a masterful solution. In more ways than either Rebecca or Dara likely imagined. Carolyn pictured the two of them, working side by side every night after a day on the set, and her heart skipped happily. Yes, this might be just the thing, for both of them. "What do you think, Dar?

Dara drummed her fingers on the table. After a pregnant pause, she broke out in a grin that nearly split her face in half. "It's perfect."

"There's only one problem," Rebecca said.

"What's that?" Carolyn asked.

"I'm in the middle of the semester. I'd need to take an immediate leave of absence, which would really leave the department in a bind. It's not fair to the students. Besides, I don't even know if the college would release me to do this."

"Are you kidding me? Think of the PR for the school," Carolyn said. "This would be great for their reputation. What other school has an American literature scholar consulting on the screen adaptation of a Pulitzer Prize-winning novel?"

"I agree with you. I'm just not sure they'll see it that way." Rebecca frowned.

After a moment's silence, Dara chimed in. "In this day and age of technology, how is it possible that we can't solve this?" She leaned forward animatedly. "What if you continued to teach the course, except you did it via satellite or Skype? You could give the lectures and interact with the students and they could send you their assignments electronically."

Rebecca's eyes lit up. "It would give the school creds for being progressive and innovative. But then there's the cost factor."

"Forget about that. The studio can foot the bill. Car, can you take a look at whatever deal they're offering Rebecca and write all this in as a stipulation?"

Carolyn nodded. "It would be my distinct pleasure."

"Wait," Rebecca said. "I don't even know your rates. I'm sure I can't afford you."

"I'll pick up the tab," Dara said.

"No need." Carolyn wanted to jump up and pump her fist in the air. "This one's on the house."

"I can't let you do that."

"It's settled. Don't argue with me, either one of you. Dara, you're in charge of clearing the table and doing the dishes. Rebecca and I have work to do."

"I'd better call my head of department, first. If he says no, this is all a moot point."

Dara walked over and kissed Rebecca on the top of the head as she cleared her plate. "That's for the ingenious idea."

Carolyn momentarily turned her head to hide her surprise. Who was this woman, and what had she done with the usually reserved, circumspect Dara Thomas?

Dara paused with Rebecca's dish in her hand. "If your department head were to say no to you, which I can't imagine… Is he straight?"

Rebecca's eyebrows arched into her hairline. "Yes."

"Good. Even if he says no to you, he won't say no to Dara Thomas, movie star." She struck an exaggerated pose and they all burst out laughing.

"Oh, my God. Are we really going to do this?" Rebecca asked.

"Yes. We really are. Get him on the phone."

"Better yet," Carolyn suggested, "The two of you should Skype him from my home office."

"I like the way you think," Dara said. She kissed Carolyn on the top of the head for good measure and whispered in her ear. "You were right. Again. She's the real deal. Thank you for sticking to your guns."

"You're welcome." Carolyn wanted to add, "And she's pretty hot too," but she could see that Dara already knew that.

"I can't believe you flirted with him," Rebecca said. "More to the point, I can't believe he responded. Alistar Nash is a serious, hard-nosed curmudgeon. I'm not sure I ever saw him break a smile before tonight."

Dara made a show of buffing her nails on her shirt. "I never met a curmudgeon I couldn't charm."

"I would've thought you, of all people, would eschew such behavior."

"Normally, you'd be right. But desperate times call for desperate measures."

"Are you ladies ready to go?" Carolyn stood in the foyer with the car keys in her hand. "Rebecca has a crack-of-dawn flight."

"Three hours sleep last night, another three or four tonight. Is this how you Hollywood-types operate on a regular basis? If so, I'm already too old for this."

"Be glad you don't have to be in a makeup chair at 5:00 a.m."

"Be glad you don't have to be sitting in front of a computer, Skype lecturing to an auditorium full of nineteen-year-olds at that hour."

Dara winced. "Yeah. That's definitely a worse deal. Is that what time your class is?"

"8:00 a.m. on the east coast, followed by a smaller seminar course on F. Scott Fitzgerald at 9:30."

"Back-to-back classes?"

"Usually followed by office hours from ten forty-five to two."

"What are you going to do about those?" Carolyn asked.

"Fit them in virtually somehow, I suppose." Rebecca felt the stress creep into the middle of her back and take up residence. It was one thing to get Alistar to agree to this arrangement in principle. It would be quite another to execute it in such a way that it was fair to Middlebury. She had no idea what her obligations would be on the set, but she felt a very deep and abiding responsibility to her students.

"Are you okay?"

Rebecca gave Dara a half-smile. "Sure. Why do you ask?"

"You just got this funny look on your face, kind of like a 'what the hell have I gotten myself into' thing."

"I can't imagine why. I'm just turning my life upside down. What could go wrong?"

Dara rested a hand on her shoulder. "It'll be all right, you'll see."

Dara's light touch sent a reassuring burst of warmth through her, and Rebecca sighed. "It's going to have to be." Rebecca's phone buzzed and she took it out to look at it. "Oh."

"Is that a good *oh* or a bad *oh*?" Carolyn asked.

"It's a 'the studio sent back a PDF of the contract with all of our stipulations accepted' *oh*...including setting up my own trailer on the set from which I can teach my classes."

Goose flesh popped up all over Rebecca's arms. This was really happening. She kept scrolling. "Oh."

"Well, that was a different *oh*," Dara said. "What does that one mean?"

"It means they don't want me to get on a plane tomorrow. They expect me to be on set first thing Monday morning. They're messengering a copy of the script to my hotel right now along with the software I'll need to install on my laptop so I can make revisions and be able to work on the script and interface with the director and assistant director electronically."

Rebecca knew her voice held an edge of panic. It was impossible. She had no clothes with her, none of her class notes, and they hadn't ironed out any of the details of how the distance-learning piece was going to work. It simply couldn't be done.

"Rebecca?"

"Hmm?"

"You're hyperventilating," Carolyn said.

"I am?"

"How about if we sit back down for a second," Dara recommended.

Rebecca allowed herself to be led to a chair. Carolyn and Dara hovered above her. "I'm sorry. It's just... I don't know how I can possibly agree to that. I don't have any of the stuff for my classes with me. I don't have any clothes. I don't have a place to live here yet. I don't..." She looked up at the two women standing in front of her. "That's a lot of *I don'ts*, isn't it?"

Dara smiled kindly at her. "It's okay. We forgive you."

"Rebecca, Dara and I can help you." A look passed between Carolyn and Dara.

"Carolyn and I *will* help you. Together we can get this done. I promise. We'll make it work. You'll see."

"How?"

"For starters, we'll answer the studio back and tell them that if that's what they expect, they're going to have to move Heaven and Earth to get your satellite office up and running tomorrow so that it can be tested and in perfect working order for your Monday class," Carolyn said.

"But I still won't have my notes for class."

"You said you have your laptop with you?" Dara asked.

"Yes."

"And is it safe to assume that your lesson plans are on a computer in your office?"

"Of course."

"Perfect. Car, put in the contract that the studio has to make any necessary modifications so that Rebecca's work computer is accessible from her laptop." Dara turned to Rebecca. "Will that work?"

"It would if they can get it done."

"If they want you on set on Monday, they'll get it done. Next, tomorrow, I'll take you shopping and we'll get you a wardrobe and anything else you need," Dara added. "That'll be at the studio's expense too, right Car?"

"Absolutely. We'll insist on it."

"When we're done shopping, I'll get my real estate agent on the job of finding you someplace to live for the next ninety days."

Rebecca simply watched Dara and Carolyn go back and forth. They made it sound so…doable. "It's too late to call Alistar back tonight," she said practically.

"You can call him first thing in the morning," Dara said. "I'll even take one for the team and flirt again, if necessary."

Rebecca laughed. "At this rate, you might have to flash him." She enjoyed that Dara's mouth formed an *O* but made no sound. She found it charming that such a suggestion, even in jest, could embarrass Dara. "And we'll never get a place that I can rent and move into tomorrow. My reservation at the hotel is only through tonight."

"That's easy." Dara waved a hand dismissively. "You can stay at my place for now."

Rebecca nearly fell off the chair. If she pinched herself surreptitiously, would either woman notice? Surely this couldn't be real. Three hours ago, Dara never wanted to see her again.

Now? Now, she was offering Rebecca a place to stay and to take her shopping for clothes and a condo? *If this were a novel, the critics would pan it for implausibility.* Belatedly, she realized she hadn't answered. "That's too generous." She made eye contact with Dara and Carolyn in turn. "All of this. You both are wonderful, but I can't ask you to—"

"Well, then, it's a good thing you didn't ask," Carolyn said. "We offered."

"Very true," Dara agreed. "We did. It would be downright unfriendly of you to turn us down, wouldn't it, Car?"

"It would."

"Let's get the pumpkin back to the hotel so she can crash, then you can drop me at home." Dara offered Rebecca a hand and pulled her up out of the chair.

It was a dream. It had to be. Rebecca followed them out the door, got in the back seat of Carolyn's car, and buckled herself in. Less than twenty-four hours ago she was sleeping in her own bed, a relatively obscure college professor with an obsession for a great American author and a broken heart. *If this is a dream, please, God, don't wake me up.*

"Rebecca?"

"Wh-what?" She jumped when she heard Dara call her name. "We're at the hotel. Time to wake up, Sleeping Beauty."

"Oh, my God. How embarrassing is that? Please, tell me I didn't fall asleep like a little kid on a car ride?"

"If that's what you want to hear..." Carolyn said.

Rebecca hid her face in her hands.

"Hey. It's understandable. It's been a long day for you."

"Uh-huh. I think I'll just go inside now before I humiliate myself any further." She scrambled out of the seatbelt, grabbed her briefcase and purse, and opened the car door. "Thank you both so much. If you'd told me this is how the last twenty-four hours would've turned out, I'd have bet against it."

"Good thing you didn't put money on it," Carolyn said.

"What's your room number?" Dara asked. "I'll pick you up in the morning."

Rebecca groaned. "What's morning around these parts?"

"I'll take pity on you. I'll get you at nine-thirty."

"Deal. Room 227."

Dara pulled out her cell phone. And your phone number? Just in case I need it?"

Rebecca gave it to her. Dara Thomas, aka Constance Darrow, wanted her digits. What a long, strange day it had been.

CHAPTER SIXTEEN

Dara knew she should be sleeping. The clock on the nightstand mocked her—2:23 a.m. If she dropped off right now, she could salvage five hours of sleep before she had to be up for her morning run.

Instead, she replayed the evening's events at Carolyn's condo over and over again, an endless loop of conflicting and confounding emotions. When she said that she never wanted to see Rebecca again, she meant it. And if only Rebecca hadn't overheard her say it, Dara's nice, ordered life could've stayed exactly as it was.

In retrospect, she was appalled at her own behavior. What the hell was that about? Surely Rebecca hadn't done anything to warrant her vitriolic diatribe. If she'd been standing outside herself, Dara would've wondered who that diva was and dismissed her as a spoiled bitch.

That Rebecca actually forgave her enough to come back inside and give her a chance was remarkable enough. But to take such an enormous leap of faith and undertake a project in which she had no personal stake? Well, it simply boggled the mind.

She tried to put herself in Rebecca's place. What would she have done? *You'd have told her to stick it where the sun don't shine.* A wave of nausea made her guts roil, and Dara threw a hand over her stomach, as if that would alleviate the sickening sensation of self-realization. *I am not that woman. I'm not a bitter, isolated, misanthrope. I'm not.*

After spending time with Rebecca tonight, one thing already was obvious: Rebecca was no Sheilah. Rebecca was insightful, passionate, sincere, thoughtful, and principled—all qualities that

171

Sheilah lacked. Fleetingly, Dara wondered why she was comparing Rebecca to an ex-lover. After all, this was just a business arrangement.

Dara closed her eyes and saw Rebecca as she'd been standing under that streetlight. Her face, even tear-streaked as it was, was near perfection. The high cheekbones and generous lips, combined with the soulful eyes, gave her a quality of vulnerability and sensuality that Dara found nearly irresistible.

Dara's eyes flew open and her heart pounded hard against her ribcage. *She's a business colleague. Maybe she might turn into a friend. That's all it is. The rest just makes the package more pleasant.*

After several moments, satisfied that she had her libido under control, Dara closed her eyes again. Finally, sleep took her. In her dreams, she held Rebecca again under the streetlight. This time, though, she didn't resist the urge to kiss her.

Rebecca jolted awake and flailed around trying to locate the incessant buzzing noise. After several ineffectual swipes with her hand, she cracked open her eyes and discovered the culprit—the alarm clock on the nightstand. She turned it off and rolled over, snuggling back into the plush covers. She just needed a few more minutes…

"Shit!" How was it possible that twenty minutes had passed? She threw off the covers and scrambled out of the bed, nearly stumbling on the way to the bathroom. Dara would be here in less than an hour.

Rebecca pulled up short in the middle of the room. Dara Thomas would be knocking on her hotel room door sixty minutes from now. The thrill of it sent shivers down her spine. She flashed back to the memory of Dara's tirade outside the condo, and those shivers turned into pinpricks of pain. If she hadn't cried and Dara hadn't felt sorry for her, she would be on a plane heading back east right now.

Your only purpose here is to give Dara the cover she needs so that she can turn this movie around and make it consistent with Constance's vision. Stay professional. Remember that it's in her

172

best interest to have you here. There's nothing personal to it. Inexplicably, that thought depressed her.

Rebecca got in the shower and stood under the spray. She let the water beat down on her tense muscles. Beyond the dynamics with Dara, there were so many other challenges.

Although Alistar agreed to the proposal in principle last night, she knew that after a night to sleep on it, he would already be re-thinking the whole idea and trying to find a way to backtrack. Sure, he was blown away by Dara and the whole star thing. Who wouldn't be? But in the cold light of day, his practical, conservative, take-no-risks technophobic side would win out.

Then there was the matter of telling him there was no time for a gentle transition, that come tomorrow morning, she'd simply be a disembodied face on a big screen. She could hear him already. Dara or no this morning, Alistar no doubt would revert to being his dour self. Rebecca had a foreboding she couldn't shake.

She toweled off, dried her hair, put on her makeup, and got dressed just in time for the knock on the door. It was exactly nine thirty. *Well, now I know she's prompt.*

"Good morning." Dara lingered in the doorway, striving to appear nonchalant. Rebecca looked spectacular in a pair of worn, low-cut jeans and a shape-hugging sleeveless v-neck top. Her lips…

"Good morning. Come on in." Rebecca stepped aside and Dara walked into the room. "Sorry. I didn't have time to make the bed." Rebecca stood, self-consciously shifting from foot to foot.

"It's a hotel. I'm pretty sure you're not expected to make it."

"Good point."

From the looks of it, Dara deduced that Rebecca preferred to sleep on the right side of the bed, and she was a neat sleeper. *And you're thinking about this, why?*

"Have you eaten anything?"

"No. I turned off the alarm and promptly fell back to sleep," Rebecca admitted.

"Well, there's a great restaurant called The Polo Lounge right here in the hotel that serves an awesome Sunday brunch."

"That sounds perfect. But I really think I need to square things away with my head of department, first."

"Of course. Maybe I should've worn something more revealing." Dara winked.

"I doubt that would help this time." Rebecca sat down heavily on the end of the bed.

"Why? What's the matter?"

"It's just... I know Alistar. He's an old-school guy who's never been a big fan of technology. Now that the thrill of talking to 'the' Dara Thomas has worn off—"

"So soon?" Dara batted her eyelashes but stopped clowning around when she saw Rebecca's troubled expression. "You're really worried."

"I really am."

Dara sat down next to her and gave her a reassuring one-armed hug. "Are you familiar with the Law of Attraction?"

"The what?"

"The Law of Attraction. The basic principle is that you attract to yourself that which you think. In other words, if you're expecting the worst, you'll get the worst."

"Let me guess. Correspondingly, if you expect the best, that's what you draw to yourself."

"You're a quick study," Dara said. "So, how about if we assume that old Alistar is fully on board with all of this and bring that outcome to us. What do you say?"

"I say, I'd love it if that were true."

"Then let's call him and make it so."

Rebecca got up and went to the window. She flipped open her Bluetooth and dialed.

"Hi, Alistar, it's Rebecca again. There have been some additional developments I need to share with you."

Dara watched as Rebecca paced around the room, seemingly no longer aware of Dara's presence, completely absorbed in trying to convince her boss that this could work. Dara cocked her head as Rebecca gesticulated with her hands, soothed with her voice, and argued a strong case. *Impressive.*

When she hung up, Dara tried unsuccessfully to read her expression. "Well?"

"He's not happy."

"But he'll go along with it, right?" *Please, say yes. Please, say yes.*

"He's given conditional approval."

"Terrific." Dara clapped her hands. "Wait. What's the condition in the conditional?"

"First, he wants to see and approve the setup the studio's putting together today. He's understandably skeptical that everything can be done in a day."

"Okay. I can help ease your mind there. These are the guys that build entire sets in a day. I'm pretty sure they can handle putting together a virtual classroom in that amount of time. Piece of cake."

"And they just happen to be in Vermont?"

God, you're even prettier with a furrowed brow. "Studios work with unionized crews. Those unions have members pretty much everywhere in the country. So the powers that be will just go down a list using a location filter, for say, New England, and they'll put a crew together in less than an hour."

"Huh. Okay. Well, maybe we can get past that hurdle. But that's just one item on Alistar's list."

"What's next?" *And why don't you come back and sit next to me again?*

"He wants assurances that I'll make myself available to my students just as I would if I were holding regular office hours."

"They don't have to be the same hours, do they?"

"No. But they have to be equivalent hours."

Dara raised her eyebrows. "Meaning three to four hours a day?"

"More or less, yes. I don't know how often I'll have to be on set, but..."

Dara calculated. Their days on set would be ten to twelve hours long. Depending on George's predilections, that could mean a fourteen to sixteen hour day for Rebecca, every day for three months.

"Too many for you to be able to keep regular office hours. That's ridiculous. He's asking too much of you."

Rebecca came and put a gentle hand on her arm. "I appreciate your righteous indignation on my behalf. I do. But it's okay. He's within his rights. My job contract requires that I offer a certain number of office hours."

"Yes, but this is an extraordinary circumstance. He should make allowances." Dara wanted to snatch the cell phone from Rebecca and redial her boss. She put her hand in her pocket. *She's just a business colleague, Dara. Relax. This isn't your battle to fight.*

"I don't have office hours every day. Usually only on days when I have classes, so it'll be all right."

"How many days is that?"

"Three, this semester. Monday, Tuesday, Thursday."

"I still think it's unreasonable."

"Noted," Rebecca said. "You know what I'd like?"

"What?"

"Breakfast. All that groveling has made me famished."

"We've got an app for that," Dara said.

"Don't I need to check out first?"

"We should have time to grab your stuff after brunch, but if you're already packed, we can do it now and throw your gear in my car."

Rebecca laughed. "It isn't like I was planning to be here for long. All I have is this." She held up a small carry-on bag.

"Okay. You make the call. Pack now or pack later."

"It'll only take me a minute. Let's just do it now and then we won't be rushed over brunch."

"I like the way you think." Dara got up and moved to the sofa to get out of the way. She observed Rebecca as she hustled from the bathroom to the bed, where the carry-on lay open, and then to the closet where she'd hung her pants and blouses. *Efficient. Organized. Neat.* Dara shook her head at herself. *What? Are you taking notes for an evaluation?*

"Okay. That's it."

Dara made a show of looking at her watch. "Less than four minutes."

Rebecca blushed an appealing shade of red. "As I said, I didn't bring much."

"Which brings us to the next item on our agenda after brunch," Dara said, as she rose and headed for the door. "Clothes shopping…"

⋖⋗

"What do you think about this?" Dara held up a pair of stonewashed skinny jeans and a silk tank top.

Rebecca blushed, again. It felt like she was doing that a lot today. Everything Dara had picked out for her so far was form-fitting and sexy. Rebecca rarely wore such things in everyday life, and never to work.

They were in a small, trendy boutique in Hollywood where Dara obviously was a regular customer. The sales staff called her by name and immediately began pulling items off the racks in her size until she stopped them and told them she wasn't the customer today.

"Just try it on." Dara shoved the items at her. "Please? Humor me."

Reluctantly, Rebecca took the items and disappeared into the dressing room.

"Don't forget to come out and model for me this time. How am I supposed to be able to gauge your style if I don't see the results?"

The jeans fit like a glove, and Rebecca had to admit the top hugged her in all the right places. Still, it was a sea change from what she was accustomed to.

"Well? Let's see it."

Rebecca ducked outside the dressing room and Dara whistled appreciatively, which resulted in yet another blush. "Really?"

"I'd never lie to you," Dara said. Rebecca might have imagined it, but Dara's voice sounded husky to her. "You look hot. If you show up on the set looking like that, there'll be a lot of heads turning in your direction."

"As if with you anywhere nearby anyone would be looking at me." It slipped out without permission. *You're an idiot. She's a business colleague. And, worse still, you just made yourself like everyone else in her life.* Rebecca wanted to cry.

"That would be their mistake," Dara said. She came and wrapped a belt she'd picked up around Rebecca's hips.

Standing this close, Rebecca could feel Dara's breath on her face. Her perfume was light and clean, her eyes vibrant and alive. *You are in so much trouble. She's just a colleague helping you out.*

She's just a colleague helping you out. Maybe if she said it often enough, her stomach would stop doing cartwheels.

"Do you like it?" Dara raised an eyebrow, cocked her head, and smiled playfully.

"Oh." *You actually need to answer her. Now would be good.* Rebecca looked down to see Dara's arms around her hips holding the belt in place. *Not helpful.* "Um, yeah. If you think it works."

"It absolutely works."

Unable to stop herself, Rebecca squirmed. She was human, after all, and could only be expected to endure so much.

Dara dropped one end of the belt and stepped back, evaluating her. "Mm-hmm. You're a babe."

"I-I'll just go get dressed. We've got enough clothes to get me through the week now. I'll fly home on the weekend and get my things." Rebecca retreated as quickly as she could. Heaven only knows what would happen if she had to stand there any longer with Dara looking at her like that.

When she came back out, the sales staff already had everything rung up for her.

"I was going to pay for it," Dara said, "but I suspect the studio might wonder why they were reimbursing me for your wardrobe when I'm not supposed to know about you."

"True." Rebecca took out her credit card. She hoped it wouldn't take too long for her to be reimbursed. The total was complete sticker shock and more than she would've paid for clothes in a year.

They walked out into the bright sunshine and Dara put on her shades. "Condo shopping next." She checked her iPhone. "Looks like my agent has lined up a few prospects for us to check out."

"Really? How did she know what to look for?"

Dara grinned. "Did you think I was grilling you about what kinds of places you've lived out of idle curiosity?"

"You mean you didn't really care?"

"Oh, I definitely cared. But I also wanted to get my agent working while we were shopping. I gave her parameters based on what you said this morning." Dara bit her lip.

Oh, please don't do that. Rebecca tried, with marginal success, not to stare at those luscious lips and resisted the urge to reach out and touch them with her fingertips.

"Is that okay? I guess it was a little presumptuous, huh?" Rebecca shook her head. "No. It was incredibly thoughtful. Thank you."

"You're welcome." Dara used her hands to mock frame Rebecca's face. "Definitely."

"Definitely what?"

"Definitely you're an ice cream kind of girl."

Rebecca burst out laughing. "You can tell that just by looking, eh?"

"From the right angle, I can tell a lot of things." Dara waggled her eyebrows. "So, how about if I take you to my favorite ice cream joint and then we'll meet my agent at the first place? What do you say?"

"Sounds perfect." *I can't imagine anything I'd rather do, or anyone with whom I'd rather do it.* Rebecca sighed happily. *I am in so much trouble.*

❧❧

Dara answered Carolyn's call on the second ring while she waited for Rebecca to come back from the bathroom. "Hi."

"Hi, yourself. How's it going?"

"Great."

"Where are you?"

"We just finished eating ice cream. When Rebecca comes back from the ladies' room we're going to check out a few condos."

"How did the shopping go?"

"She's incredibly easy."

"Excuse me?"

Dara felt the heat flow south from her belly. "She's easy to buy clothes for. She looks good in everything."

"Ah. I see. So all-in-all, a successful day."

Dara thought back to the beginning of the day. "Mostly. Seems like her boss is a bit of a problem."

"How so?"

Dara explained Alistar's demands.

"Well, she does already have a day job, Dar."

"I know that. But if he holds her to that schedule, she'll be exhausted before the first week is done. The guy's being a jerk."

"Seems to me he's just taking care of his professional responsibility."

"Maybe, but I'm worried for her." Carolyn was silent on the other end of the phone. "You still there?"

"I'm here."

"I thought maybe I lost you."

"Nope. I'm just wondering what happened to the woman who stood outside my house last night vehemently insisting that she never wanted to see Rebecca again."

Worst mistake ever. Dara closed her eyes. "Okay, I was wrong. You were right. Is that what you want me to say?"

Carolyn laughed. "I wasn't looking for that, but you could say it about a hundred more times and I'd be all right with that."

"I'm going now."

"Bye, Dar."

Dara ended the call as Rebecca emerged from the bathroom and walked toward her. *Yeah, I was definitely, definitely wrong about that.*

CHAPTER SEVENTEEN

Rebecca twirled around in the middle of the tastefully furnished, spacious living room. This was the third condo they'd checked out in the last two hours. Dara rejected the first spot, Rebecca the second.

"Do you like it?" Dara asked.

"I do. It's modern, yet comfortable. You know what I mean?"

"I was thinking the same thing. Did you see this?" Dara motioned for Rebecca to join her in the backyard. "It's got a sunken hot tub. Perfect for relaxing after a long day on the set."

Especially if I could share it with you. "That's a nice bonus." *Stay on track here.* "What happened to Stacy?"

"She's probably out front on her iPad, investigating other options for us."

The way she said it made Rebecca wonder if Dara had asked the agent to make herself scarce. But why would she? Rebecca went back inside and down the hall to have a look at the bedrooms. There were three of them. One bedroom doubled as an office. It featured a sturdy desk and a comfortable office chair and a recliner in the corner that would be a perfect spot to do some reading. The second bedroom held a treadmill, a flat screen television, and a queen size futon. The third bedroom was the master bedroom.

A large, flat-screen TV dominated the wall opposite the king size bed. A sizeable window opened onto a nice view, and the walk-in closet was large enough to house a dresser alongside a California Closet organizer for pants, blouses, dresses, and shoes.

"This is the nicest one we've se—" Rebecca stopped short and her mouth went dry when she turned around to see Dara lying on the bed.

"The bed is pretty comfy. Come try it out." When Rebecca hesitated, Dara added, "You can't know whether a place is the right one for you until you know that you can get some quality sleep in the bed." She patted the bed next to her.

Tentatively, Rebecca sat on the bed and pushed down on it with her hands. "Feels pretty good."

"Argh." Dara reached up and pulled Rebecca's shoulder so that she fell backward. Now they were lying side-by-side. "Now you can tell whether or not the bed suits you. What do you think?"

I think if I stay like this I'm ninety percent likely to do something I know I really, really shouldn't do with a business colleague.

"It's fine."

"Fine? Fine isn't good enough for ninety nights of sleeping. I'll take comfortable, or heavenly, or even yummy. But fine just isn't going to cut it."

Rebecca tried her hardest to get comfortable without touching any part of Dara's body. She scooted to her right by a few feet and wiggled around until she was in proper sleeping position. "It's comfortable, and heavenly, and yummy to boot. Satisfied?" She jumped up and stepped back from the bed.

Dara grinned like a Cheshire cat and rolled off the other side of the bed. "That's better."

Are you intentionally making me crazy? Or is that just a side benefit?

"Do you want to keep looking?"

They walked back into the living room and Rebecca spun around one last time. "I could see spending three months in a place like this. I think I'm good."

Dara nodded her approval. "I agree. Let's go see what Stacy has to say about how quickly we can get you in here."

"Right." *So why am I hoping the lease doesn't start right away?*

∽⌘∾

"So, this is my place." Dara flitted around, turning on lights. "Normally, I'd be at my beach place on the weekend, but we've got such an early start tomorrow, I thought it would be better if we stayed closer to the studio." *And why are you blabbering on like a high school girl on a first date worried about getting to first base?* "I'll show you around."

"Is this from that Williamstown Theater production of *Under the Blue Sky*?" Rebecca was peering intently at a picture on the wall in Dara's office.

Dara moved in behind Rebecca to stand over her shoulder. "You know about that?"

"Why do you sound so surprised? Of course I know about that. What kind of academic would I be if I hadn't done my homework?"

"I suppose there's something to that, but I have to say, that's a little frightening."

"Sorry." Rebecca turned to face Dara. "The last thing in the world I want to do is frighten you."

Too late for that. Dara momentarily lost herself in Rebecca's eyes. "Right. In answer to your question, yes. That shot was taken by the production's marketing folks."

"To get a role like that right out of the gate… What a coup."

For a moment, neither one of them gave ground. *If I stay here like this, I'll kiss you.* Dara cleared her throat and took a step back. "It was just an understudy role. I got pretty lucky."

"You're selling yourself short, and you know it. You don't get something like that by being lucky. That's about talent."

At that moment, Dara's computer alerted her to an e-mail. Both she and Rebecca jumped at the intrusion. "Sorry. That's probably the call sheet for tomorrow."

"The call sheet?"

"The schedule that tells everyone what time they need to be on set or in makeup, and what scenes are being shot."

Rebecca checked her watch. "They're just now sending it at seven-thirty on a Sunday night?"

"Are you kidding? That's early." Dara walked to her computer monitor to verify that it was, indeed, the call sheet. When she returned, Rebecca was staring at her phone.

"What is it?"

"E-mails. One from Alistar gushing about the crew that came and created an entire new world in what he's calling the Minton Lab."

"See? I told you everything would be fine with your boss."

"For now. Tomorrow's another day."

"What did I tell you about the Law of Attraction?"

"Right. Yes," Rebecca agreed, "everything is fine and will remain so throughout the duration of this project. Better?"

"Much. Good job."

Rebecca continued to stare at her phone.

"What else?"

"Hmm? Oh. An e-mail from the director ordering me to be on set at 8:30 a.m. and an attachment with the pages for tomorrow's filming." Rebecca's arms fell loosely to her sides. She looked up at Dara, wide-eyed. "This is really happening, isn't it?"

Dara smiled broadly. "It most certainly is. How about if we go over the pages? I'll print them out for us and you can run lines with me. Together we can work out what needs to change in the script."

"Okay. Wow. I can't believe this is real."

"Want me to pinch you?"

Rebecca shook her head. "You're a little too eager, I think."

≪⒏≫

Rebecca lowered the script to her lap. They were comfortably ensconced on matching leather chairs in Dara's library. Rebecca had her feet up on the ottoman. "Is this really helping you?"

"Are you kidding? You're a great Harold. Sam had better watch out before you steal the part from him."

"Very funny."

"Who said I was kidding? I don't usually get to run lines with someone who so thoroughly gets the ins and outs of the character she's reading, or the one she's interacting with. Most often, I'm just in my own little world with someone woodenly reciting words opposite me. So, to answer your question, yes, you're really, really helping me tremendously."

Rebecca spent a moment basking in Dara's smile, enjoying being in her company. *You're in deep trouble. Keep it professional. You're just here to help. You can't sit here and go all gaga on her. That makes you no different than anyone else in her life.*

"I thought most actors wanted that lack of affect from their reading partner? I read somewhere it throws them off otherwise if the real actor playing that other part plays it differently than it was rehearsed."

"You did, huh?"

"Yes."

Dara reached behind her, grabbed a throw pillow, and heaved it at Rebecca. "Anyone ever tell you, you read too much?"

"Hey!" Rebecca blocked the pillow and it fell to the rug. "That was completely uncalled for."

"What fun is playing fair?"

Rebecca smirked, grabbed the matching pillow behind her back, and let it fly. To her surprise, Dara caught it.

"Ha! I have mad skills."

Just as Dara was about to send the pillow back, Rebecca launched herself out of the chair and onto the floor, reaching for the pillow she'd deflected earlier. Immediately she was pinned to the floor by a body. A very warm, soft-in-all-the-right-places body. Long, delicate fingers clamped down around her wrists. Rebecca forgot to breathe.

"Don't even think about struggling."

Dara's voice was right next to Rebecca's ear. Struggling was about the last thing she had on her mind as heat radiated downward from her belly.

Still, the competitive side of her refused to surrender, so Rebecca gathered herself, pushed up onto her knees, broke Dara's grip, and flipped them over so that Dara was underneath her, her head on the pillow.

Rebecca scrambled until she straddled Dara, a knee on either side, her hands flat on the rug, framing Dara's head. She looked down triumphantly. "Never underestimate the literary nerd."

"I'm sure I wouldn't." Dara's chest was heaving. Her eyes were deep and dark, her voice husky.

All Rebecca wanted to do was lean down and kiss her. It would've been so easy. *You can't. If you do, you risk everything.* "Not anymore you won't, anyway."

Carolyn's words from their lunch in New York replayed in her mind: *Dara's life hasn't been easy. She's been badly hurt before. It's difficult for her to trust that someone wants to know her. Really know her.*

Carefully, Rebecca got her feet under her and stood up, never touching Dara in the process. She retook her seat, dusted her hands off, and tried for an air of insouciance. "Now, where were we?"

Rebecca saw the momentary confusion on Dara's face before Dara, too, picked herself up and resumed her seat.

If you're feeling what I'm feeling, Dara, you're going to have to make the move. I can't do this. You have to choose me, not the other way around.

"Act One, Scene Three," Dara said, as she put her feet up and crossed her legs at the ankle.

↩↪

An errant strand of hair fell across Rebecca's cheek, and Dara badly wanted to reach out and put it behind her ear. They were sitting side by side at the kitchen table, having adjourned from the library in order to re-work the scene.

Really, it was just easier to be huddled over the same page together someplace where they could make notes. *Uh-huh. Keep lying to yourself if it makes you feel better. Or you could be honest and admit you just want to be near her.*

"This spot here," Dara pointed to a section in the middle of the page. "This just feels wrong."

Rebecca scooted closer to see. "I think that's because it's too sterile. There's not enough emotion."

When Rebecca turned her head toward her, Dara caught a whiff of her perfume. It was spicy and alluring. *Delectable.* Dara barely caught herself before she leaned in for a kiss. Her heart beat a staccato rhythm and her palms dampened. *This can't happen. You don't even know her. Ninety days. She'll be here for ninety days. That's all.*

"Dara? Are you okay? If you're too tired…"

"No. No. We need to push through this. You're right. There has to be more punch to it."

"What about this line, here?" Rebecca tapped her finger on the page. "If instead of saying, 'I feel so lost,' Harold says something like: 'The world is flowing by, and I'm standing still on the shore.' I mean he's just lost his wife, his anchor. He's completely adrift; 'I feel so lost' just sits there. This is the crux of his story arc. It has to be stronger." She shook her fist to emphasize the point.

I can't believe how easily you completely captured what I was trying to convey.

"I'm sorry. Did I speak out of turn?"

"What?" Dara sat transfixed.

"I mean, it's your work. What do I know?"

Dara touched her fingertips to Rebecca's lips. *So soft.* With her other hand, Dara caressed Rebecca's cheek, and trailed her fingers along the strong line of her jaw. Finally unable to wait any longer, she closed the distance between them and kissed Rebecca softly on the mouth. Her lips were pliant and luscious, and tasted of the strawberries they'd shared for dessert.

She pressed, and Rebecca opened to her. Someone groaned, and with a start, Dara realized it was her. She opened her eyes and drew back until Rebecca came into focus. Her eyes were dark pools of desire, her lips were slightly parted, and the pulse point in her neck was throbbing. She was glorious.

Dara dropped her hands into her lap and pushed her chair back. "I-I'm sorry. I shouldn't have. I really am more tired than I thought and I've got to be on set at 5:10 a.m. tomorrow. Your adjustments are spot on. You don't need me for this—do what feels right to you. I trust your judgment."

She got up and started toward her bedroom. "Remember, when you meet me tomorrow, it has to look like it's for the first time." Rebecca still hadn't moved. "Well, goodnight."

Dara crossed the threshold into her bedroom, shut the door, and leaned against it. Her lips still tingled and her body was on fire. "Of all the stupid, asinine, wrong-headed, idiotic... Augh. What were you thinking? You weren't thinking. That's the problem."

She stomped off toward her bathroom, kicking off her jeans as she went. "If you'd been thinking, you never would've done that. Yes, she's hot. Yes, she's passionate and smart and fun to be around, and yes, she pinpointed the exact problem with the scene and nailed the solution in a way even you didn't think of, but..."

But...what? But you didn't want to kiss her? Of course you did. But, you haven't been wondering what that would feel like all day? Of course you have. But, you didn't enjoy the kiss?

Dara closed her eyes and felt the way their mouths had fit together, the warmth of their tongues dancing in time to an unheard beat, the velvety softness of Rebecca's lips. She groaned again as moisture soaked her panties.

How in the world was she going to be able to face Rebecca tomorrow and work closely with her every day for the next three months after this?

She didn't have any idea. But one thing she did know was that what happened tonight could never, ever happen again.

Rebecca ran her fingers through her hair and stared unseeing at the script pages in front of her on the kitchen table. Her breathing finally had returned to normal and her lips had stopped buzzing.

She didn't make the first move. Dara had kissed her. And yet, Dara was the one who ran away like her pants were on fire. *You did everything right. You kept your distance, and you maintained proper boundaries. This isn't your fault.* Then why did she want to cry?

Rebecca shook her head. It didn't matter whose fault it was, the bottom line was that Dara thought what happened between them was a mistake, and Rebecca thought it was pure magic. The question was, what to do about it now? Pretend like it never happened? Acknowledge it and move forward? Run away and go home?

She picked up the page they'd been working on. *I can't show up on set tomorrow and say I've got nothing.*

Dara told her to trust her own judgment. She reread the entire scene and marked up and altered the areas of dialogue she thought should be shored up to bring the script into alignment with the novel. Then she stuffed them in her briefcase. If she wanted to be worth anything in the morning, she, too, needed to go to bed. Tomorrow, she would master the screenplay software.

Rebecca's class was at five o'clock LA time, and she needed to be on the lot and in the specially equipped "classroom" trailer no later than four thirty. She wanted to be sure all the equipment worked with time to spare, in case any adjustments needed to be made. The studio promised her a technician would be on hand to walk her through it.

Although the studio also offered to send a car for her, Rebecca declined. If she'd given them the address, they would've known she was spending the night at Dara's house. Since she presumably didn't know Dara, the coincidence would've been hard to explain. Instead, Rebecca simply told them that she was staying with a friend and she'd catch a cab to the studio in the morning and put in for reimbursement.

Rebecca glanced down the hall toward Dara's closed bedroom door. Was she really sleeping? Could she be, after what happened?

And what would it be like when they saw each other for the first time on set tomorrow?

Rebecca frowned. It was inconceivable to her that they could leave it the way it was without any further discussion. She found a blank piece of paper and penned a note to Dara.

Dear Dara,

I hope you got a good night's rest. I just want you to know that I had a fabulous day yesterday. I can't remember when I've ever enjoyed shopping or apartment hunting more. No need to look for me or worry that I'll come out of my bedroom and surprise you— my eight o'clock East Coast class necessitated that I leave extra early. I didn't want to lead a cab to your door, so I arranged to meet it down on the corner. Thank you for your hospitality and the hand of friendship you extended.

I promise you that when next we meet, presumably on the set later today, it'll be purely professional and as if we were meeting for the very first time. I hope this will allay any concerns you might have relative to last night. I assure you, it is already forgotten.

Break a leg with the scene. I hope you'll think I've done right by the characters. Please know that I did my best.

Rebecca started to sign it, "With all due respect," but that felt too cold. She discarded "Fondly," "Yours, truly," and "Sincerely." Finally, she settled on "All the best," and signed it.

She stood up and rubbed the sore spot over her heart. She could tell Dara it was forgotten all she wanted, but she knew if she lived to be one hundred and senile, it was a moment she would always hold close in her heart.

❦

"Don't close yourself off to love, Dara."

"Mother? What are you doing here?"

"It's my fault. You spent all those years feeling unloved and unwanted, and you're afraid."

"I'm not afraid."

"Oh, but you are. You're attracted to that woman. That's why you kissed her. But you're convinced that it's not safe to give her a chance. What if she abandons you like your father and I did? Or what if she doesn't love you back, like Sheilah?"

"You know about Sheilah?"

"From this side, we can see everything. I see all the mistakes I made with you, and I see what it's done to you. That's why I'm here. It's time for me to make amends. I came to tell you not to lose faith in love. Don't lose hope. If you care about this woman, let her in. She'll heal your soul."

"What do you know about my soul? There's nothing wrong with my soul."

"Your heart is closed. Let go of fear and reach out to love, before it's too late."

"Good morning, Los Angeles, and happy Monday."

Dara started at the sound of the clock radio going off and then remembered that she'd set her alarm clock to the radio setting before she fell asleep. She turned it off and stretched. The remnants of a strange dream clung to her and she tried to put the pieces together. Her mother was there and they were having a conversation about love.

Having a conversation with you, Mother, is odd enough. But about love? As if...

Dara walked into the shower, still half-asleep. As the water hit her in the face, the entirety of the dream flooded back to her. She shook her head as if to shrug it off. It couldn't be. It wasn't real or a vision. It was just a dream.

She rinsed the soap out of her eyes. What was she going to say to Rebecca this morning? *Maybe I could just sneak out. Maybe she's still asleep.*

She's already gone.

Dara jumped as she heard her mother's voice in her head as clearly as if she was standing in the shower stall with her. She ignored it and finished washing her hair.

I know you can hear me, just like I know you heard what I told you when you were sleeping. All those years I thought you were making up imaginary people and now I know you were telling the truth. You really can see and hear dead people. The irony is not lost on me.

Dara gritted her teeth. "This is not happening to me. Not now. I shut all that stuff off years ago."

Because you thought that was what was preventing you from being loved. And that's the heart of the problem here. I didn't realize it at the time, but your father and I conditioned you to believe that no one could or would love you for who you really are. That was the message you took away when we wouldn't accept your special gifts. I'm here now to tell you that that's not true.

"I stopped worrying about what you thought a long time ago."

Maybe, but that belief stuck with you. Over the years, a new twist or two got added, and in addition to thinking you weren't free to be who you really are, you came to believe that no one could see *you for who you really are. Your romantic experiences up until now, especially your relationship with Sheilah, only reinforced that. So you shut everyone out and closed your heart to love.*

"You're an expert on the topic, are you?"

No. But I can see it all very clearly from here. And I came to try to set things right.

"Really? How?"

You're about to make a very big mistake. This woman, the one you kissed last night. She sees you, Dara. All of you. If you keep your heart closed up tight, you're going to miss out on something really special. Give this woman a chance.

"How about if I live my own life and we leave it at that? You can feel better that you delivered me the message and go on about your heavenly duties, whatever they are."

I came because I care about you and I want to help. I hope you can accept this. I'm sorry for the wounds and scars we caused you. I never realized. Being here, having to review my life, I can see with great clarity the mistakes I made. I made so many with you. Too many. I hope one day you'll find it in yourself to forgive me. Forgiveness is important for the soul, Dara. Trust me, I know.

Dara stepped out of the shower and dried herself off. Her hands were shaking. She'd made a conscious decision years ago to close off the psychic part of herself. Apart from the vision of the angel in the hospital when her mother died, she hadn't seen a spirit or held a conversation with one since she'd reached puberty.

Just my luck that it'd be my mother who haunts me.

She dried her hair, quickly donned a pair of jeans and a shirt, and prepared herself for the possibility that she would have to face Rebecca right now. When she opened the door and crept down the hall into the kitchen, she found a note on the counter. Damn her mother for being right. Rebecca had already left.

CHAPTER EIGHTEEN

Y ou look like you're lost."

"Oh my God. You have no idea." Rebecca smiled at the twenty-something young woman in short shorts and a barely-there tank top.

"How can I help you?"

"I'm desperately seeking coffee."

The woman laughed. "Aren't we all at this hour, hon? I have an app for that." She stared at Rebecca appraisingly. "You look pretty enough to be an actress, but somehow I don't picture that for you."

"You don't, huh?"

"Nope."

"Just out of curiosity, why not?"

"Not self-absorbed enough, for one thing."

"You can tell that just by the way I asked for coffee?"

"No." The woman giggled. "I can tell that because you made direct eye contact, you were polite, and you didn't act like you were more important than me."

Rebecca raised an eyebrow at the breathtakingly blunt assessment. "I didn't realize being rude was a prerequisite for being an actor."

"It's not really. I'm just being jaded this morning. So, what's your gig?"

"Oh, um." Rebecca wondered if it was okay for her to explain her presence. Well, everyone would know soon enough anyway. "I'm working on *On the Wings of Angels*. I'm—"

"Wait! Don't tell me, I want to guess." The woman cocked her head to one side, and then the other. "Given the rumors on set, I'd say you're here to fix the mess of a script."

Rebecca's eyes popped open wide, and the woman laughed at her.

"I'm right, aren't I? C'mon, by the way. The coffee is this way."

"What makes you say the script is in trouble?"

"Honey, I'm a makeup artist. We hear everything. I'm Leslie, but everyone calls me Zip."

"Hi, Zip. Nice to meet you. I'm Rebecca."

"Cool. Here we are. Brew to go."

When they'd gotten their coffee and were headed back toward the row of trailers, Rebecca asked, "So all of the actors you work with are self-absorbed?"

"Nah. Most of them are okay."

"What about the actors on this set?"

"Let's see... Most of the secondary characters think they should be playing the leads."

"And the actors who are playing the leads?" Rebecca held her breath. What was Dara like in her environment? Was she a diva? Rebecca couldn't see it and she hoped it wasn't true. *What does it matter now anyway?*

"Sam Rutledge—he plays Harold. He's a pretty nice guy. He's been around a long time. Mellow, you know?"

"Mmm."

"Dara Thomas."

Rebecca's heartbeat quickened and she willed herself not to care. Except that she did.

"She's awesome. Always kind, always thoughtful. She pays attention to details, you know? I have a little flamingo hanging off my makeup mirror and another on my keychain. Next thing I know, she shows up in my chair and hands me a flamingo bobblehead. Blew my mind. Nobody does that." Zip shook her head.

"Wow. Sounds like she's special."

"Yeah. But she seems a little haunted, you know? Like lonely, I guess." Zip waved her hand. "Don't mind me. I'm getting my degree in psychology and I have an overactive imagination."

They arrived back at the trailers. "Thank you, Zip. For showing me the ropes. It wouldn't be an overstatement to say you might've saved my life with this caffeine infusion."

"I hear you." Zip squinted and shielded her eyes as she gazed off into the distance. "Speaking of Dara Thomas, here she comes now. Early for makeup like always. I like that about her too. A lot of actors think it's just fine to keep the makeup artists waiting. They saunter in hours late and expect us to work miracles. Not Dara. She's always fifteen to twenty minutes early."

Rebecca felt the heat rise in her cheeks. First, because it was obvious that Zip was nursing a serious case of hero worship where Dara was concerned. And second, because Dara was walking directly toward them.

"Hey, I can introduce you if you want."

The heat turned to panic. She checked her watch. "No. No, thanks. I'm sure I'll get to meet her on set. I'm going to be late, I've got to run." She smiled tightly at Zip. "Thanks for the knowledge and for the company. Next time, coffee's on me."

As quickly as she could without running, Rebecca beat a hasty retreat to the classroom trailer. She didn't think Dara had seen her. At least she hoped not. She stood for a bit, gathering her wits and letting her pulse slow. Class would start in less than five minutes. *Get your head together. If this is going to work, you need to be able to be in the same space with Dara and stay detached.*

Rebecca sat down in front of the webcam and glanced at the monitors in front of her that would allow her to see the students in the classroom from several angles. Truly, what the studio set up for her was a miracle of technology. Now if only she could concentrate on her lecture. Of course, spending an hour talking about Constance Darrow's work wasn't going to be all that helpful.

"Sorry for the reclamation project," Dara said. She met Zip's eyes in the mirror.

"Tough weekend?"

"Sort of." Dara swallowed hard. Where was Rebecca now? She must be here somewhere.

Zip began spraying on Dara's foundation. "Hey. I met someone really cool this morning. I bet you'd like her."

"Oh? Who's that?" Dara closed her eyes to avoid getting foundation in them.

"A new chick the studio brought in to doctor the script. Name's Rebecca."

Dara's breath caught in her throat and she tried, unsuccessfully, to suck in air. She was glad her eyes were closed so that they didn't give anything away. *You're an actress. You can do this.* "Is that so?"

"Seems really nice. You'll probably get to meet her later."

"Probably." *When I do, God, give me the strength to be a better actress than I am right now.*

≈≈≈

Rebecca sat back and breathed a sigh of relief. The classes went better than she dared hope, but she was completely drained. The combination of the emotional upheaval of last night, the lack of sleep, the early start, and having to spend an hour talking about Dara's work while pretending not to have any personal attachment... All of it was too much.

She glanced at her watch; it was eight fifteen. In fifteen minutes, she would have to be on set, where no doubt she would come face to face with Dara. *You can do this. You have to be able to pull it off.* She took a few deep breaths to calm her nerves. What if she couldn't? *Failure is not an option.*

She took out her phone and dialed the number Stacy gave her yesterday.

"This is Stacy."

"Hi, Stacy. It's Rebecca Minton."

"Hi there. What can I do for you?"

"I'm wondering..." Rebecca cleared her throat. Could it really have been just yesterday that she'd been praying that the condo wouldn't be available for a while? "I'm wondering how soon I can get into the condo?"

"Oh. Um. You want me to push for an early in?"

"Yes, please." Rebecca swallowed her tears. She eyed her carryon bag and the additional suitcase she purchased yesterday that now held all of her new clothes. *What a mess.*

"Let me make a phone call and I'll let you know, okay?"

"Sure. Thanks." Rebecca hung up. She scrolled through her recent calls until she got to Carolyn's name. Her finger hovered over the call button, then she thought better of it and put the phone away. *Carolyn is Dara's best friend. She can't help you with this. Just keep breathing and go to work.* She checked herself in the trailer's mirror, combed her fingers through her hair to settle it, and picked up her briefcase. *Show time.*

⋘⋙

"Good morning," George said, as Rebecca stepped onto the set. "Welcome to bedlam." He gestured with his arm to encompass the bustling activity all around the set. "I'll introduce you in a second."

"Okay."

"So, this is how it's going to go. We're going to do a take or two the way the script is written. If I don't like what I see, you and I will talk about the necessary adjustments. Got it?"

"I do."

"Did you get the pages Audrey sent last night?"

"I did. I went through them and have suggestions ready, but I didn't know how to use the software, so I made the changes by hand."

"Excellent. I'm hoping we won't need them, but the way things have been going…" Someone whispered in his ear, distracting him.

"Okay. Audrey?"

Audrey yelled, "Places everybody. Let's get this show on the road. Oh, but first, George wants to introduce someone."

George stepped forward. "This," he pointed to Rebecca, "is the professor. She's going to make the script even more brilliant than it already is. Rebecca Minton, meet motley crew."

There was a round of welcoming murmurs. A distinguished-looking gentleman separated himself from the crowd. "I'm Sam Rutledge. It's a pleasure to meet you."

"I'm Rebecca. Nice to meet you too."

When Sam stepped back, Rebecca was face-to-face with Dara. She stood stock still, her heart pounding hard against her ribcage.

"I'm Dara Thomas."

Dara held out her hand and Rebecca took it. As she did, she flashed back to the smoothness of that hand caressing her cheek.

"Rebecca Minton." She hoped no one heard her voice crack.

Dara didn't make eye contact. Instead, she seemed to be looking at a spot over Rebecca's right shoulder. "Welcome aboard."

Rebecca let go of Dara's hand and immediately missed the warmth of her touch. "Thank you." She backed away and averted her gaze. It was too hard to see Dara like this.

"Okay, people," Audrey barked. "Act One, Scene Three. Let's get this show on the road."

People hustled all around her and Rebecca moved to the side, trying to get out of the way.

"Stand over here." Audrey grasped her arm and led her slightly to the right of where George was sitting on an elevated chair attached to some kind of small crane.

From this vantage point, Rebecca could watch all the action live, and she could see the monitor next to George at the same time.

The scene had Sam and Dara sitting outdoors at a table in a small, quaint café with checkered tablecloths. Extras filled in the other tables around them. Trees and potted plants surrounded the patio. A waitress stood off to the side with a tray carrying coffee cups, cream, and sugar.

"Okay, folks," George yelled. "I want just enough activity to make this look like your average café, and not so much that it detracts at all from Celeste and Harold, who are having their first meaningful heart-to-heart. Audrey?"

"Let's do this, folks."

Rebecca noticed that Audrey, the camera people, and others were consulting iPads. She peeked at one of them. On the screen was something called a "Shot List."

Someone whispered to her, "All of the camera angles and shots, lighting, and other details are determined the night before. By the time everyone gets here for the day's shoot, they all know exactly what comes next."

"Oh. Thanks."

A young man stood directly in front of one of the cameras holding up a clapboard with the name *On the Wings of Angels* at the top, along with the names of the director, the director of photography, the date and time, the scene, and the take.

"Lock it up… Settle everybody!"

"Rolling."

"Speed."

"Scene Three, Take One. 'A' Camera mark." The clapper-loader slapped the clapper.

"'B' Camera mark." A second loud clap followed.

"And, action!"

Rebecca watched in fascination as the scene came to life before her eyes. There was the low murmur of conversations around the café, waiters and waitresses serving customers, and the waitress with the coffee tray approaching Celeste and Harold's table.

"And, cut!" George called. "Okay. Let's go again, only this time…"

Rebecca tuned him out. She was not required for this part of the process, as no one had yet spoken a word of significance. Neither main character had uttered a line. The focus was on their actions.

She watched Dara. Take after take, the subtlety of her movements and expressions conveyed mountains without a single word being spoken. She was a consummate pro.

Rebecca sighed as a wave of sadness washed over her. Right now, she should be looking forward to telling Dara that tonight over dinner. Instead, they'd likely both be eating alone. It felt so wrong. A woman like Dara should never be alone.

It's not like there's anything you can do about it, so you'd better let it go.

Audrey said, "Let's take a twenty minute break for a reset."

Dara stood up and walked away in the opposite direction, without so much as a glance back at Rebecca.

Surely you didn't expect her to acknowledge you, did you? Rebecca thrust her hands in her pockets and wandered off in the direction of her classroom. Twenty minutes was enough time to answer student e-mails and respond to requests for appointments. If only it were enough time to heal the ache in her heart.

❧❧

Dara sat on the couch in her trailer, sipping from a bottle of water. The next part of the scene they would shoot was the piece that she and Rebecca worked on last night.

Rebecca. Dara recognized her clothes as one of the outfits Dara picked out for her on their shopping spree. She looked so damned sexy in it. But she obviously was tired and when they shook hands, Dara could feel the sadness radiating from her even though Rebecca kept true to her word and acted as if they'd never met before.

Dara couldn't look her in the eye. She was afraid she'd get lost there. *If only you didn't kiss her, everything would've been fine. Now...* Now, it was all wrong and there was no way to walk it back.

"Ms. Thomas? Two minutes."

"Be right there. Thanks." Dara took a deep breath. She needed to put all that aside now and focus on the job at hand. George hadn't handed them any revision pages yet, so for now at least, they were shooting the scene the way Cal wrote it. Already she felt the tightness in her shoulders, neck, and jaw. It was going to be a long afternoon.

As she emerged from her trailer, she spotted Rebecca in the distance. She was walking with her head down, her hands jammed into her pockets, and her shoulders slumped.

She looks like she's going to a funeral and this should be an exciting day for her. You did that. Dara wondered how Rebecca's first day of distance learning went and how the kids reacted. And whether or not she'd been comfortable in the guest bed last night and how she slept. *All things you're never likely to know.*

The edges of depression sank in and Dara shrugged them off. *You can wallow in it later if you must. Now, you have a job to do.*

"All right," George said. "Let's see how this goes. Dara, Sam. We're going to start with the part where Harold starts to open up to Celeste about how he's feeling."

Dara nodded and took her place at the table kitty-corner to Sam. Out of the corner of her eye, she spied Rebecca standing off to the side and she thought about her sitting in the chair in the library, reading lines as if she'd leapt from the pages of the novel and was Harold.

"Dara?"

"Hmm?"

"We're ready any time you are," George said.

Dara straightened up, took a deep breath in and blew it out. "I'm ready."

They ran through it three times; each time, in Dara's opinion, was worse than the previous one. Finally, George had had enough.

"Take fifteen, everybody. Randy? Find me Cal Whiting and get him here in the next ten minutes. He knew we were bringing somebody in to work on the script with him. Why isn't he here already? Rebecca, let's see what you've got."

Normally, Dara would've gone back to her trailer or to find something to eat. But this was Rebecca's first big moment as a script doctor, and Dara wanted to be sure she was okay. So she hovered nearby in the director's chair with her name on it, pretending to close her eyes and grab a catnap.

"Look. The footage is just dead. It's dull," George said.

"Do you want me to say something?" Rebecca asked.

"That's why you're here, Professor."

"Okay. Of course it's not coming to life for the camera. That's because the words are lackluster and don't convey the full range of emotions the characters are feeling. See this section here?"

Dara, of course, couldn't see where Rebecca was pointing, but she smiled slightly as she imagined the very spot they'd gone over last night.

"This line should be the crux of Harold's entire story arc. This is what drives his point of view, his philosophy on life from this moment forward, and all we get is a throwaway line that has no power in it."

"I'm sorry. What?"

Dara nearly jumped out of her chair when she heard Cal's tone. Her immediate reaction was to go to Rebecca's side and stand up for her. She cracked open one eye to watch.

"Professor Rebecca Minton, meet Cal Whiting, our screenwriter."

"Oh. Nice to meet you."

"George? This is who the studio brought in to work on the script?"

"That's right."

"And when they told me they were bringing someone in to work with me nobody thought to tell me she was a what, an academic?"

"I'm telling you now."

There was a tense moment of silence.

"Rebecca was just pointing out that this section here needs some work."

"Really? And the academic's credentials might be?" His tone was derisive, and the hair stood up on the back of Dara's neck.

"She's the foremost scholar of Constance Darrow's work."

"Does she have any experience working on a screenplay? Do you?"

"I…um…"

It was all Dara could do to stay seated and seemingly relaxed.

"Exactly. As I said the other day, there's nothing wrong with the script, George."

Stand up for yourself, Rebecca. Don't be intimidated by him.

"If you'd just take a look at what I'm suggesting, you'll see what I'm talking about. If you shoot it and it isn't better than what was originally written, so be it. This is one of the most critical scenes in the book—"

"That's the problem, Professor," Cal said derisively. "This isn't a book anymore and this ain't a classroom."

"You didn't let me finish. I was going to say, *and* the movie. It's also one of the most important scenes in the movie and that's just not in here right now as the script is written. I'm telling you the adjustments I've made here bring Harold's state of mind leaping off the page and lay the groundwork for everything else that follows."

Atta girl.

Silence ensued while no doubt George and Cal reviewed the changes Rebecca had made.

"I'm inclined to agree," George said. "I'm going to shoot the scene again with Rebecca's changes and let's see how it looks. I'm optimistic. Something I haven't been up until now."

Dara could almost feel Cal seething from ten feet away. *Don't worry, Rebecca, honey, I'll take it from here and sell the hell out of the scene.*

"Randy?" George said. "Get everyone back here. I want to go over a few changes with them. I think we'll be able to do this on the fly. I hope so. We've already wasted enough time and money today."

⋖⋗

Dara and Sam spent half an hour rehearsing the rewritten scene and then George declared it time to put it on film.

Rebecca, still shaking from the unexpected confrontation with Cal, wrapped her arms around herself and retreated to what she hoped was a safe distance to watch the filming. For the first time since the meeting between her, George, and Cal began, she chanced a look at Dara.

Dara was staring back at her for a fraction of a second before she turned away. Rebecca could've sworn she winked. *Now you're just imagining things.*

"Places everyone. Let's have some quiet and get this thing done."

In the end, they shot four takes, and George declared the fourth one a print.

Audrey called out, "That's a wrap for today, folks. Good work. See you tomorrow."

Rebecca started to walk away, but George stopped her. "Rebecca and Cal. I need you here for a minute."

Cal stood across from Rebecca, legs shoulder width apart, arms folded tightly across his chest. George took a position between them.

"Okay. Cal, I know you may not like it, but I don't have to see the dailies to know that we finally got something worthwhile today. That's the first time since we started shooting a week ago. I want you to work closely with Rebecca here to re-imagine the script based on the perspective she brings to the table."

"There's nothing wrong with the script the way it was written. I've been in this business a while now, George, and I've got some hits under my belt. I've got a proven track record. I have no intention of letting some literary scholar who's probably never been on a soundstage until today, rip apart my work."

"It's not my intention—"

George stopped Rebecca with a hand on her arm. "I'm sorry you feel that way, Cal. I've got a few hits under my belt too, and an Oscar or two to show for it. What you wrote is crap compared to what this 'literary scholar' pulled out of the actors this afternoon by virtue of rewriting three pages of dialogue. You don't want to work with her? That's fine by me. Because you're fired."

"Wha—What?"

Rebecca gasped.

"You're fired. Get off of my set. And don't ever plan on working on another one of my pictures. Are we clear?"

"You can't—"

"Oh, but I just did. The studio checked the terms of your contract, Cal. I'm on solid ground here. You were given an opportunity to work with the script doctor and I clearly just heard you refuse. Goodbye, Cal. Don't let the door hit you on the way out."

Cal gave Rebecca a withering look and stalked off.

"You okay?" George asked.

"Me?" Rebecca pointed at her own chest and raised her eyebrows. "Ah. Just another day at the office, right?" She smiled sheepishly.

George threw his head back and laughed. "I like you. You've got guts and I appreciate that about you. I also like what you wrote today. That was genius. You keep that up and we'll have ourselves a movie here."

"That was the idea, wasn't it?"

"That was the rumor." George guided her toward the soundstage exit.

"Did you really need to fire him?"

"That's been coming for a while, Professor. That's not on you. That's on him. He made it hard to work with him."

"Can I ask you something else?"

"Shoot."

"Is it always like this around here?"

George laughed again. "Stick around. You're about to find out. I'll have Audrey get you up to speed right now on the software and the pages for tomorrow. But to give you a head start beyond that, I'm planning for us to shoot as much in order as possible. So you might want to get cracking ASAP on the next three scenes. E-mail the changes to Audrey and cc me and Randy. I'll make sure you get all our contact information. We're going to need the next scenes as early as you can get them to us tonight so that we can get the revised pages out to the actors. I don't want to lose any time on this. I'm thinking I'll put in a late call for everyone tomorrow— maybe eleven o'clock—to give the actors time to memorize the new lines and the crew time to make any necessary changes to the setup. We can rehearse before lunch and shoot afterwards."

"Okay. I'll have a new address as of tonight in case you need that for any reason."

"Good. Give it to my assistant and to Audrey, along with your phone numbers." George patted her on the back. "You did good today. Welcome to the big time, Professor."

"Thanks. I think."

CHAPTER NINETEEN

W hen she emerged from the trailer after her shower, Dara looked everywhere for Rebecca. *I just need to know that you're okay and to tell you how proud I am of how you handled yourself today.*

Rebecca was nowhere to be found. Dara tried her cell phone, but it went directly to voicemail.

Maybe she went back to the house. Yeah, and maybe pigs can fly. It's not like you left the welcome mat out for her when you went to bed last night.

Where else was she going to go? The condo wouldn't be ready for another week. The only other person Rebecca knew here was Carolyn. Dara pulled out her phone and hit autodial. *This ought to be fun.*

"Hey."

"Hey, yourself."

"Done for the day?"

"Finally."

"How'd it go?"

"Crappy, until Rebecca got in there and duked it out with Cal."

"Seriously?"

"Absolutely. She really stood her ground."

"Good for her."

"Uh," Dara reached her car and leaned against it. "That leads me to a question."

"Yes?"

"I don't suppose you have any idea where Rebecca is, do you?" Dara scrunched up her face, imagining Carolyn's expression on the other end.

"You don't know?"

"If I knew, would I be calling you?"

"Good point."

"So, can you help me out or are you going to leave me hanging here?"

"That depends."

"On?"

"You."

"Meaning?" Dara was pretty sure she knew where this was going, but she wasn't going to give in unless she absolutely had to.

"The woman was staying at your house. Presumably you both left the house this morning. You spent all day on the same set today. And I know she gave you her cell phone number the other day. How is it you don't know where she is or where she was going?"

Dara huffed out a breath. "You're really going to make me do this, aren't you?"

"You bet your ass I am."

"Does that mean you know where she is?"

"You haven't answered the question."

"About that. It might have something to do with the fact that I did something really, really stupid last night and then I freaked out afterward and, well, the rest is history."

"What do you mean, 'the rest is history?'" Carolyn asked slowly.

Dara pushed off the car. "I don't want to stand out here in the parking lot and talk about this. Do you know where Rebecca is, or not?"

"I do not. But I might be able to figure it out if you tell me what the hell happened between you two yesterday?"

"What are you doing right now?"

"Waiting for an explanation from you."

"If you want that, come to my place. I'm on my way home now."

"I'll be there and yes, I'll bring dinner."

"I don't suppose you think there's a snowball's chance in hell that Rebecca went to my house, do you?"

"Did you try calling her?"

"It went directly to voicemail."

"Honestly, Dar, I haven't talked to her."

"Oh."

"But I have talked to Stacy."

"Oh?"

"I suspect Rebecca's at her condo."

"The one we agreed on yesterday?"

"That's the one."

"Can I change our plans?"

"No. Dar. Don't go charging over there. Come home and tell me everything and let's figure it out together, okay?"

"But—"

"Do you trust me?"

"With my life."

"Okay, then. I'll meet you at your house in half an hour."

⊰⊱

"You look like hell."

"Hello to you too," Dara said as she threw her keys on the kitchen table. "I don't suppose..." Dara peeked into the living room.

"What? That Rebecca's here? No. It's just us chickens." Carolyn unpacked dinner from a series of bags.

"Mmm. That smells good. I don't think I remembered to eat today."

"That may explain part of why you look like hell." Carolyn stopped what she was doing and leaned against the counter. "But from where I'm standing, I'd say it's more that someone didn't get her beauty rest last night." She took note of the stress lines around Dara's eyes and mouth and the slight bruising under her eyes. "Spill it."

"Now?"

"Is there a better time?"

"Can't we eat first?"

"We can eat and talk at the same time. Don't get cagey with me. I know you too well." Carolyn dished out the Chinese food from the cartons and put the plates on the kitchen table.

"Thank you for picking up dinner." Dara kissed her on the top of the head.

"You're welcome. Now let's have it."

Dara plopped down into the chair. "Rebecca and I had a fantastic day—brunch at the Polo Lounge, great conversation, fun shopping. She even let me pick out her outfits."

"The condo hunting must have gone well too, if she's already moved into one."

"The first couple weren't worth our time, but the third one, it was simply…her. It was tasteful, elegant, open, and airy. It had the perfect vibe."

Carolyn wondered if Dara was hearing herself and how her voice warmed when she described Rebecca. "So, now you're comparing her to a condo?"

"C'mon, Car. You know what I'm saying, it just fit her perfectly."

"Okay. She signed a three-month lease for the condo. What happened after that?" *As if I haven't figured out where this is going. Listen to yourself, Dar. You're gushing.*

"We came home and ran lines together for today's scene." Dara's eyes got even brighter. "I swear to God, she was Harold. It was like she was inside his skin, exactly the way I wrote him. Remarkable. That should've made it hard for me, because Sam might have read the scene completely differently, but I just enjoyed her take on Harold so much."

"And?" Carolyn raised an eyebrow.

"And then we sat down together to revise the scene."

"And?" Carolyn felt like a broken record. *Please, God. Let her get to the point soon.*

"She's incredibly sharp. She absolutely nailed the problem right off the bat and knew precisely how to fix it. I couldn't believe it. Even I didn't see it as quickly as she did."

"And?"

Dara put down her chopsticks. For a second, Carolyn thought she might cry.

"Dara Thomas. Look at me." Carolyn waited until she did. "I'm your best friend and I love you. What happened next?"

"I-I made a really, really big mistake." Dara's voice faltered and Carolyn knew there was nothing for it except to be patient. "Car," Dara's eyes filled with tears, "I kissed her." The last word was lost on a sob. Dara wrapped her arms around herself and rocked back and forth. "I knew I shouldn't have done it. But I couldn't seem to stop myself. She's so perfect and we just clicked so well. It was intense."

Softly, Carolyn asked, "Did she kiss you back?"

"What? Oh. Yeah." Dara sighed happily. "She definitely kissed me back."

"Okay. Maybe I'm being dense, but I fail to see a problem."

"You..."

"Fail to see a problem here. You're both grown women, consenting adults. As far as I know, you're both single. What's the problem?"

"The problem is... The problem is, I don't even know her. I mean, I know nothing about her history, what kind of person she is—"

"How can you say that? You just spent fifteen minutes describing her to me," Carolyn pointed out reasonably. "Let's see, you said she was tasteful, elegant, open, sharp... Have I left anything out? Presumably you're attracted to her or you wouldn't have kissed her."

"She's only going to be here for ninety days, then she'll go back to her nice, quiet life in Vermont and forget—"

"And forget you? Dara, sweetie. You can't honestly believe that if you and Rebecca start something here, she'll forget all about you when the shoot wraps. You had a connection before she ever got here, and you'll have a connection after this movie is history."

"I'm not risking my heart on some three-month temporary—"

"Who said anything about risking your heart?" *Let's try a different tack.* "Why not just have fun?"

"What? Rebecca's not... Well, she's not that kind of girl. How can you suggest such a thing?"

"How is it that you're so sure she's not 'that kind of girl' and yet you're not sure that she wouldn't use you on a whim and walk away? You can't have it both ways. Which is it?" Carolyn knew she was pushing Dara's buttons. She only hoped it would help her figure this out.

Dara sat there, eyes glistening, nostrils flaring, arms folded across her chest. "Why are you doing this? Why aren't you helping me?"

"I am helping you," Carolyn said quietly. "You've got so much fear around your heart you've forgotten how to love."

"What did you say?"

"I said—"

Dara waved her off. "Never mind. You just said almost word for word what my mother said to me this morning. And here I was trying to forget it."

Carolyn nearly choked on a sip of water. "I'm sorry? Did you say you had a conversation with your mother this morning? Are you okay?"

Dara shook her head. "I don't know what I am, Car. I had this dream last night after I ran away from Rebecca."

"Wait. You ran away?"

Dara grimaced. "Yeah. Pretty much. I ended the kiss, told her she was on her own and that when we met on set today it had to look like it was for the very first time. Then I escaped to the bedroom."

"Oh, Dara."

"Don't even." Dara wagged a finger at Carolyn. "Anyway, I had this very vivid dream that I had a conversation with my mother about love."

"Okay, that's just wrong on so many levels I hardly know where to start."

"Too true. But she said the same thing you just said. That I need to let go of fear and open my heart to love."

"I never thought I'd say these words, but your mother is right."

"Oh, my God. Don't say that again. It's frightening. She said it was her fault, hers and my father's, that they shaped me to believe that it wasn't safe to be my true self—to let myself be seen. And that later on, my experience with Sheilah added a twist to that, so that I came to believe that nobody saw me for who I really am or cared who I am beyond the superficial stuff and nobody ever would."

Carolyn whistled. "That was some dream."

"Except that it wasn't." Dara picked up her chopsticks again and pushed the brown rice and chicken with broccoli around on her plate. "After I was up and in the shower, she kept talking to me, saying the same things. She said she came to make amends and that it was ironic that I was telling the truth as a child, that I really could see and hear dead people."

"You've got to be kidding me. How many years have you waited to hear that?"

"I wasn't waiting anymore. I simply shut down that part of my life and I was okay with that."

"And now?" Carolyn tried to put herself in Dara's place. Her psychic abilities caused her so much pain, so much anguish as a child. Carolyn well remembered the many times Dara cried in her arms and prayed that the visions and visitations would stop and that she could just be normal, like everybody else. Eventually, she stopped talking about it and Carolyn didn't want to bring up a painful subject, so she stopped asking about it too. What must it be like, after all this time, to have that switch turned on again, and by her mother, of all people?

"I don't know. So far, my mother's the only one I've seen. Maybe it was just a one-time deal. Like a special dispensation from God for her to have one last conversation with me."

"I guess you'll find out."

"I guess I will."

"Anyway," Carolyn said, "back on topic here. Your mother is right. Sorry, I had to say it again. You've been protecting your heart so fiercely for the last ten years that you've forgotten any other way to be."

"That's not true. I just haven't met anyone who interested me on that level."

"Don't you dare sit there and tell me that all these years you've been open to the possibility of a relationship. You know that's a lie."

Dara looked as if she would argue the point, then thought better of it.

"And don't tell me now that you aren't romantically attracted to Rebecca." Carolyn pointed her chopsticks at Dara.

Dara sighed. "Honestly? I'd wanted to kiss her all day. Finally, I just ran out of willpower."

"Okay. We can work with that. Admitting that you have it bad is the first step."

"Very funny." Dara let the chopsticks clatter to the plate and looked beseechingly at Carolyn. "I can't do this. I don't know how to let someone in, even if I wanted to." Her eyes held confusion and pain.

"I've never known you to back away from a challenge. Don't start now. Right this instant. Close your eyes and tell me the first impressions that come to you about Rebecca. Don't stop to think, just speak."

"Sexy." Dara smiled. "Passionate, stunning, bright, fun, honest, open, great kisser, sincere."

"Okay. You can open your eyes now. How does your heart feel when you rattle off those impressions of her?"

Dara put her hand over her heart. "Full."

Carolyn reached across the table and took Dara's other hand. "It's a pretty special feeling, isn't it?"

"It is."

"I'm not going to tell you that opening your heart to love isn't scary as all get out. It is. Love involves risk. So does living. You've been simply existing for so long now, you've forgotten how to live. You have to learn how to do that now."

"What if…"

Dara didn't need to finish the sentence for Carolyn to know where it was going. "Rebecca is not Sheilah. Don't make the mistake of comparing the two. Only time will tell, but I believe with all my heart that Rebecca really does see all of you. Maybe more clearly than you see yourself. She's very astute."

"I know. She's blown me away more than once. And you should've heard her on the set standing up to Cal. She was polite, but she didn't give an inch. It was really impressive. Her first day, facing off against a seasoned screenwriter and an Oscar-winning director. Spectacular."

"I wish I'd been there."

"You'd have loved it. The thing is, she wasn't doing it from her ego. She was arguing because she believed in Constance Darrow's vision of Harold and she wanted that reflected in the movie. She was fighting for me, Car, even after what I did to her." Dara choked up. "Who does that?"

"Someone genuine. Someone very special."

Dara nodded and blew her nose. "What do I do now? I've screwed this up so badly."

"No, you haven't. We need a game plan."

Before Carolyn could say another word, her cell phone rang. "Hello?"

"Hi, Carolyn. This is Rebecca Minton."

Carolyn almost laughed out loud. Rebecca's ears must have been burning. "What can I do for you, Rebecca?"

When she said the name, Dara nearly jumped out of her seat. Carolyn put up a hand to stop her.

"Um…I hate to bother you."

"It's no bother. What's up?" Dara motioned for Carolyn to put her on speaker, and Carolyn waved her away.

"I know this is silly, but I can't seem to find an e-mail address for Dara."

"An e-mail address for Dara?"

"Yes. I-I want to send her the pages I revised for tomorrow and I want to be sure she's okay with how I interpreted the interaction before I send them to the director and assistant director."

"I see. Can I ask you a question?"

"Sure."

"Why aren't you two working together on the changes in the same place tonight? I thought that was how you were planning to get it done?"

"Oh, uh, it was just that my condo came available earlier than expected and I got tied up with getting all that squared away and I still don't have a car, so by the time I could get over to Dara's, it would be pretty late and everyone is waiting on these pages. I don't want to let anyone see them before Dara has a look, so…"

Carolyn shook her head in wonder. *Oh, my God. You're a horrible liar. And that's a really good thing.* "Sure. I can give you Dara's e-mail. She probably checks darathomas@gmail.com more often than any other e-mail address. That's your best bet."

"Thanks. You're a lifesaver."

"Do you want her phone num—"

"No." Rebecca got the word out before Carolyn had even finished asking the question. "I mean, that won't be necessary, and I'm pretty sure that's not something Dara gives out, right? I mean, that's about her privacy. If she wanted me to have it, she would've given it to me."

"Maybe she forgot."

"Well, if she did, she can give it to me next time I talk to her."

"Okay. Do you need anything else?"

"No. Nope, I'm good."

"How'd your first day go?"

Rebecca chuckled. "It was…interesting."

"Is that 'interesting' in the Chinese sense?"

"The director fired the screenwriter right in front of me. Is that the sort of thing that happens around here every day?"

Carolyn's eyebrows disappeared into her hairline. "No. I think it's pretty safe to say that's a really, really rare occurrence. What happened?"

"I don't want to go into it, really. Let's call it creative differences and leave it at that."

"How very diplomatic of you."

"Well, I'll let you go. I'm sure you're busy and I really want to get these pages to Dara before it gets any later."

"Okay. Hey, Rebecca?"

"Hmm?"

"How are you planning to get to the studio in the morning if you don't have a car?"

"Oh, I'll catch a cab."

"Don't do that."

"No, it's okay. Really."

"Let me send a car to pick you up."

"Like I said—"

"Please? I'll feel better."

"Okay. If you're sure."

"I'm sure. What time do you need to be on set?"

"I have to teach a class at 5:00 a.m. our time, so I need to be at my trailer before then. Which royally sucks since the cast isn't going to have be on set until eleven."

"Eww." Carolyn's wheels were spinning. "I'll have a car get you at 4:15. Will that be enough time?"

"Plenty. Thanks. Tomorrow, I'll work on the car issue."

"Sounds like a plan. Let me know if you need any help, and good luck with the script changes tonight."

"Thanks. Carolyn?"

"Yes?"

"Thanks for everything. You've been really great to me."

"You're very welcome. Goodbye, Rebecca."

"Good night."

When she disconnected the call, Dara practically was in Carolyn's lap. "Well? What did she say?"

"My God. You're worse than a teenager." Carolyn put the phone down on the table. "You should be getting an e-mail momentarily with Rebecca's revisions. She didn't want to send them to the powers that be without your approval first."

"Wow. She doesn't have to do that. I mean, I told her last night that I trusted her judgment, she should just do what she thought was right."

"Well, I guess she still wants to include you in the process and make sure you're on board."

"That's generous."

"From what you told me, it certainly is," Carolyn said.

"Please don't make me feel worse than I already do. What else?"

"She was very circumspect about the reasons why you two aren't working together in person tonight. She completely covered for you, and you'll be happy to know, she's a really, really bad liar." Carolyn smiled. "I'm pretty sure you'll never have to worry about whether or not she's being straight with you about anything. You'll know."

"She didn't want my phone number?"

"Interestingly, no. She was very uncomfortable about it. Another plus in her favor. She didn't want to violate your privacy and although she didn't come out and say so, I could see that she didn't think you'd want her to have the number, so she wouldn't take it."

"Wow. That's…wow. I don't know what to say."

"Say that she's unique and more principled than most people you'll meet."

"Definitely. What did she say about her day today?"

"Oh, that was interesting. Did you know George fired Cal? Right in front of Rebecca?"

"What? No. That didn't happen in the conversation I overheard."

"Well, I suspect you'll get a memo about it soon. Rebecca chalked it up to 'creative differences' and asked me if things were always like this on a movie set."

"Poor Rebecca. What a day." Dara leaned forward in her chair. "That brings us back to the question we were solving when she called. We need a plan."

"I think I just may have one. But you're going to have to sacrifice some sleep to make it work."

"I'm listening…"

CHAPTER TWENTY

Rebecca reread the same scene for the fourth time, saying the dialogue out loud to herself as she paced back and forth around the family room. Each time, she changed the emphasis on a word, giving the line a different spin. Finally, she marked up the page. She was working on her fourth scene of the night, trying to stay ahead of the curve. Dara had said they generally shot a scene a day or every two days, so Rebecca figured she was making good progress.

In her mind's eye, Rebecca saw Dara as she was last night, sitting so close to her she practically could feel the warmth of her skin. *This was so much more fun when I was doing it with you.*

Rebecca sighed miserably. *Suck it up. That's never going to happen again.*

Her computer chimed, letting her know she had an incoming e-mail, and Rebecca's heart skipped. She sent the pages for tomorrow to Dara nearly forty-five minutes ago. She hustled over to the desk and clicked on her inbox.

Rebecca,

I really like the direction you've taken this scene. It's far closer now to the original vibe. I appreciate all your efforts. You're doing great. I made one minor adjustment to Celeste's line on the third page, only because I have trouble saying the word 'unequivocally' in dialogue without screwing it up. Trust me when I tell you, changing that out will save George at least five takes! Otherwise, you're good to go.

Thank you for sending the pages to me first for my input. That means a lot to me. Keep up the good work. See you tomorrow.

D.

Rebecca reviewed the e-mail three times trying to catch any hidden meaning, anything personal. *Sometimes a professional e-mail is just a professional e-mail.*

Yet the tone was more casual than that, and Dara made a point of complimenting Rebecca's work. That was something, wasn't it? Plus, relating her issue with "unequivocally" to Rebecca was a friendly aside. Would she have revealed that to Cal? Rebecca didn't think so.

"Oh, my God. Get over yourself. She sent you essentially a one-paragraph response. Don't analyze it to death. Just take it at face value, make the correction, and send the damn e-mail to Audrey and George."

When that was done, Rebecca reopened Dara's e-mail. She should probably answer it, shouldn't she? That would be proper etiquette, wouldn't it?

"How old are you? Do what you would do for any other colleague and stop obsessing."

Dara,

Of course I wanted you to see the changes first. A collaboration was the way we envisioned this process working all along.

I'm glad you're okay with my treatment of the scene. I'm sure you'll play it tomorrow with unequivocal aplomb. <g> I look forward to watching the dialogue come to life.

See you on the set.

R.

She sat back and went over her words. "This is ridiculous. You've anguished more over word choice in these few lines than you did on your entire PhD dissertation. She allowed the pointer arrow to hover over the Send button for a second longer, then clicked on it.

"Let's get back to more secure ground, shall we? Time to review the material for tomorrow's classes." She saved and closed the script file and opened up her notes for the eight o'clock lecture.

❧❦

"Just breathe. Everything will be fine. Just breathe." This sounded like such a good idea when Carolyn proposed it last night. Now, however...

Dara checked herself in the rearview mirror at a stoplight. Normally, she wouldn't have applied any makeup, leaving the makeup artists with a blank slate on which to work. But nothing about this situation was normal. She fluffed her hair with one hand.

At this hour, traffic was fairly light and she made good time. *One block left to go. You still have time to pull out.*

The light turned green and Dara saw a car approaching from behind. She stepped on the gas to pull through the intersection and tried to ignore the butterflies in her stomach. *Be casual.* "No," she admonished herself, "be real."

The sun was not up yet, and a light was on in the master bedroom as she pulled into the driveway. She checked her watch—fifteen minutes early. Dara rested her head on the steering wheel. Should she sit there? Should she ring the doorbell? *Maybe you should just go home and go back to bed and pretend you were never here.*

A knock on her window startled her so badly that she almost hit her head on the roof. She put a hand to her chest, where her heart was beating wildly, and lowered the window.

"Dara?"

"Ah...hi."

"What are you doing here at this hour? I'm waiting for a car Carolyn was sending to take me to the studio. I've got my eight a.m. class."

"I know. I'm your ride."

"You are?"

"If that's okay with you, I mean. If not, I can call you a ca—"

"No. It's fine. I'm just surprised, that's all Just give me a second, I'll get my things."

Appreciating her curves and the way the slacks hugged her ass, Dara stared after Rebecca's retreating form and swallowed hard. If she was nervous before, the desire welling up inside her only made her more so.

In short order, Rebecca was back with her briefcase, which she placed on the floor in the back. She settled in the passenger seat and put on her seatbelt, then turned sideways to look at Dara.

"What?"

"You know you're not due on set until eleven, right?"

"Yes."

"Did the ride Carolyn was getting me fall through and she needed backup?"

"No." Dara looked over her shoulder for oncoming cars and pulled away from the curb.

Rebecca scrunched up her face, clearly perplexed. "I don't want you to take this the wrong way, because I'm very, very grateful for the ride. But why are you here? And by you, I mean you, particularly?"

There it was. Dara took a deep breath and gripped the steering wheel more tightly. "I wanted to apologize to you." She glanced over to see Rebecca staring intently at her.

"You did? I mean, you do?"

"I do. I behaved very badly the other night and you deserve so much better than that."

"It's okay, Dara."

"No. It's really not. I made a mistake—"

"I get it," Rebecca said, waving her hand as if trying to stop Dara from finishing the sentence. Her voice was tight. "You didn't mean for what happened to happen. It's not what you want. You didn't mean to do it. I get it. As I said in my note, it's forgotten. You don't need to worry about it."

Dara took a hand off the steering wheel and wrapped her fingers around Rebecca's forearm. "Stop." Rebecca's arm was shaking, and Dara's heart sank. "Please." Dara checked her mirrors, pulled to the side of the road, and turned on her hazard lights. She had to make this right. Now.

"What are you doing?"

She faced Rebecca fully and took both of her hands. "I did make a mistake that night." Rebecca's hands flinched and Dara rushed on. "But the mistake wasn't what you think." She squeezed Rebecca's hands. "I meant to kiss you. I'd been wanting to do that all day. So much so, that I frightened myself." Dara ran her thumbs across the backs of Rebecca's hands. "The mistake I made was running away. If it's okay with you, I want to fix that." Dara looked in her rearview mirror then checked the rest of their surroundings. They were completely alone on the road. She leaned over and touched her lips to Rebecca's.

She meant only for it to be the briefest of caresses, but as soon as she felt the softness of Rebecca's mouth, she couldn't stop herself. She leaned in for more. The sweetness of the moment nearly undid her.

This time it was Rebecca who pulled back. "Dara."

"Mmm?"

"As much as I want this—as much as I want you—we're out in the open here, exposed. It's too risky for you."

Dara blinked as the world around them came back into focus. Rebecca was right, of course.

Rebecca freed one hand and ran the backs of her fingers across Dara's cheek. "I'd really, really like a rain check, though, someplace more private."

Dara cleared her throat and sat back properly in the driver's seat. "Thank you for worrying about my reputation." She turned again toward Rebecca, although keeping enough distance so that she did not touch her again. "I know I don't deserve it, but I'd like a do-over. Rebecca Minton, will you have dinner with me tonight?"

"Just to be clear, are you asking me on a date?"

Dara shoved down the rising panic. "I am." She nodded. "Rebecca Minton, will you go on a date with me?"

"Absolutely. I'd love to have dinner with you tonight."

"You would?"

"I would."

"Okay, then." Dara turned off the hazards, and pulled back onto the road. She snuck a peek at Rebecca, who was smiling broadly. "You're sure you want to do this?"

"I'm very sure."

"Okay." Dara nodded and tapped her fingers merrily on the steering wheel.

"Dara?"

"Mm-hmm?"

"What the heck are you going to do between now and eleven?"

Dara grinned as a bubble of happiness filled her stomach. "Any chance I can sit in on your classes? I'd love to watch you work."

"I'm sorry, what? I could've sworn you said you wanted to watch me teach."

"That's because I did. Would that be okay?"

"I-I guess so."

"If you don't want me to…"

"It isn't that. I'm just trying to wrap my mind around teaching a course on Constance Darrow with Constance Darrow sitting alongside me just out of view."

"Surreal, eh?"

"That would be an understatement."

"I think it'll be a lot of fun."

"You would." Rebecca was quiet for a moment. "Are you going to slip me notes if I get something wrong?"

Dara laughed. "Maybe. Or maybe I'll learn something new about my own work." She pulled up to the studio gates and the guard, recognizing her and her car, waved her through. The day was off to a good start.

⋘⋙

"Good morning, everybody."

"Good morning, Professor Minton."

"I'm glad to see you haven't found a way to disable the microphones in the room. Yet. You all are looking bright and chipper for a Tuesday."

"If you don't mind my saying, Prof, you look a little worn out."

Rebecca checked the monitor on the left. "Yeah, Sky? Well, let's remember it's five in the morning here and I'm only on my first cup of coffee."

"Noted."

"Hey, Prof?"

"Yes, Dan?"

"Before you get rolling, how's it going out in Tinseltown? Are you setting the place on fire yet?"

Rebecca was hyper-aware of Dara, seated just a few feet away, out of range of the webcam. "I don't know about that, but I will say it's been most stimulating and enlightening."

Dara's eyes shone with amusement.

"Are you, like, going to introduce us to any major stars or anything? I mean, it would be relevant, since you're working on a movie adaptation of a work we're studying and all. Call it interactive teaching."

Rebecca smirked. What would the kids think if Dara moved her chair over about three feet and into their line of sight?

As if reading her mind, Dara passed her a note. Rebecca glanced down at it. *Want to have some fun with the kids?*

Rebecca pursed her lips in thought. Since Dara most often was sitting in the makeup chair at this hour, there might never be another opportunity like this. On the other hand, it would completely blow up her lesson plan. Beyond that, what if Dara accidentally slipped and said something that only Constance would know? She wrote on the paper, *Are you sure?*

Dara nodded.

"As a matter of fact," Rebecca said. "I might just be able to pull a string or two."

"Yeah? Never mind the guy who plays Harold. We want to meet Dara Thomas."

"Now, Clint, that's only because you have a thing for Celeste, right?" Rebecca raised an eyebrow and pointed into the camera.

Clint feigned innocence. "Well, duh. Why else?" He smiled mischievously.

Rebecca grabbed the scrap of paper back. *Seriously? You know that there are teenaged boys in my class, right?*

I'll be fine.

"Well, since you asked so nicely, and since I know you will all comport yourselves like the ladies and gentlemen you are, let me snap my fingers here and, since this is Hollywood, maybe I can make something, or someone, magically appear."

Dara scooted her chair over so that she and Rebecca were side by side in front of the webcam.

"Holy shit!" Clint exclaimed.

"Profound, Clint. Everyone, please meet Dara Thomas, who is playing Celeste."

Dara waved into the webcam. "Hi, folks. Welcome to Hollywood, where we can take any three hundred-plus page book and boil it down to two hours that might or might not bear any resemblance to the novel you're studying right now."

"Obviously, this changes the lecture I so painstakingly prepared for today. So, how about if I open up the floor for questions. Raise your hand if you have one, don't just talk over each other. And here are a few more ground rules. Confine your questions to something remotely related to *On the Wings of Angels*—the book or the movie. I'm pretty sure Dara is very familiar with the novel." Rebecca stole a glance at Dara, who remarkably kept an absolutely straight face.

"I've read the book a few times," she said. "Look, when you're working on an adaptation, any adaptation, you have to treat the material as if it is original. Still, I think it's valuable and important to understand the source material. I'd love to play Celeste as true as possible to the character as she was originally written. I'm counting on your professor, here, to help make that possible."

Rebecca blushed. "Okay. So, if you ask a personal question, we're done. Is everybody clear?"

The students answered with a chorus of "yeses."

"Who wants to ask the first question?" A dozen hands shot up. Rebecca silently evaluated each of the kids, zeroing in on the ones she thought would ask the most responsible, most interesting questions. "Christie?"

"Ms. Thomas—"

"Call me Dara, please."

Christie smiled shyly. "Okay. Dara, what was it about Celeste that made you want to play her?"

"Good question, Christie. For me, Celeste is this very layered, rich character. At first glance, she seems pretty straight-forward—she's just an aimless, unmotivated, unfocused thirty-year-old doing everything she can to avoid life. Then we see her interacting with Harold, and all of a sudden we realize that there's a lot more there than meets the eye. She's totally misunderstood.

"As an actress, I love the challenge of peeling an onion like Celeste scene by scene until the audience has this 'aha' moment where they finally 'get' her."

God, I could listen to you talk about your work forever and never tire of it. "Aaron, you have a question?"

"Dara, since you've obviously read the book carefully, what happens if you get on set and the director, or the screenwriter, or the guy playing Harold, directs, writes, or plays the scene differently than the way you envision it?"

"Wow. You've got sharp students," Dara said to Rebecca. "Well, Aaron, that's an excellent question. The shit hits the fan." She winked into the webcam and the class erupted in a ripple of laughter. "No, seriously. The director has final say. He's the boss on the set, so if he doesn't like the way something looks, he has the power to order it to be rewritten or to explain to the actors what he wants them to do differently. It's our job to make his vision a reality."

"So you don't get any say?"

"I didn't say that. Depending on the director, he might listen to our opinion about a line or what we think our motivation is in a scene. If he agrees with us, great. If not, we have to suck it up and do it his way."

The questions and answers about the film, acting, and adapting a book into a film continued for the better part of an hour. Finally, Rebecca held up a hand to the webcam.

"We have time for one last question. Make it count. Lisbeth?"

"Dara, I saw on *Extra* last night that there's trouble on the set. They said the screenwriter got fired and that there's dissention on the set."

Rebecca jumped in. "If you have time to be watching trashy television, obviously I'm not assigning enough homework." She opened her mouth to dismiss the students, but Dara put a hand on her knee out of sight of the camera.

"Sometimes, although rarely," Dara said, "the director and the screenwriter don't see eye-to-eye about how a script needs to be revised and something has to give. In this case, we were extremely fortunate in that we had someone with extraordinary vision and a real feel for the story to set the script to rights." Dara jabbed her thumb in Rebecca's direction. "That would be your professor. I am completely confident that the movie will be a huge success, largely because of her work here."

Again, Rebecca blushed. "Okay. I think we're done. On Thursday, we're going to talk about the weather... As in weather as a metaphor in this novel. Until then, do try to keep yourselves out of trouble. I want to thank our very special guest, Dara Thomas, for her time and her generosity in stopping by to spend time with us, even though she isn't due on set for another five hours."

"Thank you, Dara," the kids all said in unison.

"You're welcome, guys. Before you go, I want you to know that Professor Minton is the real deal. You're so lucky to have her. Make sure you treat her well."

"I'll see you all on Thursday. Bye, guys." Rebecca clicked out of the session and sat back. "Well, that was different."

"Different bad or different good?"

"Different, as in the thrill of a lifetime for me and for these kids. Thank you so much for being so generous with your time and your answers. They'll be talking about this morning for a long, long time."

"That was fun."

"Uh-huh."

"No, really. It was. Plus, I got to see you in action." Dara's smile was radiant.

"Not exactly. Seeing me in action would require that I do something other than play traffic cop for you. Speaking of which, sorry about that last question."

"It was no big deal. Goes with the territory on a movie set. And it gave me an opportunity to put in a plug for you."

"That's good, because you know, my creds were in question."

"As if," Dara said. "Now what?"

"Now we talk about Gatsby with a bunch of seniors…"

CHAPTER TWENTY-ONE

The intent here is for Celeste to realize for the very first time that Harold needs her as much as she needs him. It's the moment that gives her a new lease on life, a new purpose. This line," Rebecca pointed to a place on the script, "is the most critical piece of dialogue in the scene."

"I agree," George said. "Okay, so we'll shoot those lines in tight and if we have to lose something, what about this right here?"

Dara caught herself staring at Rebecca and busied herself pretending to go over the script.

"She really seems to know her stuff, eh?" Sam leaned against Dara's chair.

"Hmm? Oh, you mean Reb—the professor? She does." *Oh, yes indeed. She certainly does.*

"What about that mess with Cal? Crazy stuff. I can't remember the last time I ever saw something like that on a set."

"It was wild, but I have to say, I'm liking the new direction of the script." Dara looked up at Sam to gauge his reaction. "Did you read the novel?"

"As a matter of fact, I did. Loved the book. That's why I signed on to play Harold. I'd read the novel and I heard they were looking to bring it to the big screen. I knew it was the best role I'd get at this age." He winked at Dara. "You're not nearly there yet, but trust me when I tell you that when you get to be this old, really well-written, meaty roles are much harder to come by. And," he said, pushing off as the conference between George and Rebecca broke up, "I agree with you. The changes accentuate the depth of the original material in a way Cal's version simply didn't. Nothing against Cal, of course."

"Of course."

"I heard this was the professor's first ever look at a screenplay. Could've fooled me. She's like an old pro. I'll have to remember to tell her that if I get a chance."

Dara smothered a grin. "I bet she'd appreciate hearing it from you, Sam. I imagine all this is pretty overwhelming to her. Knowing that we're behind her might give her a real boost. I'll remember to say something to her too."

"All right. Why is everybody standing around?" George joked. "Back to work with the lot of you. Here's what we're going to do…"

❦

"If you keep mooning like this, everyone on the set is going to know something's going on," Rebecca mumbled, admonishing herself. It was a conversation she'd been having with herself, with limited success, most of the day.

Rebecca couldn't help herself. Dara was astonishing in the part, now that it was written as she'd intended it to be played, and the shooting was going exceptionally smoothly.

At the moment, Dara and Sam were sitting on a park bench, watching some trained pigeons peck at breadcrumbs on the manufactured sidewalk in front of them. Three cameras focused on the action while Harold spoke of longing for his wife as he dropped off to sleep at night and the unfairness of losing her while they still had so much living left to do.

"And, cut! Print that," George yelled.

"Okay, everybody," Audrey yelled, "that's a reset for the extreme close-ups. Take ten." As everyone started to move away, she added, "But be back here on time! Ten means ten."

Dara walked directly toward her, and for a moment, Rebecca thought she would pass without acknowledging her. Instead, she stopped right in front of Rebecca.

"I just want you to know that you're doing a fantastic job with the script. You've created evocative dialogue that makes it a pleasure to play the character."

230

Rebecca beamed. "It's easy to envision writing dialogue for a great actress who breathes life into every word and whose expressions alone speak volumes."

"Is it okay if I join this mutual admiration society?" Sam slid between Rebecca and Dara and put an arm around each of them. "Dara is a great actress, and believe me," he stage whispered to Rebecca, "I've seen and worked with my share of those. But what she says is true—an actor is only as good as the material he or she has to work with. You've done wonders with the pages so far. Keep up the good work." He patted her shoulder and walked away, leaving the two women alone together again.

The scent of Dara's light perfume wafted toward her, and Rebecca inhaled deeply. "Was that rehearsed? The two of you, I mean?"

"No. In fact, Sam was the one who wanted to say something to you first." Dara looked over Rebecca's head and her expression changed, becoming more closed. "Well, as I said, thank you for excellent adjustments. Keep up the good work."

Rebecca tried to process the reason for the change in Dara's demeanor. When George walked right past them, she understood. *Oh. Remember where you are, Rebecca, and remember who she is here on the set.*

Dara nodded to her one last time, and took off in the direction of her trailer.

"Let's just get one last set of extreme close-ups and we can call it a day," George said. "Dara, we're going to start with you. Take it from the line, 'Life is what happens when you're looking the other way.' Got it?"

Dara closed her eyes and breathed, summoning up the emotion that would be necessary to play this scene. With the camera positioned literally right in front of her face, every blink, every facial tick, every shift of the eyes, every emotion would be plainly visible. She needed to be fully, completely immersed in Celeste.

Which means you have to stop stealing glances at Rebecca and thinking ahead to tonight. Stay present. Stay focused. Isn't that the message that Celeste is trying to get across to Harold? You should take her advice.

Watching the ease with which Rebecca interacted with her students and the obvious respect and esteem in which they held her warmed Dara's heart. Seeing her interact with George on set all day and problem-solve lines on the fly was downright sexy.

"Dara," George said. "Whenever you're ready."

Dara schooled her expression. In this moment, she was imparting to Harold the most important lesson she'd learned while traveling around the world. *The sooner you get your head in the game, the sooner you can spend time alone with Rebecca.* That was more than enough incentive to get the scene right in as few takes as possible.

⋖⋗

Rebecca gathered her things and checked around to make sure she had everything she needed for the night.

Knock, knock.

Rebecca flew to the door and opened it to see Dara on the other side, still in full makeup.

"Hi."

"Hi, yourself."

"Um, I didn't have a chance to give you my phone number this morning, so…" She handed Rebecca a slip of paper. On it was her phone number and her address.

"Thank you."

Dara looked around nervously. "I'm going to be about half an hour to forty-five minutes while I get the makeup off, shower, and change. You can wait for me and we can ride together, or—"

"I'll wait. Unless you don't want me to. If you don't want to be seen driving together I can catch a cab."

"No. I don't want you to have to take a taxi. That's ridiculous. Wait here and I'll come get you when I'm ready. If that's okay with you."

I hope we're not going to be this careful with each other all night. "That's fine. I'll work on the next scenes until you're done. That way, I'll be free and clear for the night as soon as you sign off on the pages. Unless you want to work on them together."

"No. No. You did a great job today. I'll look forward to seeing what you do with tomorrow's pages."

"Then I'll see you in a little while."

"Count on it."

She shooed Dara away from the door. "Hurry up, will you?"

Dara's laughter echoed in her ears as she shut the door. Rebecca pulled her laptop back out of her briefcase and got to work. Based on the adjustments she and George made during today's shooting, she scrolled through the next few scenes and tweaked various lines and setups that she created last night. Then she did the same for the other two scenes she had worked on, as well.

Just as she finished, Dara knocked on the door again. "I hope you're decent in there, because I'm coming in."

The door flew open as Rebecca reached it and the two women were standing inches apart. "Good thing I was. Decent, I mean. That wasn't much notice."

"Good thing." Dara's eyes sparkled with mischief. After several seconds she said. "Okay, then. What do you say we blow this pop stand?"

"I'm not the one who's been holding us up."

"Oh, sure. Blame it on me."

"Who else would I blame it on?" Rebecca packed up the laptop and the briefcase, turned out the light, and locked the door behind them. "You look and smell very nice, by the way." And she did. Dara was wearing a low-cut tank top that showed off ample cleavage and her toned arms, a pair of stylish stonewashed jeans, and worn cowboy boots.

"Thank you. You don't clean up so bad, yourself."

"I'm wearing the same thing I was wearing at four o'clock this morning."

"And your point is?"

"Never mind, I'm sure I didn't have one."

"Since you're not from around these parts," Dara affected a southern drawl, "I thought maybe I'd take you for a drive and show you the sights. Then we could grab some dinner and dessert."

"That sounds amazing." Rebecca bit her lip. "What about the pages for tomorrow?"

"That's easy. You're going to read them to me on the way so that by the time we get to dinner, where there will be WiFi, by the way, you can just e-mail them to Audrey and George."

Rebecca hesitated.

"You don't like that plan?"

"No. It's… You want me to read every part to you? Me?"

"Absolutely. Not only that, but I want you to read it in character."

"You've lost your mind, you know that?"

"You wouldn't be the first person to tell me that."

"And probably not the last, either. Okay, if you're sure that's what you want."

"I'm sure." Dara unlocked the car. "And they better be good. Did I mention that?"

"No. You conveniently left that part out. No pressure here."

As they pulled onto Sunset Boulevard, Rebecca opened the laptop and began reading the pages. She continued reading through Beverly Hills, Holmby Hills, Bel Air, and Brentwood, occasionally looking up when Dara pointed out some significant landmark. Finally, she finished reading when Dara took a short turn and stopped the car at a scenic overlook at the Bel Air Bay Club just off Sunset.

Dara put the car in park and applauded. "Brava! Brava!"

"Very funny."

"I'm serious. I got all of the intonation and the intent of the scene. It was inspired. I loved it. All of it. And there wasn't one U-N-E-Q-U-I-V-O-C-A-L-L-Y in the entire scene."

"I can add one in, if you'd like?"

"What I'd like," Dara said, gazing deeply into Rebecca's eyes, "is to find a WiFi spot so that you can e-mail the file and stop working for the night."

Rebecca swallowed hard. "Oh. Okay." She glanced out the window at the ocean and the darkening sky. "Do you have a spot in mind?"

"I do."

Dara threw the car in reverse and headed back out onto Sunset and then down the Pacific Coast Highway. "I really think you're going to like it."

"I'm sure I will." Rebecca admired the breathtaking scenery, soaking in the hues of the skyline as the sun set into the ocean, setting it on fire. "This is gorgeous."

"I'm glad you think so."

The car stopped and Rebecca glanced around. They were parked in the circular drive of a spectacular beach house. Rebecca glanced around in confusion. "Who lives here?"

"I do," Dara tossed over her shoulder as she hopped out of the car. "Remember? I told you I had a beach house. Are you coming in, or do you just want to sit there? And bring the briefcase."

Rebecca scrambled out of the passenger seat. "This is your little beach house?"

"It is."

"Holy crap."

"That was profound, Professor. Hurry up and get in here. We're losing the sunset."

Rebecca hustled through the front door with her briefcase in hand.

"I'll type in the WiFi password for you. You send the file while I put a few things away." Dara snatched the briefcase from her and got to work. "Okay. You're in. Make it snappy." She moved away and into the kitchen.

Rebecca logged into her e-mail, pulled up the next scene they would shoot tomorrow, attached it to an e-mail with a brief note to Audrey and George, and hit Send.

"Are you done?"

"I am."

"Good." Dara grabbed her by the hand. "Come with me."

They headed out a set of sliding glass doors at the back of the house and out onto a deck.

"You might want to roll your pants up a little and take off your shoes," Dara advised, as she removed the cowboy boots and rolled up her jeans.

When Rebecca complied, Dara took her hand again and led her down the steps of the deck and onto the beach. "If we hurry, we can just catch the last of it."

They reached the shoreline just as the sun dipped below the horizon, leaving streaks of orange, red, pink, and yellow in the sky. Not a word passed between them as they stood, hand in hand, watching the sky transform from day to night, listening to the rhythmic sound of the waves lapping gently against the shore and the occasional cry of a gull.

"Did you enjoy that?" Dara asked, when the last vestiges of light faded away.

"That was awe-inspiring. The stuff of poetry." She turned to Dara and took her other hand. "Thank you for sharing that with me."

"I-I haven't wanted to share that with anyone in many, many years. Too many to count really. But all day long I kept thinking about how much I wanted to share it with you."

"I'm so glad you did."

"Me too." Dara rubbed her thumbs over the backs of Rebecca's hands, sending chills up her arms. "If I'm right, I think there are many things I'm going to want to share with you. But I'm a very private person and this doesn't come easily for me. For right now, though, I need for you to understand something about what happened between us the other night."

"You don't owe me any explanations."

"Shh. I want to explain. To understand why I reacted the way I did the other night, you need to know that you're the first woman I've kissed in a very, very long time."

"Oh."

Dara looked away toward the ocean for a moment. When she turned back to Rebecca, there were tears in her eyes. "When I was acting in that first Williamstown production, I met a woman. Her name was Sheilah. She was older, and sophisticated, and she wooed me with flowers and love notes and lavished attention on me." Dara let go of Rebecca's hands and wrapped her arms around herself. "I was young and naïve, and I thought we were very much in love."

Dara met Rebecca's eyes and in that instant, Rebecca saw raw pain and anguish. She wanted to pull Dara close, but sensed that Dara needed to finish this.

"I was so wrong. Belatedly, too late for my heart, I discovered that Sheilah was only interested in window dressing. In the end, I was nothing more than a pretty thing she wanted as a trophy—something to make her friends and business colleagues envious."

"Oh, Dara." Rebecca couldn't stand it anymore. She pulled Dara to her. Although she was met with some initial resistance, Dara capitulated and allowed herself to be held. "I'm so, so sorry for that. I know how devastating that can be."

"Yeah, well," Dara straightened up and pulled back a little. "I learned a lot from that experience. She wasn't the first one with ulterior motives, although she was the first woman. But I'll tell you this," Dara's gaze was piercing. "She was the last. I promised myself then that I would never be used like that again. And I meant it." Dara's voice shook.

Rebecca could feel the waves of confusion and anger emanating from Dara. "So when you kissed me the other night, you were afraid that I'd be just like Sheilah."

Dara nodded and hung her head. "Yes. I'm not proud of that. And I realize that I kissed you, not the other way around. But you're only here for ninety days, then you'll leave here and go back to your real life, and I'll be nothing but—"

"Please, God, tell me you weren't about to say a notch on my belt. You weren't, right?" Now it was Rebecca's voice that shook. "Let me tell you a little bit about myself, Dara. I had my own Sheilah. Her name was Cynthia. I didn't catch a clue until I found her in our bed with our landscape designer. I know what it feels like to be used. To be treated like a toy that's easily discarded when something or someone else comes along. If you think I could be remotely capable of being like Cynthia, or Sheilah... Well, the thought makes me sick to my stomach.

"If you couldn't tell from my letters and from our short time together so far that I'm not that kind of person, then I really shouldn't be here." Rebecca turned and ran, tears spilling out of the corners of her eyes.

"Hey! Hey! Wait. Rebecca, please wait." Dara caught her around the waist and held her from behind. "Don't go. Please, don't go."

Rebecca struggled for another few seconds, then dropped to her knees on the sand. "Dara. I was in love with you before I knew who you were, before I knew what you looked like. I didn't care. I fell in love with your words, and your mind, and your soul, which was so evident in the pages of your books. Then, when you answered my letters... I fell even more in love. You were passionate, and smart, and funny, and humble." She took a shaky breath. "I knew that I could never find anyone in real life like Constance. And then when I figured it out and you freaked, I mourned you. I mourned losing Constance. Not Dara, because I didn't know her yet. But Constance, with whom I was, ridiculously, madly in love."

She held up a hand as Dara came around and knelt in the sand in front of her.

"Don't. Let me finish. When I got the call from the studio and came out here and learned what they wanted from me, all I wanted to do was to get back on a plane and go home. The idea of spending time around you, knowing you would never feel the way I did, was more than I was ready to bear."

"Rebecca—"

"But then I met with Carolyn. I didn't tell her how I felt about you—about Constance. It seemed absurd and childish. But she convinced me that I should sit down with you. So I did. I believed that Constance needed my help. Not you. Dara would be just fine, whether it was this project or another. But Constance couldn't get her movie made unless I subjugated my feelings for you and got the job done. And that's what I intended to do.

"Spending the other day with you, shopping and playing, and working, all I wanted to do was kiss you. But I didn't do it. No, I knew I needed to put my feelings aside and stay professional. And then you kissed me and…" Rebecca sobbed.

Dara pulled her into her arms. "I'm sorry. God, please don't cry. Don't cry, baby. It's okay. It's okay."

Somewhere in the deep recesses of her mind, Rebecca heard the term of endearment, but it didn't stick. She wanted to pull away, to disappear, but the feel of Dara holding her tight—of Constance, holding her in her arms—the allure of it was too strong. She gave in and allowed herself to be held until all her tears were spent.

When Rebecca stopped fighting for air, Dara put a palm to her cheek. "I think I knew I loved you when I saw that first video of you teaching my work on YouTube. We'd been corresponding a few times by the time I stumbled across it. I was transfixed. I never envisioned someone, anyone, could so totally and thoroughly understand my work—could understand me. And yet, there you were.

"But I knew I could never have you, or let you know who I was, because I couldn't find my way clear to trust again or to open my heart to love. And then you showed up at Letterman and I had no idea what to do with that. My fight or flight instincts kicked in and, well, the rest is history." Dara shook her head.

"When you turned up here, completely out of the blue, I felt cornered. Without you, there would be no movie. With you? Every day I'd have to face the one person I believed might really see me for who I am." She laughed mirthlessly. "I didn't even make it a day without giving in and kissing you. Not even one day. Nobody gets through my defenses like that. Nobody." Dara framed Rebecca's face with both hands. "Nobody except you. And right here, right now? I wouldn't have it any other way."

Before Rebecca could say another word, Dara kissed her. Softly at first, her lips gentle and probing. But as their hearts caught up to their mouths, Rebecca deepened the kiss, her movements mirroring her emotions. Dara matched her stroke for stroke, until they were moving and breathing as one.

CHAPTER TWENTY-TWO

C an we—"

"Take this inside?" Dara asked, breathless. "Yes." But she resumed right where they'd left off.

"Dara?"

"Yes? Oh. Inside. Right." She struggled to get to her feet without relinquishing Rebecca's lips. They tasted so sweet.

Finally, Rebecca put a hand on Dara's chest. "If you don't stop kissing me right now, we're going to make love out here and end up with sand in too many unmentionable places to count. Could make for an uncomfortable day on set for you tomorrow, picking sand out of—"

Dara smothered Rebecca's next words with another kiss. Without losing contact, she murmured, "Got it. Heading inside, right now." It took all her willpower, but she managed to step back.

"Why are you standing still?" Rebecca teased, as she grabbed Dara's hand and ran toward the house.

Dara barely managed to close and lock the glass doors before she whipped off Rebecca's blouse and bra. "Far enough," she breathed, pushing Rebecca up against the glass. Her hands skimmed the soft skin at the base of Rebecca's breasts and the two women groaned in unison. Without missing a beat, she relieved Rebecca of her slacks and panties too.

Rebecca's mouth found her nipple before Dara realized her own bra and top were gone. At the first touch of Rebecca's warm tongue, Dara's knees wobbled. She surged forward, pushing further into Rebecca's mouth. *How could I have forgotten what it feels like to be loved and to want to love in return?*

Dara wanted to keep control, wanted to be in charge, but Rebecca's ministrations undid her.

"Reb—"

Rebecca stopped her with a finger on her lips. "I don't want you to talk right now. I want you to know, deep inside, everything I feel for you—for all of who you are. Let me show you."

Dara's breasts heaved and her heart swelled as Rebecca unbuttoned and unzipped her jeans, easing them off her hips and letting them pool around her ankles.

Slowly, lovingly, Rebecca ran her hands along Dara's waist and down her hips, teasing her fingers around the edges of Dara's lace panties.

Moisture pooled in Dara's center as Rebecca lowered herself until she knelt in front of Dara. When she paused to kiss Dara through the material, Dara arched backward and dug her nails into Rebecca's shoulders. "Oh, God."

Gentle hands helped her untangle her feet from the jeans and step free. Feather light kisses and caresses created a trail of desire at once so sweet and so powerful that Dara wanted to weep. Never in her life had anything felt so right, and they'd barely begun.

Carefully, without a word, Rebecca guided her to the floor, sliding Dara underneath her as her thigh pressed into Dara's center.

Dara's heart stuttered at the look of naked adulation and love in Rebecca's eyes, and she recognized something she'd never seen with a lover before—the look was for her. Not the movie star, not the pretty face—simply her, with all her flaws and vulnerabilities. Tears filled her eyes.

"I love you, Dara Constance Darrow Thomas," Rebecca said softly. "I love everything about you."

Dara's lips trembled as Rebecca removed her panties and lowered herself to drink. There was nothing hurried or frenzied about it, just long, languid movements that told Dara she was cherished. She rose up to meet Rebecca, her hips rising and falling to the rhythm of Rebecca's tongue, until she crested on a whisper and a prayer.

She closed her eyes, savoring the moment, as Rebecca covered her with her body and kissed her deeply on the mouth. Never had lovemaking felt like this.

Rebecca's thigh insinuated itself once again between her legs, and Dara's body rocked against the long muscle. She'd never been capable of multiple orgasms.

"Oh. *Oh.*" Dara tried to swallow and catch her breath all at the same time, but it was impossible. Her hips arched up and she opened to accept Rebecca's delicate, delectable fingers as they curved up into her, creating waves of sensation that rolled through her, taking her out of her body to a place she'd never been before, and never knew existed.

When she came back into herself, Rebecca was smiling down at her, smoothing wisps of damp hair away from her face.

"Are you okay?"

"Mmm." Dara wanted to say more, but couldn't catch the words as they floated by. Instead, she wrapped her fingers around the back of Rebecca's neck and pulled her down for a thorough, soul-shaking kiss.

As she regained her equilibrium, Dara rolled them over until she was on top. With slow, deliberate movements, she teased and tested, probing for sensitive spots with her fingers and her tongue.

Rebecca's responsiveness nearly unraveled her again, but Dara resisted all attempts to distract her. She met Rebecca's gaze, locking onto the intensity and desire held within. And then she noticed something else—a razor's edge of fear.

"Are you okay? Is this—"

"I… Since Cynthia, I haven't been able to—"

"Shh," Dara soothed. "Stop talking. Stop thinking. And focus on me. Just me. There's no one else. No ghosts, no shadows. No broken promises. Just me, and you, and love. I promise you love." She bent her elbows so that their breasts brushed against one another, then settled her body more firmly on top of Rebecca and smoothed her hand down Rebecca's belly and in between her legs. *Oh, my God, babe. You're soaked.*

Dara rubbed gentle circles on Rebecca's swollen clit, rejoicing as she shuddered at the contact. Then she slid down, lifted Rebecca's hips, and ran her tongue through velvety folds, sampling the sweetness within.

"Oh, my God. Dara, please don't stop."

"Never." Dara tried to remember ever feeling more alive than she did at that moment. Rebecca levitated off the floor. Her back arched as she pushed her hips forward, seeking deeper contact. She came, calling Dara's name, the sound echoing off the glass doors.

After the last shudder, Rebecca grabbed for her with a fierceness that rocked Dara and nearly made her come again. For long moments, they held each other tightly, breathing heavily, sated and sure of the only thing that mattered right now—they both were loved.

ⰎⰎ

Rebecca propped herself up on an elbow to watch Dara as she slept. They made it to the bed in time for several more rounds of lovemaking and, exhausted, fell asleep in a tangle of arms and legs and soft sheets.

Now it was almost three o'clock, Dara had to be on set by five, and they still hadn't gone over the pages for today. Dara looked like an angel with her hair splayed across the pillow, and Rebecca couldn't bring herself to wake her.

So she slipped out of the bed and tiptoed out into the living room to find her clothes. They were strewn haphazardly near the doors to the deck, tangled together with Dara's tank top and bra.

Rebecca caught her reflection in the glass of the doors. Her hair was tousled and she looked as relaxed and sated as she felt. Could this be real? It certainly felt like it was. Multiple times during the night Dara had told her she loved her. Was that only about lust?

Well, it's certainly about a lot more than that for me. Rebecca had had her share of lovers over the years. Making love with them felt nothing like what happened between her and Dara last night. There was a balletic sensuality and an emotional richness to their lovemaking that pushed the experience far beyond lust. The night wasn't about having sex, as often was the case with first-time lovers, even if the relationships lasted well past that initial night. No, there was something far deeper at work here.

Or maybe we were just healing each other from past wounds. But Rebecca didn't think so.

She jumped and then relaxed as long arms wrapped around her from behind and soft lips kissed the juncture between her neck and shoulder.

"I didn't want to wake you."

"I missed you." Dara's body was warm from the bed and her nipples tightened against Rebecca's back.

Rebecca turned in the circle of Dara's arms and kissed her full on the mouth, reveling in the taste of her.

"You know we're going to have to make love again if you keep that up, right?"

"Mmm." Rebecca reluctantly relinquished Dara's mouth and instead ran her fingertips over her lips, her cheekbones, and her jaw line. "I want to tell you how beautiful you are, but I'm afraid you'll misconstrue my meaning."

Dara's eyes crinkled as she smiled and she shook her head. "Not coming from you. From you, it's heartfelt. I can see that in your eyes, and I can feel it here." Dara put a hand on Rebecca's heart.

"Yes, it is." Rebecca tucked a strand of hair behind Dara's ear. "I love you, Dara. I know I said it while we were making love, but I want you to know that I didn't just say that in the heat of the moment. I truly feel it and mean it from the bottom of my heart. Maybe it's too soon and you're not ready—"

Dara's mouth covered hers in a kiss that nearly stopped Rebecca's heart. Dara pulled back and gazed deep into Rebecca's eyes. "I love you, Rebecca. It's not too soon. It's about time. I feel like I've been waiting for you my entire life."

"I know I have." Rebecca felt the tears welling in her eyes and willed them not to spill over.

Dara caught one on her fingertip. "Why are you crying?"

"If anyone had ever told me I'd grow up to be loved by the most remarkable woman in the universe, I never would have believed it."

"You deserve every good thing. Why wouldn't you think you'd have it?"

"Do you remember at dinner the other night when Carolyn asked me why I wanted to become a professor? I said I had a hard time as a kid. That was a bit of an understatement. At school, I spent most of my time being pushed into walls, having my books knocked out of my hands, or cleaning graffiti off my locker."

"Oh, honey."

Rebecca held up a hand. "It's okay."

"No. It's not."

"You're right, it's not. What I mean to say is—that was a long time ago. Going to school frightened me. Every day brought more emotional and verbal abuse. There were days when I didn't think I wanted to go on anymore."

Dara gasped and pulled Rebecca closer, resting her head on her shoulder. "I'm so glad you chose to stay."

Rebecca swallowed hard. "Me too."

"Where were your parents in all this?"

"My dad died in a small plane crash when I was five. My mother's way of grieving was to lose herself in a bottle of booze."

"You were on your own all those years?"

"More or less. Yes."

"Oh, God. I'm sorry." Dara's voice caught on a sob. "I know exactly what that feels like."

"You do?"

"Mm-hmm. My parents had me late in life and let's just say they weren't too happy to have me around. I was meant to be seen and not heard."

Dara tensed in Rebecca's arms and Rebecca rubbed circles on her back. "I'm sorry." She knew there must be more to the story, but she didn't get the sense that Dara was ready to talk about it. *Tread carefully.* She thought about the story she'd read in the gossip rag at the airport terminal. "Your mom died pretty recently, right?"

"She did. I was her only child and my father already was dead, so it fell to me to be there. That's why I was in New York and why I was available to do the Letterman show."

"So, what you're saying is, I was a gift from your mother."

Dara straightened up. "What?"

"Your mother drew you to New York, otherwise you never would have come, right?"

"True."

"And if you hadn't come, you wouldn't have been on Letterman when I was in the audience."

"True."

"And if none of that had happened, I wouldn't have known who you were. Well, not the Constance part, anyway."

"Uh-huh."

"And you wouldn't have lobbied for the part on national television. Not that you wouldn't have gotten the part anyway, but who knows? Maybe if you didn't do that, the movie wouldn't have gotten made and I wouldn't be here now, standing in your arms, the only place I ever want to be from this moment to the end of time."

"Huh. Neatly done, Professor."

"In summary, then, your mother did you one last positive turn. Maybe bringing us together was her way of making amends for the way she treated you when she was alive. At least, that's how Celeste would look at it."

Dara seemed distracted for a moment, looking over Rebecca's shoulder.

Rebecca turned her head to look. "Something out there I should see?"

"Huh? Oh, no. Just the ghost of my mother agreeing with you." She winked.

Rebecca narrowed her eyes. "Why is it I believe you?"

Dara kissed her lightly. "Another story for another day. Right now," she took Rebecca's hand, "we have about half an hour to run lines and get me ready for today."

"You know I need to get dropped back at the condo so that I can shower and change clothes before you go to the set, right? Or I could take a cab there after you go to the set, since I don't have to be there until eight thirty this morning. I'll be okay to get to the studio on my own once I get to the condo. Apparently, I finally have my own car. I'm told it's in my driveway."

"Don't worry. I've got it all covered"—she stopped and pulled Rebecca in tight so that almost every part of them was touching— "except for you. Right now, all I want to do is cover you with my body."

Rebecca felt the stirrings deep in her belly. *Every day for the rest of our lives, if I have anything to say about it.*

✧✧

"Are you sure you want to do this?"

"Rebecca, this the fourth time you've asked me since we boarded the plane. We're cruising at 33,000 feet, halfway across the country. Don't you think it's a little late for me to rethink whether or not I want to come to Vermont with you?" All Dara wanted to do was to reach over and smooth the worry lines away from Rebecca's forehead. "I'm the one who had to talk you into letting me come along to pack up your things, remember?"

"I do, but you were in a weakened state at the time."

Rebecca smiled warmly and Dara knew exactly what she was thinking about. Following an early morning run on the beach, they'd just finished making love in the shower, when Rebecca reminded her that she would be heading to Middlebury on Friday to get the clothes and other items she would need for the three-month shoot.

Dara corralled her in the corner of the shower, boxing her in with her arms. "You're not going anywhere without me."

"It's only two nights."

"I don't care if it's two minutes. No can do." Since their first night of lovemaking, they hadn't spent a night apart all week.

"I need my clothes."

"Then I'm coming with you."

"What? You're crazy. The weekend is your only time off. I'll be back Sunday night."

"Not happening."

"You're not being reasonable."

"And you're not going anywhere without me." Dara had kissed her hard, setting off another round of lovemaking before they finally got clean and out of the shower.

Dara turned to stare out the window at the inky darkness. If she kept looking at Rebecca, she'd want to kiss her right here. She could just imagine the tabloid furor over that. Instead, she curled up with her head on the airplane pillow and closed her eyes.

"Hey. Hey, we're about to land." Dara was dimly aware of Rebecca shaking her. "Sleepy head. Time to get up."

"What?" She cracked an eye open. "We're here already?"

"Already? You've been asleep for hours."

Dara straightened up and put her seat back up. "It's a red-eye. You're supposed to sleep. What were you doing while I was doing the sensible thing?"

"I was script-doctoring. I figured it would be a good time to get ahead of next week's schedule."

"You did, did you?" Dara reached for Rebecca's laptop. "Are you going to let me see the pages?"

"Ah, ah." Rebecca playfully held the laptop out of reach. "All electronic devices must be turned off and stowed."

Dara loved that Rebecca couldn't stop staring at her lips as she pouted. She felt the first twinges of arousal and crossed her legs. How was it possible that she still couldn't get enough of Rebecca? They'd made love more times in a week than Dara had in a lifetime. With each successive round of lovemaking, Dara felt the pain of past betrayals fade into nothingness. In those precious moments of physical connection with Rebecca, she found emotional healing…a solace and a freedom she'd never known. Until now.

Dara thought about what her mother said about opening her heart to love. *I hope you're enjoying this, Mother.* And she knew her mother was. Not only had Dara seen her over Rebecca's shoulder the night she and Rebecca made love for the first time, she'd seen her two times in dreams since.

The re-emergence of her mediumship abilities was profoundly uncomfortable. How critical was it for her to share that piece of herself with Rebecca? Dara felt a wave of nausea at the mere thought of telling her. What would Rebecca make of her psychic gifts? What if it sent her running for the hills? Dara swallowed hard. She didn't have to tell her. At least not yet.

She poked Rebecca. "What's your friend's name again? The one who's picking us up?"

"Natalie. She's a history professor with a specialty in the Nixon years."

"And what does she know about us?"

"She knows that I'm working on the movie and she's a fan of your movies. She also knows all about my correspondence with Constance and that I was completely crushed out on the author."

Dara grinned. "Oh, you told her that, did you?"

"I didn't have to tell her. It was written all over my face."

"Does she know about the Letterman thing?"

There was a hitch in Rebecca's stride as they walked toward the airport exit. "No."

She said it so quietly, Dara had to strain to hear her.

"Dara, I meant what I said back then. I never told a soul. Not even my best friend. And I never would. Even if we don't end up working out, I would never say a word. I hope you know that by now and trust it."

Dara smoothed her hand down Rebecca's arm. "I do. I'm sorry. That was a stupid, thoughtless question."

"It's fine."

But Dara could tell that it wasn't. "I'm just nervous."

"Don't be," Rebecca said. "Natalie is good people and I haven't said a word about our status. We haven't discussed how you want to handle people knowing about your sexuality, or us, and I would never presume to speak for you or violate your privacy. As far as Natalie knows, we've just bonded and you volunteered to come help out a friend."

"Hey." Dara pulled them to a stop. "I'm really sorry. I trust you with my life and with my heart. If I could, I'd shout I love you from the rooftops for everyone to hear." Dara was cognizant of people pulling out their cell phones to snap pictures of her. She dropped her hand and lowered her voice. "Right now, that's not in either of our best interests."

"I'm okay with it, Dara." Rebecca started walking again and Dara followed. "I knew this wasn't going to be easy."

"Are you out at school?"

"Yes. I was very upfront about my sexuality before the college hired me. I wanted them to know what they were getting."

"You're far braver than I am."

"I'm in a far lower profile position than you are. And yes, I see that people are gawking at you and taking your picture. Do you want me to move farther away?"

"Absolutely not."

"Are you sure?"

"Positive."

"Well, here we go." Rebecca waved to someone as they emerged outside of security. "Hey."

"Hey, yourself, big shot."

"As if." Rebecca turned to Dara. "Dara Thomas, this is my BFF, Natalie. Natalie, meet my new West Coast BFF, Dara."

Natalie mimed being shot in the heart. "I'm so easily replaced. That totally sucks. On the other hand, it's incredibly cool." She shook Dara's hand. "Thank you for taking good care of my friend. Rebecca's special."

"I know that." Dara tried to keep any hint of intimacy and love out of her voice.

"And besides," Natalie said as she clapped Rebecca on the arm, "it's only for a few months, right?"

Dara's knees wobbled momentarily and she very nearly stumbled. *Oh, God, please let this be forever. I don't know how I could go back to living without Rebecca.*

"What happened at the faculty meeting this morning?" Rebecca asked. Dara was heartened that she changed the topic, deliberately ignoring Natalie's comment.

"Your distance learning experiment was the talk of the town. Everybody's buzzing about what a breakthrough it is for the college. Of course, Alistar is taking full credit for it."

"Of course."

"Seriously, this is big. And your sitting in on the class the other morning blew up all over social media on campus," Natalie said to Dara. "That was major."

"The kids were cute and asked intelligent questions," Dara said.

They spent the rest of the nearly hour-long drive from Burlington to Middlebury chatting amiably about nothing of consequence. It was obvious to Dara that Rebecca had warned Natalie not to pester her with a lot of questions about Hollywood or her personal life. *Remind me to kiss you later. As if I wasn't going to do that anyway.*

"Here we are," Natalie said, as she pulled into a driveway.

"Wow. This is gorgeous." And Dara meant it. The shrubbery and flowers were vibrant and lush, the rolling lawn was perfectly cut, and a wrap-around porch surrounded the house. A couple of Adirondack chairs situated side by side near the front door rounded out the perfection.

"Thanks. It's home." Rebecca leaned over and kissed Natalie on the cheek. "Thanks for coming to get us."

"You're welcome. Miss you. Don't be a stranger and think about my invitation to dinner tonight."

"We'll consider it. Honestly, there's so little time and so much to pack. I'll let you know."

"It was very nice to meet you, Natalie. Thanks for the ride," Dara said as she got out of the car.

"Are you kidding? The pleasure was all mine. If I don't see you again, good luck with the movie, though I know you won't need it."

"And that's as close to a fan girl as you're allowed to get, my friend," Rebecca said, as she tugged on Dara's arm, closed the car door, and stepped back.

"C'mon," Rebecca said, as Natalie drove away. "If we stay out here, the neighbors are going to get a helluva show." She unlocked the front door and let them inside.

"Okay. I'll let you have your way this once," Dara teased. "But after that we're getting to work. The faster we get you packed up, the more time we have to...explore." She waggled her eyebrows suggestively.

"Exactly."

CHAPTER TWENTY-THREE

Rebecca rolled over and gently pulled Dara to her, kissing her shoulder.

Dara stirred. "What time is it?"

"Shh. Go back to sleep. It's the middle of the night." She stroked Dara's silky hair. *How is it possible that three months could fly by so quickly? I'm not ready.*

Dara leaned up on one elbow and ran her fingers along Rebecca's collarbone. "Why are you up?"

"No reason." Rebecca's voice broke.

"Sweetheart? What is it?" Dara turned to face her fully. "What's going on?"

"Nothing. Really."

"This doesn't feel like nothing." Dara put a hand over Rebecca's heart. "Talk to me."

Rebecca kissed her softly. "After today..." She cleared her throat. "After today, everything changes. When the movie wraps at the end of the day, my work here is done. They're sending me home." She could barely say the last word.

Dara sat up against the headboard and fluffed a pillow behind her back. She beckoned for Rebecca to join her and Rebecca settled into the crook of her arm. "If you want this as badly as I do, we'll make it work."

"I want this," Rebecca indicated their entwined bodies, "and you, more than anything in the world."

"Then we'll be fine." Dara ran a palm up and down Rebecca's arm.

Rebecca wanted to muster up the same confidence Dara had, but old insecurities crept in. "You'll be here finishing up the

253

voice-overs on the picture and I'll be back in Vermont teaching the next batch of students all about Constance Darrow."

"We have Skype and there's this nifty little invention called the airplane. Maybe you've heard of it?" Dara kissed her on the forehead.

"I've heard vague rumbles about a piece of metal that could fly like a bird."

"I'm here to tell you it can. And I'll be testing out the technology as often as I can."

"Will you now?"

"You know I will." Dara nibbled on Rebecca's lower lip and pulled it into her mouth.

As always happened, Rebecca was instantly wet and ready. "You unravel me."

"I love you, Rebecca."

Rebecca's heart soared. "I love you, Dara."

The lovemaking was slow and sweet. The poignancy of it filled Rebecca to overflowing.

"I've got a five-thirty makeup call." Dara said eventually, her thigh still pressed against Rebecca's center.

"I know."

"Why don't you go back to sleep, babe? You don't have to be on set until eight thirty and there's no class today."

"Nah-ah. The bed's not the same without you in it." Rebecca slid down and ran her tongue around Dara's swollen clit.

"Oh." Dara's hand found the back of Rebecca's head and held her firmly in place.

Rebecca reveled in the taste and smell of her and the delicious sounds Dara made—sounds that resonated throughout her being and took up residence in her heart. *Please, God, let me always have this in my life. Let me always have Dara in my life.*

"What's next for you, Celeste?"

Dara smiled wanly at Sam, who was doing a masterful job of infusing Harold's words and expressions with just the right combination of sadness and pride.

It was the last scene in the book and the movie. When Dara wrote it, she meant it to represent a divergence of paths, the two characters having learned the life lessons they were intended to learn from each other and now ready to let go of each other and their pasts and move on.

The original version of the movie script failed to capture the essence of the scene. But Rebecca—Rebecca's version was sensitive, deeply moving, and perfect.

Dara summoned up the tears the scene called for. It wasn't hard, as they'd been near the surface all day. As much as Dara had put a positive face on it, today was heart wrenching for her. For the first time in her career, she wanted to bring someone to the wrap party. She wanted to tell the world how in love she was with the most extraordinary woman in the world. But she couldn't do it and not just because outing herself was bad business.

If she confirmed that she and Rebecca were an item, it would raise questions about whether Rebecca slanted the script to benefit Dara in any way, and whether Dara had pushed for Cal's firing in order to promote Rebecca. Dara wasn't willing to allow Rebecca's integrity to come into question.

I love you, Rebecca. I wish with all my heart I could tell the world that my heart belongs to you. The tears spilled over for real. "I'm not sure, Harold. I wish I could see that far ahead. The only thing I can say for certain is that, wherever I go, I'll carry you and our friendship in my heart." Dara leaned forward and kissed Sam on the cheek. "You changed my life. You taught me what it means to care about something larger than myself, and I'll never forget that. Goodbye, my friend, and Godspeed."

"Goodbye, Celeste. Wherever your journey takes you, know that you made a real difference in this old man's life and I'll be forever grateful." Sam raised his hand slowly and held it up in a weak wave as Dara's Celeste rose from the same park bench where Celeste and Harold first met and walked away into the distance.

When Dara had taken about ten steps, George called out, "Cut! Print it, and that's a wrap everybody!"

The set erupted in applause. Dara took a moment to compose herself. Her hands were shaking.

"Are you okay?" Sam came alongside her and put an arm around her shoulder.

"I am if you are." Dara sniffed.

"It's been a true pleasure working with you these past few months. You're a consummate pro, Dara. I hope we get the opportunity again."

"Likewise, Sam." She kissed him on the cheek.

"See you at the party?"

"You bet." She wiped away a tear. Thank God the last scene involved deep emotion. Otherwise, she wasn't sure how she would've gotten through it.

Dara stood on her tiptoes, searching, seeking for Rebecca in the crowd. Before she could find her, more people crowded around her. George gave her a warm hug.

"That was great stuff. Great work. I can't wait to direct you again."

"Thank you, George. I look forward to it."

"Nice going, Dara. It was a pleasure to work with you."

"Thank you, Audrey. You too." With a sinking feeling, Dara conceded that finding the one face, the one person she most wanted to see in all the chaos, would have to wait.

⋘⋙

Dara was besieged with well-wishers. Rebecca was so proud of her. It was a bravura performance; one she hoped very much would win Dara an Oscar. If only she could tell her so. Instead, Rebecca shoved her hands in her pockets and walked off the soundstage and out into the fading sunlight of a Hollywood evening.

"Rebecca! Rebecca, wait!"

Rebecca turned to see Sam hustling toward her.

"I'm so glad I caught you."

"Congratulations, Sam. You were masterful."

"Thank you, my dear. The point is and the reason I'm chasing you down like a dirty old man, which I am not for the record, is to tell you that none of it would've been possible without you."

Rebecca blushed. "That's awfully kind of you to say."

"I'm not blowing smoke here. I read Darrow's book. I loved it. It's why I signed on in the first place, before I even saw the treatment. Then I saw the script, and although I was dismayed, I hoped the material was better than it looked on paper. It wasn't. At least not until you came in and brought Darrow's book into it. Now, we've made a movie I believe we all should be very, very proud of. And you're a big part of that."

"I don't know what to say."

"Say thank you and promise me you'll come to the wrap party."

"I don't know, Sam. We'll see."

"I assure you, it's a once-in-a-lifetime experience."

"I'm sure it is."

"Rebecca." George joined them.

"Well, this is my cue to exit stage left," Sam said. He gave her a kiss on the cheek. "Come to the party," he whispered, and then he walked away.

"Before you disappear into the sunset or get buried under a snowdrift in the northeast," George said, "I just want to say how impressed I am with your work. For someone with no experience in this business to walk in under these circumstances and do what you did—well, that's mighty rare. You have my admiration and respect."

"Thank you, George. And thank you for your kindness and patience in helping me through the learning curve. Working on this movie is an experience I'll always treasure."

"When do you leave for Vermont?"

"In the morning."

"Going home in time for Christmas, eh?"

"More like going home in time to administer finals before Christmas break."

George laughed. "In which case, I'm sure you'll be very popular with your students."

"Or not," Rebecca replied. "Thank you for this opportunity, George. It's been a great honor."

"Who knows," George shrugged, "maybe we'll do it again sometime." He patted her on the shoulder. "Anyway, I didn't want to let you slip away without expressing my gratitude."

"Thank you, George."

With a wave he was gone, leaving Rebecca alone again. She glanced back hopefully in the direction of the soundstage door. Dara was nowhere to be seen, so she continued on to her trailer to pack up her things.

"Oh, my God. What's this?" On the desk were dozens of the most gorgeous red and white roses she'd ever seen. They took up every available inch of space. Rebecca inhaled their scent and opened the envelope that came with them.

Darling,

The beauty of these roses pales in comparison to your exquisiteness. There are ninety roses here. One for every day of making magic with you.

I love you with all my heart. Now and forevermore, I am yours.

Dara

"Oh, sweetheart. I love you, Dara."

"I'm sorry. Could you say that again, once more with feeling?"

Rebecca whipped around toward the door to see Dara standing there, framed in the last vestiges of daylight. From this angle, it appeared that she had a halo around her head.

Rebecca threw herself into Dara's arms just as Dara managed to get the door closed. "I love you. I love you. I love you. So much more than words can say. I am yours. Now and always."

"Now that's what I love to hear."

"What are you doing here? You've got to get to the party."

"No party, in fact, nothing in the world, could be more important than being right here with you, right now."

"Sweetheart, you're expected. You're the star. You have to show up."

"I will. But not before I properly thank you." Dara kissed Rebecca breathless. "Thank you for fulfilling all of my dreams, both personal and professional. Thank you for coming into my life and restoring my faith in love. Thank you for being the most amazing person I've ever met."

"I am so grateful for you. You've made my every wish, my every whispered hope, come true. I am so blessed to have you in my life." Rebecca buried her hands in Dara's hair. When their mouths met again, the feeling was electric. "Wait," Rebecca said, as Dara moved them toward the futon. Rebecca's blouse was halfway unbuttoned. "Wait."

Dara stilled her hands. The desire in her eyes nearly cleaved Rebecca in two.

"You really do need to go to the party. If you're late, it will look horrible."

"Damn you for being practical." Dara smiled.

"I know. Also, before we get lost in each other again, a common phenomenon any time we're alone, I want to say something."

"Okay." Dara sat on the edge of the futon.

"You know I had a crush on Constance long before I ever got here."

"No secret there."

"Let me finish." Rebecca quickly kissed Dara and then danced out of reach. "But being here, watching Dara work, has been nothing short of life-changing. Your performance in this movie was so far off the charts I don't even have the superlatives to describe it."

In a rarity, Dara blushed.

"Never in my life have I met anyone with so many skills, so many talents, so many attributes, so much grace and beauty, inside and out."

"You're a little biased, you know."

"Not this time." Rebecca shook her head. "Honestly, Dara, if you don't win an Oscar for this performance…"

"Shh." Dara rose again and pulled Rebecca into her arms. "We don't talk about those kinds of things. It's bad luck."

"I didn't peg you for superstitious."

"I'm not, really. I'd just rather focus on us. On this. Our time together is so precious. I want to spend every moment loving you."

"Then hurry up and go to the party, already. I'll be waiting at home for you." Rebecca kissed her thoroughly once more and resettled Dara's hair. She stepped back. "Thank God for movie-grade lipstick that never moves. Thank you, Zip."

"Okay," Dara said, and kissed Rebecca one more time. "I'm really going now."

Rebecca pushed her playfully toward the door. "Go. I'll just be getting a crane to get these flowers back to the house. I'll probably still be unloading them by the time you get home."

⤚⥲

Rebecca closed her eyes and inhaled the scent of the dozen fresh roses on the coffee table. *I miss you so much it's a physical ache, babe.* She opened her eyes to evaluate the fully decorated Christmas tree in her living room one last time. She'd debated whether to keep her tradition of trimming the tree the night before Christmas. Her heart wasn't in it this year, with Dara stuck all the way across the country. Still, tradition was tradition...

The sound of carolers outside the door drew Rebecca to the window. They approached, carrying candles to light their way. It was a uniquely beautiful Christmas Eve sight, especially with the light dusting of snow.

The carolers, well insulated from the cold with heavy parkas, face scarves, hats, and gloves, were singing *Hark the Herald Angels*, one of her favorites. Rebecca opened the front door before they rang the bell. The melodic sounds of a dozen voices raised in harmony wafted into the night air and Rebecca clapped her hands in delight.

As the last notes of the song died away, one of the group called out, "Merry Christmas, Professor."

Rebecca tried to see if she could recognize anyone, but the many layers of clothing made it impossible. "Merry Christmas to all of you. Thank you for making my night."

The group moved away, but one person from the middle of the pack stayed behind.

When the person said nothing, Rebecca asked, "Do you need something? A hot drink? A bathroom?"

The person stepped forward, closer to the porch light, shedding a hat and face scarf as she went. "What I need is you."

Rebecca opened her mouth to speak, but what came out was a squeak.

"Can I come in?"

Rebecca stepped aside and mutely trailed behind Dara. As the door clicked closed, strong arms lifted her off the floor, spun her around, and set her back down.

"I love you so much. I couldn't bear for us to be apart on Christmas." Dara threw the hat and scarf on the floor and struggled out of her gloves and heavy jacket.

"How did you—" The rest of the question was swallowed up in a tangle of tongues, moans, and hammering hearts.

"I love you." Tears swam in Dara's eyes. They mirrored the moisture Rebecca felt on her own cheeks.

"I love you too."

Hand in hand they went to stand in front of the Christmas tree.

"It's gorgeous, and it smells good." Dara took a deep breath in.

"Douglas fir. After all, I live in the land of Christmas trees. Do you really like it?"

"I love it." Dara squeezed her hand. "But there's something missing."

"What?" Rebecca's stomach dropped.

"Hold on a second." Dara let go of her hand and walked out the front door. Curious, Rebecca followed. Dara was rooting around behind the bushes that bordered the porch.

"What are you looking for?"

"This." Dara returned with a wrapped present and an overnight bag.

"How did you...? When did you...?"

"I'm sure there's a question in there somewhere just dying to get out." Dara laughed. "Now can we go back inside? It's f-freezing out here."

When they were safely back inside, Dara placed the present under the tree.

Rebecca stared at it for several moments.

"No cheating. I can see that you want to shake it. Don't. That would be cheating."

"But..."

"Nope."

"Can I open it tonight?"

"Would you rather open the present tonight or open me tonight?" Dara's voice was a seductive purr.

"Um. Uh." Heat suffused Rebecca's cheeks and radiated downward throughout her body. "Can I have both?"

"Oh. Greedy, greedy, greedy. But if you open this tonight, what will you open tomorrow morning?"

"I'll worry about that tomorrow."

"Very well." Dara retrieved the large box from under the tree and handed it to Rebecca. For the first time, she seemed to notice the fire crackling in the fireplace. "How about in front of that?"

"Sure. Hang on." Rebecca put the present down and retrieved a couple of couch cushions and a blanket. She laid them out on the floor and patted one of the cushions for Dara to sit on.

When they were fully situated, Rebecca examined the package, looking at it from all sides.

"Have any guesses?"

"Not a clue." The box was light, but big.

"Don't you dare shake it. That would be cheating. Just open it."

"Okay." Rebecca teased the tape from the corners and eased it off without ripping the paper.

Dara impatiently drummed her fingers on the floor. "I should've known you'd be one of those."

"One of what?"

"A careful opener."

"I'm just savoring the experience."

"Of course you are."

Rebecca continued to worry at the tape until the paper fell away. Inside was a large plain shipping box. She got up and retrieved a pocketknife with which to slit open the packing tape. When she looked inside the box, there was another wrapped box.

"Oh, my God. You've got to be kidding me."

"The way you're going about this, it'll take all night. If you ever want to unwrap this present," Dara indicated herself, "you'd better speed it up."

The admonition was sufficient incentive for Rebecca to slice through the next round of wrapping paper to reveal yet another box, and then another.

"There is a real present in here, right?"

"Patience is a virtue. I promise you'll be rewarded."

Three boxes later, Rebecca finally held something in her hand that didn't feel like a box. She hefted it experimentally.

"Open it carefully."

"Okay." Rebecca slit the tape and gently smoothed the paper away. "Oh, my. Is this...?" She looked at Dara for confirmation and Dara nodded, her eyes gleaming.

Reverently, Rebecca turned it over in her hands and ran her fingertips over the surface of the raised letters. The book jacket read: *Love Above All Else*, a novel by Pulitzer Prize-winner Constance Darrow.

"This is only a review copy. The actual finished retail version won't be out until—"

"February 14th. I know." Rebecca caressed the cover. "I don't know what to say."

"Open it." Dara scooted closer until their shoulders and hips were touching. She eased the hardcover open and skipped past the first few pages. When she let go, Rebecca could see that the book was open to the dedication page. "Read it."

Rebecca read the writing centered in the middle of the page.

To the world's preeminent Constance Darrow scholar, Professor Rebecca Minton. Thanks for challenging me always to be my very best. Your loyal fan, Constance Darrow

"Oh." Rebecca put trembling fingers to her mouth and tears sprang to her eyes. She tried to focus on the words as she reread them. She sought Dara's eyes, which glittered in the reflected light of the fire.

"Do you like it, darling?"

"L-like it? I'm speechless. Did you really..." She read the words again. "I can't... I don't..."

"I love you, Rebecca." Dara lifted the book from Rebecca's limp fingers, closed it, and set it aside. "Now, if you don't mind too terribly much, I'd like to unwrap my gift." Slowly, with painstaking care, she unbuttoned Rebecca's shirt and peeled it off, followed seconds later by her bra, shoes, and socks. Finally, Dara unzipped Rebecca's pants and removed them, along with the lace panties.

When Rebecca was completely naked, Dara raked her eyes over her body. "Now that's what I call the perfect Christmas present."

CHAPTER TWENTY-FOUR

O pen it." Dara vibrated with excitement. She nudged the small wrapped box toward Rebecca.

"Now?" Rebecca asked. She sat in front of the large makeup mirror and put the finishing touches on her makeup. "I've never been to a big movie premiere. I don't want to be late."

"I promise you, we won't be late. The limos won't even be here for another twenty minutes."

"Surely this can wait."

Dara caught Rebecca's reflection in the mirror. "At Christmastime you couldn't wait to open your present. Now you want to get all shy on me?"

"What's the rush?"

"You're going to need what's in the box to complete your outfit for tonight."

"I am?"

"Absolutely." *And if you don't hurry up and open it, I swear, I'll open it for you.* "You look perfect." Dara wrapped her fingers around Rebecca's hand and stopped her as she tried to apply lip gloss on top of her lipstick. Her eyes pleaded. "Open it, please."

Rebecca put down the gloss and picked up the box.

By now, Dara was used to the care with which Rebecca did everything. She stifled the urge to bounce on the balls of her feet. Finally, she could stand it no more.

Dara leaned over and kissed Rebecca's fingers as she pried them off the box. She ripped off the paper to reveal an elegant black velvet jewelry box, which she palmed as she swiveled Rebecca to face her.

Dara turned the box toward Rebecca and opened it. "Rebecca Minton, I have waited all my life for you and I want to spend the rest of my days walking hand-in-hand with you by my side. Please, Rebecca. Will you marry me?"

"Will I...?" Surprise registered on Rebecca's face, then she looked down at the open box and back up at Dara. She opened her mouth to speak, but no words came out. She put a trembling hand to her heart.

"Will you marry me, sweetheart?"

"I—" Rebecca's voice shook. "You're all I ever wanted. You're all I'll ever need. Yes. Yes, I will marry you. Absolutely, yes."

"Yes?" Tears streamed down Dara's face and she thought vaguely that she would have to fix her own makeup.

"Oh, yes." Rebecca rose up and wrapped her arms around Dara's waist, kissing her deeply. With their lips still touching she repeated. "Yes. Yes. Yes."

Dara pulled back from the circle of Rebecca's arms, carefully removed the 3-carat diamond ring from its velvet nest, and slipped it onto Rebecca's left ring finger. It fit perfectly and Dara said a silent prayer of thanks.

"Now you can add the lip gloss." Dara grinned broadly.

"Not just yet." Rebecca kissed her again.

Mindful of the time, Dara extricated herself. "You're the one who was worried about being late."

"Right. Do I need a wrap?

"We won't be outside long. Besides, I like looking at your hot body." And Rebecca did look hot in an elegant Versace gown with a plunging neckline and an open "V" back. She ran her fingertips over Rebecca's exposed skin. "Are you sure you're okay riding in a separate limo with Carolyn?"

"We've been over this, sweetheart. It makes perfect sense for me to arrive with Carolyn. This is your moment on the carpet. The paparazzi are going to go wild. You've never arrived at a premiere with a date. Now is not a good time to break precedence."

Dara frowned. She knew Rebecca was right, but she didn't like it. A car horn sounded at the gate and she entered the code to let the limos in. Then she sat down and repaired her makeup. "How do I look?"

"Like a glamorous Hollywood movie star," Rebecca said, encircling her waist from behind.

"Always good to look the part."

"You don't need to play a part, darling. You are the part. You look amazing. As always, you take my breath away."

Dara waggled her eyebrows. "Oh, no. Not yet. I'm planning to do that later."

"I sincerely hope so."

Dara answered the knock on the door to admit Carolyn.

"Wow. You two look incredible." Carolyn's eyes traveled down and settled on Rebecca's finger. She looked from Rebecca to Dara and back again. "Something you want to share?"

Dara shoved her toward the door. "Rebecca can tell you all about it in the car on the way to the theater."

Dozens of flashes erupted and television camera klieg lights lit up the evening as the driver opened the door to the limo. Rebecca, whose limo had arrived minutes earlier to no fanfare, watched from a safe distance at the entrance doors to the famed Grauman's Chinese Theater, now the TCL Chinese Theater. "Who sells naming rights to one of the greatest landmarks in the history of Hollywood?" Rebecca idly mumbled.

Dara stepped out of the car with the help of the driver, revealing a long expanse of leg. Somehow, she managed to glide flawlessly down the red carpet, although Rebecca imagined that the lights must be blinding her. Microphones were shoved in her face. And she paused a few feet from the entrance to chat with a television reporter.

"This is *Entertainment Tonight*, coming to you this Friday evening, May 17, 2013, from the much-hyped premiere of *On the Wings of Angels*. With me is the star of the film, Dara Thomas. Dara, there's already Oscar buzz around this film, including the possibility of a Best Actress nod for you. What do you think about that?"

Dara smiled dazzlingly. "I think we ought to at least see the movie first, don't you?" She nodded graciously to the reporter and took a few more turns while posing for all the cameras, then she was whisking past Rebecca and Carolyn. Surreptitiously, she brushed her fingers against Rebecca's thigh on the way by.

Rebecca shuddered, then turned and followed behind at a safe distance.

She and Carolyn found seats a few rows behind Dara, Sam, George, and the studio executives.

"Are you nervous?" Carolyn whispered.

"About the movie or the engagement?" Rebecca whispered back.

Carolyn laughed. "Both, I guess."

"If you're asking if I'm sure I want to marry her, the answer is I'm more sure of that than my own name."

Carolyn smiled. "I'm so happy for both of you. She was a wreck, you know. I don't think I've ever seen her that panicked, except for maybe when we pulled up outside my place and she learned she was going to have to come face-to-face with you the day the studio brought you in."

Rebecca allowed her puzzlement to show. "Why in the world would she be nervous about asking me to marry her?"

"I think she wasn't sure you'd say yes."

"You're kidding, right?"

"Not in the least."

"How could she not know that?"

"She hates that she can't hold your hand in public, or proclaim you her fiancée. She doesn't want you to have to hide the relationship, either. It's not fair to you and she doesn't want to saddle you with a life like that. She knows it'll be hard."

"It's already complicated and hard. But I understand. Right now the timing is just wrong. I don't have a problem with it."

"But she does. Don't you see? It eats her up inside. It never bothered her before not to say anything about her sexuality because there was nothing to say. It wasn't like she was dating anyone. It was a non-issue. Now, she wants to be who she is. She's incredibly proud of you."

"And if our relationship had come about under different circumstances, she'd be holding my hand right here in this theater, but it's too complicated and too easily misconstrued."

Two women hugged Carolyn and sat down in the two seats she'd been saving. "So glad you two could make it."

"Are you kidding? We were thrilled to get the invite from Dara."

"Let me do the introductions here. Renée Maupin, Yahzi Begay, this is Rebecca Minton. Rebecca, this is Renée and Yahzi."

"How do you do?"

"Nice to meet you both."

"Renée grew up with Dara and me. Yahzi is her wife."

"Ah. Then it's truly a pleasure to meet you." Rebecca turned to Carolyn. "Does this mean I get to hear all about what you and Dara were like as kids?"

As Rebecca pretended to rub her hands together in glee, the next teasing question died on her lips. Renée was looking at Carolyn with something akin to panic. Rebecca leaned close to Carolyn and whispered, "I'm sorry, did I ask something I shouldn't have?"

Just as Carolyn was about to answer her, the lights started to dim.

"I'll explain later."

"It really is nice to meet you," Rebecca said quickly to Renée and then her focus turned fully to the screen.

Her stomach did a flip. As she'd told Carolyn, she wasn't nervous about marrying Dara, far from it, but seeing the movie for the first time was a completely different matter.

Dara had seen the Director's Cut back in late January, but that was just a preliminary version shown to a select audience to gage what more needed to be done to get the picture ready for wide release. And no matter how Rebecca tried to wheedle the information out of her, Dara wouldn't tell her what she thought of the first screening.

Next week, the film would open around the country. The box office from that first weekend was crucial to determine how well the film was received by the public. The studio had been promoting the movie heavily, and Dara was scheduled to do *The Tonight Show with Jimmy Fallon* on Tuesday. Reviews from advance press screenings would appear in the *LA Times*, *Variety*, *The New York Times*, and dozens of other newspapers and online outlets in conjunction with next weekend's opening.

Rebecca's knees started to bob up and down, a sure sign of stress. There was so much riding on all of this.

Then the theater went completely dark and the opening credits rolled and she lost herself in the world of Celeste and Harold. It was all there on the big screen, everything she dreamed and hoped it would be. Tears streamed down her face as the music swelled and Celeste walked away from Harold for the last time.

When the house lights came back up, the theater was completely silent. Rebecca closed her eyes as her heart sank. And then it started. First it was a wave of applause, then whistles, and finally a standing ovation. She sprang to her feet along with everyone else, yelling, "Bravo, bravo!"

She watched as Dara, Sam, and George turned to face the audience, joined hands, and took a bow. Rebecca's heart burst with pride.

Then Dara looked directly at her, her eyes glistening with tears, her smile radiant, and they might have been the only two people in the room. She mouthed, "Thank you."

Rebecca gave a small nod of acknowledgment and blushed, understanding that the words came not only from Dara, but from Constance, as well. *How on Earth did I get so lucky?*

"How did I get so lucky?" Dara stroked the side of Rebecca's breast.

"Is that a rhetorical question?" Rebecca turned toward Dara and pulled her on top, running her fingers over the supple skin of Dara's back.

"You know we don't have time to make love again, right?"

"Uh-huh." Rebecca kissed her shoulder.

"Sweetheart, how bad would it look if you missed the faculty processional at graduation and I was late to the podium to receive my honorary Doctor of Arts?"

"Killjoy."

Rebecca pulled Dara's lower lip into her mouth one more time, and Dara's insides melted again. She rolled to the other side of the bed before anything more happened.

"What are you doing all the way over there?"

"You're the one with a king size bed. Why do you have such a big bed, anyway?"

"Saves on having to have more bedroom furniture."

Dara laughed. "Ah, very sneaky."

"You know, if you came out as Constance today you could get a two-fer."

"Oh? How so?"

"A Doctor of Arts for Dara and a Doctor of Letters for Constance. How cool would that be?"

Dara reached over and mussed Rebecca's hair. "You've lost it."

"Come on. It's genius."

"Hey, genius," Dara said, turning serious. "Have I told you today how much I love you?"

"I love you too, baby."

"When we were sitting in the theater last week and the audience reacted so strongly at the end of the movie, all I wanted was to tell the world that the movie was only that good because you fixed the script."

"I wasn't up there on the screen, darling. You and Sam were phenomenal. It was pure magic."

Dara cupped Rebecca's cheek and choked back a sob. "Thank you, for bringing Constance's vision to life. I don't know what I would have done if I had to go through with making the movie Cal wrote. It was breaking my heart."

"I know. I could see that. It's why I fought so hard for the changes."

"You know I was listening to that entire exchange, right?"

"What exchange?"

"The one that very first day between you, George, and Cal. I was ready to jump up and rip Cal's throat out."

"You were, eh?"

"I really was. I was so proud of you for standing your ground."

Rebecca shrugged. "Constance needed to be heard. I was her voice."

"That's what you were thinking?"

"It was."

"Wow. Just, wow. After the way I treated you the night before—"

"We're not going there, sweetheart. Let's stay right here, in this moment, where I'm lying in bed naked and well loved by my gorgeous, indescribably talented fiancée, who is about to receive an honorary doctorate from my college. How proud am I?"

"You know, there's something I never told you."

"I'm guessing there are a lot of things you've never told me."

Dara's breath caught and a wave of guilt washed over her. She flashed back to a recent discussion with Carolyn.

"You can't let her marry you and not tell her about the rest of who you are. You have to tell her you see and talk to dead people."

"I will tell her. I promise."

"When?"

"Not right now. When the time is right."

"You have a love child stashed somewhere?"

"What?" Dara shook herself from the reverie. "Very funny." Dara swatted Rebecca lightly on the arm. "I'm serious."

"Okay. What is it?"

"Many years ago, when I was a young, aspiring writer and just before my acting career took off, I applied to attend the Bread Loaf Writers' Conference."

"You... What?!"

"I applied to Bread Loaf."

"As Constance?"

"No." Dara shook her head. "Constance didn't exist back then. Dara Thomas applied."

"You're serious."

"I am."

"Did you go?"

"I would've, except they rejected me."

"They..." Rebecca paused and cocked her head to the side. "I'm sorry. I could've sworn you said they rejected you."

"That's because they did."

Rebecca sat straight up. "Middlebury College's Bread Loaf Writers' Conference rejected Constance Darrow's application?"

"No." Dara drew the word out. "They rejected Dara Thomas's application."

"Same writer. Same talent. Of all the moronic, idiotic... Oh, my God. Do they know they did it?"

"You mean is there a record of it?"

"Yes."

Dara shrugged. "I have no idea what kind of record keeping they do on applications they turn down." Dara could see Rebecca's wheels spinning.

"What was your writing like back then? Do you remember what you sent them?"

"Why?"

"Please tell me you didn't send them anything that eventually ended up being published under Constance's name."

"Oh." Dara hadn't considered that. If something like that ever came to light, either Dara would have to come out as Constance or be accused of plagiarism either as Constance or Dara. What a mess that would be.

"No. I was so distraught about being turned down that I was convinced my writing was horrible. I burned what I sent them in a ritual in my backyard. As far as I know, I never kept a copy of it."

"Thank God," Rebecca said.

"You know, when I received your very first letter, I remember saying out loud that I wouldn't hold a grudge against you just because your school gave me the cold shoulder."

"I'm very glad you didn't hold me responsible. Especially since I wasn't here at the time." Rebecca kissed Dara's forehead. "How ironic that now they want to give you an honorary degree. Guess you get the last laugh."

"Guess I do, but I don't think I'll be telling them the story any time soon."

"No. I'd recommend against that." Rebecca glanced at the bedside clock. "And now we really do have to get going."

"Last day of school, Professor."

"Last day of school, and I get to spend my summer vacation with you."

"Perfect. Care to shower with me?"

"Always. Very environmentally friendly and I hear this is that kind of campus."

On the way to the bathroom and with her conversation with Carolyn still top of mind, Dara considered and discarded a half dozen opening lines to ease into the discussion about her childhood. Somehow, the time just didn't seem right. *I'll tell her soon; maybe over the summer when we don't have any distractions.*

CHAPTER TWENTY-FIVE

They were on time in the end, just barely. Rebecca marched in wearing her hood and robe with the other professors and Dara, having marched in at the front of the parade with the other degree recipients, got to watch. She sighed contentedly from her spot on the stage. She could see Rebecca beaming at her from the left side front row when she collected her hood and degree. *Thank God I didn't trip.*

After eight months together, she had to pinch herself every now and again to trust that this was real. To think that she found the one person in the world who saw her completely for herself... It was more than she believed she'd ever have and all that she knew she'd ever want. *I love you, Rebecca Minton. I can't wait to marry you.*

She can't see you completely for yourself until you show her all of you.

Dara started as she heard her mother's voice in her head. "Oh, my God. Not now, Mother," she mumbled.

You can't keep putting it off. She deserves to know.

Panic began to bloom in Dara's chest.

"Are you coming?"

"I'm sorry, what?"

"The band is playing our song," one of the other honorees said.

When Dara glanced around, she realized the recessional was about to start and she needed to parade out. When the recessional ended, she searched for Rebecca. Along the way, she signed many autographs for new graduates and their parents.

"I'm sorry. I need to go find someone," she said, apologizing to the now rather large throng of autograph seekers.

"Looking for me?"

Dara turned to see Rebecca leaning against the tree to her right, watching her. "As a matter of fact, Professor, I was."

"Walk this way. I promise to protect you from the mob." Rebecca winked.

As they ambled across the verdant lawn, someone called out to them. "Dara! Rebecca! Wait."

Dara pulled them up short. "I could swear that sounded like Carolyn."

"Nah." Rebecca urged them forward.

"Wait, damn it!"

"Definitely Carolyn," Dara said. She pivoted in the direction of the voice. Indeed, it was her best friend.

"My God, I thought you'd never stop." Carolyn put her hands on her knees, catching her breath.

"What in the world are you doing here?" Dara asked.

"It was easier to drive up here from New York than it was to fly to LA to see you tomorrow."

"Why would you need to do either?" Rebecca asked reasonably. "Doesn't your phone work?"

"Very funny. You can't sign something over the phone."

"Sign something?"

"What am I signing that's important enough to make you drive almost six hours to bring it to me?" Dara asked.

"Never mind that," Rebecca chimed in. "If you just drove up now you had to start at the crack of dawn. What's going on?"

"Business is going on. Is there somewhere we can talk?"

Dara looked to Rebecca. "Sure. We can either go to my place, or I can treat you both to lunch at Mr. Up's. If we hustle, we can beat the bulk of the graduation crowd."

"This could be somewhat delicate." Carolyn checked their surroundings. "I'm thinking your house might be best under the circumstances."

"Okay. How about if I drive us? We can come back and get your car later."

"Perfect."

Rebecca pointed out the sights for Carolyn on the way to her place.

"It's beautiful. Bucolic."

"Peaceful," Dara said. And it was. She enjoyed her visits here because it was so different from the hustle and bustle of LA.

"This is it."

"It's lovely," Carolyn said, as she turned in a circle in the foyer.

"Thanks. It's home."

When they were situated inside the living room, Dara couldn't wait anymore. "Why are you here? Don't get me wrong. You know I love you to pieces. But what gives?"

"The studio gives," Carolyn said. "A lot. As in money. As in the potential benefits here are astronomical."

"What are you talking about?"

"I'm talking about the phone call I got from Randolph Curtain in what was the middle of the night for him last night and what was way too early this morning for me."

Rebecca brought iced tea for all of them.

"He said the front end of the weekend box office was out of sight. So much so that he didn't even want to wait for the full weekend numbers. He was satisfied that Friday's take would only multiply on Saturday and today."

"That's fantastic," Rebecca said. "Right?"

Dara laughed at her and kissed her on the cheek. "Right, Ms. Hollywood movie expert. Okay. So the numbers are good. We'll all be rich thanks to my most excellent business manager who negotiated Dara and Constance incredibly generous contracts that included a piece of the box office take. Why does Randolph have ants in his pants?"

"He wants to option Constance's latest book right away before anyone else jumps in."

"He wants the rights to *Love Above All Else?*"

"Yes, and he wants it tied up today. He sent a contract he had his people draw up at one o'clock this morning."

"Wow. That's serious. The terms?"

"I'll push for a bigger share of the box office this time, but otherwise it'll be the same as *On the Wings of Angels.*"

"That's awesome, isn't it?" Rebecca asked. "I mean, you could pull off the same setup. Dara is the right age to play the lead, even though the character ages during the course of the story. They've got makeup for that and prosthetics, right?"

Dara sat very still.

"Say something," Rebecca said.

"I'm thinking."

"I can see that. Think faster."

"Okay. Here's what I think." She sat forward. "Put two stipulations in Constance's contract. If he really wants this book so badly, he'll have to agree to them."

Carolyn took out her iPad.

"Stipulation One—Dara Thomas plays Courtney."

"Okay. You know that's not done. The author doesn't get to pick the actors."

"She will this time. And Stipulation Two—Constance will only sell the rights if Rebecca Minton is the screenwriter."

"What?" Rebecca and Carolyn exclaimed in unison.

"You heard me." Dara knelt in front of Rebecca and took her hands. "What you did with *On the Wings of Angels* was genius. We saw what happened when I trusted the studio to hire the right screenwriter for the project. No one understands my characters and my stories better than you do. You truly are the preeminent Constance Darrow scholar."

"But..."

"Constance dedicated the book to you. It would only be natural that she would want you to write the treatment. Especially knowing that you were brought in to doctor *On the Wings of Angels.*"

"How would she know that? I didn't get a screen credit."

"That doesn't matter," Carolyn jumped in. "She would've heard. I'm business manager to both of them. I would've told Constance."

"There you go." Dara closed her eyes, trying to organize what she wanted to say to Rebecca. "You're my life—the one person who sees inside me and understands my heart and the context for my work. I can't imagine trusting Constance's words to anyone else. I won't sign if you're not part of the package."

"It would give you the perfect cover to be spending a lot of time together again," Carolyn added.

Rebecca bit her lip. "It would likely mean I'd have to give up my professorship. Once was a fluke they were willing to work with. Twice..."

Dara nodded sadly. "I understand. It's a lot to ask you to give up your life here." She started to get up and Rebecca held her in place.

"It's not what I'm giving up that matters," Rebecca said quietly. "It's what I'd be walking into and the awesome responsibility of it. I've never written a screenplay. It's one thing to fix something that already exists. It's quite another to create something from scratch."

"I believe in you, Rebecca. I trust you."

"We could do it together. You could help me write it."

Dara shook her head. "No. You don't need me for this. I've seen you in action. You understood what to do with that script better than I did. You saw better solutions. Your writing was crisp and clear. Your dialogue was pitch perfect.

"I write novels. They ebb and flow and meander. A screenplay is a completely different genre and it requires a different mindset. I can't bring a fresh mindset to something that exists within me in a fixed format. I need you."

"What happens if I let you down? What happens if I write a flop?"

"You won't."

"I could ruin your career. I couldn't live with myself."

"I can't live without you. My career comes in a distant second if I have to choose."

The words were out before Dara could process their implication, but in her heart she knew that was the truth, and it felt freeing. "And if you want and you can get them to grant you a sabbatical for the year to make the movie, I would take a year off after the film and we could live here together while you teach. Who knows, maybe Constance could get another book written while gazing out at the mountains."

"You can't take a year off at the height of your career. I won't have it," Rebecca said. "When you win the Oscar for Celeste, and you will, you're going to be in even more demand than you are now."

"What did I tell you about saying that kind of stuff out loud?"

"Aha! So, you really are superstitious."

Dara wagged a finger at her. That's beside the point and don't change the subject."

"Carolyn? If you proposed these terms to the studio, do you think they would accept?" Rebecca asked.

"Given that Randolph thought it was important enough to bring his lawyer out in the middle of the night on a Saturday night to draft the contract, my professional opinion would be that he might go for it."

Carolyn turned to Dara and then to Rebecca. "Rebecca, can you give Dara and me a minute?"

Dara said, "That won't be—"

"Sure. I'll be out on the deck."

When Rebecca was out of earshot, Dara whispered fiercely, "What are you doing?"

"Did you hear yourself? You told Rebecca she understood you completely, she understood what was in your heart. But there's this one pretty significant thing about you that she doesn't know—you're a medium. Or did you tell her?"

"Damn it, Carolyn." Dara jumped up to pace.

"So, you didn't tell her. You can't ask this woman to turn her whole life upside down without being completely honest with her. It's not fair."

Dara turned beseeching eyes to her best friend. "What if it's a deal breaker? What if she can't accept that part of me?"

"Don't you think you should find that out now?"

Tears sprang to Dara's eyes.

Carolyn got up and put her hands on Dara's shoulders. "I'd like to think I'm a good judge of character. Rebecca is one of the genuinely nicest human beings I've ever met. She's never given any indication that she's anything but open and accepting about anything to do with your life. Why would this be any different?"

Dara swallowed down a sob. "Why can't I just keep that to myself? It's not like it happens all the time and it's not like I'm going to talk about it anywhere."

"You mean it's not like when you were a kid. You've learned to keep your mouth shut about it," Carolyn said quietly. "Sounds an awful lot to me like there's a very scared little girl in there." She tapped a finger against Dara's heart.

Dara closed her eyes tightly as a tear leaked out. Her lips started to tremble. "I'm scared, Car. Rebecca is the one. She's the person I've been waiting for my whole life."

"Then trust her with this." Carolyn wiped a tear from Dara's cheek. "Have faith. It'll be fine. You'll see."

"You really think so?"

"I do. And I think she deserves to know before she makes any decisions about her career or her life."

Dara nodded resolutely. "I'll go out there and talk to her."

∽৯৵৵

"Everything all right?" Rebecca asked, when Dara joined her on the deck.

"Sure."

"You've been crying." Rebecca pulled Dara to her and held her close. "What's wrong?"

"It's nothing. I-it's… There's something I need to tell you. About me. Something I should have told you a long time ago."

Rebecca's heart hammered. She let go of Dara and stood at the railing, looking out over the backyard. "You don't want to be with me anymore. You just couldn't figure out how to let me down gently." Rebecca tried to swallow, tried to breathe, but she couldn't. *Please, God, I won't be able to stand it if this ends.*

"What?" Dara grabbed her from behind and whirled her around, holding her tight. "Why on Earth would you think that? Did you hear everything I just said to you in there? You're my life, Rebecca." Dara rocked them from side to side. "That isn't it at all. It's about who I am. Or at least, about a part of me I haven't shared with you until now."

"I'm listening." Rebecca's voice sounded strained, even to her own ears. She pulled away from Dara's embrace and sat down in one of the chairs.

Dara sat on the edge of the other chair and faced her. "Do you remember Renée Maupin? You met her at the movie premiere. She and her wife, Yahzi sat with you and Carolyn."

Rebecca nodded. "You grew up together."

"Right." Dara fidgeted in the chair. "Carolyn told me afterward that you asked Renée a question that she never answered because the movie started."

Rebecca thought back to that night. She had teased Carolyn about finding out more about her and Dara as children. *And the look on Renée's face was sheer panic.* "I remember. I thought Renée's reaction was odd."

"That's because she didn't know what to say to you. You see, my relationship with Renée back then was...contentious."

"Meaning?"

"Meaning she was my worst nightmare. Remember how you told me you got bullied at school?"

"Yes."

"And I told you I knew exactly how you felt, but I said that was another story for another day?"

Rebecca nodded. "I let it slide because I knew you were a very private person, and it felt like the topic might be painful for you."

"Oh." Dara touched Rebecca's arm with her fingertips, then let her hand drop. "You are the most sensitive, perceptive person I know. I love you, Rebecca."

"I love you too."

"I hope— I hope you still feel that way when I'm done telling you this."

Again, Rebecca's heart rate increased as she struggled not to let her insecurities get the better of her. *What is it? This big thing? Surely this time was different.* "Please, Dara. Just tell me why I'm not right for you."

"What? Sweetheart, where does this stuff come from? This has nothing to do with you and everything to do with me. You're perfect for me in every way."

Rebecca wanted to believe what Dara said, but that part of her that still looked in the mirror and saw the overweight, awkward teenager nobody wanted to be around, wouldn't fully accept that someone like Dara could want her.

Dara took a deep breath in. "The reason I got bullied by Renée and others was because I saw dead people. It's the same reason I had so much trouble with my parents. Well, one of the reasons, anyway. They thought I was obstinate and crazy. So I just stopped talking about it. And I willed myself to be normal." Dara sat back.

Rebecca could see that she was trembling. She went to her, knelt and put her hands on Dara's knees. "They rejected you because you had a gift they couldn't understand?"

Dara nodded.

"Oh, baby. I'm so sorry for that. It must have been so lonely for you."

"Did you hear what I said?"

"You said you're able to communicate with people from the other side. I heard you."

"And that doesn't bother you?"

"My God, Dara. Why would that bother me? It's a remarkable gift. It makes you all that much more special."

"Why don't you sound surprised?"

Rebecca laughed. "How could I read *On the Wings of Angels*, read Constance Darrow's written comments to me about angels and ascended beings, and not recognize that the author had a deep and abiding understanding of metaphysics? I'm just sorry you found it so difficult to tell me."

"I just thought... I was worried..."

"What, that I'd walk away if I knew? Oh, sweetheart, if you thought that you still have a lot to learn about me."

"I hope I'll have a lifetime to do research."

"I'm counting on it." Rebecca stood up and climbed into Dara's lap. "I love you, Dara. All of you. Everything about you. Unless you're secretly an ax murderer or you're cheating on me, there isn't anything you can do that would make me turn away."

Dara wrapped Rebecca in her arms. "What was all that about you not being right for me and me wanting to walk away?"

"My own childhood scars rearing their ugly heads. Don't worry about it."

"Don't worry about it? How can I not worry about the woman I love thinking she's on shaky ground with me."

"If I showed you childhood pictures—"

"Please tell me that you don't think that appearances matter to me. After everything you've seen me go through, after all the objectification and underestimations, do you really think I'd be so shallow?"

"Well, I don't look like that now."

"Even if you gained every ounce of weight back that you lost, you'd still be you. It isn't the window dressing with you, Rebecca." Dara's voice shook with emotion. "Yes, you're a gorgeous woman. But I fell in love with who you are, not what you look like. So unless you're planning to have a lobotomy, and maybe even then..."

Rebecca leaned in and kissed Dara. It wasn't a passionate embrace, it was an acknowledgment that they'd crossed an important threshold in their relationship. After a minute, she pulled back.

"So, why was that woman at the premiere?" Her eyebrows drew together in consternation.

"Renée?"

"Yes."

"It turns out the reason she was bullying me was because she was just like me. She figured if she was the loudest bully, no one would point fingers at her."

"Okay. But that still doesn't answer the question."

"Carolyn reintroduced us a while back and we had a nice chat. She apologized for everything and I accepted her apology. We've been mending fences ever since. She's nothing like what she was as a kid."

"Good thing." Rebecca gave her best tough look and made a fist and Dara laughed.

"Now that we've got all that squared away..." Rebecca ran her fingers through Dara's hair. "Let's get back to the business discussion. If this deal with the studio is what you truly want, then I say go for it. I'm with you. Now and always. Wherever you go, I'll be there beside you every step of the way."

She kissed Dara softly on the mouth. "Plus, Carolyn's right—this would give me the perfect cover to spend lots of time with you without arousing any suspicions."

Rebecca tried to ignore the pang she felt in her gut every time she thought about them having to hide their love for each other. She wondered if Dara felt the same way.

CHAPTER TWENTY-SIX

I wish you were riding in the limo with me. I wish I could walk arm-in-arm with you right up the red carpet."

"I know you do, and that's all that matters."

"Not to me."

Rebecca walked into the bedroom from the bathroom. "What are you doing under there? Not that I'm minding the view." Rebecca tilted her head to one side to stare at Dara's ass as she crawled around under the reading table in the sitting area near the window.

"I'm looking for my earring."

"As in the borrowed-for-the-night, Harry Winston, two-million-dollar earring?" Rebecca got on the floor with her.

"Yes, that one."

"How did you lose it?"

"I was having trouble getting it in my ear because my hands were trembling too badly, so I dropped it."

Rebecca pulled Dara into her lap. "Come here."

"I have to find it. The limo will be here in less than an hour and I'm not even dressed."

"Have I told you how adorable you are when you're nervous. When you win that Oscar tonight—"

"Oh, my God! How many times now have I told you not to say that?"

Rebecca laughed and kissed Dara on the nose, careful not to spoil her makeup. "I love you so much. Since I imagine you'll be swallowed up in crowds for most of the night, let me say congratulations right now." She held Dara fast as she squirmed.

"Congratulations for being a winner in my book. Congratulations for an unbeatable performance. Congratulations for being, I'm confident, the only Pulitzer Prize-winning author who is also an Oscar nominee for Best Actress. I am bursting with pride for you."

Tears pooled in Dara's eyes. "I will not cry. I will not cry. I will not cry."

"How's that working for you?"

Dara cleared her throat. "Just fine, thanks." Dara hugged Rebecca tight. "How did I ever live before I had you in my life? I love you beyond all measure. I am so looking forward to working on *Love Above All Else* with you."

"Me too. But first you have to finish the Speilberg movie, and I have to finish writing the script."

"Details, details."

"Speaking of details, were you looking for this?" Rebecca held up the missing earring.

"How did you...? Where did you...?"

"Chalk it up to magic for a magical night." Rebecca let go of Dara so that she could get up. "Now you really do have to hustle. You need help getting into the dress? I mean, what there is of a dress."

Dara poked her in the arm. "You said you loved it."

"And I meant it. Classy, elegant, and sexy all at the same time. You're a triple threat tonight."

"You're not too bad yourself."

"Well, my dress isn't custom-made."

"No, but it's custom fit." Dara winked.

"I'm glad you like it. Now hurry up. I'll go get the shoehorn to help you into the dress."

⇜⇝

Rebecca turned on their TV to watch the coverage of the early red carpet arrivals. Since she wasn't a celebrity, she didn't need to arrive for a couple of hours.

"Good evening and welcome to the red carpet outside the Dolby Theater in sunny Hollywood, California, where the 87th annual Oscars will be presented tonight. It's a crisp, clear day here in Hollywood, and the stars are out to shine tonight. Let's get started…"

Rebecca watched the parade of A-list stars step out of limos and walk the carpet. All of the nominees looked lovely, but there was only one arrival she cared about. And there she was.

"Here is the ever-stunning Dara Thomas. Hi, Dara."

"Hello."

"You look amazing. Our fashion mavens are saying you're the best-dressed woman so far."

"Well, thank you for that."

"What are you wearing?"

"This is Donatella Versace."

"Beautiful."

The camera caressed Dara's curves like a lover, and Rebecca tried not to think about the millions of male and female viewers everywhere who were tweeting and Facebooking about what Dara was wearing and what they wanted to do about it.

"You're up for Best Actress tonight for your performance as Celeste in *On the Wings of Angels*. What do you think your chances are?"

"What kind of question is that?" Rebecca asked. "What do you think she's going to say to that?"

"This has been an extraordinary year for movies. I'm just thrilled to have been nominated in the same category with these fabulous actresses."

"Thank you, Dara. Good luck tonight."

"Thank you." Dara turned and walked away, and Rebecca turned off the television.

◈◈

The theater was packed and the night dragged on. Dara continued to smile brightly in case any cameras were trained on her. All she wanted was to find Rebecca. She texted her.

Where are you?

I'm here. Don't worry. Almost your category. I love you.

I love you too. Give me your location.

Balcony, stage left. Don't worry about me. Turn off your phone. You're up after the commercial break.

Reluctantly, Dara turned off the phone and stowed it in her pocketbook. So far, it had been a good night for the movie. It took awards for Best Film Editing, Best Production, and Best Original Score. What it hadn't taken was any of the acting awards.

"And now the award for Best Actress in a Leading Role. The nominees are..."

Dara was so nervous she couldn't hear the names. She knew they must have mentioned her, because there was a camera about two feet from her face.

"And the Oscar goes to... Dara Thomas, *On the Wings of Angels*."

The crowd erupted in a huge ovation and George and Sam lifted Dara out of her seat. Sam hugged her. "You won. Go get it, girl. You deserve it."

The announcer was saying, "This is Ms. Thomas's second Oscar nomination and her first win."

Dara covered her mouth with trembling fingers and made her way to the stage. Well-wishers—some of the best actors in the world—grabbed her hands on the way by to congratulate her.

Someone took her elbow and guided her up the stairs. Vaguely, she was aware that she'd brought her purse with her and wondered why.

When she reached the microphone, last year's winner for Best Actor handed her the statuette and the winner's envelope. She tried to see out into the crowd, but the lighting made it nearly impossible.

"Oh, my. I honestly never expected to win this. The actresses in this category are of such extraordinary caliber and the performances this year were exquisite. Thank you to my fellow nominees. I salute each and every one of you. Thank you to the Academy and to my fellow actors. This is an incredible honor. Thank you to my team, my business manager and best friend Carolyn Detweiler who has been there for me since kindergarten, my agent, Rick Church, and my PR guru Colin Lafferty. You all rock. Thank you to 722 Films, and to my fabulous director, George Nelson, and my wonderful co-star Sam Rutledge. Thank you, as well, to the rest of the cast and crew."

Dara took a deep breath, the first one since she'd stepped to the microphone. She hoped she appeared far more composed than she felt. "Thank you to Constance Darrow, the author of the novel from which this film was adapted, for creating a dynamic, deep character like Celeste." She smiled, wondering if Rebecca just fell off her chair.

"And one more, very special thank you. You know, in this business, script doctors, as we call them, don't often get recognized. You'll never see their name in the credits. They toil in near obscurity, and yet they play such an important role. Well, believe me when I tell you I noticed the script doctor on the set for this movie. When she started, she was a professor of American literature—a scholar without an ounce of filmmaking experience. But her knowledge and understanding of the characters is part of the reason I'm standing up here right now."

Dara hesitated. *If you do this, there's no turning back.* She glanced up toward the balcony, stage left. The lights were blinding.

"She's sitting someplace up there." Dara indicated the area. "Her name is Rebecca Minton. I hope you'll remember that name, because she's writing the screenplay for my next movie. More importantly, after next week, she'll be my wife. I love you, Rebecca, with all that I am and all that I ever will be. Thank you."

Dara's heart pounded as she blindly made her way off the stage. Backstage, she was accosted by several media outlets. She posed for pictures with the statuette, did interviews with the stars of the top television entertainment programs, and accepted congratulations from several presenters and other award winners.

In truth, she had no idea what she was saying. Only one thing mattered. Only one face mattered. Dara exited the backstage area and shouldered through a set of doors into the lobby. She needed a plan, and she had none. *It's not like you can go charging up to the balcony.*

The brightness of the lobby was in such contrast to the darkness in the backstage area that she paused for a moment to allow her eyes to adjust. She did a double take. She could've sworn she saw...

"I love you." Rebecca swept her up in her arms and held her tight. "I love you so much. I'm so proud of you."

"I love you too. And now the whole world knows it."

"Yes, they certainly do. No question you did that with style and panache."

"I always say, if you're going to do something, go big or go home."

"You've lost your mind, you know that?"

"No. My mind is just fine. What I lost is my heart. The first time I read the very first line in your very first letter. Thank you, for coming into my life and seeing me—all of me. You show me what it means to live every day. And I'm forever grateful."

"Thank you, for teaching me what it means to really be loved and cherished. My life is so rich and full because I have you in it." Rebecca stepped back for a moment. "Which reminds me…" She fished in her purse. "I was going to save this for later, but since you've made discretion a moot point…" She took Dara's purse, the winner's envelope, and the Oscar, set them down at her feet, and handed her a small jewelry box. "Originally, I was thinking that at least you could wear this when we were alone. But now…"

Dara opened the box to reveal a spectacular diamond band. She swallowed hard. "This… This is…"

Rebecca removed the ring from its nesting spot and slipped it on the ring finger of Dara's left hand. "I hope you like it."

"Like it? I love it." Dara launched herself back into Rebecca's arms.

"I know I'm a week early, but tonight is a magical night I know we'll both always remember. Dara Thomas, you are the love of my life. This ring symbolizes my promise to you. I promise to love, honor, and cherish you always. I promise to spend all the rest of my days by your side, reminding you who you are and how much you are loved. Now and always."

"Always and forever," Dara agreed. As she kissed Rebecca passionately on the mouth, a photographer's flash went off in her face. *And now the whole world is a witness to our love. Well, you did say that was what you wanted.* Dara smiled as unrestrained joy filled her heart and soul. For the briefest second, she could've sworn she saw her mother applaud.

THE END

About the Author

An award-winning former broadcast journalist, former press secretary to the New York state senate minority leader, former public information officer for the nation's third largest prison system, and former editor of a national art magazine, Lynn Ames is a nationally recognized speaker and CEO of a public relations firm with a particular expertise in image, crisis communications planning, and crisis management.

Ms. Ames's other works include *The Price of Fame* (Book One in the Kate & Jay series), *The Cost of Commitment* (Book Two in the Kate & Jay series), *The Value of Valor* (winner of the 2007 Arizona Book Award and Book Three in the Kate & Jay series), *One ~ Love* (formerly published as *The Flip Side of Desire*), *Heartsong, Eyes on the Stars* (winner of a 2011 Golden Crown Literary award), *Beyond Instinct* (winner of a 2012 Golden Crown Literary Award and Book One in the Mission: Classified series), *Above Reproach*, Book Two in the Mission: Classified series, and *Outsiders* (winner of a 2010 Golden Crown Literary award).

More about the author, including contact information, news about sequels and other original upcoming works, pictures of locations mentioned in this novel, links to resources related to issues raised in this book, author interviews, and purchasing assistance can be found at www.lynnames.com. You can also friend Lynn on Facebook and follow her on Twitter.

Other Books in Print by Lynn Ames

The Mission: Classified Series
Beyond Instinct – Book One in the Mission: Classified Series
ISBN: 978-1-936429-02-8
Vaughn Elliott is a member of the State Department's Diplomatic Security Force. Someone high up in the United States government has pulled rank, hand-selecting her to oversee security for a visit by congressional VIPs to the West African nation of Mali. The question is, who picked her for the job and why?

Sage McNally, a career diplomat, is the political officer at the US Embassy in Mali. As control officer for the congressional visit, she is tasked to brief Vaughn regarding the political climate in the region.

The two women are instantly attracted to each other and share a wild night of passion. The next morning, Sage disappears while running, leaving behind signs of a scuffle. Why was Sage taken and by whom? Where is she being held?

Vaughn's attempts to get answers are thwarted at every turn. Even Sage does not know why she's been targeted.

Independently, Sage and Vaughn struggle to make sense of the seemingly senseless. By the time each of them figures it out, it could be too late for Sage.

As the clock ticks inexorably toward the congressional visit, the stakes get even higher, and Vaughn is faced with unspeakable choices. Her decisions will make the difference between life and death. Will she choose duty or her own code of honor?

Above Reproach – Book Two in the Mission: Classified Series

ISBN: 978-1-936429-04-2

Sedona Ramos is a dedicated public servant. Fluent in three languages, with looks that allow her to pass for Hispanic, Native American, or Middle Eastern, she is a valuable asset to the super-secret National Security Agency. When she accidentally stumbles upon a mysterious series of satellite images revealing activity at a shuttered nuclear facility in war-torn Iraq, somebody wants her dead.

With danger lurking at every turn and not knowing who among her colleagues might be involved, Sedona risks her life to get the information to the one person she can trust—the president.

The implications of Sedona's discovery are clear and quite possibly catastrophic. Potential suspects include foreign terrorists, high-ranking Cabinet members, and assorted others. Whomever the president picks for this mission must be above reproach.

Vaughn Elliott is enjoying her self-imposed isolation on a remote island, content to live in quiet anonymity. But when old friend Katherine Kyle brings an urgent SOS from the president of the United States, duty trumps comfort.

Time is of the essence. Vaughn, Sedona, and a hand-picked team of ex-operatives and specialists must figure out what's really going on outside Baghdad, stop it, and unmask the forces behind the plot. If they fail at any point along the way, it could mean the loss of millions of lives.

Will Vaughn and company unravel the mysteries in time? The trail of clues stretches from the Middle East to Washington. The list of people who want to kill them is long. And the stakes have never been higher...

Stand-Alone Romances
Eyes on the Stars
ISBN: 978-1-936429-00-4

Jessie Keaton and Claudia Sherwood were as different as night and day. But when their nation needed experienced female pilots, their reactions were identical: heed the call. In early 1943, the two women joined the Women Airforce Service Pilots—WASP—and reported to Avenger Field in Sweetwater, Texas, where they promptly fell head-over-heels in love.

The life of a WASP was often perilous by definition. Being two women in love added another layer of complication entirely, leading to ostracism and worse. Like many others, Jessie and Claudia hid their relationship, going on dates with men to avert suspicion. The ruse worked well until one seemingly innocent afternoon ruined everything.

Two lives tragically altered. Two hearts ripped apart. And a second chance more than fifty years in the making.

From the airfields of World War II, to the East Room of the Obama White House, follow the lives of two extraordinary women whose love transcends time and place.

Heartsong
ISBN: 978-0-9840521-3-4

After three years spent mourning the death of her partner in a tragic climbing accident, Danica Warren has re-emerged in the public eye. With a best-selling memoir, a blockbuster movie about her heroic efforts to save three other climbers, and a successful career on the motivational speaking circuit, Danica has convinced herself that her life can be full without love.

When Chase Crosley walks into Danica's field of vision everything changes. Danica is suddenly faced with questions she's never pondered.

Is there really one love that transcends all concepts of space and time? One great love that joins two hearts so that they beat as one? One moment of recognition when twin flames join and burn together?

Will Danica and Chase be able to overcome the barriers standing between them and find forever? And can that love be sustained, even in the face of cruel circumstances and fate?

One ~ Love, (formerly *The Flip Side of Desire*)
ISBN: 978-0-9840521-2-7

Trystan Lightfoot allowed herself to love once in her life; the experience broke her heart and strengthened her resolve never to fall in love again. At forty, however, she still longs for the comfort of a woman's arms. She finds temporary solace in meaningless, albeit adventuresome encounters, burying her pain and her emotions deep inside where no one can reach. No one, that is, until she meets C.J. Winslow.

C.J. Winslow is the model-pretty-but-aging professional tennis star the Women's Tennis Federation is counting on to dispel the image that all great female tennis players are lesbians. And her lesbianism isn't the only secret she's hiding. A traumatic event from her childhood is taking its toll both on and off the court.

Together Trystan and C.J. must find a way beyond their pasts to discover lasting love.

The Kate and Jay Series
The Price of Fame
ISBN: 978-0-9840521-4-1

When local television news anchor Katherine Kyle is thrust into the national spotlight, it sets in motion a chain of events that will change her life forever. Jamison "Jay" Parker is an intensely career-driven Time magazine reporter. The first time she saw Kate, she fell in love. The last time she saw her, Kate was rescuing her. That was five years ago, and she never expected to see her again. Then circumstances and an assignment bring them back together.

Kate and Jay's lives intertwine, leading them on a journey to love and happiness, until fate and fame threaten to tear them apart. What is the price of fame? For Kate, the cost just might be everything. For Jay, it could be the other half of her soul.

The Cost of Commitment
ISBN: 978-0-9840521-5-8

Kate and Jay want nothing more than to focus on their love. But as Kate settles into a new profession, she and Jay are caught in the middle of a deadly scheme and find themselves pawns in a larger game in which the stakes are nothing less than control of the country.

In her novel of corruption, greed, romance, and danger, Lynn Ames takes us on an unforgettable journey of harrowing conspiracy—and establishes herself as a mistress of suspense.

The Cost of Commitment—it could be everything...

The Value of Valor
ISBN: 978-0-9840521-6-5

Katherine Kyle is the press secretary to the president of the United States. Her lover, Jamison Parker, is a respected writer for Time magazine. Separated by unthinkable tragedy, the two must struggle to survive against impossible odds...

A powerful, shadowy organization wants to advance its own global agenda. To succeed, the president must be eliminated. Only one person knows the truth and can put a stop to the scheme.

It will take every ounce of courage and strength Kate possesses to stay alive long enough to expose the plot. Meanwhile, Jay must cheat death and race across continents to be by her lover's side...

This hair-raising thriller will grip you from the start and won't let you go until the ride is over.

The Value of Valor—it's priceless.

Anthology Collections
Outsiders
ISBN: 978-0-979-92545-0
What happens when you take five beloved, powerhouse authors, each with a unique voice and style, give them one word to work with, and put them between the sheets together, no holds barred?

Magic!!

Brisk Press presents Lynn Ames, Georgia Beers, JD Glass, Susan X. Meagher and Susan Smith, all together under the same cover with the aim to satisfy your every literary taste. This incredible combination offers something for everyone—a smorgasbord of fiction unlike anything you'll find anywhere else.

A Native American raised on the Reservation ventures outside the comfort and familiarity of her own world to help a lost soul embrace the gifts that set her apart. * A reluctantly wealthy woman uses all of her resources anonymously to help those who cannot help themselves. * Three individuals, three aspects of the self, combine to create balance and harmony at last for a popular trio of characters. * Two nomadic women from very different walks of life discover common ground—and a lot more—during a blackout in New York City. * A traditional, old school butch must confront her community and her own belief system when she falls for a much younger transman.

Five authors—five novellas. Outsiders—one remarkable book.

All Lynn Ames books are available through www.lynnames.com, from your favorite local bookstore, or through other online venues.

You can purchase other Phoenix Rising Press books online at www.phoenixrisingpress.com or at your local bookstore.

Published by
Phoenix Rising Press
Phoenix, AZ

Visit us on the Web: Phoenix Rising Press

Here at Phoenix Rising Press, our goal is to provide you, the reader, with top quality, entertaining, well-written, well-edited works that leave you wanting more. We give our authors free rein to let their imaginations soar. We believe that nurturing that kind of unbridled creativity and encouraging our authors to write what's in their hearts results in the kinds of books you can't put down.

Whether you crave romances, mysteries, fantasy/science fiction, short stories, thrillers, or something else, when you pick up a Phoenix Rising Press book, you know you've found a good read. So sit back, relax, get comfortable, and enjoy!

Phoenix Rising Press
Phoenix, AZ